Published by:
CsiMec Inc.
Abilene TX, 79606

The Symphony of Leif is a work of fiction. Names, characters, places and incidents are the product of the author's imagination and/or are used fictitiously. Any resemblance to actual events, locations, or persons, living or dead is entirely coincidental.

First Edition: January 2010
Printed by arrangement with Book Surge

ISBN 978-1-60365-004-5

Book design by Paul Y. Csige

PRINTED IN THE UNITED STATES OF AMERICA

The Symphony
of Leif

A Novel

PAUL Y. CSIGE

CSIMEC INC • ABILENE, TEXAS

in memory of friends lost

ACKNOWLEDGMENTS

Thanks to Lauren for first planting the idea of penning this book in my head. Thanks to John for helping me remember things I can't believe I forgot. Thanks to Mecca, Geza, and Dana; without a family to support me, I don't think I would have even attempted this. Thanks Nicole for being my best friend. Thanks to Kara, Luis, Ulf and everyone who read earlier drafts and gave suggestions. Thanks Joni and Barb for getting the book on its way, and a special thanks to Kathleen Istudor for your friendship and technical assistance.

The Symphony
of Leif

The Lamia School

Leif
Csuba

Prelude

I lay perfectly still on my bunk listening for any signs of movement in the hall outside. Rain tapped against the small window near the ceiling. A weak shaft of light punctured the glass, casting a silvery square on the floor.

Was that a click at the door? I listened. Nothing. I realized I was holding my breath and let it out slowly. I wasn't that chick down in the well from *Silence of the Lambs*. Screw this crap!

I gingerly tiptoed to the door. I pressed my ear against it, listening. The only sound I could hear was my own blood rushing through my veins. I prayed that the dumb, balding sentry was gone. For a brief moment I wondered how many others were imprisoned down here behind similar blank doors.

I reached down and turned the handle. It would not twist. I strained harder but it didn't budge. They'd locked it! It had been open all day. That must have been the click I heard. Son of a bitch!

I turned to the window. It was too high and too small to crawl out. Shit! I sat back down on the bed. My stomach was twisted with hunger and frustration. I wanted to get out of this fucked up place. Was it only January? God! That meant I had 126 days left.

Then I remembered my reminder, the secret keepsake I'd smuggled into this godforsaken place. It was the only real thing that kept me sane. That it was close by gave me some solace and I relaxed a little.

My stomach still stung with the injustice of it all. I was going to get out of here. I was.

Movement I

summer

CHAPTER I
Adults and the New World

I HATED MY SCHOOL!

I don't mean a particular teacher, or a bully, or the peer pressure. No. I hated the institution. I hated the structure. I hated that I had to run from one class as soon as it ended so I wouldn't be late to the next. I hated the fact I had to bring homework back with me when I had finally escaped from that goddamn place for the day. I hated school, PERIOD.

By my second semester of 8th grade I couldn't stand it anymore. I told my parents I didn't care if I passed the finals and was accepted into high school. They would physically have to drag me to class and chain me to the desk to keep me there. They had heard me make elaborate threats before but they could see I was serious this time.

I failed most of my final exams but through my mom's influence, Kamuela conceded to let me enroll in 9th grade. I prepared myself for the inevitable battle with my parents over attending high school when they sat me down and presented me with an alternative solution.

"Leif," my mom began. "Istvan and I have been looking around and found a pretty remarkable school."

"Oh, really?" They were all the same.

"I think you may like it," Rebecca continued. "It's located in the Northwest. There are no teachers."

"No teachers?" I perked up.

"No. They have something called Supervisors. They are only there to answer questions. What you do is sit down with your workbook and learn at your own pace, one subject at a time. It's pass or fail. Either you know it or you don't. No grades."

"Man!" It seemed too good to be true.

"The only thing is, it's a boarding school, so you'll have to live there."

"If Mercedes can do it in Europe, so can I," I said confidently.

"Do you really think he can handle it, Bec?" my dad asked.

My mom gave my dad a quick look and he said no more.

This school sounded perfect to me. My mom made the arrangements and I was accepted for the fall. I was thrilled. No more school crap. Education the way it should be; my way. I could start fresh. No unshakable reputation, just what I made for myself. In August I was going to leave Kamuela and enroll in the Lamia School. Sure the Northwest was far away, but I'd get used to it. Hawaii was getting boring anyway. It was definitely time for a little mainland action.

No, I'm not Hawaiian, at least not by blood. Istvan's from Hungary and my mom's from New Jersey. Rebecca tries to speak well but her Jersey accent comes back when she's angry. Istvan has always had an accent, but I can't hear it anymore. He's lived in America for 40 years. I was born in Los Angeles. My family moved to Hawaii when I was three.

"You're from Hawaii?" people ask. The next question is always the same, "Why did you leave?" It's right up there with, "You're from Hawaii? Do you surf?" People surf in France. Stupid questions.

Hawaii is great if you're a kid, with its rainforests and hundreds of beaches to surf, or if you're old and looking for a place to relax before you die. But if you're young and want to do something important, Hawaii is not the place to be. Hawaii is my home and home is almost always boring.

I was really looking forward to starting my new life. I couldn't wait for music camp to finish. I flew back to Hawaii to pack up all my stuff and in the third week of August I left for Jackskeep. I had never really left home before, not like this. I was more psyched than nervous.

My mom had some friends from her old business who lived in Jackskeep. We stayed with them that first night. The Petersons were okay, for adults. John Peterson was the only old guy I'd seen with braces. He always wore a baseball cap and had a thin mustache. Ruth Peterson was like those moms I'd seen on *Nick-at-Night*. She looked and acted like the 50's had never ended. It was kind of funny. They had a son, Jack, who was about two years older than me. My mom told me to hang out with him but two years is like a generation gap when you're that age. At 14, I would never hang out with a 12 year old. 13 was pushing it.

While the adults talked, Jack and I took a ride in his Camero. He blasted his music way too loud, drove too fast and hooted at girls on the street. I liked classical music and just talking to girls was difficult. I was glad when he finally pulled the Camero into the driveway.

Before we left the next morning John Peterson wished me good luck.

"Thanks," I said, shaking his hand.

"Hey," he went on, "if you ever want to come and stay for the weekend just give me a call."

"Is that okay, Bec?" I asked her.

"It's perfectly alright."

Maybe once a month I'd take a break from school and come out here. Whatever.

Bec and Isht took me to Costco to buy things my admission papers said I would need - things like towels, sheets, long pants for cold weather, and sneakers. All I owned were sandals.

"Can I get a boom box?" I asked Rebecca looking down the electronics aisle.

"Sure," she said.

"What about this one?" I asked.

It wasn't too expensive but had all sorts of extra features like a radio, clock and a tape player. Also, the design was cool.

"That looks fine."

I was just about to pull the box from under the shelf when Rebecca stopped me.

"Wait." She riffled through the admission papers, "You can have a boom box but it can't have a radio under any circumstance, and all music must be of a pleasant nature so as not to disturb other students."

Bummer. I liked that one. I searched the rest of them and finally found one without a radio. It was small and not as cool but it still played CDs.

"This one is good. Can I get some Beethoven symphonies, too?"

"Of course," Rebecca replied.

New CDs, a new place, and a new life. I was totally psyched. Rebecca was more anxious about school than I was. It was kind of funny.

"You're going to be living in a dorm with a roommate." Rebecca was wringing her hands. "Do you think you'll be okay?"

"Sure," I stated confidently. "It's just a roommate. I had to, like sleep in the same room with Mercedes for years. As long as he doesn't kick my bed at night, I'm cool."

I have an older sister. At this exact moment she was at boarding school too, but in Switzerland. My mom wanted me to go there, but after they read my permanent record they told her that military school was the only place I should be sent.

Mercedes and I had a normal relationship while growing

up. She beat me up and I cried to my parents. She was tall for a girl and I could never win a physical fight. I asked my mom why she did it.

"She's bored. It's just something for her to do."

Wish she'd just talk on the phone more or something. Sometimes I would start the fights but most of the time it was her fault. I'd just be sitting there watching TV when she'd suddenly run off with my blanket, my most prized possession until 8th grade when my mom made me throw it in the trash. So unfair. Anyway, I'd chase after Mercedes and attempt to stop her before she could get to her room and lock me out, but sometimes she'd turn on me and I would be the one being chased. I could never get away. She'd pin my arms down with her knees and pull out my hair. I can still give my hair a good yank and it doesn't hurt.

The strange thing was that she never let anybody else hit me. There were lots of kids at school who wanted to wail on me, up until 6th grade, but she always protected me. I never understood this until later. At the time I thought she just wanted my pain all to herself.

When I was 11 she really got into middle school life and our fights died down to verbal bickering. By the time I was 13, Mercedes was always on the phone and we rarely even spoke any more.

As we drove through the low rolling hills of the Pacific Northwest my parents listened to the news on the radio. I hated the news. I never watched it or read the paper. It never made any difference in my life.

"This cloned sheep is only the beginning," Istvan said when the report had finished, "By 2005 they'll have the human genome mapped and be in a position to create super soldiers for the military. The wars of the 21st century will make the ones in this look like a paintball fight."

"Just like *Wrath of Khan*," I thought.

"I think Dolly is a wonderful achievement," Rebecca replied. "Just think what genetics will do for medicine - new livers and hearts-"

"That's ridiculous," Istvan said cutting her off. "The government gets way too many kick backs from the drug companies to ever let that happen. I'm sure there's already a cure for cancer but the pharmaceutical companies make more money on treatments. There is no justice in this country, just look at O.J. Simpson."

I tried to ignore these adult discussions but Istvan was too loud to block out.

"Are you sure this isn't a waste of money?" Isht said, changing the subject.

"Please, don't say that," Rebecca cautioned.

"Let me put it to you this way: Both of them are going to boarding school. That's a lot of money. The U.S. economy is on the brink of collapse. I was just asking if this whole education idea is reasonable."

"You've been saying the world's going to end since I was eight, Isht," I quipped.

"You just wait and see. We could be saving this money and converting it to gold. That's the only currency that will matter when the biker gangs are roving the nation."

Istvan isn't crazy, at least not in a dangerous way. He grew up in Hungary during the Soviet occupation. His family was very wealthy. One day, without warning, the secret police confiscated all their possessions and put my Grandpa in prison. He escaped in 1956 when a tank shell blew up half the jail. He grabbed my father and they escaped into Austria. Istvan told me stories of having to jump over bodies in the streets of Budapest and bullets exploding the bark off nearby trees as they ran for their lives. He was only nine at the time. I'm sure that's why Isht has such a dark outlook on governments and the future.

"You didn't have to say it that way," Rebecca scolded.

"What do you mean?" Istvan asked, genuinely confused.

"You didn't say that about Mercedes when she went off to school."

"That's completely different. Your son will probably be nothing more than a gas station attendant anyway."

Mom didn't respond. These words probably would have devastated a normal kid but they barely bothered me anymore.

When I was little my dad tried to teach me to play soccer but I wasn't any good. Afterwards he dragged me by the arm to my mom.

"This boy has absolutely no talent."

"He's five, Isht. You can try again tomorrow. He just needs more practice."

"It's pointless. Your son will never be more than a gas station attendant."

My mom narrowed her eyes at him.

"What's a gas station *atennent*, Mom?" I asked.

"Nothing, honey. Why don't you go play outside?"

I could tell she was angry so I left as quickly as I could.

"What?" I heard a perplexed Istvan say as I left the house.

Whenever I did something wrong after that, Istvan would always give me these long lectures about how that event would define the rest of my life. Pumping gas took no thought and that would be the only thing I would ever do well. The only father-son thing we did together was fish.

I don't hate my dad. I just don't want to argue with him. If I did, he would lecture me until I admitted he was right. He could go on for hours. There was no way to win. I learned to agree with whatever he said, even if I thought he was completely wrong. It wasn't worth the time to argue. Second to my hatred of my last school, an absence of Istvan from my life made the idea of boarding school that much more appealing. I wouldn't have to deal with his crap anymore.

A sharp, unpleasant odor brought my attention back to the car.

"What the heck's that?" I asked, looking out the windows for the source.

"Right," Rebecca said, "You wouldn't know. That's a skunk."

"Really?" I'd seen them in cartoons but never in real life. I looked out the window trying to spot it.

"Oh, you won't see it. It's probably a mile away."

I wrinkled my nose.

"It's really strong."

"That's why you don't want to get sprayed."

"Yeah." I remembered an episode of *Lassie* I'd seen where a kid had to take a bath in tomato juice because a skunk got him.

We continued on past the smell. What always struck me most about coming to the mainland was the unfamiliarity. Hawaii was small, so I knew every road and every town. I couldn't go anywhere without running into somebody I knew. This place was like going to a party where you didn't know anybody. No matter how many times I came, it was always different. The land just went on and on. It made me feel small and insignificant.

"There it is," Rebecca said, pointing. I looked out the window and saw it - a faded red brick building far atop a hill.

"Dude," I responded. It didn't look like much at the time.

We drove up this winding road to the top of the hill. As we climbed higher I looked around the expansive landscape. We were really far from everything. We passed the nearest town a half hour ago. It would take hours to walk there and this hill would suck to have to climb. Students weren't allowed to have cars.

We drove onto the school grounds. There was a long straight road flanked on either side by a row of strange trees.

"Bec, what are those?" I asked.

"Weeping willows."

"Ah, like Mr. Toad."

"Right. You know, they make aspirin from the bark."

"Really?" I didn't know that.

To the right of the willows was a large soccer field. Next to it was a big square building with the sign, 'GYM' over two large metal doors. To the left of the road was a smaller field. Then we drove through a grove of maple trees. Above, flickers of sunlight darted between the broad green leaves. And then I saw the school, a three-story building in the shape of a large W, with a tall tower extending another floor. There was a small sign over the doorway that read *The Lamia School.* This was it.

"It's not so bad," I said.

We parked and went in the front entrance. A woman met us in the lobby. She gave Istvan a quizzical look before taking us to meet some admissions person. I was sure it was because of my dad's clothes. My dad's "uniform" was several layers of plaid shirts or an argyle sweater vest over a white t-shirt, grey sweatpants and white sneakers. He'd been wearing this same ensemble all my life so I didn't even think about it until we met new people. He had a large nose and a hairline an inch from his eyebrows.

My mom on the other hand was always well dressed and very beautiful. She had long, dark, brown hair and fine features. They were a strange match. Even though she was 47 most people assumed she was 15 years younger. Regardless of her youthful appearance she was very sensitive about her age.

Once, standing in line at Sizzler, I stated very loudly, "So, Mom. You're going to be 37 next week."

My mom whipped around and glared at me.

"Sorry. Sorry, Sorry! I meant 32, 32!" Everybody around us laughed. Rebecca was not thrilled.

I looked around at my new home as we followed the Lobby Lady. Nothing too out there. There were high ceilings and linoleum floors. One thing I did notice was how quiet it was. There were always kids yelling or running around at my last school. This place was like a church. We entered a small office with a tall horse-faced woman sitting behind a counter.

"Rebecca? I'm Becky Hort," the Admissions Lady said, extending her hand. Bec shook it.

"And you must be Istvan?" she said holding out her hand to my dad.

"*Ishtvon*," he corrected her, refusing to shake. "S is pronounced SH in Hungarian. So it's *Budapesht*, not Budapest."

"Oh," Mrs. Hort said, lowering her hand, "I'm glad to know."

"And knowing is half the battle," I said quoting *G.I. Joe*.

"Leif," my mom scolded.

"It's fine," Mrs. Hort said. "I need to give Leif a little placement test. Is that okay?"

"Sure," I answered.

She took me into a small office and began to question me.

"So, Leif. It says in your file that you are taking Ritalin?"

"What? No. I took Ritalin when I was seven but I haven't taken it for four years. I hated that crap. I got sick every-"

"Very well, Very well," she interrupted. "Let's move on."

So what if I took Ritalin? Doctors tried to explain my bad performance in school by saying I had A.D.D. Even back then I thought it was bullshit. I couldn't stand those pills. For years I begged my mom not to make me take them. When I was ten she said if I didn't overreact for a week she'd agree. I kept my calm and she didn't make me take them.

"Come on," I told her when the next week was over, "I didn't overreact all week! Please don't make me take them!"

"Okay. But if you lose control, it's right back on."

And so it went. Every time I started to get unfocused or too excited she'd threaten to give me a pill. I would immediately calm down. After a year she didn't have to coerce me any more and I got over my A.D.D by threat of medication. If my problem was a chemical imbalance then I couldn't have done what I did. So HA!

Becky Hort asked me more questions. Where was I from? What did I want to get out of school? Was I happy? Would being at Lamia make me happy? It was nothing too unusual until one question caught me off guard.

"Are you sexually active?"

"Ah… What do you mean?"

"Have you or are you having sex with anybody, messing around, oral sex?"

"No, I'm 14," I answered almost laughing. I'd only become interested in girls a little over a year and a half ago. What kind of question was that?! I knew what sex was, even though I didn't understand all of it. I'd seen lots of R-rated movies and Rebecca had explained the birds and the bees to me when I was three.

"Are your parents?" Mrs. Hort went on.

"Sexually active? Ah… they're still married, so yeah. I think so." My bedroom was right next to theirs and I heard them sometimes. I didn't like thinking about it so I definitely wasn't going to talk about it with this lady.

"Do you do drugs?" Mrs. Hort asked. I was thankful she'd been satisfied by my previous answer.

"Well, Tylenol, when I have a headache." This was true. I'd never even tried a cigarette.

"I see," she said, writing something down. "Do your parents do drugs?"

I answered honestly, "I don't know. If they do, they don't tell me." She was weird, but it was the mainland. Maybe all adults here were like this.

Rebecca had told me she'd done drugs in college. She was a hippie and had done everything that made the 60's the 60's - free love, drugs, protests. Not my dad though. He didn't even drink, not since I was 11 and a half and that was only a glass of wine at dinner.

"Have you ever been in a fight?" Mrs. Hort asked.

I felt a tingling in my stomach. I had been in a fight. I didn't want these people to know, but I had paused too long to say no.

"Some older kids tried to throw me in the shower once with all my clothes on and I punched one on the chin." This was true but it had happened a very long time ago. It was kind of my fault. I could be very annoying sometimes.

She gave me a long look.

"Very well," Mrs. Hort said, putting my file down on the desk. "We'll get you set up in your dorm room. Why don't you go sit with your mommy and daddy?"

I'm glad her back was turned because I had a very condescending look on my face. I'd never called them mommy or daddy. I called them by their first names: Rebecca or Bec, Istvan or Isht. My sister thought it was rude, but my parents didn't mind, so why should I?

"So what was your test like?" Rebecca asked when I came back.

"Okay. They asked some weird stuff though."

"Like what?"

"Like if you were sexually active or did drugs."

My mom laughed.

"What did you say?" Istvan asked. He never told anybody anything about himself if he didn't have to.

"I said you didn't tell me so I didn't know."

"Good answer," my mom said.

A man walked up. His name was Duane Something and he did tours. He gave me my key and showed me to my room on the third floor.

It was a nice sized room. There were two windows side by side, two beds on opposite ends of the room and a stack of shelves by the door. There was nobody there but the other bed was made up and things were already on the bottom shelves. He told me that my roommate's name was Robert

Foe. He then walked us downstairs.

"The students are down at lunch. So, when you're unpacked you can join them."

"Okay," I said.

He stopped then and looked at my parents.

"You do know that we were apprehensive about letting somebody in who's been on medication."

"Yes," Rebecca replied.

"But someone influential has vouched for your son and I guess we can accept that."

Rebecca nodded.

"I'm glad."

"Then here is where I'll leave you. Welcome and good luck, Leif." Duane shook my hand and walked away, leaving us there in the lobby.

"What was he talking about, Bec?" I asked.

"They didn't want to let you in because of the Ritalin."

Oh, so that explained the strange questions about it.

"I had one of my friends in my women's group talk to Lamia's board. She's a member of their faith and donates a lot of money."

I didn't realize that my being here was so complicated.

"Oh. That was nice of her."

Rebecca had run a large business in the 70's. Istvan had actually worked for her. She was one of the first women to own a company that large and she was still a part of her businesswomen's group. She'd even met President Reagan because of it. She sold the business a long time ago so she could be a full-time mom. Had she kept it we would be millionaires, but I'd probably never see my parents or get to know them. Who knows how screwed up I'd be. We weren't rich, but hey, that's life.

We got my stuff up to my room pretty quickly. The only heavy thing was my computer and monitor. Can't be without that. My handwriting was terrible. I couldn't even read it. Typing was the only way I could write my school stuff.

Soon my things were unloaded and I looked out the windows. If the school was shaped like a W, I was inside the right courtyard. The center prong of the W was a partially subterranean hallway. The bottom of the W held the classrooms and the arms were the dorms.

I went down to the lobby to say goodbye to my parents. My mom was crying.

"Call me often," she said around the sobs.

"I will, Bec. I'll be fine."

Istvan gave me a brief hug and told me to stay focused. My parents went out to the car and drove away. Almost immediately the car was out of sight. I was alone, except for the Lobby Lady. It kind of hit me then that this was real. I was actually on my own. What to do?

I didn't feel like lunch yet. I decided to go back up to my room. If you weren't loading heavy things you couldn't use the elevator, so I walked the stairs to the third floor. I took a left into the boy's dorm. The other side was the girl's. Duane had instructed me that nobody from either side was allowed to go to the other.

I opened my door and Robert was there. He was chubby - but not evenly distributed, like a pillow that had been sat on wrong. He wore thick glasses and had freckles. He was reading at his desk. I walked up to him.

"Hi, I'm Leif."

"Rob," he said and shook my hand. He had some book open - *Learning How to Study* or something.

"Is this your first year here?" I asked.

"No."

I waited. He said no more.

"Do you like it here?"

"Sure."

He seemed preoccupied with his book. I didn't want to interrupt, but I was new.

"How did you hear about Lamia?"

"My mom's a Supervisor. She's in the Lower School.

"Oh, really? She lives nearby?"

"Faculty apartments. First floor, right wing."

"Why don't you live with her?"

"Students aren't allowed downstairs in the right wing." He hadn't looked up from his book the whole time.

I wasn't getting much out of him. "I don't really know my way around. Do you think you could, like, help me and show me some stuff?"

He finally raised his eyes. "No. I'd like to look this over and get ahead before classes start." He wasn't mean, just not very nice.

"Okay." The whole exchange was weird. I had to live

with this guy. We'd become friends and all would be well. I left the room and began to wander. I didn't know where I was going, just trying to get the lay of the land.

First, I went up to the tower to check it out. I followed the stairs to the top. There was a windowless corridor and a single door that said Ethics Office. I probably shouldn't go in and with no windows it was boring. So I went back down.

There wasn't much going on anywhere so I decided to go to lunch and see all the kids. I walked down the dark hallway that was half underground and into the cafeteria. It was still crowded. The food counter was to the right and behind it were two big swinging doors that led to the kitchen. The whole left side of the room was tables and chairs. I grabbed a tray and started to fill my plate. It didn't look too bad. I was used to saimin and teriyaki chicken with rice, but this mainland food would do.

There was a boy in line ahead of me. He was kind of heavy and had dark brown hair down to his ears that was parted in the middle. He turned and looked at me. I gave him a small smile and nodded my head. He scanned me up and down.

"You know," he said, "I don't like you. I'm going to walk slow in front of you."

What the fuck? I couldn't tell if he was joking or not. He was smiling, but not in a humorous way. I decided to ignore him. I tried to go forward, but he wasn't moving. When I tried to move around him he sped up and got in the way. The only way to go anywhere was to get out of line. So

I did. I grabbed some bread and looked for a table. I could hear his laughter from the serving area. What was his problem?

I noticed somebody waving towards me as I was looking for a table. It was a group of three older students, probably seniors. I looked behind me first to make sure I was the one they wanted. They motioned for me to come sit with them. Some people are nice here. I sat down.

I introduced myself and told them I was new. They were amazed to hear where I was from.

"Hawaii?" a boy said, "Do you surf?"

"In the winter, when the waves are big."

"That's the bomb!"

"Do you know who he is?" I asked, pointing to the kid from the food line. He'd just sat down at a table. He was sitting with a short kid with even sandy hair and a tall one with a long face. They all seemed to be the best of friends.

"Oh, that's Derk Johnson," the tall, pretty girl named Alexandria said. "He's an asshole. Just don't take what he says personally."

"Okay."

"So, what high school did you transfer from?" Alexandria asked.

"I didn't. I just finished 8th grade."

They all looked at me, and then turned to each other.

"How old are you?" the boy asked.

"14."

"You look like… 17 or 18," Alexandria said.

"Cool," I responded.

They all looked at each other again. What was going on?

"I don't want to sound mean," the other girl said, "but we thought you were a senior. Could you sit someplace else?"

I felt a pang in my chest. I didn't know these people but I had thought they were nice. It hurt, but I wasn't going to show it.

"Okay," I said as nonchalantly as possible. I got up and looked for another table. The cafeteria was clearing out so one wasn't hard to find. I sat down at an empty table. I took a deep breath and swallowed a small lump in my throat. I hadn't cried since I was 11 and I wasn't about to start now.

I looked at my empty table. This wasn't the way it was supposed to be. It was supposed to be exciting and fun - a place to start fresh. I thought of going home but that would mean high school in Kamuela and living with Istvan. That would be much worse than being here.

I was just jumping the gun. I'd only been here a few hours. I hadn't even started classes. It was just some bad luck - the seniors, my roommate, and that asshole in line. I'd stick it out. Things had to get better. Everybody here couldn't be bad. I hoped.

CHAPTER II
I Need To Do a Method Three on You

It was Sunday, the day before classes started. Things weren't any worse, but they weren't any better. My roommate, Rob, would respond to my questions, but would never elaborate more than he had to. So much for making friends with him.

I got a notice in my mailbox. My school chore was evening kitchen duty between 6:30 and 8:00. I asked Rob what that meant.

"There are no janitors or cooks at Lamia. The students do all the work."

"That sucks."

"Every year we get a different chore. Worst job is the Trash..." he suddenly stopped. He looked like he was afraid he'd said too much.

"Trash what?" I prompted.

"I had scullery duty last year. Didn't like it much." He

stopped talking and buried his head in one of his books. I wasn't going to get any more out of him. What the hell was scullery? I wasn't sure I wanted to know. No custodians? We were paying to go here and we were forced to do manual labor? Even slaves didn't have to pay to pick cotton. There was nothing to do about it right then so I said no more.

Over the weekend I'd explored the school and found out some history. Lamia used to be a monastery. That's why it's so far from everything. Those willows I'd seen on the way in had been planted by monks over a hundred years ago. It was interesting, but I didn't really care.

If you walked from the main entrance straight through the lobby you'd end up in the old chapel. I usually wouldn't have cared, but the piano was there - a big, black grand piano. I liked to play but I only knew two songs. I'd only started taking lessons and playing piano in January but I was good for the amount of time I'd been playing.

I'd gotten into music when I was 13. I'd attended a ukulele festival and this kid picked out that famous Mozart piece. I'd never really cared about music before, but after that performance, I wanted to do what he'd done. I practiced on the uke every moment I could and within a year I'd gone beyond Mozart to Bach and Beethoven. It was the first time in my life I was actually good at something. However, I found the ukulele limiting for classical music so I switched to piano.

I gave my first performance at my 8th grade graduation. Our class sang "Stand By Me." I played the rhythm part on the piano. I didn't get it down until the day before the ceremony, but it was a lot of fun. Only the front of the piano was onstage so I could see the audience, but they couldn't see me. I liked it that way but Rebecca was pissed I couldn't be seen. Moms are like that.

At Lamia, we had bed check every night at 10:00 p.m. Everybody had to stand at their doors and we weren't allowed to leave until everybody was accounted for by one of the Rovers. Every week several older students were selected to be Rovers. They would wander the school day and night to make sure kids weren't trying to sneak out. It seemed pretty dumb to me. Where the hell were we supposed to go?

I looked around at my neighbors. To my left was a tall skinny kid named Curtis. If you looked up 'nerd' in the dictionary, his picture would be there. Down to my right was the only black kid I'd seen. His name was Stan and his roommate was Will. That one kid I'd seen at Derk's table, the short one with sandy hair was across the hall from me. His name was Jude Adams. Derk was far down the hall and I was glad of it.

Everybody was accounted for, so we were allowed to go into our rooms. The Rover told us there would be room check at 7:15 a.m. every weekday. That was way too early!

I awoke the next morning and tried to get a shower in before the check. We had a common bathroom at the end of the hall but the showers and sinks were all taken. There was even a line. Shit, I wanted to shave. I'd started shaving my upper lip right before I turned 14. There wasn't much there but it made me feel manly.

I went back to my room and used my little hand mirror to do it. I never asked Istvan how to shave because I didn't want a lecture. All I wanted was a demonstration but he couldn't *just* do that. I took the razor, placed it at my lip and drew up. I felt the ruff scrape of the steel on my skin. It wasn't so bad without water.

"What are you doing?" Rob asked.

I looked sideways.

"Shaving - SHIT!" I'd caught the blade on my lip and sliced an inch wide cut. "FUCK!" I yelled, trying to stanch the flow of blood.

"You shouldn't go against the grain."

"Doesn't do me any fucking good now. Goddamn it!"

It really hurt. This is how I was going to start my first day of school? Rob chuckled and left to go to the bathroom.

"Asshole," I thought. When I was sure he'd gone, I took my colored Clearasil and dabbed it on my pimples. It barely did anything to hide them. I used to use my sister's makeup, which worked really well, but Istvan caught me putting it on one time.

"Boys don't wear that shit," he lectured me. "Do you want people to think you're a frickin' fag?"

So I had to use this Clearasil crap. Being a guy sucks sometimes. I don't want to be a girl but sometimes it seems they have so much more freedom.

I looked again at the bumps on my face. I hated my zits! It looked like somebody had dipped a brush in red paint and flicked it at my face. I just wanted them to go away. I had some 'Polo' aftershave and dabbed it above my lip. The stinging always reminded me of *Home Alone*.

One of the Rovers came in at 7:15 sharp and looked around.

"Bed's not made," he said to me.

"Sorry. Didn't know I had to." I saw Rob's was made up. Why didn't he tell me?

The Rover marked something on a clipboard and left. I wanted to say something to Rob but didn't bother. "Don't worry," I told myself, "You'll fall into a rhythm here."

I dressed and went down to breakfast. The food quality had dropped considerably since the day before. The fried eggs looked like those novelty plastic food spills. It was nasty but there was nothing else, so I ate it.

What had happened? The food had been okay this weekend when our parents were dropping us off. Could it have only been a show for our folks?

"No," I thought, "that's just stupid." The Kamuela cafeteria had good and bad days, too.

After that unsatisfying breakfast I went to my room and got ready for class. My lip was still hurting but there was nothing I could do about it.

I grabbed my notebooks and some pencils and made my way up the stairs. I was wearing my $2 Locals - my flip-flops. I had to go up the stairs on the front of my feet so they wouldn't plop down so loudly. I heard laughter behind me.

"Look how he walks up the steps!" I looked back to see

four guys laughing at me and pointing at my feet. I glanced down. What the hell?

I pulled the door open to the strangest classroom I'd ever seen. It was one large room. There were rows of tables arranged in five columns. Four people could sit at each table. In front of each column was a desk with a Supervisor. All of the Supervisors seemed to be wearing the same blue shirts and dark pants. Over to my left were the older kids. To my right were what looked like Koreans and Japanese.

I couldn't see any signs to direct me to where I needed to be. I tapped somebody on the shoulder.

"Where's the 9th grade tables?"

"Don't know what you're talking about, man." The guy looked at me like I was an alien and moved away.

I walked to the middle of the room and looked around. A big clock on the wall by the door said 7:58. I still had a few minutes before class started. A very beautiful girl was looking around too. She was tall with long blonde hair, amazing breasts and impeccable taste in clothes. Maybe she was new as well.

"Do you know where the first years go?" I asked trying another tactic. I hoped I'd get to sit next to her.

"You mean Form Six?"

"Yeah." They apparently didn't have a 9th grade, but this Form thing sounded good to me.

"It's back there." She pointed to a far section of the room separated by columns.

"Where are you? I asked.

"Form Seven," she replied, smiled and pointed to another part of the large room. Oh, well.

"Thanks," I said, walked over and sat down. I settled in.

A bell went off and everybody quieted down. I'd never been in a school with a bell. Cool, just like a movie. The Supervisor at the front of our tables took out a checklist and started to read off names.

"Jim Anderson?"

"Here," a boy in a tie called.

"Clint Arnold?"

"Here," another boy called. And so on. I waited but as he moved on to the D's without calling my name I felt a small pang of fear. By the time he finished, I was freaking out. Was I in the wrong room or something?

"What's your name?" the Supervisor said, looking at me.

"C-S-U-B-A. *Chooba. Leaf Chooba*," I pronounced for him. People could never figure out Hungarian.

The Supervisor looked down his list. Then he shook his head.

"I don't see your name here."

What the hell? I glanced around. Everybody was looking at me. I hated this. What was going on? Just then a rotund woman with a short 80's hairstyle poked her head in through the columns.

"There you are, Leif." She sounded relieved to find me.

Who the hell was this? Who cared? She probably knew where I was supposed to go. I got up from the table and followed her. She took me to the area near the foreign kids.

"Get a little lost?" she asked.

"Yeah. I thought that was 9th - ah - first year of high school or something."

"It's okay," she said soothingly. "You're in Form Six Entry, not Form Six."

This made no sense to me but the other kids were waiting. I didn't want to ask just then.

"Here's the last one," she said, "I'm Constance Friend, your Supervisor. You can take your seats now."

The others made their way toward the tables.

"Mrs. Friend -" I began.

"Don't call me that," she said sternly.

"What?" I asked startled by her sudden change of tone.

"Call me Connie. Students don't call Supervisors by their last names."

I had no idea what to say. I'd always said Mr. this or Mrs. that. The idea of calling a teacher by their first name was just bizarre.

"Sure I can't call you Mrs. Friend?"

"No," she stated firmly. "What's your question?"

"Ah, what do I do, exactly?"

"Reading, for the first two hours. Go pick out a book from the back. Make sure it's on your list. Then we have an hour of writing. After lunch it's workbook."

She handed me a list of books and another list of what I guessed was workbook courses.

"So, any book on this list?" I asked.

"Not exactly. You start with the lower levels. One, two,

and three, then move up from there. You can't learn if it's too steep a gradient."

Made sense. I nodded and made my way to an empty seat. Not the best start but things were going okay now. I sat down next to a wiry guy with a big head.

"Hi," the guy said, taking my hand. "I'm Austin."

"Leif Csuba," I said shaking his.

"New here, huh?" He had a very nasally sounding voice but he seemed nice.

"Yup."

"I was in middle school last year but I didn't finish. That's why I'm in Form Six Entry."

"Yeah. What is that?"

"It goes by forms, not grades, here. Form One and Two are Lower School. Three through Five are middle. They're on the third floor, right below us, and Six through Eight are Upper. Form Six Entry is kind of a limbo form before Six. It means you know more than a middle schooler but not enough to be an upper schooler. We'll probably be over there in Form Six by next semester."

It was strange but it was their system.

"So this whole area is Form Six Entry?" I asked motioning.

"Us and the English as a Second Language students there. They'll move to Six when they finish their tests, too."

That explained why all the foreign kids were in one place.

"For a second I thought Lamia was segregated."

Austin didn't get my joke. He just cocked his head.

"Never mind," I said quickly.

Everybody else was reading so I guess I had to. I never liked reading. I'm more of a movie person, if you hadn't guessed. I looked over the lower levels on my book list. Most of them I'd never heard of, like *Watersky* and *The Book of Three*. I'd heard of *The Hobbit* and *Lord of the Rings*. They were like book versions of the movie *Willow*, but I couldn't start with those because they were level five. I went back to level one. AH! *The Black Stallion*. I'd heard of that. Well, I guess I had to start.

It's not that I don't enjoy books. I wasn't allowed to watch TV so Rebecca would read novels aloud every night to Istvan and me. My favorite book was *Ender's Game*. It was the story of a little boy in the future being trained to battle an alien force. Bec read it to us every year. When the doctor 'diagnosed' me with A.D.D. he also said I was dyslexic, which turned out to be true. I didn't need a mirror to read, but I could never remember anything I read.

Most people think dyslexia means we read words backwards. It's not that simple. I mix words up in a sentence or, if the word is too long, my brain will just take a guess from some of the letters. If I'm writing, I'll spell *rubbing* - r-u-p-p-i-n-g. It really sucks. I don't know I'm doing it. When I get to the bottom of the page I can't remember what I just read. I can still recall the doctor telling my mom and me just before I turned seven.

"Your son's dyslexic, Mrs. Csuba."

"Abbot," she corrected. "I kept my maiden name."

That was kind of true. The fact was my mom didn't like the name Csuba for herself.

"Sorry, Mrs. Abbot."

"Is there anything that you can do?"

"Not really," he said, leaning back in his chair. "Nope. If he's born with dyslexia, he'll die with it. That's it."

My mom was pissed at the way the doctor put it, but I didn't care.

I've found ways around my disability. I developed a great auditory memory and could memorize almost everything the teacher said in class, like deaf people who can read lips. I've always felt envious of people at airports who were reading to pass the time. If only reading could be easy and fun. That would be the greatest thing in the world.

I'd been psyched when Bec told me there were no teachers here but, thinking about it now, without somebody to hear, how was I going to learn anything?

These books on my list would be fine as long as I wasn't tested on them. I picked out *Black Stallion Legend* and started to read. I hadn't delved more than a few pages into it when Mrs. Friend came over.

"Where's your dictionary?"

"What, Mrs. Fr - Connie?"

"You can't read without a dictionary. What if you come across a Misunderstood Word?" Was she speaking English or did I just warp jump to another country?

"Come here," she said seeing my expression. I followed her to a row of books behind her desk. She pulled out a thick maroon dictionary and gave it to me.

"You must have a dictionary with you at all times."

"Oh," I said, nodding, "Can I keep this one?"

"No," she said putting her hands on her hips. "This one is too advanced and too heavy to carry. You need to buy your own from the library downstairs."

Great. My mom told me she'd left some allowance money with the Resident Director on my floor. I'd have to ask her for some. Dictionary, what a waste of money.

I thanked Mrs. Friend for the dictionary and sat back down. I looked at the massive volume. Like I need this! I wasn't stupid. I could figure words out by context. I continued reading my book. It was an okay story. The main dude was making way too big a deal out of this girl's death. It wasn't the end of the world. It was just love. I cracked my back and gave a nice yawn. I was about to keep reading when an older boy appeared over me.

"Did you get enough sleep?"

"Ah… I guess."

"Did you eat breakfast?"

Not really, but I wasn't going to criticize the food to him.

"Yeah."

"I need to do a Method Three on you. Could you come with me?"

I got up and followed him without question. I'd find out what was happening soon enough. He took me to this out of the way back room. The kid had a very athletic body, but the worst case of acne I'd seen. It kind of made me feel better about my own.

"I want you to start reading aloud," he commanded.

I hated reading aloud. Was this a test? Shit! I'd only read ten pages of the Black Stallion thing. I started to read.

"No," he stopped me. "Something simple."

He got up from the table and went to a bookshelf. He pulled a thin children's book out and handed it to me.

"Read this."

Was he joking? He didn't look like he was. I swallowed my disdain and began to read.

"Once upon a time there were three ducks. The… first was the best at-"

"Stop," he said.

"What?"

"You paused in that sentence."

"Huh?"

"You paused. You have a Misunderstood Word."

"What?" I was totally confused now.

"I want you to define every word in that sentence until we find your Misunderstood Word. That's the cause of your learning problem."

"Why?"

"That's what a Method Three is," he said exasperated, like I was an idiot. "After this, I need you to sign off that I was thorough."

"Okay. Okay." I surrendered, holding up my hands. "Just chill out. Okay. Duck… a bird that flies south in the winter.

First... starting-"

"What's the definition of *the*?"

Definition of *the*? Who gives a shit?

"It's just a word that goes between things."

"Look it up," he commanded.

I opened my massive maroon dictionary.

"The... the definite article in the... grammar of-"

"Stop. You paused. You have a Misunderstood Word in that definition. Define each word."

And so began the word chain. If I didn't know a word exactly, I had to look it up. Word after word after word. Definition after definition. Then I had to back track and keep going. It got so complicated I had to take frickin' notes. After two days of this I had only made it through a page and a half of the kiddy book. I was really frustrated. I was seriously contemplating strangling that kid.

On the third day he said, "We're done." He closed the kiddy book. He must be frustrated with me, too. Good.

"Thank God! I'm never doing a Method Whatever again."

"You don't have a choice," he said, "I saw you yawn. That's why I asked you. Yawning is a sure sign of a Misunderstood Word. Also, slouching and looking dazed. If somebody asks you to do a Method Three, you can't say no."

"Yeah, right." He then gave me the strangest look. I don't know how to describe it, but it was like I was a spy who'd been caught. He walked away without another word. I made my way back to my table.

Three days and I hadn't even started my course work yet. That Method Three was one of the worst experiences of my life. Unfortunately, there would be more to come at Lamia.

CHAPTER III
Followed

I showed up to the cafeteria for work detail at 6:30 and went through the double doors into the kitchen. Other kids were already there and the Supervisor was going through a list of names. He gave out assignments when he'd accounted for all of us.

"Alex," he said to a tall Korean kid, "mopping and sweeping. Clint, scullery."

I finally saw what the scullery was. It was a large conveyer belt that ran into a big machine. It was for cleaning dishes. The machine sprayed water everywhere and the scullery kids had to wear big aprons to keep from getting soaked. Rob was right. That was a bad job. I prayed that I didn't get that.

"Leif C... Scu..." the Supervisor said, struggling to pronounce my name.

"Leif Chooba," I finished.

"Right. Boilers."

Boilers? What the hell were those? When he was done giving out all the assignments he showed me the boilers. They were three huge aluminum vats for cooking large quantities of food. One was clean and empty, but the others were not. One had spaghetti, hard and caked to the insides. The other one was filled with baked beans. It made me sick to look at it.

"You clean these," he said to me, "and get them ready for tomorrow."

There had to be something else I could do. My mind raced. Then I looked at the kids with scullery duty. One of the girls was holding a hose and it was spraying a wide mist into the air. Her hair and clothes were dripping wet. It could be worse.

So, I began to clean the vats. I tackled the spaghetti first. I had to use the scraper from the grill to get that shit off. The vat was so big I had to stand on a milk crate so I could lean in and get to the bottom. It was not a good time.

I then turned to the vat filled with beans. I couldn't clean it filled up like that. I'd have to throw them out. I dragged a trashcan over and began to ladle out the beans.

"What are you doing, Leif?" the Supervisor yelled as he came over.

"What? I have to clean this thing."

"Don't throw food in the trash. Find a container and put it in the cold locker."

I looked down at the cold hard beans.

"But they're old. You really want to-?"

"That's what we do here. We don't waste food. What's not eaten today is served tomorrow and so on until it's gone."

Then I realized that these beans could be weeks old by now. I hadn't eaten much that day, but after that statement, I wasn't hungry anymore.

"Okay. Sorry."

The Supervisor left. I began to scoop the beans into a large white bucket. When I'd extracted as much as possible I waddled the heavy container to the cold locker. The locker smelled like cleaning fluid and old vegetables. I came back and looked into the mostly empty vat. The remaining beans had burnt to the bottom. It would take forever to get that clean.

I don't mean to sound spoiled but I felt very low class doing this. I did chores at home - vacuuming and sweeping. I cooked sometimes, but nothing like this. This was disgusting! I came here for school, not to do slave labor. I knew I couldn't argue. They'd say some bullshit about learning responsibility. Fucking adults!

Scrubbing the bean vat over and over wasn't so bad but the smell was terrible. It was like fermented dirt. I tried to breathe through my mouth so as not to get sick. I wasn't done by 8:00 so I had to stay longer. The front of my shirt was very damp from leaning over the sides of the vats. It was the first of countless days of kitchen chores.

A few days earlier I'd found a little slice of heaven at Lamia, the Rec Room. It was down near the laundry, almost in the basement. It wasn't big, but it didn't matter. It had a pool table, air hockey and foosball. The best part was the food counter: chips, pretzels, and soda. You had to pay for it, but I was so hungry I didn't care. I don't know why but for some reason the bright lighting and stark white walls in that place reminded me of the *Wonka Vision* room.

I ordered a Blue Sky cola and a soft pretzel with melted American cheese. I know this sounds weird, but it is the best way to eat a soft pretzel. I only had an hour before study hall so I enjoyed my time with a game of pool. I wasn't great, but my Grandpa had shown me a few tricks and I could hold my own. Without the simple pleasures of this room, kids would have revolted a long time ago.

Serving snacks out from behind the counter was a very plain looking girl with mousy brown hair. All she did was hand out food. I asked her how she'd gotten this chore. This was the job I wanted but I was sure it was given out by seniority or something.

"No. I'm in Form Six. They give the jobs out randomly."

Shit. I would have to work in the kitchen until next year.

I arrived at 10:00 for bed check. When that was over, I crawled into bed with my clothes on. I was so tired. I'd only had that one hour in the Rec Room to rest from both mental and physical work. The Petersons said I could call them any time I wanted and they'd bring me to their house for the weekend. I was definitely going to take them up on that offer soon.

"So, Leif," Rob began once the lights were out, "What's

up?"

He'd never initiated a conversation before, but I was too exhausted right then.

"I'm kind of tired. Can we talk another time?"

"I noticed you have a Mac."

"So what?"

"IBMs are better."

"No, they're not."

"All the great games are for IBMs."

"But Macs are easier to use. Just plug and play. You have to install your operating system on an IBM."

"But Windows '95 is the most stable operating system out there."

"But the desktop-" I was about to keep arguing, but I stopped myself. Where could this go? There was no way to prove either point.

"Look," I said, "Macs are better for some things and IBMs are better for others. Can we leave it at that?"

"No. IBM's are better everything."

"GOD!"

"Keep it down in there," a muffled voice called from outside the door. One of the Rovers on patrol.

"Please let me sleep," I begged Rob.

"IBMs are better," he almost sang.

And so it went on. I only got a few hours of sleep that night. The next morning I was dying on my feet. I don't think I've ever felt this miserable, even when I broke my wrist.

Odi, my best friend from Hawaii, and I had been playing at a waterfall about a mile from my house. Odi kept jumping from the top but I was too scared to make the 40 foot plunge, so I swam in the pond. I was getting out when I slipped on some moss. I instinctively tried to catch myself as I fell backwards. My left arm made a loud cracking sound under my full weight but it didn't hurt. I stared at my arm. There was this huge bump under my skin just behind my wrist.

"Holy shit!" Odi cried when he saw my arm.

I tried to bend it but it just twitched. I didn't know it was broken yet.

"I think I cracked my wrist," was all I could say. An x-ray at the hospital showed what the doctor called a 'greenstick' fracture. He explained that it only happened in kids when the bones weren't fully solid yet. The break isn't clean but jagged, like when you try and break a fresh *greenstick* from a tree or plant. Of course, the doctor didn't explain to me how he was going to fix it.

"Hold him," the doctor told the nurse.

The doctor put his thumbs on either side of the bone and pushed hard. I have never felt such horrendous pain in my life. I could barely keep myself from screaming. My arm ached for a whole week and when I got the cast off, the skin was so tight I couldn't bend my wrist. At least my mom was there to tell me it would be all right. Here, I had nobody.

When I came back into class from lunch I didn't feel like starting my workbooks. *Learning Techniques for Adulthood? Learning How to Read?* What kind of fucked up courses were those? Even though the books were all in the library I couldn't borrow them for the few weeks I'd be using them. I had to buy my own copies.

I just kept reading fiction books from my list. It was my way of protesting. If they knew how I felt about reading, they'd see how seriously I didn't want to do their dumb courses. But they didn't know.

When it came time for writing I asked if I could use the computer but Mrs. Friend said I had to take a typing test first. I needed 90% accuracy for two minutes at 50 words a minute. If I passed, they'd let me use the computer for writing. I went to the computers and tried, but couldn't even come close. Mrs. Friend said I'd have to write things out by hand. No way. I had to show her I needed a computer.

I wrote a guide to the best surfing beaches on my island - Mahai'ula's, Pine Trees, and Lyman's, but didn't even try to make my words clear. I gave her the paper and waited for her response.

"Your handwriting is illegible," she finally said.

"I know. That's why I need the computer."

"No computer until you pass the test. And you can't use your own for class work."

Great.

"So, what do I do?"

She brought me Lower School cursive books and told me to practice with each letter. This was a nightmare! I'd hated this crap in elementary school and I certainly didn't want to do it again.

I read the entire day. I had to yawn a lot but I soon got very good at suppressing them. My jaw ached by the time the final bell rang but it was better than getting another Method Three. As I was getting up to leave for the day Mrs. Friend came over to me.

"You didn't turn in your Cleared-List again."

"Huh?" My mind was way too mushy to deal with their lingo.

"The list students make for all the words they've Cleared that day," she prompted.

Is she fucking kidding? I hadn't looked up anything.

"I didn't do one."

"Leif," she said slowly shaking her head, "The Cleared-List is one of the most important aspects of our education system. How can you fix a Misunderstood Word if you don't remember it?"

Who cares?

"Sorry," I said, "I didn't know."

"That's not an excuse. Every time you read make a Cleared-List. Even when you're not in class."

"Okay." Now leave me alone. She walked off. God, I was so tired and hungry.

That night something sort of good happened. I met a girl at dinner. She was from Austria and this was her first year, too. This was also her first time on the mainland, so I kind of felt a kinship with her. She wasn't beautiful but she was kind of pretty. Her name was Constanze.

After dinner we walked the halls, talking. I asked her why

she'd come here.

"This is school which go by teaching of my faith." She had a heavy accent, but hell, I could only speak one language. Who was I to criticize?

"You mean like Catholic, or Baptist?" I remembered Rebecca mentioning this was a religious school before she left but I hadn't seen any bible classes or whatever religious schools did.

"No. Scientology."

I'd never heard of it.

"What's that?"

"We no believe in medicine. You, you heal yourself."

"Interesting." I didn't believe it, but if it got them through the day, whatever. I wanted to impress her so I told her wild stories about the music camp I'd gone to that summer.

"This one kid was totally crazy," I began, "I remember coming back to our cabin and this spacey kid, who kept talking about killing himself, was on the bed crying. He was naked except for a towel. One of the counselors was yelling at the crazy kid. The spacey kid was, like, allergic to aerosol spray. When the spacey kid was taking a shower, the crazy kid came in and sprayed Lysol in the stall so the kid couldn't see. Then, the crazy kid came at him with a pair of scissors. He tried to cut his dick off Bobbit-style. The kid ran out of the stall, blind and screaming. They found him in the field."

"That is terrible!" she said, covering her mouth. I had her. This was the jewel in my collection of stories.

"Yeah. That kid was totally gone. He had to take these

pills or he would start vomiting blood."

"Ugh!" she said, her face bunched up.

I knew these were guy stories, but I wanted to make an impression. When we reached the hall near the empty middle school on the third floor, she said it was late and had to go to bed. I asked if she wanted to sit with me at dinner the next day. She said sure and, after saying good night, I went to my dorm room.

The next morning there was a pink slip in my mailbox. I'd never seen anything like this.

> *Ethics Violation: Discussing drugs*
> *with another student.*

"What the hell?" I said aloud.

Some of the other kids in the mailroom looked at me. What was this crap? The bottom of the slip was signed by Connie Friend, my Supervisor. Classes were starting in 10 minutes. I'd talk to her after the roll call.

"What's this?" I asked, holding up the pink slip.

"It's an Ethics Report," she stated matter-of-factly.

"I wasn't discussing drugs with anybody." The only drugs I'd ever seen in my life was when D.A.R.E. had visited our school and brought examples.

"Don't deny it. I heard you."

"When?"

"Last night, with Constanze."

"Last night?" My mind was spinning.

"You were discussing the medication of another boy."

Did she mean the crazy kid and his pills? That wasn't discussing drugs. This slip made it sound like I was a pusher or something. Then a strange thought hit me. That was 9:30 at night.

"But that was after class. How did you…?"

"I was following you."

The noises of the room seemed to die away. I looked at her to see if this was a joke or something. She just looked back at me. No humor. No guilt.

"Ah… what?"

"We always follow new students when they first arrive."

All new students? I remembered the empty corridors with Constanze. There was nobody there. She must have been lurking. I felt a prickling on my scalp. She spoke like this was an everyday conversation.

"Why?" was all I could say.

"To make sure you're not doing anything you're not supposed to. Now, go to the Ethics Office and be dealt with."

In a kind of daze I turned and left the room. Even I knew exactly where Ethics was. I climbed the stairs to the 5th floor and went into the Ethics Office. It was a small, blank room with four chairs and another door. Two kids were sitting there, just staring at the wall. Weird. Was this it? Or was there more than one Ethics Office?

"This is Ethics, right?" I asked.

"Shhh," the girl hissed. Then in a whisper, "You're not allowed to talk."

I shut up and sat down. I looked at the two kids. They were staring blankly at the walls like during that boring lecture about tariffs in *Ferris Bueller*. It was strange. I looked around the bare room. There were no magazines or anything. I should have brought something for the wait. It wasn't too late.

I stood up to leave when the other door flew open. A fat lady, with a stern face and pulled back grey hair, glared at me.

"Where are you going?"

"I was just going to get a book or something."

She stomped over, took my shoulders, and sat me back in the chair hard.

"No books, no work, no talking. You will sit here and think about what you've done."

"But I didn't-"

"No talking!" She stomped back, closing the door behind her. This Ethics Lady must be like the principal around Lamia. I caught a peek inside before she shut the door. There was nobody else in there. She was keeping us waiting on purpose. This had to be a joke. It was too... *Oliver Twist* or something. Sit and think about what I've done?! I didn't do anything wrong. In two seconds I was finished thinking about it.

And so I waited. Eventually the other kids went in. I heard muffled voices and drawers opening and closing, but nothing specific.

It was over an hour before my turn came. She closed the door behind me. Her office was very small and cramped with filing cabinets. There was one big window overlooking the bland Northwest landscape. I could see the road I'd come in on far in the distance.

The Ethics Lady was looking at a folder with my name on it. Then she read another pink slip. This one had much more writing on it. She put it down and looked at me. I stared right back into that fleshy face.

"This is your first year at Lamia, Leif Csuba." She pronounced my name perfectly. For some reason it creeped me out. "Why were you discussing drugs with a student?"

"I wasn't." I told her about telling Constanze the story of the crazy kid. She never moved. She just stared at me. It was unnerving.

She looked me up and down. "So you admit you were discussing drugs?"

Was she wearing earplugs or something?

"No. Drugs are illegal things like pakalolo or whatever. This was prescription. I don't even know what it was called."

"There is no difference between illegal and prescription. They are all drugs."

I didn't know how to respond to that.

"So you were discussing drugs," she decreed.

"If you put it that way then, I guess." I wanted to get out of there as soon as possible. It felt like the filing cabinets were about to fall in on me but I wasn't going to admit I'd done anything wrong when I hadn't.

"It was just a story. I wasn't telling her to go buy some."

She just looked at me. Then she opened my folder and wrote on it.

"What are you writing?"

"Don't ask questions. I'm glad you admit to discussing drugs. We can now correct the problem."

What? Hadn't she heard me?

"But I- "

"Are we going to have a problem?"

I looked at her.

"This being your first offence, I'm willing to let you off with a warning, if you admit to it. Yet, if you keep denying it, I can find a suitable punishment for lying."

Jesus Christ! Was she serious? She looked it. I hated the idea of admitting I'd done something wrong but a warning sounded better than a punishment.

"I… I'm sorry I discussed drugs with a student," I finally managed to get out.

"Good. You are never to talk about any type of drug. Understand? Not even headache medicine."

"What about the willows right outside? You know aspirin is made from the bark."

Her eyes narrowed for the briefest of moments. I realized it was a dumb thing to say.

"Sorry. I won't discuss any type of drugs with students." I never really had in the first place, so that wouldn't be too hard.

"If you do, there will be serious consequences."

She put my folder back in the filing cabinet and kicked the

drawer shut. The sound made me jump. Then she opened the door. I left as fast as I could without trying to look like I was.

What was the point of that whole thing? She had already decided I was guilty before she saw me. Fucking waste of time! I tried to forget about the whole thing. I went back downstairs to class, but as I was walking, I looked over my shoulder to see if I was being followed.

CHAPTER IV
A Brief Escape

My first week was over. I still wasn't doing my coursework. I just kept reading books in my own silent protest. I made a bogus Cleared-List every day. I randomly wrote down words and their definitions. I also opened my dictionary from time to time to give the appearance of determining words. It worked. Mrs. Friend never said anything.

Work detail was exactly the same. Every night at 6:30 I'd show up at the kitchen to clean those frickin' vats. Sometimes only two of the three had been used but it still took me the whole time to get them done.

Rob was still keeping me up every night asking me strange questions and provoking arguments. Sometimes he'd ask me elaborate riddles. I've never been one for those things. I tried to figure them out, but it was getting irritating.

I tried talking to Constanze at dinner, but she avoided me.

I wondered why. A day or so later I was walking to the cafeteria when I noticed something new. On the wall by the entrance was a large bulletin board covered by a pane of glass. It was for official use and could only be opened with a key. It had been empty until now, but taking up almost half of the space was a list entitled: Ethics Infractions and Repentance. There were three names on it. I didn't know the first two, but recognized the last one.

> *Leif Csuba: Ethics Violation– On the night of September 2nd discussing drugs with another student. Leif was turned in and admitted his guilt.*

What the hell was this shit? Everybody could read this. I went into dinner and found Big-head Austin.

"The EIR," Austin replied.

"The *Ear*?" I asked.

"The Ethics Infractions and Repentance list. They post a list with the names of ethics offenders on it."

He said this so calmly.

"Why?"

"So you know what people have done wrong."

This pissed me off. There was no point other than to embarrass us.

"But I wasn't disci..." I stopped mid-sentence. The Ethics Lady's words about some suitable punishment for continuing to deny it came back to me. There was nobody here I could complain to.

"Didn't what?" Austin prompted.

"Never mind."

Every day after class we had gym. The gym had a volleyball court but it was for the varsity team. All we did was lift weights. It sucked.

Derk was there at the same time I was.

"What kind of fucked up name is Scuba?"

"It's not Scuba," I tried to explain to Derk. "The letters CS are like CH in Eng-"

"I said, what kind of fucked up name is that?" he cackled loudly.

Near by other kids snickered. I felt a flicker of hot anger in the pit of my stomach, but ignored it.

"Man! *Leaf*?" Derk went on, "if Scuba wasn't stupid enough. Did your parents never want you to get laid?"

I'd been teased before about my name and knew how to deal with it.

"My dad's from Hungary," I began, "and he thought Leif..."

"I don't give a shit about your gay-ass father. You're dumber than Scrubs." Derk shook his head and walked away.

What the hell was Scrubs? Idiot! Derk should be glad that Istvan wasn't here. Istvan detested Homosexuals and any association with him, even a joke, would not be tolerated. Isht would have no qualms about wailing on a 14 year old kid. My dad probably wouldn't have stood by me, so I wasn't about to defend his honor or anything. I decided I would just try my best to ignore Derk for the rest of the year.

I was hungry all the time. One day I tried to eat the sloppy joes, but I almost vomited right there in the cafeteria. It was just so rancid, like pouring straight vinegar on my tongue. The bread was the only thing that was consistent. Toast became my only sustenance.

Even though there was a television, there was no cable or broadcast. The television was hooked up to a VCR in a small TV room on the 2nd floor, but we could only use it on the weekends and only to watch PG movies. Unless you arrived hours in advance and staked it out, you could never watch anything you wanted. Guys would always put on martial arts films or, if chicks got a hold of the VCR, they'd put on stupid shit like *Moll Flanders.*

Down in the basement was a small room with three pay phones. We didn't have any phone lines in our rooms and only rich Hollywood people had cell phones, not like they would work out here in Boony Land. I used the calling card my mom had given me.

"So, Honey, how was your first week?" my mom asked, "Did you make any friends?"

"Not really, Bec."

"Oh, don't worry. You're new. It just takes time."

"I don't know. People can't even pronounce my name."

"Leif Csuba, right?" A boy, walking by right then said.

"Ahh… yeah," I was astonished. Who the hell was he?

"Cool," he nodded, and walked away. What was going on here?

"Leif? Are you there?" Rebecca was still on the line.

"Yeah. Sorry about that, Bec."

"So, how are classes?"

"Ah, okay," I said, unenthusiastically. "It's really strange here. I was foll-"

A dial tone buzzed in my ear.

"Bec?" I'd lost the connection. Damn! Now I'd have to enter in all those calling card numbers again.

"I guess we got cut off," Rebecca said when I got her back.

"Yeah. Long distance."

"Is it nice having one subject at a time? Going at your own pace?"

I'd forgotten that that's the reason I came here.

"I guess. I got my name on this list called the-"

Dial tone again. Jesus! The phones in this place were shit. I was about to dial again but stopped. My hand hovered over the buttons. I looked around the divider. People were on the other two pay phones, talking away happily about how nice school was and what great friends they had. I felt a chill in my gut. It was strange how the line disconnected like that. It cut off just when I was about to tell her about... I thought of Mrs. Friend being told to follow me. Were they listening?

I put the phone back on the hook and stood up. This was impossible. This was a school. But what if they were listening? My breath was coming short and fast. I needed to get out of here now. But how? I was in the middle of nowhere. Then I remembered. I picked up the phone and dialed the Petersons. A few minutes later I hung up with a smile. I was going away. Mr. Peterson said they were going to the beach that weekend and would pick me up Friday night. Beach sounded good. Too bad I didn't have my board with me.

I was about to leave the basement, but realized I'd never been down here. I should check it out. I began to wander. It was a maze of corridors like in *The Labyrinth*. I kind of liked it, except for the odor. It smelled like that gray stuff you pull out of the dryer.

Nobody was down here. I found a big room with kiddy drawings of suns and happy faces up on the walls. Must be the Lower School where Rob's mom worked. Their classroom was down here? That sucks. At least we had windows in ours.

I heard a clanking sound from down one of the hallways. This one wasn't as well lit as the others. As I moved forward I began to notice a different smell, a mixture of smoke and putrefaction. There was an old metal door that wasn't placed well on its hinges. You could see through the sides and into the room without opening it. The smell was worse than that skunk. What the hell was in there? I looked inside.

The room was filled with dumpsters. At the bottom of nine steps, the floor was alive with cockroaches. Flies were buzzing around everywhere. In the center of the room was a large furnace pulsing with heat. Pipes like a network of arteries, led up into the ceiling. Even from here it was sweltering. But, it wasn't the bugs or smell that held my attention.

Two kids with shovels were scooping garbage off the floor or out of the dumpsters and tossing it into the furnace. They were covered with soot, smeared from their constant perspiration. Flies were crawling all over them. They looked like coal miners with bubonic plague. I even saw some flies crawling out of their noses, but it was their eyes that chilled me. Dead eyes, like those kids in Ethics. My throat felt suddenly cold, like I'd swallowed refrigerant. I knew now exactly what Hell was supposed to be like.

I backed away and ran. I ran until I found the door to the outside. I burst free into the open air in front of the right wing.

So that was the Trash Room chore. Suddenly my vats didn't look so bad. Thank God I hadn't been randomly assigned there. Those poor kids. I kind of felt bad for my own glee. Like trying to get my name off the EIR, there was nothing I could do for them. I found the door that would take me to the dorms and went back inside.

The next week passed much as the first. I didn't have any friends and I still wasn't doing my course work. I did call my parents, but didn't talk about being followed or the slave labor. I'd tell them when I could call from another phone.

It seemed that Friday would never come. At bed check on Thursday we were told that our hall was selected for Sunday chores. We had to mop the linoleum on the first two floors and vacuum the carpets. Suckers. I'm not going to be here.

During class on Friday some boy came up to me with a

clipboard asking which study hall I was taking that weekend.

"I'm not."

"You have to."

"Sorry," I corrected quickly, "I meant I already signed up for Saturday."

"Oh. Okay," he said and moved off. I was glad he hadn't double-checked.

I was down in the lobby at 6:45. I wasn't going to miss Mr. Peterson by a second. It was raining but I was raised in the rain so I didn't pay it any mind.

"Where are you going?" the Lobby Lady asked.

"Nowhere," I lied. "Just waiting for someone." I only had a backpack with me, so it looked like it could be schoolwork.

I waited. Mr. Peterson was late by an hour. Where was he? I'm sure it looked kind of strange to the lady with me just sitting there. Then I saw headlights through the downpour and I rushed outside.

"Excuse me," the Lobby Lady said as I flew by. I didn't stop. I ran out the door and jumped into the passenger seat before the car came to a stop.

"Hey there, Sport," Mr. Peterson said, smiling through his braces.

"Let's go," I said, eyeing the door. What if the lady came after me? Go, go, go!

"Sure thing. Jack and Ruth are waiting for us at the beach."

We took off. I looked back as the school melted into the

dark, rainy night. I slumped in my seat.

"Thanks for coming."

"You bet. You like Yanni?"

"I guess." I had no idea what that was. He turned on some strange music, but I didn't care. I had escaped. I looked around the car. It was like an oversized Jeep.

"This is a pretty big car."

"Thanks. It's an SUV."

SUV, huh? Whatever got me away from here. I wondered what SUV stood for - Super Uber Vehicle, probably. I liked that. We drove on through the night.

The beach wasn't like the beaches in Hawaii. It was dark and cloudy. There were waves, but you couldn't go in the water because it was too cold. The beach was made of rounded rocks, not sand. It hurt to walk on. Was this what going to the beach on the mainland was like? Major suckage.

We spent most of the time at the little beach house playing board games on the floor. Jack and John talked constantly about football. I never followed the game so I didn't have much to add. Mrs. Peterson bustled around cleaning things that already looked pretty clean.

They asked me about school, but I didn't go into any details. After several one or two word responses they sort of stopped trying. I wanted to talk to Rebecca first. There was no phone at the beach house and I hadn't brought my calling card, so I'd have to wait to call Bec when I visited their house the next time. I know I should have been more polite, but I was just so glad to get away from Lamia. I didn't care if

Saddam Hussein had come and picked me up.

Saturday night we went to a seafood restaurant and I gorged myself. They were surprised at my voracious appetite, but didn't scold me.

They took me back on Sunday afternoon. I didn't want to return, but I felt I could handle it. Those few days away had been like popping a mint to clear a bad taste from my mouth.

"Call me anytime you want to come over," Mr. Peterson said as I got out of the car.

"Thank you, Mr. and Mrs. Peterson. See ya, Jack."

They drove away and I walked inside. The Lobby Lady got up from her desk when she saw me come in.

"Where were you? Your parents were worried."

The Petersons had told me they'd talked to my mom before they picked me up.

"My mom said it was okay for me to go with them. They're old family friends."

"You just can't leave without telling the school."

"Sorry. I didn't know." *Can I go now, bitch?* I wanted to say, but didn't.

"Your Supervisor wants to speak with you."

I tried not to groan aloud but it slipped out. I went upstairs and waited for her. What were they going to do? My mom said it was okay. I had to hear this.

Mrs. Friend came in and sat down across from me.

"I heard you went away this weekend."

"My mom has friends who took me to the beach."

"Mmm," Mrs. Friend said, studying me. "Are you going

away next weekend?"

I hadn't thought about it, but that sounded good to me.

"Sure. I'll probably go every weekend."

"No, you're not," Mrs. Friend said, looking hard at me.

"Why?"

"You're falling behind in your class work. You need to take the study halls over the weekend to catch up. And hall chores on the weekends are necessary to maintain the school."

That was logical but I had a feeling that wasn't really the reason.

Mrs. Friend went on, "I'll have to talk to your mom about this. Tell her it's important that you remain here as much as possible. We'll ask her to talk to her friends, too."

"It's only a few days and it's the weekend," I protested. "There's nothing about me having to stay here the entire time."

Mrs. Friend thought for a minute. "True, but I'm going to limit your trips to twice a month until you catch up with your work. I'm sure your parents will agree."

I didn't know what else I could say or do.

"Fine."

I got up and left. I made my way back to my dorm room and lay on my bed. I closed my eyes. Twice a month. Oh, well. At least it was something. I took some comfort in the fact that they probably didn't want me to leave at all. I smiled. It wasn't a victory, but I hadn't lost either.

Then I thought of the phone call the week before. If they were listening, then they would have known about the trip to the beach. I knew I was over reacting. But what if they suspected I knew and didn't want to tip their hand? Or they only monitored my home number so the Peterson's number didn't... AH! I physically shook my head. I was going to drive myself crazy with this. There was no way to really know. All I knew is I'd get to leave this godforsaken place twice a month. That was all that mattered.

CHAPTER V
26 Days

I thought they were joking when I was told that masturbation was forbidden at Lamia.

"Come on," I said. "How are they going to enforce that?"

Oh, but they did. Anytime you left class you had to mark the reason and what time you left. The Supervisor checked it. If you said you forgot a book and weren't back in two minutes, they'd come looking for you.

A kid named Daniel tried it. He ran down to his room and tried to beat off in one minute. It's not impossible, but it's no easy task. Unfortunately, his roommate walked in because he had actually forgotten a book and caught him. Daniel was sent to Ethics. I don't know what his punishment was. Probably some extra chore or something.

Narcing was encouraged at Lamia and rewarded. If you learned somebody was doing something they weren't supposed to, you were obligated by the rules to tell. You then were praised throughout the school as a model student. I didn't know every single rule at the school and was always on edge because I never knew when that little pink slip could appear in my mailbox. I'm sure that same fear kept the other students in line.

Room check was at 7:15 a.m. After classes you had gym, an activity, dinner, then forced labor, and study hall. You only had about an hour of free time a day. Your roommate could be in the room then and, if he wasn't, he could come back at anytime.

One kid tried during that hour of free time when he knew his roommate would be away. He went to the bathroom to get some toilet paper. On the way back to his room he ran into a Rover.

"What's with the toilet paper?"

"Ah, I spilled some soda on the floor in my room. Just wanted to clean it up."

"That won't do. Go back to the bathroom and get the mop and bucket."

The kid returned to the bathroom and waited. When he peeked out and saw that the hallway was empty, he ran back to his room and proceeded. Just as he was getting to the climax the closet door opened and the Rover came out. He'd suspected what the boy was going to do and hid. He popped out at the worst moment, just before release so the kid couldn't finish. The boy was also sent to Ethics.

How do I know all these stories? The offenders were all posted on The EIR, but the details were circulated by the

Rovers and Supervisors to all the students. They wanted to embarrass the offenders and keep others from doing it. They had a system and it worked.

I've known how to jerk off since I was five. Istvan explained the procedure. I guess he was trying to impart some fatherly advice or something, but I was too young to comprehend. After the lecture I tried it but didn't understand why I was doing it. It wasn't until many years later that I really began to feel the urge to pick it up again.

Odi and I used to have races, to see who could climax the quickest. I usually won. Odi blamed it on the fact that I was three months older. We never touched each other or anything like that. We're not gay. We were 11. We weren't thinking about sex or any of that shit. It just felt good. Plus, at that age you don't have to worry about cumming all over the place.

By the time we were 13, our races began to feel awkward. We were starting to get interested in girls and girls always complicated things. We agreed to go our own separate ways in the jacking off department. I missed the time when it was just something for fun. Now it was a necessity.

By the fourth week of school I was getting pretty tense. I went to sleep with an erection and woke up with one. Sometimes just the movement of crossing my legs in class caused a stiffy. I then had to surreptitiously tuck it up under my waistband so it wasn't obvious. It sucked. My face constantly felt flushed and I could hear my heart beating in my chest all the time. I just wanted the tension to go away, but didn't know how. Males produce over 100 million sperm a day and it continually builds up.

That line in *Vice Versa* finally made sense to me. A father and son magically change places. When they realize it could be permanent, the father says how terrible it will be that he'll have to go through puberty again.

I found the only way I could take a shower was at random times in the afternoon and only about twice a week. Mornings and nights were always too crowded. There was only one warm shower, the third one from the right. The others were tepid at best.

One day, while taking a shower, I got the idea. I could do it here. I looked down at the stained tiles. No way. I was not sitting on that. I'd never tried standing up. I leaned against the wall and went for it. It was not easy. By ten minutes my arm was getting tired. I tensed my whole body trying to find some release. The warm water pouring on my head was distracting, but I'd get too cold turning it off. Come on, please let this happen.

I moved my hand as fast as possible. Then I climaxed. It felt as if a sand bag was taken off my chest. I took a deep long breath. 2.5 billon sperm. That felt so good! Using my foot I washed the cum down the drain. Perfect. Nobody will ever know. Then it occurred to me that I probably wasn't the first guy to think this up. I looked down at the grayish tiles. I was even more glad I hadn't sat on them.

I left the shower and went back to my room. Rob was there. I squinted against the harsh fluorescent light.

"Can we turn that light off? I have a desk lamp over here."

I told everyone I didn't like bright lights. Adults thought I was photophobic and kids thought I was a Gremlin. I didn't care. There was more to it though. I didn't want the lights on because I didn't want people to see my pimples.

"No," Rob said, with a smile, "I like the light."

"Well, I don't."

"Light switch is on my side of the room."

"Are you serious?"

"Yes. That side is yours, and this is mine. You can do whatever you want on that side."

Was this Kindergarten? It was so stupid I didn't know how to argue. I went over and closed the window. My hair and skin were still damp and a cold breeze was causing chicken skin to pop up on my arms and legs.

"Don't touch my window!" Rob yelled, jumping up.

"What? It's cold outside."

"That's my window. Put more clothes on."

"Why should I? Your cold air is coming onto my side of the room," I said, trying to use his logic.

"Not my fault. You can keep your window closed, but this is mine. I like the cold." He was doing this just to bug me.

"Fine." I wrapped up in my blankets. Rob went back to reading his learning books. Soon my mind wandered back to that great jerk and how good it felt. God, how much more relaxed I was. 26 days without jerking off. I'd never gone that long before. It wouldn't be the longest though.

I closed my eyes and reveled in the feeling. I wanted to sleep now, but soon they'd be here for bed check and I'd have to get up. But that was fine. I finally felt normal.

CHAPTER VI
The Piano Student

I hung out a lot in the chapel. Had I been religious I probably would have been praying to God for help, but I was playing the piano. As I played, I kept stealing glances at the front of the room hoping somebody, anybody would come to see me.

Back at Kamuela I'd practiced the piano every afternoon, hoping girls would hear and come talk to me. I could just imagine it:

"I like your playing," some insanely gorgeous girl would say, walking into the music room.

"Thanks. It's for you," I would say, leaning against the piano with a knowing smile on my face.

"Really? That's so sweet of you. Play something else for me."

No girls came and neither did anybody here. I just kept practicing the two pieces I knew over and over again. Playing the piano at Lamia I felt more alone than at any time, but I kept coming back day after day. I hated being alone, but playing music was the only time I really felt like myself.

Sometimes I just laid my head against the piano and wished I could cry, just to get some attention. But I was a guy and that wasn't right.

Why would anybody give a shit about me or what I had to say? I wasn't smart or cool. I had pimples. My hair was a frizzy brown bird's nest and I weighed 165 pounds. Even Rebecca said I was too heavy. Was feeling sorry for myself going to make anything good happen? No. Fuck!

"Hello?"

I stopped playing. A girl was standing in the shadows of the doorway.

"Hello?" I called back. My voice echoed off the hard walls.

"Sorry to interrupt you."

"No, it's cool." Who was she?

"Can I turn the lights on?"

I really didn't want the light, but I wanted to see who she was more.

"Go for it."

The lights in the high ceiling went on and there she was. She was very cute, with a big smile and shiny dark hair.

"What's up?" I stammered, "I'm Leif."

"Camila," she said, walking toward me. "You're very good."

"Aw, I only know a few pieces." Come on, I told myself.

More confidence.

"What was that one you were just playing?" She was standing only a few feet from me now. She was even cuter than at a distance. My heart began to race.

"Beethoven. Moonlight Sonata."

"I like that." She was now standing right next to me. Her arm brushed against mine. I could feel a stiffening in my pants. Not now! Go down! Go down!

"I always wanted to play," she said, tilting her head and looking down at the piano. I prayed she hadn't noticed my erection.

"Um, I can show you, if you want?"

"Really?" she asked, looking into my eyes. "I can't read music though."

"I'm not so good either. I sort of picked this up by ear. Yeah, just sit down here."

She sat down next to me. She smelled like Herbal Essence Shampoo. This was it. This was what I had always wished for. Why couldn't I be all cool and confident like I was in my mind?

"Just put your right hand here." I moved her hand over the G#, C# and E keys. "And just do this." I played the notes.

She repeated what I did.

"With your left just play this octave." I showed her. She played the whole thing.

"I did it!" she said, smiling and bouncing.

"See. Easy as pie, simple as cake."

I showed her how to play the first few bars of the piece.

This small achievement made her very happy. I was psyched to be the cause of it. Every time she was concentrating on playing I stole the opportunity to check out her tits. They were very nice.

After an hour she said she had to go, but could I show her some more tomorrow night? I heartily agreed. She left the chapel. I checked out her ass the whole way out. I didn't even mind she hadn't turned out the lights. My dreams had finally come true. I knew things would be better here.

The next day at lunch I saw her at a table. I was walking over to sit with her, but this big Korean kid dressed like a rapper sat down next her. She smiled and hugged him. I felt my heart drop hard. She had a boyfriend. I should have known. The good ones are always taken. I looked around for another seat. She spotted me standing there.

"Leif!" she called out, "Come, sit."

Should I? I couldn't think of an excuse not to. I sat down across from the Korean kid. He was even bigger than I was. He had lots of gold chains around his neck, a sideways baseball cap, and spoke in loud but broken English.

"This is Jae," Camila said, "Jae, this is Leif."

He shook my hand very roughly. He then gave me a cool look. For the rest of the meal he talked continuously about sports and other things. I didn't get a chance to interject anything. It was almost like I wasn't there. When I was done with my buttered toast I left. Better to leave them alone. She probably wasn't going to come tonight. I felt my heart drop some more. Oh, well. It was kind of nice while it lasted.

I came to the chapel anyway that night. What else was I going to do? I started to play the piano. I needed to cheer myself up. "Fur Elise" would do it. I really like the B section of the piece. It reminded me of something you'd hear in an Old West saloon.

The chapel door closed. The sound echoed around the room. I turned. There she was. I smiled and felt my sprits lift.

"There you are," I said, trying to sound like the cool Leif in my mind, "You ready?"

"Sure." She came over and sat next to me. She'd forgotten everything I'd showed her the day before, but I didn't mind demonstrating again. Maybe she'd forget about that Korean guy and become my girlfriend. Chicks like musicians. That guy was just big and cocky. I had depth.

A girlfriend. That would make everything right. It wasn't just the physical part I craved. I wanted somebody I could tell how I felt and who would care. I hadn't had a girlfriend in over a year.

I'd met her at summer camp up in Puget Sound. It was a fun relationship. Erin was the first girl I ever French kissed. But then camp ended and she went back to Pennsylvania and I went back to Hawaii. We never exchanged information, so that was it.

You may not believe this but for most of my life, girls had always liked me. I kissed my first girl when I was in preschool and by the time I was 12, lots of girls were asking me out. I didn't even have to try. I was on my way to becoming "a player."

A few months into 8th grade, puberty hit me hard and, aside from the physical abnormalities, I became very introspective and depressed. I didn't understand why I felt this way. It felt as if I knew something about the world that nobody else did or could. I would see people going about their lives and just wanted to shout at them, "Stop! Don't you even think about what you're doing? You have a life and you don't even know it!" I felt separated from everybody.

After the winter break in 8th grade I stopped eating lunch with others in my class and sat alone by the Art Room. Nobody seemed to care that I was gone. That only made me feel more depressed. Even girls stopped seeking me out. I would sit there in silence, day after day, playing out in my head exchanges and conversations.

Camila was different. She wouldn't be here if she didn't like me, right? She would make the year since Erin worth it.

We'd been there practicing for about 20 minutes when the door to the chapel flew open. I looked up and Big Jae was standing there blocking most of the light from the lobby with his size. He stomped down the aisle toward us. Camila stopped playing and looked at him with curiosity. I stood up and took a few steps toward him.

"Hi," I said.

Jae kept coming straight at me. He quickly came up the few stairs to the stage. I should have done something but I only stood there, waiting to see what he was going to do. Jae put his palms out flat and shoved me hard. I wasn't expecting the impact on my chest and launched backwards. I tried to stop myself from hitting the concrete floor but I couldn't. My right knee slammed down hard followed by the rest of me.

"Shit!" I yelled, holding my knee. The pain was excruciating.

"You fell?" Big Jae said, genuinely perplexed.

"Jae!" Camila scolded, "Why'd you do that?"

"I push my friends all the time and don't fall. I don't know he falling down. Here."

Jae walked over and extended his hand to help me up. I didn't take it. I pushed my way to my feet. My knee was on fire.

"Why weren't you ready for it?" Jae asked, looking down at me.

"What the hell do you mean?" It took superhuman effort to control my anger and not strike out. The fire in my knee seemed to spread through my insides. The pain made it difficult to get words out.

"How would I know you'd shove me across the room!"

"Wow," Jae said, "You should be more ready."

"Are you okay?" Camila asked.

"Yeah, I'm okay." I was trying to act more macho than I felt. I took a step and pain shot up to my groin.

"Are you sure?" she said, watching my expression.

"Fine." I walked out of the chapel without another word. I could hear them talking behind me but didn't listen. What the fuck? What the fuck! *Why did you fall*? Fucking idiot!

My stomach burned in anger.

I hopped up the stairs to my room. I was glad Rob wasn't there. I sat on the bed and rubbed my knee, hoping that would ease the pain, but it didn't. Wish they'd let me have some Tylenol. I was in pain and I was hungry. Fucking Lamia. This was the same knee I hurt in a car accident a year ago.

I'd been sitting in the passenger seat with my knees to my chest when a drunk driver swerved in front of Rebecca. She managed to miss him but slammed into a car parked along the side of the road. I had a seat belt on, but still hurled forward. I cracked the dashboard in half. It was my first car accident. It was much more jarring than movies made it out to be. Cars always rolled and skidded in slow motion. Real accidents are over before you can even prepare yourself. I didn't break my knee but I was in an Ace Bandage for a few weeks. I can still remember limping out of the crumpled car and seeing this green fluid all over the ground.

That same knee was hurting now. Even if Camila had never come tonight, I'd always have the good memory of the night before. This incident tainted the whole experience like adding salt to soda. She later came to me and apologized for Jae's behavior.

"Are you, like, going out with him, or something?" I asked.

"No, but he thinks we are. He feels threatened by you."

"Great." I couldn't imagine anybody believing they had to out do me. Who was I?

I still talked to Camila occasionally after that but Big Jae was always with her. The less I was around Big Jae the better off I felt I was. That was the beginning and the end of my career as a piano teacher.

CHAPTER VII
The Reminder

Cleaning the vats still sucked, but I was getting faster. Before, I barely finished in 90 minutes, but now I could get it done in an hour. The first time I finished early I tried to leave the kitchen.

"Hey!" the Supervisor called after me. "Where you going?"

"I'm done with the boilers." I turned to leave again.

"Oh, no you don't." He walked around in front of me.

"You must stay here the entire hour and a half."

"Oh, man! But what do I do?"

The Supervisor led me to this four-rack oven that was taller than I was.

"Clean this. See all that grime and brown stains? Get those off."

The Supervisor walked off to check on the scullery girls. Dickhead. I retrieved my sponge and began to wipe the oven.

There was a hissing sound and suddenly it felt like I'd been bitten. I dropped the sponge.

"Damn!" I yelled, holding my hand. My palm was red and painful. I looked down at the sponge. It was smoking.

The Supervisor came back in response to my yell.

"The oven is still on," he said, as though I should have known this. "You have to put a piece of plastic between the sponge and your hand to clean it."

"Why don't you just turn it off?"

He shook his head.

"It's too old. It would never come back to full heat. At night, we just turn it to low so it's ready for breakfast. It hasn't been off since the school opened 20 years ago."

The pain in my hand finally abated. I found this plastic thing to hold the sponge and began to clean the hot oven. It was an *old* piece of machinery. The indicator lights on the control panel looked like they were left over from the set of the original TV *Star Trek*.

I had to keep returning to the sink to wet the sponge because the heat would evaporate the water. I singed my knuckles a few times, but managed to wipe it down. It still didn't look very clean. I walked over to the scullery.

"Can I borrow the hose?" I asked one of the girls.

"Just for a minute," she said, wiping water from her face.

The hose had one of those gun handles you pressed to shoot the water. I washed down the front of the oven. It was a wide spray and made it look all shiny. I took the hose back and found the Supervisor.

"Good job," he said. "Let's make this oven part of your kitchen chore. Take care of it after the boilers."

Oh, shit! I came back to my room that night cranky and tired. My knee had only stopped hurting a few days ago, but that didn't make me feel any better. Rob was mumbling lessons from one of his books to the wall. He had his window wide open again, and the room was cold.

"Could you please close the window?"

"I like the fresh air," Rob replied, with a smile.

Fuck it. I didn't want to deal with his shit any more. I changed into my long pants. I had never owned any until I came to Lamia.

I didn't even brush my teeth before bed check. Back in the room and in bed, I pulled the covers over my head to block out the light. Rob took his sweet ass time undressing. Finally, the light was out and I heard the springs creak as he lay his hefty bulk down.

"How about a riddle?" Rob asked.

"No."

"It's a good one. There's a drowned man. A pile of clothes is on the beach next to an alarm clock. There's a buoy far out to sea. How did the guy drown? Only yes or no questions."

"I don't feel like it," I said, between gritted teeth.

"Why not?"

"I just want to sleep. Please, shut up."

"No need to get hostile."

"Leave me alone!" my voice was rising and I mentally checked it.

"Ask your first question. I'll give you a hint. There's a bell on the buoy."

"Shut the fuck up! I want to sleep. What's so fucking hard to understand?"

"The riddle will make you feel better," he said calmly. I was about to yell again when I finally understood. Rob didn't care about the riddle. Everything Rob did while I was around was to provoke me. He enjoyed my suffering. It was like my sister starting all those fights. It was my reaction he craved and fed off of. If I could handle Mercedes, I could deal with Fat Rob.

"Leif?"

I didn't say anything.

"Leif?"

I smiled to myself. I made a rumbling noise to fake a soft snore.

"You can't fall asleep that fast."

Keep talking. I'm not going to say another word for the rest of the night. Fucker.

"IBMs really are better than Macs and classical music sucks."

I was starting to relax. I could handle this. Fat Rob went silent. I'd won. The dickhead.

"So," Rob began. "I haven't seen you with any girls."

What was this? He was really reaching.

"So, are you gay?"

I tensed. I'm not gay. Don't say anything, that's just what he wants.

"Yeah, I thought so."

I could almost hear the smile in his words. Don't say anything, I kept telling myself.

"You don't mind if I tell the others on the floor? They'd probably want to know, in case you try something while they're in the shower."

I was starting to shake with rage. I trembled like I was being stung by hundreds of bees. I hated him!

"I know it's embarrassing. But I need an answer, Leif."

I was going to explode any second.

"If you're gay, don't respond."

"SHUT THE FUCK UP!" I screamed.

Rob laughed. Fuck this godforsaken place! The door opened. It was a Rover. "What's going on in here?"

"Leif had a nightmare," Rob said, innocently. "I think he misses home."

It took all of my will to keep from strangling that bastard right there. It would be hard to get my hands around that fat neck but I'd find a way.

Then I thought of the last time I'd lost my temper. Never again. Don't lose your cool. Just think about surfing at a deserted beach. I turned over in bed, putting my back to Fat Rob.

I was not in a good mood the next morning. Breakfast consisted of oily slices of ham. I just couldn't do it. I went over to the toaster and dropped in two slices of white bread.

Bread at every meal.

After a minute it popped and I spread some butter on it. I was tired of buttered toast. I needed to spice it up. I looked at the condiments. Salt, pepper, salad dressing, parmesan, oregano - parmesan! That could be interesting. I sprinkled some on my toast and tried it. Not bad. Actually, it was pretty good - a new recipe by Leif Csuba. This creation should have perked me up but I was too tired and hungry.

My day got even darker when I went to the mailroom. Another pink slip.

Ethics Violation: Not completing course work.

At least they were right for once. I couldn't see how that came under the heading of an ethics violation. The slip said to report to Ethics immediately after roll call.

This time I was alone in the waiting room. There were no voices from behind her door, only the opening and closing of file cabinets. She was by herself but she kept me waiting a good half hour. Why? I was going to fight this place, starting with her. I didn't care what she said about the class work.

The door opened and that bull of a woman stood there, looking at me. The Ethics Lady.

"Come in, Leif," she said. After I came in, she closed the door and walked back behind her desk. I sat across from her. She opened my file and read through it, slowly turning the pages. I waited and waited. She just kept reading.

"I can come back later if you need some time." I

immediately regretted it as the last word passed my lips.

The file slowly lowered and she looked at me. I'd caught a whitetip shark once fishing with Istvan. Her eyes looked exactly like that predatory fish.

"Why aren't you doing your course work?"

"I don't know. I just don't believe in it. I'm reading and doing my hand writing stuff, though."

"What do you mean you don't believe in it?"

"Come on," I said, "*Misunderstood Words*, *Learning How to Read*, *Method Three's*. It's just weird."

"Those are the teachings of L. Ron Hubbard. It's proven and it works."

"For some kids. Not me."

She smiled. It was not a pleasant sight.

"I know how hard it is being a teenager. I understand the desire to stand out and be unique. Believe me, we don't want carbon copies here."

What the hell was a carbon copy? She kept going.

"All things aside, you are enrolled here and you will continue your course work as we direct."

"Really?" I don't know why I felt so bold. Fat Rob and work detail were pushing me to the limits of what I could take. "I'm not part of your faith or whatever you call it. I don't believe in it. I'll call Rebecca and tell her."

"Why would your mom help you? You're just a failing student and a violent delinquent. That's why your parents sent you to us."

"What are you talking about?"

"I'm talking about that boy you almost killed at your last school."

I froze in my seat. Fear pulsed through my veins.

"What?"

"Do you really think we don't know everything about you, Leif?"

"But…" How did she know? It was true. One day in 6th grade, while the teacher was out of the room, a boy started provoking me. For no reason at all, he punched me in the arm. This was kind of normal for guys so I didn't do anything, but he kept it up.

"Little Leiffy," the boy mocked, "You like this? Huh?" He punched me again.

I tried to hit him back, but he was faster than I was and he grabbed my wrist. He hit me again - harder. My rage began to build, but I still tried to ignore him.

Then, from out of nowhere, a rubber band hit me in the eye. It hurt like a bitch. My eye started watering. The whole class began to laugh at me. They laughed and laughed. With my good eye I could see the kid smiling and laughing with the others.

My stomach was on fire. I just wanted to hurt him. Nothing else mattered. I reached into my backpack and pulled out my drawing compass. It was an old fashioned metal one. With absolute clarity I knew what I had to do.

When the boy turned his head I leapt up onto my chair and jumped through the air, knocking him to the floor. I had the sharp metal point within an inch of his eye, pushing down with all my strength. I still remember the look of total fear on his face when he realized he couldn't hold it back.

Before I could pierce the soft jelly of his eyeball, I was lifted through the air. Three other boys were pulling me off him. They threw me to the side. I backed up against the wall and looked around the class. Everyone was staring at me, their faces white. I looked down at the compass in my hand. I relaxed my fingers and let it drop to the floor.

I began to cry. I was in 6th grade and I'd tried to murder somebody. I'd *really* tried. My friend Odi was the only one who came over to comfort me.

"He deserved it," Odi said, his arm around my shoulder. "Hitting you like that and the rubber band, was not cool. It's not your fault."

But I just kept crying.

The teacher was supposed to be in the room and she would have gotten into a lot of trouble. Since nobody had been badly hurt, no official report was ever made. But everyone knew what had happened. All of the kids at school were afraid of me, except for Odi. When I'd walk down the halls, they'd move as far to the walls as possible. Even the 8th graders avoided me. I wanted to explain to them, "I'm not dangerous. I just lost my temper. That's all. I'm sorry. I'm not."

When I told my parents, my mom was shocked that her baby could do such a thing. As for Istvan, it was the first time in my life he was actually proud of me.

"You have to be like Ender," my dad said, "Next time,

not only win, but make sure it can never happen again." I didn't know what to make of that, but right then I made a promise to myself that I would never lose control again.

But how did Lamia know about it? It was never on record. The Ethics Lady's smile widened at my stunned expression.

"You are not special, Leif. I've seen kids like you come through here before and now they're one of us."

This was crazy. She couldn't be real. She was like a Roald Dahl villain.

"My mom trusts me."

The Ethics lady picked up the phone.

"I can call your mom right now and tell her you beat a student up. I can even let you speak to her afterwards. Who do you think she'll believe?"

Jesus Christ. She was nuts!

"You are just a 14 year old boy. Why would anybody listen to what you have to say? We are educators. Parents always put our integrity above their children's."

Shit! My mind raced trying to think of a solution to this. Kids on TV always figured out some cool elaborate plan to fix their situations. Not one brilliant idea came to me.

I finally realized she was right. My parents couldn't help me. The teachers wouldn't. Neither would the students. Nobody would. I was alone. These people were far more cunning than any school I'd ever attended. Lamia was a gingerbread facade. They tricked you into believing this was the ultimate paradise for students, the greatest school in the world. When they had you isolated and alone, they pulled off their smiley masks and prepared to bake you in their authoritarian oven.

"So," she went on, "Are you going to do our lessons or do we need to find other work? Perhaps an additional chore? We can always use more kids in the Trash Room."

The air in her office seemed to get colder. Not the Trash Room! I'd kill myself if I had to work there. Is that why they had such a horrible place? Lamia's own Room 101. Were those kids I'd seen not randomly chosen? I could still see those dead eyes.

I'd lost. There was nothing I could do. I was alone and naked against an enemy that didn't fight fair. Like when King Kamehameha pushed the entire opposing army off the cliffs in Oahu. I could join the institution or fall to my death. I couldn't think of a way out. I was no Ender. Istvan was right not to believe in me.

I was about to concede defeat when a thought occurred to me - *Istvan*. I remembered all his lectures about what a fuck up I was and how I'd gotten through them. In a moment of clarity, I knew how to beat Lamia.

"Okay," I said, as if I'd lost. "I'll start my class work."

"Good," the Ethics Lady stood up. "I'm glad you're smart enough to see the right path to becoming a fruitful adult." She kicked one of the drawers shut again but I wasn't startled as much as last time.

I walked out of the Ethics Office looking dejected, but inside I was bubbling with triumph. I couldn't fight the way

I'd always had, resisting in the open. I'd have to keep it inside. Like with my father, I had to agree with what they said and just wait it out until I left. There would be no battles, just a long silent war. Thank you, Istvan. Inadvertently, he had taught me how to win here. Lamia would never suspect a thing.

I don't have to believe, I just have to give the appearance that I do. It was so simple. I understood this was a major turning point in my life. It was my first glimpse at how the world really worked and I had made the leap on my own.

Before I went back to class I stopped at my room. I rummaged around in my top dresser drawer until I'd found it. I'd brought it as sort of a souvenir of home, but now I saw a perfect use for it.

There was a danger in my strategy. Because the battle was to be fought in my mind I knew there was a possibility I could forget. This token was the perfect reminder to me of what I was doing. I placed it on my shelves near the door so I would see it every time I left my room and entered their world.

I nodded to myself. I just hoped that Fat Rob wouldn't take it. I doubted he would. He ignored my stuff. Nobody would suspect its true meaning.

I thought about my visit to the Ethics Office. I can beat you, just you wait and see. I'd never have to go back up there again. Unfortunately, it wouldn't be the last time I'd have to deal with Ethics.

I took one last look at my reminder before I left my room.

Go along with it until you don't have to. That's all I had to do. I returned to the fourth floor to start my course work.

Movement II

fall

CHAPTER VIII
A Graduation

Almost immediately, after that last round of Ethics, things got better. They weren't perfect, though. Fat Rob wasn't letting up on my sleep deprivation and work detail now included that stupid oven, but, overall, things were more tolerable.

I started my first course, *Learning How to Read.* It went into great detail about the Misunderstood Word and how to fix it. It sort of made sense but the book made it out to be the only reason for all learning problems. Having dyslexia, I knew that was bullshit, but, with my new attitude, I went along with it.

I soon found out Lamia were liars, too. Connie came up to me as I began my course work.

"I'm glad you've started that."

"Well, it's at your own pace. I just needed a little time to adjust."

"Well, adjust more quickly. You have a lot of catching up."

"What do you mean?"

"You are scheduled to go into Form Six by May. You're a month behind."

"I thought it was, like, however fast we finished?"

"Yes and no. If we let students do it that way, they'd never leave school."

That almost made me laugh.

"While learning is at your own pace, we do have a schedule to keep. So chop-chop." She walked off.

Keep their schedule at your own pace. That was a total contradiction to everything I'd been told coming in, but I didn't question it or complain. I was going to go along with it until I didn't have to.

The next improvement was sports. We were out of the gym and playing soccer. We kept score for the first 30 minutes or so, but by the end, nobody knew who'd won. This was actually fun.

I played mid-field or fullback. I wasn't fast, but I had the size to stop the forwards. I'd just walk in the way and they'd have to run into me. They'd always yell to the Supervisor that it was a foul, but since I didn't do anything except stand there, I never got carded (or the school equivalent). The only problem to this strategy was the Koreans.

I was used to slender Japanese back in Hawaii but the Koreans were not of the same mold. Not only was Big Jae there, but some of the others were just as huge as he was. If I tried to get in their way, they'd plow me down. I never got hurt too badly but I did get the wind knocked out of me a few times. It's not like football where you were trying to smash the other person. I'd never play football again after what had happened last time.

In 7th grade I was tackled without a helmet and got a concussion. A concussion is the strangest feeling, like breaking through glass into a pool of water. There's a jarring pain, then all is quiet and slow. This game was in the schoolyard, so no official precautions were taken.

I lay there on the field unable to get up. I had trouble seeing, but could hear the others continuing the game around me. If my body got in the way of a play, the others would yell at me to move and give me a kick. About a half an hour went by before some girls on the sidelines ran in and carried me off. I wish I could remember who they were, but I can't. Except for Odi, they were the only ones at school who were nice to me after the compass incident. Soccer was my sport of choice now.

We did have some good players at Lamia, though. Edward, the kid with the bad acne who'd given me the Method Three, was very good. He could dribble the ball with his feet in mid-air while running down the field. Jason looked and sounded like a Scottish warrior from *Braveheart* and could run faster than anybody. He could give *Forrest Gump* a run for his money. Dylan could kick the ball from one end of the field to the other. Everybody wanted him on their team, except for one problem. Dylan had the worst B.O. in school.

He could make Pepe Le Pew run for the hills. If he didn't shower that day you couldn't get within 20 feet of him without wincing. I wondered if it was a sports tactic to keep opponents away. The worst player was Derk Johnson. He laughed at anybody when they screwed up, but he couldn't do shit if he got the ball. It sort of canceled out the effects of his jeers.

Fat Rob kept at his riddles, Mac vs. IBM, and why classical music was crap, but now I heartily engaged him. I never got angry and even went along with his riddles. I'd just have to be tired the next day. I could see he was confused at my interest. By the beginning of October our "conversations" began to trickle down. I wanted to shout, "In your face!" but didn't.

I kept trying the typing test, hoping to pass and use the computer for writing, but I couldn't do it. They weren't making me practice cursive anymore, but that didn't make it any better. I now had to write an essay every day. If I misspelled one word, I'd have to write the whole paper all over again.

The only upside was we could write about any subject we wanted, so to get back at them, I'd write about the symptoms of the Ebola Virus or the effects of nuclear bombs exploding in the area; bleeding from the eyes, defecating your own bowls, the nuclear vacuum sucking the air from the lungs, and the degree of burns, depending on the distance from ground zero.

The look on Connie's face every time she read one of my

papers was priceless. She'd finish and look at me like, "Are you serious?" I'd just smile back. If my grammar and spelling were correct, there was nothing they could do about it. Suckers!

I was getting very good at pool down in the Rec Room. I'd never compete in Las Vegas or anything, but I could definitely see myself improving. I was playing pool one night with one of Derk's posse - the small one with straight, sandy hair.

The way the pool table worked was there was a champion player. A line would form to compete against him. Kids would play him until he was beaten. Then that kid would be the champion player. Lots of times you never asked for your opponent's name or even talked at all. You just played. This night the Rec Room was empty, the small kid and I played game after game. After half an hour, he spoke up.

"You're Leif, right?" he asked after missing his shot. I walked around the table and took aim at the 11 ball near the side pocket.

"Yup." I sank my shot. "What's your name?"

"Jude. How did you get a name like Leif?" He looked completely serious. I couldn't see any mockery in his expression. Maybe he wasn't like Derk.

"My dad's from Hungary. He wanted his first son to have, like, a strong American name so that's why I'm called Leif."

Jude looked puzzled.

"American name? I don't get it."

"You know, Leif Ericson. The Viking. The first guy to discover America."

"Oh," Jude said, with a small laugh, "That's... kind of weird."

I shrugged.

"Eh, he's Hungarian. What the hell can you say?"

Jude nodded and took his shot. He was cool about my explanation. Too bad he was Derk's friend. I kind of liked him.

"What's Scrubs?" I asked.

"Huh?" Jude looked up from the table.

"One day in gym Derk said I was dumber than Scrubs. Is that like a mainland thing?"

"Oh." Jude said nodding. "He was talking about George Scrubs. He's a middle schooler. He's the dumbest kid at Lamia."

Ah, okay. That made sense. Kind of like how in Hawaii all our jokes make fun of the Portuguese.

"He's on the EIR again this week," Jude said.

"Really?" I'd stopped reading the EIR after my name appeared on it.

"Stupid kid." Jude shook his head. "A few nights ago he was chosen to be a Rover for the 2nd floor, but he didn't feel like it. So after roll call he took off and came down here to play air hockey."

"Jesus." I said, smiling. Everybody knows who's a Rover on their hall and the Rec Room's not exactly isolated. Jude went on.

"One of the middle schoolers saw him down here and reported him to Ethics."

I chuckled and shook my head.

"That is dumb."

We started to talk about things or, at least, I did. Jude was kind of quiet. He laughed at my jokes, but his face was always so stolid. He seemed intent on acting like a grownup. His short stature made the display almost comic.

Jude was an army brat so he'd lived everywhere.

"Germany was my favorite place," Jude said, his eyes lighting like a kid on Christmas. "They had a whole theme park based on *The NeverEnding Story*. I got to sit on the Rockbiter's lap."

"Sweet! It would be cool to live all over the world like that."

The light quickly disappeared from Jude's face.

"Sort of."

Eventually the conversation came around to my area of expertise. Nuclear bombs. Jude was amazed at my vast knowledge on the subject.

"Sixty megatons is the biggest that was ever tested," I said, shooting at the eight ball and missing. "Soviets dropped it. Vaporized everything for a hundred miles."

"Man. What's the largest bomb ever made?"

"Who can say?" I waited for Jude to sink his last solid. "Classified. But let me put it to you this way: the Hiroshima bomb was 12 kilotons in 1945. By 1962, they had a 100 megaton bomb. That's about... 4,000 times more powerful than Hiroshima. 4,000 times was the technology leap in 15 years and they haven't stopped developing bombs. 1962 was over 30 years ago, so you do the math."

"Jeez, man. That would be, like… the Death Star." Jude sank his last solid.

"Could be a gigaton bomb. Something like that could never be tested on earth, but nobody knows."

I enjoyed impressing people. I didn't get to do it often. When I was 12, I got into this big destruction phase where I became obsessed with knowing how guns and bombs worked. My mom was a little freaked out, but since I was reading she didn't stop me. I never asked for a gun or built any of the bombs I researched. It was just fascinating to me.

"I even know how to build a nuke," I boldly stated.

"Come on." Jude lined up for the eight ball.

"I don't mean I could, like do it right at this moment, but if I had some plutonium and a few other components I could. All you need to do is compress the core with explosives. I don't even need to buy C-4. I can make it from scratch."

"Cool." Jude nodded and made the eight ball. I'd lost.

"Yes!" Jude said, triumphantly.

"Ah, man!"

"I'm getting too old for this," Jude sighed.

"Another?"

"Yeah, sure," he replied as I racked the balls.

It was a few days into the new month. I brushed my teeth like I always did. The sinks are all connected and jut out far from the wall. Even if you leaned forward, you're always at least three feet from the mirror. It made it a bitch to pop pimples. There were several people in the bathroom that morning, but I didn't talk to them.

After I was done, I returned to my room. Fat Rob was up and making his bed for room check. He wasn't talking to me much anymore since I wasn't getting ticked off, or at least giving the impression I was. To get back at him, I talked as much as possible or played my music anytime he was there.

"Turn that stuff off," he'd say to me.

"Why? I think Tchaikovsky falls under the heading of 'pleasant music.' Don't you just love his first piano concerto? Did you know that Russian composers didn't like him because they thought his music was too Germanic? Listen to those strings. Aren't they the bomb?"

Fat Rob just growled and ignored me. This morning I didn't feel like music just yet, so I decided to cheerfully ask if he had a good night's rest. I used to do this with my sister. She's a terrible morning person. She'd trudge into the kitchen with her hair all over the place. I'd say very politely, "So Mercedes, how did you sleep?"

"Shut the hell up you little fuckface!"

"Mercedes!" Rebecca would yell.

"He's being an asshole!"

"I was just asking if she slept well," I'd say, as if hurt by her reaction. My mom knew exactly what I was doing but couldn't reprimand me for being polite. It was always a sure thing. I hoped it would work here.

"So, Ro-" I began, but stopped. My voice had ground to

a gurgling halt in my throat. Fat Rob heard it and looked at me.

"What was that?"

I rubbed my throat thinking I just hadn't swallowed the sleep grogginess.

"Wha-" I tried again, but with the same effect. My speech sounded like gravel. It was low and would catch in my throat like a skipping CD.

"What are you doing?"

"My voice," I finally said. I had to speak much more forcibly than I'd ever had to before to get those words out. What was going on? Was I sick? I felt fine.

"Yeah. It sounds pretty weird." Rob went back to fixing his bed.

I kept repeating a few words trying to relearn how to talk again. Rob kept looking over like I was a freak, but I was kind of worried. By room check I'd figured out how to talk again, but not very well. The whole thing was very disturbing. My voice sounded foreign to my own ears. Must be the weather. Autumn was coming soon and I'd never been in a season change. Could the seasons change overnight? Yesterday I'd been fine.

During roll call the whole class looked at me when I called out my name.

"Are you okay?" Connie asked.

"My voice is kind of gravely."

"Very well," Connie replied, and went on.

Everybody who came to talk to me was startled by my

new voice. They would ask what was wrong, but I didn't know. The ESL kids were the most confused. While technically, they were part of Form Six Entry, they had a different program to help them learn English.

The ESLs would come up to us and ask us grammar questions or to read sentences from their course books. We had to stop whatever we were doing if they did. It was required. I didn't mind the interruptions, at least at first but soon every ESL kid would come to me for help. Sometimes there was a line of them. My course progress was suffering because of it. I finally asked Mopping Alex why he and the others always came to me.

"You easy understand," he said. "Very careful you talk."

My mom was a part time English teacher and never let me or my sister use poor English. Her grammar corrections at dinner always bugged me, but I guess they'd actually helped in the long run. Alex continued.

"You say lessons many time. Others say only one time. You help pass course easy."

And now the poor ESLs were trying to understand this new Leif.

I was getting better at speaking like this, but I didn't want to try too hard. I kept telling myself it would go away in a few days. I didn't realize it, but that morning in early October was the day my voice dropped to what it would be for the rest of my life.

When I was eight, I asked my mom what all kids ask at some point.

"Mom, when will I be a grownup?"

"Well. You'll grow hair on your face. Your voice will slowly get deeper. When you sweat you'll smell bad and-"

"Like dad?" I asked, horrified.

My mom smiled.

"Yes. Like dad."

My dad was big into sports and would come home from basketball with his shirts completely soaked with sweat.

"Come give Stinkor a hug?" he'd call out holding his arms out for an embrace.

"NO!" My sister and I would scream and run. Istvan would laugh and chase after us.

I was very big into *He-Man* at the time and one of my action figures was named "Stinkor: The Smell of Evil." My dad, utilizing his natural tendencies, took it upon himself to become the embodiment of this character. He could be funny sometimes.

The school bell rang. I looked up at the clock. It was 10:40. What was going on? Perhaps a fire drill? The bell stopped and pulsed like a ringing telephone. Everybody got out of their seats and stood against the back of the room. I decided to follow. The bell and the jostling were too loud for me to ask what was happening. As I was getting positioned near the back wall, the doors to the room opened and the entire middle school poured in. What the hell was going on? For a second, I wondered which of them was Scrubs.

There was a "Shhh!" from the crowd and all went silent. We waited. Back in Kamuela I'd sometimes "Shhh" in assemblies long before the principal would arrive. Everyone would quiet down and look around, but nobody was there. Odi and I always got a big laugh out of our ability to control a crowd like that.

The bell stopped ringing. The only sound in the room was the rustle of kids' clothing. From my left, I heard one of the doors to the room open and everyone broke into applause. I stood on my toes and saw one of the Form Eight kids walking up to the front of the room. He stood at a small lectern that I'd never noticed before. The room quieted and he began to speak. He spoke of what a great time this had been, how fortunate he was to have this kind of education. He thanked his parents, his teachers, his friends, etc. I had to know what was going on.

"What's happening?" I asked a kid standing next to me.

"What?" he said distracted from the speech.

"Who is he?"

"He just graduated."

"Graduated? Just now?"

"Yeah." I could see the kid wanted to listen to the graduate, but I had to know more.

"He just graduated, like right now?"

"They ring the bell when you finish your last exam. You come up here, make a speech, and then you leave. Finished with school."

At your own pace. The kid returned his attention to the lectern. I looked around at all the faces turned to the graduate. They were proud and hopeful. As I gazed upon the boy I too felt hopeful, but not in the same way as the others. This kid had made it through the system. It was possible for anyone to do it, even me. That boy represented a future me, finished with school for good and proudly standing for all to see. For a brief moment, I wanted to finish school at Lamia. "Four more years" then flashed through my mind and that light of promise inside was extinguished.

The speech had gone on now for 15 minutes. He must have prepared it or something. To pass the time I looked around the room to see who else was there when I froze. Standing by one of the bookcases was the most gorgeous girl I'd ever seen. She was blindingly beautiful. Her long dark hair fell to her shoulders like black silk. Her eyes were dark and she had flawless skin. Her curvy figure was magazine perfect. She stood there like she was the only one in the room. I couldn't look away. Why had I never seen her before? She must be a middle schooler. So fucking what? She was amazing!

Just then she glanced around and caught my eye. Our eyes locked and I tensed. I tried to wave or something, but couldn't. She gave me a smile before she returned her attention to the lectern. I was suddenly very hot and my chest felt like there was a horse galloping around inside. She'd smiled at me!

After the graduate finished, everybody went back to wherever they'd come from. I lost sight of her in the crowd, but I would never forget that face. I sat down at my desk and tried to focus on my course work. It was impossible. I kept thinking about her and that smile. I had to find out who she was. I needed to know everything about her. I'd never felt feelings for a girl this strong before. Not even for any of my girlfriends. This was something I'd never felt before. I didn't know what it was, but I liked it.

CHAPTER IX
A Recipe for Friends

I was really looking forward to my next visit with the Petersons. It had been a while since I'd gotten away from Lamia and I needed a rest. Being a good student wasn't easy. With chores, study halls and roommate riddles, I needed a break.

Mr. Peterson picked me up in his big SUV Friday night. We listened to Yanni again the whole way to his house. It sounded like 80's synthesizer movie music. It was strange, but since it was his car, I said nothing.

I had to sleep on his son's extra bed. Even though I didn't like him very much, 16 year old Jack was a much better roommate than Rob. He only came to his room to sleep. The rest of the time he was out with his friends. When he did come back, he was conked out in two minutes. I wish I could fall asleep that quickly. No matter how tired I was it always took between 30 minutes to an hour of lying there before I fell asleep.

I was looking through the Peterson's fridge when I found something called Hot Pockets. It was like a frozen burrito filled with pizza or ham and cheese. I warmed one up and ate it. It tasted like frozen food but it was easy to make and I was so hungry, I had some more. Soon the entire box was finished. I felt full for the first time in months. I remember a book my mom had read to me about this perfect society where some kid told his teacher he was starving. His teacher had snapped at him, "You are not starving and you never will be starving." If I ever said I was starving after that, Rebecca would always use that line on me. I thought about it now. I was always hungry at school, even when I ate my toast. I *was* starving. It was a strange thought.

I gave my mom a call. I could talk to her and know for sure nobody was listening.

"Hi, Honey. How's my baby doing?"

"Not hungry."

"Remember to thank Mrs. Peterson for feeding you."

"I will. I will." I took a deep breath. "Rebecca, there's something I have to talk to you about."

I told her about how weird this Misunderstood Word thing was. I told her about cleaning the vats and being followed. I told her about my asshole roommate. When I was done, I waited for her response. She'd come and get me. I knew it.

"Leif," she began. "I know the learning style is different there, but that's why you wanted to go."

Not exactly the response I was looking for.

"I know about your kitchen chores, too."

"You do?"

"Yes. Lamia called me and told me how you're doing. I had to do chores and take care of my five brothers and sisters all the time, when I was growing up. I didn't like it, but it had to be done. I know we never made you do many chores at home, but I think this will help you later in life. Taking responsibility is important."

They'd gotten to her. They probably called her the moment they knew I left the school. Preemptive strike. Damn! They must do this sort of thing with all the parents. No way moms and dads would have let their kids be subjected to the Trash Room.

"And I'm sure you weren't followed," Rebecca continued. "You must have misunderstood her."

The Ethics Lady's words came back to me. "We are educators. Parents will always believe us." Shit. Nothing I could say would convince her. Rebecca went on.

"I'm sorry about your roommate. Sometimes you get assholes like that. Just know you're a better person than he is."

"I do." God, what I wouldn't give for Mercedes kicking my bunk bed from underneath. At least she got bored after a few minutes.

"The school also told me you've read over 10 books."

"What?"

"Is it true? Are you reading?"

Oh, Christ. I couldn't tell her I was reading to protest

their dumb courses. This made me look like a blossoming student under their system. Fuck!

"Yeah," I said, dejected.

"That's wonderful! I knew you had it in you. I'm so proud of you. Istvan is too. Aren't you glad you chose to go there?"

They were good. My parents would eat everything Lamia fed them. Slave labor was a character building chore. Forced doctrine was an unusual learning style. My parents couldn't help me. I had to keep fighting the Lamia war on my own.

I told Rebecca I loved her. She told me to keep up the good work. I hung up and thought for a moment. It was like that book I'd read last year in Kamuela, *Animal Farm*, where the pigs kept changing the rules. The other animals were too stupid to realize it.

That night Jack took me to see the movie *Scream*. It was a dumb horror flick with big-breasted girls running away from a masked knife wielding psycho. The big-breasted chick part didn't bother me. It was the lack of sophistication. My parents had let me watch any movie I wanted since I was three. That's how I was able to see *Stand By Me* when it first came out. All the kids in kindergarten wanted to come over to my house because they could watch grownup movies their parents wouldn't let them see.

Like other parents, the Peterson's censored Jack, too. It had stunted his taste in film. I expected more quality from my movies than *Scream* could deliver.

We raced home in the dark along winding roads at close

to 90 mph. Jack turned the stereo to full volume and I was forced to listen to a rap version of that song, *"Staying Alive"* from *Airplane*. He also popped the clutch any chance he got, so he could peel rubber. It was not fun. We flew over a hill and there was something in the middle of the road. We didn't even have time to brake. I heard a crunch under the tires and felt an impact on the undercarriage.

"Dude, what was that?" Jack asked.

It didn't take more than a few seconds to find out. A repulsive stench filled the car. It just grew stronger and stronger and wouldn't go away. I knew that smell - skunk.

"Oh, man! That smells like ass!" Jack said, waving his hand around his face.

"You should slow down!"

"No way, man! I want to get home and see if it fucked up my Camaro."

It hadn't, but Jack was pissed about the smell. I was just glad to be away from him and his car. I hoped I wasn't like that at 16. They shouldn't give driver's licenses to kids like him. It could have been a deer in the road. If we'd hit that, his stupid sports car would have been totaled, and who knew what would have happened to us. Most cars didn't have airbags in those days.

Right before I left on Sunday, Mrs. Peterson went through the fridge, getting lunch ready for everybody.

"Huh?" she said, perplexed.

"What is it?" Mr. Peterson asked.

"I thought we had a full box of Hot Pockets in the

freezer."

"Oh," I said, feeling a little embarrassed. "I'm sorry. I ate them."

They both looked at me.

"You ate 20 Hot Pockets?" she asked in amazement.

"I was hungry."

"But 20? And you didn't get sick?"

"Nah, I'm fine."

The Peterson's exchanged glances then laughed. I relaxed. Had it been 20? That sounded right. At least they weren't mad.

"If you're that hungry, dear, I'll cook for you." She smiled and shook her head. "20."

By mid-October, another chore was added to my forced labor. I had become too fast at cleaning the vats and the oven. Now, if I finished both of those, I had to help clean the grill or mop the large cafeteria floor. I preferred the latter.

Scraping a grill caked with burnt fries and meat was nasty. At least mopping you could talk to the people around you. I'm not sure how it happened but all the moppers were Koreans. They were much more friendly and willing to talk to me than the American kids, but with English being their second language, they mostly talked amongst themselves.

One day after soccer I could tell that summer was over. I'd never witnessed autumn, but I could just tell. It wasn't just the changing leaves like I'd seen in the movies. Standing there, watching the setting sun I felt no warmth from its rays. Physically the day was no different than any other but I could feel a change. I stayed after almost everybody had left as if I could hold on to the lost season.

I saw that Derk and his posse had remained and were now approaching. I waited to see what they wanted.

"Hey, Leif," Jude said.

"What's up?"

Derk looked bored but the other kid, the tall one with the long face and brown hair, was looking at me intently.

"You're the Piano Guy. I, like, hear you every time I walk by the chapel."

The Piano Guy. I guess that was my niche here. I liked that.

"That's me."

"I hear you know how to make C-4."

"What?"

"You told me you did," Jude said.

"Oh, right!" I remembered the conversation about atomic bombs. The tall boy went on. He had a slow deep voice, like a California surfer.

"So, like, could you tell me the recipe, man?"

"Sure." I settled into my seat of knowledge, "First, you need fertilizer."

"What kind?"

"Have you ever seen those little white balls they put on plants?"

"Yeah?"

"That's it. You can buy it at a gardening shop."

The kid was staring at me in amazement. Even Derk was intrigued.

"Then grind it to a powder. A coffee grinder will work."

"That's it?"

"No, not quite. You need to get black powder or something like it. Hunting section at a sporting goods store will probably have it. You mix two parts fertilizer with one part black powder. Get a little bit of Vaseline and roll the mixture into a ball or any shape you want. BOOM! You got C-4."

"That's totally awesome!"

"So have you ever made any?" Derk asked.

"No way! Over half the people who work with explosives have been killed or crippled. I'm not as dumb as Scrubs."

"Ah!" Derk yelled, "I knew he was full of shit. Come on." He began to walk off. Jude followed, but the other kid stayed behind.

"Do you know how to make other explosives?"

"Yeah, all sorts. Chemical bombs are easy to make, too."

"Do you think you could, like, teach me some time?"

"No problem."

"Oh, I'm Nick Hendrix, by the way."

"Leif Csuba." We shook hands.

"See ya, man," Nick said, and ran to catch up with his posse. It felt good to impart my knowledge. Nick had seemed friendlier than the others. Maybe he could help me find out who that girl was. I still couldn't get her out of my mind. That figure and that smile...

I walked back to the dorms day dreaming about conversations with her. I looked back at the sun. It had finally set. I didn't realize that would be the last time I'd ever see that luminous orb over Lamia.

CHAPTER X
The Posse

"Her name is Katrina Skinner," Nick said, after I pointed her out. We were sitting in the cafeteria for lunch.

"Katrina," I said, dreamily. Very pretty name.

"She's, like, in the choir and stuff." Nick picked up his slice of limp pizza.

I wanted to ask more, but I didn't want anybody to know how I felt. At least I knew her name. I'd find out more about her on my own.

"How can you eat that crap?" I said to Nick, "It tastes like wet cardboard."

"I know. That's why I have salad dressing. You dip the pizza in the Ranch dressing and it makes it better."

I watched Nick cover his slice in the thick, white, substance and take a bite. I cringed.

"That's sick."

"Try it, man."

"I don't think so." I continued to eat my toast with parmesan. Even if I ate the pizza here there's no way I'd ever put Ranch dressing on it. That's just wrong.

Nick swallowed and licked his lips.

"Mmm. The best way to eat pizza!"

Derk walked over from the water dispenser and plopped his tray down loudly next to Nick.

"What are you fags talking about?" He took a monster bite of his hotdog. I was about to tell him that those hotdogs were over three weeks old, but didn't.

I was kind of getting used to Derk. I'd been hanging around them a lot. Nick kept coming up to me asking me how to make different bombs and bringing the posse with him. I told Nick about iodine crystal explosives, black powder and other stuff. Nick kept asking why I hadn't built a bomb, if I knew all this.

"I told you. Almost everybody who works with explosives has been killed or maimed."

"Aren't you just a little curious, man?"

"I was, but not anymore. When I was 13 I helped some construction guys down in Kona set explosives to blow up a large rock. We drilled and dropped charges. The bombs smelled funny."

"Like what?

"I don't know how to describe it."

"Try."

"Ah, like, ah, like wet dirt mixed with Pine Sol. Anyway, we rigged them with detonators and blew it up. This rock, the size of a house, went, like, 20 feet straight up and came down in pieces. It was cool."

"Dude, that's sweet."

"After that my interest in bombs sort of tapered off."

I hung out with them more and more and before I was even aware, I was part of their posse. I never would have guessed two weeks ago.

"Pizza is pizza," Derk continued. "What more can you say?"

"It's the best food in the world," I said. "Countries should be judged by how good their pizza is. If the pizza sucks, then the country sucks."

"You said it!" Nick said, holding up his left hand. I high-fived it.

"If there could be only one topping," I continued, "it would be pepperoni, man. It's the best."

"Don't be a kweef," Derk said. "Sausage is the best. Everything else is for fags."

Derk became devil's advocate just to get a reaction from others. But what had he called me?

"What the hell is a kweef?"

"You're a kweef!" Derk cackled loudly.

"Smart and handsome?" I answered. "So, you're not one."

"I'll fuck you up!"

"No, dude," Nick said. "A kweef is, like, the sound a vagina makes when you're having sex and air gets inside. A pussy fart."

I tried to wrap my mind around the image, but I couldn't put it all together.

"That's kind of lame."

"No, you're lame, kweef face!" Derk yelled back.

I ignored him, looking across the room at Katrina. I could stare at her for hours. Derk followed my gaze.

"Why're you looking at the middle schoolers?"

"Leif's in love with Katrina," Nick said.

"Shut up! I'm not!"

"She's a middle schooler," Derk said with a 'they're beneath us' tone. "And she has a fat ass."

Anger burned inside of me. Don't you say that about my girl! But I calmed myself. It was just Derk.

"Dude, she's almost 14," Nick said. "She is kind of hot."

"Do you know who's hot?" Derk asked. "Winona Ryder."

"Jesus Christ!" I said, "Yeah. Like you'll ever end up with her."

"Shut the fuck up, dickface!"

"So what actress do you think is hot?" Nick asked me.

"You don't know her. She was in a small movie a few years ago."

"So, just tell us, man," Nick said.

"Okay. Kellie Martin."

"Who?" They both said in unison.

"When I was into my destructive phase I rented every movie with atomic bombs going off. There was this one called, *Matinee*. It had cool explosions, but soon I noticed her. She has this adorable cute thing going on. She's sort of like my fantasy girl."

"That's lame," Derk said. "Fantasy girls should be fucking unbelievable not cute. Like Jessica Hopemann."

I followed his gaze to a table of Form Seven girls. Everybody knew who Jessica Hopemann was. I'd met her my first day of class when I was looking for my Form. She was generally considered to be the hottest girl in school. She was very nice, but to me she didn't even compare to Katrina.

"Cool explosions?" Nick said, his mind still on *Matinee*. "Dude, I think I have to see that movie."

I looked from Derk to Nick. Not a normal group of friends, but what could I expect here at Lamia?

Suddenly Derk's hands shot forward and before I could react he had my hands bent backwards.

"Say Mercy!" Derk commanded.

"AH! Mercy! Mercy!" It fucking hurt!

"Come on! It's only been five seconds!" Derk pushed harder.

"MERCY!" I screamed.

Derk cackled and let go. I cradled my left wrist. It couldn't take that much backwards force. I hoped it wouldn't go out.

"Fucker."

Derk turned to Nick but his hands had disappeared under the table before Derk could make his move. I guess I wasn't Derk's first Mercy victim.

Derk was from Bakersfield, California and the third of

five brothers. His mother was a hygienist or something. Derk refused to talk about his father, though. Nick thought it was because he used to beat Derk as a kid.

Nick was from Seattle. Although he acted like Sean Penn from *Ridgemont High*, he wasn't a pothead or stupid. It was just the way Nick was. Nick wasn't as fucked up as the other kids here. I told him so.

"Good. I'm not a Scientologist. I think it's kind of weird. My mom and dad are members, so that's why I'm, like, here."

I immediately liked him more. Anybody who didn't believe in this crap couldn't be half bad.

"So you've, like, been here a while?"

"About three years."

"Why is it called Lamia?" I'd been wondering that for a while now.

Nick tilted his head. "It's named after some city in Greece, I think. It was, like, a center of learning or something during Alexander the Great's time."

It made about as much sense as anything else around here, so that would have to do.

I was screwing around on the computer a few days later, trying the typing test again. I got up to 35 words per minute, but couldn't go faster without messing up the text I needed to follow. It was pissing me off. They probably set the standards so high to force people to write work out by hand. It was so old fashioned and pointless. People invented word processors to make writing easier. It's like saying that learning how to drive a horse and buggy will help you on the freeway. Dumber than Scrubs.

There were eight computer workstations at Lamia. The machines weren't connected to the Internet, but nobody cared. At that time, the Web wasn't much of anything. I could still remember the first time I'd seen it.

I was 11 and my dad sat me down at his computer.

"Leif, I want you to check this out." My dad loved showing off his new gadgets. I pretended to be interested. He opened up a program called Pipeline and hit the connect button. There was a funny sound from a small box on the floor.

"What's that?"

"The modem's dialing."

After a minute of waiting a blank page appeared.

"Okay, cool." I said. I had no idea what I was seeing.

"It's the World Wide Web," my dad said, triumphantly. "It was invented by CERN in Switzerland."

"What does it do?"

"Let me put it to you this way: you type in addresses here and you can see information people have put on the Intercontinental Network."

"I don't know any addresses."

My dad typed something. After waiting about 30 seconds crammed text slowly filled the screen from top to bottom.

"This is a university on the east coast. See, they have some published papers for you to read. We can read them all the way out here."

I looked at the page of text. I hated reading.

"No pictures?"

"The Web can't support pictures. Just text."

"Cool," I said, but didn't mean it. "I'll check it out later."

I never did. I didn't even want to read real books and this Web thing seemed so pointless and slow. Waiting 30 seconds for each page to load sucked.

By the time I was 13 there were pictures online and I began to print out nuclear bomb photos. Now that was cool. The Internet is where I found all my explosive recipes. I also found papers on the effects of hemorrhagic fever and would bring them to English class for my teacher to read aloud. The look of utter revulsion on people's faces as she described the liquefaction of organs was priceless. I'd never heard of e-mail or purchasing things online until my late teens.

The computer beeped at me. I failed my typing test again. Fuck it. I give up. I started looking through the programs. All the computers were IBMs and it was hard to get used to them. I wanted to tell Fat Rob they sucked and that I couldn't find anything, but I knew he'd spin it to his advantage.

I found this program called Virus Wars. It sounded cool. I checked it out. It was a program that let you write viruses and battle them against each other. Like Ebola vs. HIV. I liked it. I didn't know how to program so I started cutting code from pre-existing viruses in the database and piecing them together.

The object was to fill a screen with your virus. But if the other virus had a stronger code it would eat yours. So you had to protect yourself with a defensive code, but others protected themselves and so on.

"Ah, Virus Wars," the computer Supervisor said, coming up behind me.

"Yup."

"You like it?"

"It's kind of cool."

"How would you like to be part of the Virus Wars Club?"

"Ahh…" I hadn't expected this.

"It can take the place of a study hall. You meet here with the other members and write programs, then pit your viruses against each other. At the end of the year we go to Jacskeep and compete against other clubs in the Northwest. It's just for fun."

It sounded kind of geeky. I hope he didn't think I was a nerd because I had a calculator watch. I liked its functionality. But something to replace a study hall sounded fine.

"Okay, I'll do it."

"Excellent. I'll sign you up."

The next day I met the other members. There was Curtis, the boy who lived next to me, Willem, a kid who looked exactly like a computer programmer should and, to my annoyance, Fat Rob.

"So," Rob said, "Part of Virus Wars?"

"Yeah." He looked like a nerd. I should have guessed.

"Well, you see IBM's are better?"

Oh, great. How could this get worse?

CHAPTER XI
Locked Doors and School Trips

It was raining every day now and getting colder. My right knee ached every morning when I got up. It wasn't just the fall in the chapel. The pain was probably compounded by the frigid air flowing in through Rob's open window. He kept it open all the time now. When I went outside I could see my breath. This was a novelty for me. It had only been this cold once in Kamuela.

In 4th grade, there was a huge winter storm that came through Hawaii. The temperature dropped down to 50 degrees. The buildings don't have insulation and no one had warm clothes so schools were cancelled all over the Big Island. Seeing my breath was fun, but the sucky thing about this place was that the clouds never went away.

Nick said this was normal for the Northwest. It had rained everyday back home in Waimea, but all you had to do was drive 15 minutes and there was always sunshine. I liked that there was no bright light but the perpetual clouds and drizzle were depressing. It was like *The Nothing* was coming. Too bad I couldn't ride a luck dragon out of this place.

Playing soccer in the rain without cleats isn't very fun either. I was constantly slipping in the mud and I was frozen and damp by the time I got back to the dorms. If the Varsity kids had practice for an upcoming game, we had to move to the smaller field near the road. It wasn't flat and the goals were only four feet high. I was made goalie, which I would usually have liked but, because of the goal's small size, I couldn't use my hands to stop the ball. I was really the last defender because their forwards could still kick the ball from me. Cold, rainy, falling down muddy soccer was the most fun I was having at Lamia.

Before the graduation I'd usually leave the cafeteria as soon as I was done with my toast, but now I waited the entire hour just hoping to get a glimpse of Katrina. The middle schoolers had a different schedule than we did. Most times when I waited she never came, but those few times we were there together were special. Her beauty was mesmerizing. I wanted to sit with her and strike up a conversation, but I didn't know what to say. She was always with her friends. I didn't want them around if I approached her. I felt like they were an audience waiting for me to screw up. Scottish Jason from soccer was the only guy I ever saw her with, but I knew he had a girlfriend. He was going out with Jessica Hopemann, so I felt there was a chance for me and Katrina.

Instead of talking with her I daydreamed about her during

class and before I went to bed - that dark hair, that smile she'd given me. I'd do anything for her to like me.

I never actually thought about her sexually. Okay, I did, but I always felt guilty. I know it sounds stupid, but you can't help how you feel. While the idea of kissing or feeling her up caused the blood to flow to my groin, I really just wanted to be with her, to talk to her and to hold her.

It was announced that there would be a school trip to Jackskeep in the beginning of November. Nick and the others didn't seem as excited about it as I was.

"These trips are lame," Nick said.

"Why?"

"They do one, like, every year. All we do is go to some crappy restaurant then go to a stupid PG movie. The rest of the time is a two hour bus trip there and back. And not only do you have to pay for everything but you have to give the school five bucks to go. It sucks. I haven't, like, done one since my first year."

"At least we get away."

"Pshaw," Nick shrugged.

Nick didn't want to go, but after a while I persuaded him. The rest of the posse followed suit.

Nick was what I called a 'hub' personality. People like Jude, Derk and I would never normally be friends, but Nick was one of those guys who just drew people together. Like the hub of a wheel, he cemented the spokes of our posse and made it possible to navigate the treacherous road of this institution. I'm not sure we could have managed on our own.

My course work was slowly catching up. I wasn't "on schedule" yet, but I was moving along as fast as I could. I looked over all the workbooks I needed to read. They were all written by that L. Ron Hubbard guy the Ethics Lady had mentioned. He must have invented this Misunderstood Word bullshit. I was reading one of my last assignments from *Learning How to Read* when I stopped. I must have read it wrong. I read it again. I hadn't. I took it to Connie.

"No. You're right," she said.

"For half an hour?"

"Yes. Why don't you ask one of the ESL students? Chop-chop."

I asked a Japanese kid if he could help me. He agreed and came over to my table. We sat across from each other and stared. That was the assignment. We had to stare at each other for half an hour. No talking or moving. It was weird with a capital W.

I looked at his eyes for a while, then his hair, then his neck, then back at his hair. I wasn't sure what the fucking point was. What the hell did this have to do with learning how to read? He was staring right back. This didn't seem strange to him.

Staring so hard at another guy made me feel very uncomfortable. I should have picked a cute girl but thinking again, that probably would have been worse. I was sure she'd focus in on my pimples then go tell all of her friends.

Time dragged on and on, like being stuck on the event horizon of a black hole. The clock was behind me, so I couldn't turn and look. I had to wait for Connie to tell me I was done. It really sucked and I was glad when it was over.

Luckily for me, Fat Rob barely talked to me in Virus Wars. I felt out of place there anyway. I wasn't a programmer. I was stealing ideas from others and getting lucky. I just kept telling myself I could be in study hall so just go along with it. I did make one mistake, though I didn't realize it at first.

One night after lights out Rob spoke up again.

"You like *Star Trek*?"

I'd mentioned it during Virus Wars that day.

"My dad's a big fan and it sort of rubbed off."

"So do you watch the one with Kirk and Spock?"

"Yeah. The movies mostly." The first movie I'd ever seen in a theater was *Star Trek IV*.

Istvan lived through the 60's but didn't get into it as much as Rebecca had. The only thing Istvan had ever protested back then was the cancellation of the TV series *Star Trek*. He was out there in front of the studio with the other five geeks who watched the show holding up signs.

Where was Fat Rob going with this?

"Do you watch *Next Generation, Deep Space Nine, Voyager*?"

"Not really," I said.

"They're much better than that retro crap."

I wasn't going to let this go. I had a plan.

"I think the movies are better, but we don't have TV at our house so you may be right. Yet, without a comparison, I can't say." What do you say to that, dickhead?

"Oh." Rob was quiet for a moment. "Let me tell you about the new *Star Treks*."

Oh, shit. He would be talking for hours now. Goddamn it!

The boys' dorms are made up of two halls like a big "L" with the bathroom at the joint. Nick lived in the other hall. Nick's room would have looked out on the gym and the road, if any of the rooms on that side had windows. The floor didn't have carpet on his side either and all of the beds were bunked. I was glad to be on my side. It would suck if I had to sleep over or under Fat Rob.

One night, Nick, Jude and I walked to Nick's room to chill out. I'd been playing pool with Jude and I had won. We'd gotten into a small argument over whose turn it was if you sank a solid and a stripe at the same time, but Nick made the peace.

We saw Nick's door was slightly ajar. The rooms here didn't lock automatically like my hall, and Nick never locked his door. We pushed the door open and saw the strangest sight.

There was Derk. He was on his knees with his back to us. Nick was about to ask what he was doing when we saw the rhythmic movement of his right arm. Derk was jerking off right there in front of us. Nick was about to yell, but I held my finger up to be quiet.

"Oh, yeah," Derk was saying. "That's the stuff."

I cupped my hand over my mouth trying not to laugh. I

could see Jude was shuddering, holding back his laughter. Nick had a disgusted look on his face.

"I'm the man," Derk said. "You know it."

Jude couldn't take it and ran down the hall to laugh. I was on the verge of losing it, too. Derk tilted his head back.

"Keep it coming, keep it coming."

"WHAT THE HELL ARE YOU DOING!?" Nick finally bellowed.

I let out a monster laugh. Jude came running back. Derk whipped his head around.

"Oh, shit!" he fumbled, trying to get his fly up.

"Don't stop," I yelled. *"Keep it coming."* Jude and I bellowed with laughter.

"Oh, man!" Derk got his jeans zipped and stood up. I could see the bulge in his pants.

"What the hell are you doing in my room?!"

"My roommate's in mine."

"So you came here?!"

"He *came* alright," I said. "Doesn't it hurt your knees on the hard floor?" Jude and I laughed again.

Nick was pissed but he wasn't really angry. How could you truly get angry at Derk?

"You came in here and got jizz all over my floor?"

"I was going to clean it up."

"Better hurry before it gets dry and sticky!" I called out between gasps. I was crying it was so funny.

"I'm too old for this!" Jude said through his laughter.

I'd never seen Derk look so meek. He was always acting so tough, but he looked like a dog that had been caught shitting on the carpet. It was a sight I'd never forget. After that, Nick locked his door every time he left his room. The whole incident still makes me laugh to this day.

Derk assumed we'd reported him to Ethics. We hadn't. We didn't see the point. Derk didn't know that, though.

I found out the next day that later that night Derk went into the TV Room to be alone. It was a weekday so you couldn't use the TV but you could still sit in there. A couple was in there to get some privacy so they ignored Derk. Derk wasn't in a great mood after being caught.

"I guess you've heard," Derk said to the couple.

"Yeah," they said, not really paying attention. They just wanted to get back to their petting.

"You know," Derk continued, "if you squeeze your balls it comes out faster."

The couple stopped. They slowly turned to him. The girl had the most horrified look on her face. The guy just glared at him.

"What the fuck are you talking about?" the guy asked.

Derk realized they didn't know, but wasn't going to miss this opportunity.

"You know. Squeezing your balls when you're whacking off. Do you ever help him with that?" he asked the girl.

"Gross!" the girl said.

Derk slapped his thighs, cackling with laughter.

"You asshole!" the boy screamed.

Derk just kept laughing. He had regained his "Derkness." Derk never had dignity.

The trip to Jackskeep was just as Nick said it would be. It took forever to get there. Then, we went to a restaurant that took just as long to serve us. The only movie they'd let us see was *The Spitfire Grill*. It was lame. I don't know how else to describe it. The only interesting part was when the girl drowned at the end, and that wasn't even that cool. I'd rather be back in Lamia than do one of these lame expensive trip things again. Maybe if Katrina had come it would have been worth it, but she hadn't.

After the total suckfest was over we headed back. The city lights were disappearing into the darkness behind us. The bus was full of about 50 tired kids. I sat with Nick, while Jude and Derk sat in front of us. Some girls across the aisle from us were listening to a small 'girly' pink boom box. Some chick song lyrics blared, "I love you always forever." It was annoying all of us, but Derk was the only one to say something.

"Can you turn that stupid shit off? It's making my dick become an inny."

"You're an asshole, Derk," the brown haired girl said to him.

"So what does a kweef feel like?"

"Ooh!" she screamed. Derk cackled.

"Can't you think of something new to say?" I asked.

Derk leaned back over the seat. "Shut up, kweef face."

"I give up on him. He's hopeless." The bus went over a

large bump, bouncing us in our seats.

"At least he didn't jack off on your floor," Nick said.

"Thank God."

"It was just one time," Derk defended himself.

"One time too many," Nick said.

Time to change the subject. It was funny, but I'd heard enough of this over the past weeks.

"That movie sucked. A chick flick would have been better."

"It was pretty lame, dude," Nick replied.

"I'd rather watch *Night Train to Venice* for the rest of my life," I said.

"What's that?" Nick asked.

"The worst movie ever made."

"You've seen every movie, right?" Jude piped up.

"Not every one but I've seen a lot."

"What's the best movie?"

"The best?" I thought for a moment. Not an easy question. "I guess it would have to be *Stand By Me*."

"Dumb!" Derk interjected. "*Mission Impossible* is the best and Tom Cruise is awesome!" He raised his hands like he'd made a goal, which he never had.

"He was good in Top Gun. Now, that's a sweet movie," I said.

"It's, like, cool that they can do so many computer effects today, like *Jurassic Park*," Nick said, "but there's nothing like filming real jet fighters."

"Hell, yeah." I agreed. Nick and I high-fived. "Did you

know they filmed *Jurassic Park* in Hawaii?"

"Cool." Nick said nodding.

"What about the best TV show?" Jude asked me.

"I don't watch TV."

"No TV?" everybody said together, looking at me.

"Jinx," I said. "Can't talk now."

"Shut up," Derk sneered. "That's baby shit."

"My parents turned our TV off when I was 10. They said it was all crap. Movies are all I get to watch."

"Dude, that sucks," Nick said.

"But when I did have TV, *Teenage Mutant Ninja Turtles*, was my favorite."

"*Bevis and Butthead* was the best," Derk interjected. We ignored him.

"I can't believe Clinton won," Jude said abruptly.

"What?" I asked. How had Jude gone from TV shows to that?

"Clinton won the election."

"So what?" Nick said to him.

"I just thought that Dole would win."

"You really thought Dole Pineapple would win?" That was the joke back in Hawaii. "Imagine him as President." I put on my best monotone voice, "Bob Dole understands the Misunderstood Word. Bob Dole will send you to Ethics. Bob Dole. BOB DOOOOOOLE!"

Derk and Nick were laughing, but Jude wasn't.

"I just don't like Clinton."

I shook my head.

"You're such an old man."

"Politics sucks," Derk said, "Now shut the fuck up!"

Nice going Derk. I didn't give a shit about Clinton either. What the hell was that Bosnian War about anyway? Did we even shoot anybody?

I looked out the bus window into the dark. There were no more lights. We were far into the countryside. Beads of rain trickled diagonally across the glass. I was feeling good about this place for the first time. I had friends. Strange friends, but friends nonetheless. Then I remembered my reminder in my room. Lamia was still the enemy. I couldn't let myself forget.

"Dude?" Nick asked.

"Yeah, Nick-meister?"

"What's the most fucked up movie you've ever seen?"

"Most fucked up?" I thought for a moment. I'd seen a lot of weird films like *Angel Heart*, but something else immediately flashed into my mind. "*Clockwork Orange*."

"What?"

"It's this old movie from the 70's. It was, like, the most violent film ever. Really bizarre."

"Tell me about it."

We had an hour to go before we got back, so I told him.

"This guy, Alex DeLarge was a leader of a gang in England. They would go around beating people up and raping women. They beat this one man up while singing, 'Singing in the Rain.'"

"Alex was obsessed with Beethoven and referred to him as Ludwig Van. Then one day his droogs ousted him from the gang and he was put in jail. While he was there he heard of this treatment to cure violent behavior and manipulated his way into the program. They gave him injections and used this helmet thing to hold his eyelids open. They played Beethoven's 9th and made him watch terrible images."

"Like *The Simpsons*," Nick interrupted.

"What?"

"There was, like, this episode where Burns gets a hold of Santa's Little Helper and did exactly what you described to turn him into an attack dog."

"Really?" I'd never seen *The Simpsons* but I did know of it. When it first came out, all these moms at Kamuela had protested it because Bart was a bad roll model.

"Yeah, I remember," Nick continued, "They had the eye drops and the music. This movie is just like it."

"*Clockwork Orange* came out over 25 years ago so *The Simpsons* was, like, borrowing the idea. Anyway," I went on.

"Soon Alex began to get very sick anytime something violent happened. He was released from prison and tried to integrate back into the world, but everything had changed. His parents didn't want him anymore and his gang members were now part of the police. They took him to a field and beat the shit out of him. He managed to crawl to a house to ask for help, but it was the 'Singing in the Rain' guy's house. The man locked him up in a high room and blasted Beethoven until Alex jumped from the window."

"That's fucked up," Nick commented.

"Told you."

"Tell it again," Nick demanded.

"What?"

"You're like having my own personal VCR. You can remember everything. We still have a while to get back. Tell it again," Nick begged.

"Ah, okay." I started again. Nick was enthralled by my story telling. I'd only seen the film once, but could remember about 70% of all the dialogue. It usually took at least two or three viewings to get it all down. When I rented the movie Rebecca gave me a funny look.

"Oh, I remember this," she said, cringing. "It was not a happy film."

"The kids at music camp told me to watch it," I said.

"It's all yours. I never want to see it again."

After I watched it, I understood why. Now I was reliving the deranged movie, but what else was there to do on this dumb bus? It wasn't like there was any scenery to watch. That was probably why Nick wanted to hear it again. It was the least I could do for dragging him along on this lame ass trip.

CHAPTER XII
Things From Above

I was in my room finishing up a Hyper Card and listening to some Chopin when Nick came in.

"What's up, dude?"

"Not much," I answered. "Just a little Hyper Card action."

"What's that?"

"It's a program I use to make cartoons. Check this out. I'm almost done."

I showed him the cartoon I'd made. It was Lamia getting blown away by a twister. The program was great but it wasn't designed for animation. You had to draw each frame. The cartoon was only a few seconds long. As the tornado moved away, all that was left of Lamia was a chimney.

"*There is no escape*," I said dramatically. "*Death is the only escape.*"

"You're dark, man. How long it take you to do that?"

"A few hours, but I've been making these toons since I was 12. Here's the first one I ever made."

I opened up a cartoon of the Titanic hitting the iceberg and sinking.

"Sweet. Is there a movie about the Titanic?"

"I'm not sure. I think there's an old flick from the 50's, but I've never seen it."

"Oh." Nick seemed disappointed. "Wouldn't that be cool seeing that ship sink with today's CG?"

"I guess," I said focusing back on my cartoon.

Nick walked over to the shelves and began examining their contents. I twisted my left arm and every joint cracked.

"Man!" Nick said. "Doesn't that hurt?"

"Nope. I broke my wrist when I was 12 and it, like, does this when I twist it." I twisted again and Nick cringed at the sound. "Crackage."

"Dude, stop. You'll screw your arm up."

"It's already screwed up. My left wrist will always be weak so I can't lift heavy things with this arm. This can't make it worse."

Sometimes I wish my arm was normal again, but there's nothing that can be done. Some mistakes you just have to learn to live with.

"I guess you always have to use your right then," Nick said, smiling.

"Shut up."

Nick continued exploring the shelves. I went back to the beginning of the cartoon to add some finishing touches like people being sucked out of the windows and torn apart. It's those little things that make the difference.

"Holy shit!" Nick called out.

"What?" Nick was standing by the door with his back to me looking at something.

"Is this what I think it is?"

"I have no idea. What are you looking at?"

Nick turned around holding something in his palm.

"Oh, yeah. My pog."

"Damn." Nick examined the slammer. "I haven't seen one of these in, like, years. They were banned in school."

"It was the only fad to come out of Hawaii," I stated with pride.

"No way."

"Yes way. Inside bottle caps were these round pieces of cardboard coated in wax to seal in the Passion, Orange, Guava juice. P.O.G. You'd collect them and use the thick plastic slammer to flip them. The winner keeps them all. It's a Hawaiian game from the 30's or something, but a couple of years ago it came back and, like, spread to the mainland. Hawaii all the way!"

"I've never seen one like this." Nick held it close to his eyes. I pointed out the details to him.

"It's a Menehune Warrior."

"What's a Men-a-hoon-ee?"

"A mythical being. You never notice them, but they work at night to make life better for people. That thing cost me, like, four bucks. That's the silver one. They had a gold one, too."

"That's the bomb, man." Nick put it back. "Do you really want to leave it here? You could go to Ethics if they find it."

Nick was probably right, but if he hadn't been sure what it was, I was positive they wouldn't figure it out.

"I think it's fine."

Nick looked out the window.

"Dude, it's snowing."

"What?" I whipped my head around. Sure enough, it was. I walked over to the window and stared. Big white flakes were coming down everywhere.

"Not much snow in Hawaii," Nick said.

"Actually, we get snow every year on Mauna Kea. One kid's dad from my old school works up there in the ski patrol during the winter. One day, he came back to Waimea with the back of his pickup truck filled with snow. We had a snowball fight, like, right there in the warm sun. It was awesome!"

"Really? Bitchin'!" Nick went back to poking at my belongings, but I continued to stare out at the snow. For some reason, I couldn't look away. I'd never been in a place that had no snow when I'd arrived and then it did.

"Let's go play in it, man." I walked over to the closet to get my jacket.

"Nah, you go ahead. I've seen too much snow."

"Suit yourself. See you at dinner?"

"Right."

"Can you turn my music off when you leave? I don't

want Fat Rob touching my stereo."

"No problem," Nick called out as I walked out the door. Why didn't he want to play in the snow? I was going to make a snowman just like in the movies. It was going to be perfect.

It was a lot colder outside than I'd thought. Snow was accumulating in the grassy courtyard. The leaves had almost completely fallen from the trees and what hadn't been scattered by the wind had accumulated in the corners of the courtyard. Nobody else was out there. Fine by me. I started to pack snow together to make a snowman.

It wasn't as easy as I thought it would be. The snow kept crumbling off the ball I was trying to make. Soon my hands and feet were numb. I looked down at my sandals and realized I should have put sneakers on. I'd have to buy gloves and a real jacket too. An unbuttoned dress shirt doesn't keep you very warm on the mainland.

I tried for about an hour to build my snowman, but couldn't make it work. My hands were hurting now and my hair was wet from the falling snow. I gave up and went to the cafeteria. The interior warmth never felt so good. I didn't feel like playing in the snow anymore today. I'd try again over the weekend.

Unfortunately, there was no weekend. The snow only fell that night and melted by the next day. It never snowed again at Lamia, but that one moment in November when the snow first fell was a special one for me.

A few days later an actual miracle happened. We were standing at Connie's desk for roll call when a name she read off caused me to snap to attention.

"Katrina Skinner?"

"Here," a soft voice answered. I looked back and there she was. Katrina was here, now, in my class. I didn't know what to do or say. I was stunned. I couldn't pull my gaze from her. She was my sun in this cloud obscured institution.

Everybody sat down at the tables, but I couldn't keep my eyes off of her. She was right there, two tables away. Katrina was wearing a tight, long sleeve shirt and jeans. She was flawless.

"Isn't she, like a middle schooler?" I asked Big-head Austin, pointing to her. "Why is she here?"

"Probably just to get used to upper school before she takes her exams for Form Six."

So, she was here to stay. My luck was astounding. I would have thanked God if I still believed in him.

For half my life I was a faithful Catholic. On Sundays I'd go to church with my mom and my sister. Every night I'd pray by my bedside.

"... *should I die before I wake, I pray the lord my soul to take*." That kind of stuff.

One day when I was seven, my parents and I took a drive and I asked them both a question that had been on my mind.

"Mom, Dad, can a person's spirit escape from a black hole?"

"Of course it can, dear," my mom answered.

"Don't tell him that, Bec. Nothing can escape a black hole, even light."

"But a spirit isn't matter, Isht."

"Neither is light. Let me put it to you this way: nothing can escape the gravity of a singularity. If a spirit is some form of energy, then it will get sucked in and crushed infinitely small and infinitely hot, just like everything else."

"But a spirit is a child of God."

"Then God created black holes, too, and he made them so nothing could escape."

And on and on it went. My mom was very religious and had even gone to Catholic school as a child. My dad, on the other hand, had worked in the physics department of USC and was a strict atheist.

I listened to them going back and forth, waiting for an answer, when a strange thought occurred to me. There was no right answer. As a seven year old, this idea shocked me. Things were always either right or wrong, black and white. For the first time, I understood that no correct answer could ever be reached.

The more I thought about it the less and less sense spirituality made to me. Soon I stopped praying by my bed and within a few weeks I told my mom I didn't feel like going to church. Rebecca had never forced me to go. It was always my choice. After a while I stopped thinking about God as being real.

When I told people this, the first question they asked was, "So, what happens to you when you die?" I never had a good answer. Sometime during my second semester of 8th grade, in one of my introspective daydreams, I finally realized what death was like. It was so simple. What was your first memory? Now, what was it like before that first memory? That's what death is like. Twelve billion years passed before you were born. The only difference is that now you know the nothingness is coming. Most people find this depressing when I explain it. They'd rather believe in the idea of Hell? So if you fuck up in any way during life, you'll go there forever? *That's* depressing.

Katrina was going to be sitting a few feet from me for several months and then she'd be just across the way in Form Six. I had to talk to her, but what was I going to say? Hi, I'm Leif. I like you. Do you want to be my girlfriend? That was pretty lame. Why do movie guys always seem to know the right thing to say? In movies women even seem to like losers like Hugh Grant. But, this wasn't the movies and I was not cool. Nothing was going to happen if I did nothing.

I made up my mind. After lunch I'd move my stuff across from her and finally talk. I'd tell her my name and ask for hers, even though I knew it. Then I'd try to make it go somewhere from there.

I was sweating on the way back from lunch. I saw her sit down at her seat. I grabbed my stuff, but couldn't lift it. Just do it, I told myself. I took a few quick deep breaths and picked up my stuff. Then I told myself to just sit down, that's all I had to do. Just sit.

I walked over to her table and set my stuff down across

from her. I was doing everything to avoid looking at her. I tried to act like this was all normal. My breath was coming fast. My heart was hammering against my ribs. Shit! Shit! Shit! What was I doing?

I slowly moved my eyes in her direction. She was reading her course book. Thank God! I was so freaked out. I was sure she'd be looking right at me with contempt and would say, "Why are you sitting there?" I could just see my heart withering away like a raisin.

What should I do now? Should I say something? No, she was reading. I'd talk to her when class was over. Kids often talked to each other then. It would seem normal. I could smell her perfume from here. It was amazing. I began to test some conversation ideas in my mind.

"How do you like Form Six Entry? You get used to it. Me? I'm from Hawaii. No, really. Thank you. I really like it there."

I looked over at her again. She was utterly breathtaking. Jessica Hopemann couldn't come close to measuring up. I just wished I knew what to do to make her like me the way I liked her.

The bell rang. Class was over for the day. My heart started to drum again. Just relax, I told myself. You're just going to ask some normal questions, that's all. She was putting her things in her backpack.

"What's up?" I finally asked.

She looked over at me.

"Nothing."

I hoped she didn't notice my zits.

"So…" I started but didn't know what to say next. Shit! I'd had it all worked out. I couldn't meet her eyes. I jammed my books into my bag and tried to control my breathing. When I finally looked up she was gone.

You really screwed the pooch on that one, Leif! It was a first try. I'd do better tomorrow. Just take it slow. You're a nice guy. Girls like nice guys, right?

I was so grateful that she had come to my class. Until then, I'd had no idea how to approach her. Now she was right here and without her friends to judge me. My luck was almost unbelievable. She was like a gift from above. I zipped up my bag and left the room with a smile on my face.

CHAPTER XIII
The Common Bathroom

"Well, well," Nick said, in a bad British accent as he sat down with us for dinner, "If it isn't my three droogs. Viddy well. Ready for a bit of the old ultra-violence?"

Derk glared at me.

"I'm going to kill you, Leif."

"I just told him about the movie," I said, around a mouthful of toast. "I didn't tell him to become the frickin' thing."

Nick smiled and examined his glass of milk.

"Milk plus vellocet or is it drencrom?"

"Only *you* have that fucking memorize-every-movie bullshit." Derk said, scathingly.

"I'm getting a flash in my gulliver," Nick went on, "Let's find some weepy young devotchka and have a bit of the old in out, in out."

"It's really freaking me out," Jude said. Nick just laughed.

I don't know how it happened, but Nick had suddenly become obsessed with *Clockwork Orange*. He now swaggered about the school doing this British accent and quoting lines from the movie. The weird thing was he'd never seen it. He was only repeating what I'd told him. I was glad he liked my telling, but Jude was right. It was freaky.

When I was six, I dressed up like Speedy Gonzales and ran around yelling, "*Andale! Arriba!*" But I was six. Nick was 14.

"What do you want me to do about it?" I asked the others.

"Shut the fuck up forever!" Derk yelled at me.

"I am Nick DeLarge! Our gang of droogs will rule Lamia!"

"Oh, fuck!" Derk buried his face in his hands. Derk embarrassed was a rare occurrence.

A few days later Nick came to my room.

"What's up, Nick-meister?"

"Nick DeLarge," he corrected.

"Right," I said, trying to hide my sarcasm.

"Hey, you need too... what are you listening to?" Nick motioned to my CD player.

"The best comic album in Hawaii, *Poi Dogs with Crabs*."

"What?"

"This one guy, Rap Replinger, like, does all the voices. It's the funniest shit. Listen to this." I held up my hand for silence. I repeated the words in perfect synchrony.

"...*Po'a gasoline top yo head and light one match*!" I laughed.

Nick looked at me curiously.

"I guess you like that because you're Hawaiian."

"I'm not Hawaiian. I was born in L.A."

"No, man. You're Hawaiian."

"Christ." I shook my head and Nick laughed at me. I would never claim to be Hawaiian. I'd get beat up. The album was still playing.

"... *Maybe yo girlfriend's one dog* ..."

"So, he's speaking Hawaiian?" Nick asked.

"No, that's Pidgin. It's the local dialect of Hawaii."

"You can speak it?"

I shrugged.

"Eh, yes and no. I can do it, but I wouldn't in front of locals. They'd think I was insulting them or something."

"Dude. Can I borrow it?" Nick pointed at the stereo.

"The CD? I guess. I don't know how much sense it'll make. It's local *kine* humor." I popped out the CD, snapped it back into the case and handed it to him.

"Thanks, man. Now come on. You have to see this. It's the coolest." We made our way to his room.

"What do you think?" he said, standing back looking at me.

"Oh, my God." On the wall above his bed was a huge poster of *A Clockwork Orange*. Alex DeLarge, with that one huge pair of eyelashes, was holding a knife like he could reach through the poster and gut you.

"I, like, had my mom and dad get it for me."

"It's… very big." I didn't know what else to say.

"I know." Nick stroked the glossy paper. "My parents got the movie for me too, but I can't see it here. I'll watch it over Thanksgiving. Are you going back to Hawaii?"

"Na. My parents think it's kind of far to fly back for four days. I'm, like, staying with the Petersons."

"That sucks." Nick turned back to his poster. His face lit up. "I would never have known about it without you."

I guess it was a compliment, but the whole thing was crazy.

"Thanks. Oh!" I said, remembering, "I just got a movie from my mom and dad."

"What?"

"It's a surprise. I'm going to show it in the TV Room tonight. I put up a note, like staking it out."

"It's not going to be something like that big Hawaiian dude again?"

"His name is Israel and he's the best musician in Hawaii. No. It's nothing like that."

"Good."

A few weeks ago I'd tried to show a video of an Israel Kamakawiwo`ole concert. I was feeling a little homesick and I thought people would be interested. They weren't. I was practically booed out of the room. He's an amazing singer and ukulele player. I thought it was better than watching stupid Kung Fu movies every weekend.

"I've been planning this since that night," I went on. "I know what makes a movie good."

"Whatever." Nick just stared at his poster.

At 8:00 Nick and I made our way to the TV Room with my VHS.

"Are you humming *This Land Is Your Land*?" Nick asked me skeptically.

Was I? I hadn't noticed.

"Not exactly. It's a version Odi and I made up at my last school."

> *"This land is my land and only my land*
> *I got a shotgun and you don't got one.*
> *If you don't get off I'll blow your head off*
> *This land was made for only me."*

"Sweet," Nick nodded. "*Blow your head off.* Bit of the old ultra-violence."

There were about 10 people waiting around in the TV Room. Smelly Dylan from soccer had the whole middle sofa to himself. He groaned as he saw me peal the note off and stick in my VHS.

"Oh, no! It's not more of that Hawaiian shit, is it?" The others in the room groaned too.

"No, it's not. You'll like this." I pressed play.

"What is it?" Dylan asked.

"Don't worry. It's good."

"Just tell us, man!"

"If you don't like it, I'll take it out." I wanted to see

everybody's first reaction. I turned off the lights and sat as far away from Dylan as possible. He didn't smell as bad as when he played soccer, but it still wasn't pleasant. *He* needed a bath in tomato juice.

A skull appeared on the screen, and then the camera zoomed into the eye socket. It moved back and the title appeared. The room filled with cheers. I looked around. Even Nick was smiling. I let out my breath. There was some normalcy to these Lamia kids after all. As every character appeared, the room cheered their names. Mama! Data! Chunk! It was better than I'd imagined.

"Do the truffle shuffle!" Dylan yelled when Chunk wanted to get into Mikey's house.

"*Hey, you guys!*" some kid screamed when Sloth slid down the sail. When the movie was over, everybody applauded. It was perfect. By the time Nick and I left the room, I was floating on air. Nobody could doubt my taste in film now.

"A classic," Nick said, smiling. "A totally awesome movie."

He was right. For us, the Whatever Generation, there is no more beloved movie than *Goonies*. There may be better films out there, but *Goonies* is special. I'd never had more fun watching a movie than that night.

"Fucking-A," I responded.

"Even Nick DeLarge thinks it was viddy cool."

What a weirdo, but it was all good. It was a great night. At least until bed check.

After roll call, the Rover made a grim announcement.

"Several of you have been chosen to clean the floor's common bathroom."

Everybody moaned.

The Rover read his duty roll. "Stan."

"Yeah," a miserable voice to my right said. "They always call on the brother," he mumbled under his breath.

"Derk," the Rover said.

"Fuck yooooou!"

We all laughed.

"Knock it off!" the Rover barked.

"Jude, Curtis and Leif."

Oh, damn! It's always me. We all trudged to the bathroom.

"At least we get to stay up an extra hour," Derk chimed.

"Cleaning shit out of toilets," Curtis scoffed.

"Don't bitch. You can use your bare hands. They used to make you lick the shit out."

"Ugh!" Curtis winced. Derk laughed.

Unfortunately, I was assigned to cleaning the toilets. Stan was to mop the floors. Derk and Jude had to wipe down the sinks and mirrors and Curtis was scrubbing the urinals. It was not fun work for any of us. The sinks were covered in shaving files. Most guys don't flush the urinals, which reeked and, when people took really big dumps that wouldn't go down, they just left it in there and the crap kept piling up. I wished Lamia had those self-cleaning seashell things from *Demolition Man.*

I was on my knees using Comet to get the shit smears out of the bowl. I talked to the others to keep myself from thinking about what I was doing.

"Curtis Man!"

"Yo!"

"What's the worst thing you've ever seen?"

"Ah... what?"

Even though he was in Virus Wars with me and lived next door, the only thing he talked about was how many cacti his mother owned. I felt this was a perfect question to break the ice and get to know him.

"What's the most horrible thing you've, like, ever seen with your own eyes?"

"Oh, Jeez. I don't know. I don't usually think about that stuff."

"You're weird, Leif," Jude called out.

"Chill out, Old Man. Come on, there must be something."

"Well, my parents and I were driving down the freeway and there was a guy on a motorbike in front of us. There was a big truck next to him. The truck changed lanes, but didn't see the bike dude. He got knocked off and slammed into the guardrail. It was sick. Looked liked somebody splashed a bucket of red paint on the road. I really wish I'd never seen that."

"That's sick," Jude said. "How old were you?"

"10."

"That's screwed up," I responded. It was horrendous, but I like extreme stories, like Arnold Schwarzenegger films.

You just knew he was going to snap somebody's neck with his bare hands. Derk was laughing.

"I can just see it, man!" He made a screeching sound and slammed his hands together. "Stupid biker. That's funny."

"Na, man," Stan said. "That's some bad times."

I was done with this toilet, five more to go.

"Stop getting shit on my floor," Stan shouted to Derk as I entered the next stall.

"I'm wiping, you're sweeping. Shut the hell up."

I ignored them. This toilet had been clogged for several days. It looked like a chocolate frozen yogurt machine had exploded in there. All my thoughts were on breathing through my mouth so I wouldn't puke as I scrubbed.

"I said stop it!" Stan yelled again.

Derk giggled. I heard water hit the floor.

"Stop! How would you like it if I shook my broom off in your sinks, Fat-ass?"

"Shut the fuck up you fucking nigger!"

I jumped to my feet. Had I really heard that? The next thing I heard was screaming and sneakers squeaking on the tiles. I ran out of the stall. Jude and Curtis were holding Stan back. Stan was struggling, with fists raised, trying to get at Derk.

"I'LL KILL YOU, MOTHERFUCKER!"

What the hell was happening? Things had just gone *Twilight Zone.*

"LET ME GO!" It was taking all their strength to hold Stan back. "I'M GOING TO FUCK THAT COCKSUCKER

UP!"

The hairs on my arms stood up when I looked over at Derk. Stan was two feet from him, ready to really kill him. Derk wasn't running or apologizing. He was laughing.

The Rover flung the bathroom door open. "What's going on in here?"

Nobody knew where to start. The Rover and Curtis pulled the struggling Stan out of the room.

"Nobody go anywhere!" the Rover ordered as the door swung closed. The bathroom felt very empty, even with the three of us there. The only sounds were the hum of the florescent lights and Derk's giggles.

"Derk," Jude began, "that was not cool."

"Did you see him?" Derk was grinning ear to ear. "He couldn't get away from you and you're a shrimp. Ha!" Derk slapped his thighs with glee.

"You called him a..." I couldn't finish. "Why?"

Derk shrugged, "I don't know."

I knew Derk wasn't a racist. He just liked to rile people up, but this?

"That was over the line, man," Jude said.

"It was," I sided.

"Don't be such pussies."

We were all quiet. There was nothing else to say.

The incident confused me. At my school in Hawaii, they taught us about the equal rights movement on the mainland. When Martin Luther King was shot all the prejudice went away and everything was perfect. Anytime I saw a movie like

Boyz in the Hood, which showed the separation of blacks and whites, I thought it was just made up, for dramatic effect. This was the modern age. How could race still be an issue? For the first time, I saw that the problems of the 50's and 60's still existed on the mainland. Even if Derk had been joking, he should have apologized.

Derk was sent to Ethics for the incident in the bathroom. It was the first time I thought somebody deserved to go there. Derk was exactly the same when he got out, as if nothing had happened. Stan didn't want to kill him anymore, but he refused to acknowledge Derk's existence.

I felt bad for Stan, insulted because of the color of his skin. At my last school, almost everybody was from somewhere else. There were Japanese, Chinese, Filipino, Europeans, and Hapa; kids who were a mix like Odi, who was half Japanese and half Hawaiian. Even I wasn't originally from Hawaii. There wasn't a majority of any race, so nobody ever made comments like those Derk had made. The thought would never have entered our minds. Even so, Hawaii isn't some utopia.

Being a white kid growing up in Hawaii wasn't always a peachy time. I was on my way to Odi's house once and decided to take a shortcut through a local neighborhood. It was a bad idea. A couple of local guys saw me and tried to run me down with their car. There was no reason other than I was there. I managed to run into a grove of trees where their car couldn't follow, but they got out and surrounded me.

"You fucking, haole!" the biggest kid yelled. "What the

fuck you doing in our fucking neighborhood! We're going to fucking kill you!" They had to be 15 or 16 and I was only 10 years old. I was pretty sure that I was dead.

"Hey! What's happening?" I looked down the street and, to my utter relief, saw Odi approaching. He must have been wondering where I was.

"You know dis haole, Odi?" the big kid said, grabbing my shirt.

"Yeah, he's cool." Odi stood next to me. "Once he unscrewed the tire valves on a busload of tourists. They were stuck and couldn't go nowhere."

Actually Odi had done that, though I was with him at the time. I was grounded for two weeks when my mom found out. I'd been angry at Odi for getting me into trouble, but now I was happy to take the blame. Screwing over tourists was always appreciated by locals.

"Why didn't you say so?" the biggest kid said, smiling and smoothing out my shirt. "Any friend of Odi's is a friend of ours. Even if he is one haole." I couldn't tell if his sincerity was real, but I was so glad to be alive I didn't care.

The technical definition of haole is somebody with no breath. In ancient Hawaii, breath was thought to be the source of life, so the word really means a human without a soul. Most people don't know the exact translation. They just use it because it's always been used.

Yet, it's not always like with the kids and the car. I was on an airplane and some local guys handed out fresh jerky, played their ukes and got the passengers to sing along.

Things like the guys trying to run me down were rare occurrences, but they did happen.

White people are the minority on the Big Island, but they have most of the wealth. Angry locals usually take it out on the tourists. They'll scan items twice at the supermarket or talk pidgin so you can't understand them. I never blamed the locals for things like that.

It was the haoles who destroyed and took the land from the Hawaiians. My ancestors hadn't. Hungary wasn't one of the great colonial powers. Hungarians had been under occupation by one empire or another since the 15th century, but that didn't change the color of my skin. I spent as much time as I could in the sun trying to make my color as dark as possible. Mercedes would never date white guys. I tried not to think of myself as white, but there were always little incidents that reminded me. My skin color was so frustrating. Why couldn't I have been born dark? There were even some schools I couldn't go to because I didn't have Hawaiian blood.

It was something I had learned to deal with. But hearing Derk call Stan a nigger was wrong. Blacks hadn't done anything to the haoles. I understood my place in Hawaii, but no matter how much I thought about it, I couldn't understand what had happened. I guess race was still a problem that everyone had in common.

CHAPTER XIV
Accident Prone

Another day in Hell's Kitchen. It was sloppy joe day again, and the vats were brimming with the smelly crap. I finally emptied them out, but the tomato juice had cooked to the inside. It took repeated brushing to get it all off. It peeled away like wet toilet paper.

When I was finally done, I looked up at the clock. Thirty minutes to go. Damn! There was still time to clean the oven and scrape the grill. Although the vats were disgusting to work with, I'd almost hoped they'd take longer so I wouldn't have to do anything else. Oh, well. There were only four more days until Thanksgiving. My first vacation since I'd arrived here. I was psyched.

I found my plastic sponge holder and scrubbed the front of the burning hot oven. The stains on the oven weren't too bad today. After I scrubbed off as much as possible, I went to the scullery to retrieve the spray hose.

Usually during this mindless cleaning, my thoughts revolved around Katrina, but today my mind was on turkey and stuffing. The stuffing was always my favorite part of the meal. I loved to help my mom cook it. Cutting up the dried bread, sautéing the onions and mushrooms with butter and spices. My mouth was watering at the thought of it. Real food!

I finished spraying the oven down and took the hose back. I noticed something strange when I crossed in front of the oven on my way to the grill. I stopped and took a closer look. One of the green indicator lights on the oven control panel was missing. There was a hole with dimly visible wires. Had that always been like that? I wasn't sure. I had just sprayed it with water. Wouldn't that be bad?

As if to answer my question, a column of smoke began to bleed out of the hole. Oh, shit! My mind raced to find a solution. I rushed to the Supervisor.

"I think there's something wrong with the oven."

"What?"

"Just come." He followed me. I didn't want to tell him about the hose unless I had to. Maybe it was just a small thing that could be fixed. I stood in front of the oven, pointing out the hole. A steady stream of smoke was still coming out.

"What happened?"

"I think some water got in while I was cleaning it." The Supervisor leaned in to examine the control panel.

There was a loud crackling and the edges of the panel lit

up like a light bulb flaring out inside. The Supervisor jumped back. I just stared - mesmerized. A stream of jet-black smoke blasted out of the hole like a rocket plume and the oven shuddered loudly. Everybody in the kitchen stopped working and was looking.

In an explosion of sparks, the entire control panel blasted away from the oven. It clanged to the floor and came to a stop near the wall. Flames burst outwards and roared to the ceiling.

"Holy shit!" I screamed and jumped back as the heat hit me full in the face. I could see the rubber on the electric wires melting and dripping away. The whole oven was on fire.

The Supervisor ran to the breaker box and hit the kill switch for the oven. It occurred to me that, until this moment, the oven hadn't been shut off in 20 years. The flames were still consuming the inside of the oven.

"Everybody out!" The Supervisor yelled. Kids ran for the swinging double doors, coughing from the smoke. I wanted to follow, but I wasn't sure if I should stay and help.

The Supervisor tore the fire extinguisher from the wall and blasted the oven with the white spray. I'd always thought extinguishers were filled with gas, but this was a fine powder. The oven was now covered in white. I tasted chemicals on my tongue. The powder was suspended in the air. It probably wasn't good to breathe. It definitely was time to leave.

I ran behind the others into the cafeteria and tried to catch my breath and rub the taste off my tongue. It took a moment before I noticed that everybody was staring at me. Somebody slapped me on the back.

"Good job, Leif." It was Clint from scullery.

Everybody applauded.

"No!" I closed my eyes to shut them out.

"You just got us out of kitchen duty for the day. Thanks, man." Clint Continued. People were now cheering.

"I didn't mean to! Oh, shit!"

"So, what do we do?" a girl asked.

"Leave! They're not going to be letting us back in today," Clint answered. "Come on."

All the kids started to file out. There were additional slaps on the back as they passed. Shit! Shit! A few more "Thanks, Leif." Shit! Shit! Shit! I was soon standing there alone. I looked back at the kitchen doors. Should I stay? It was my fault, but he did say for everybody to get out. The last of the kids were turning the corner of the hall and going out of sight. I looked back to the kitchen doors. Fuck! I didn't want to go back in there. I ran after the other kids. I hoped I was doing the right thing.

I waited for Nick's reaction when I finished telling him what happened. He began to laugh.

"Oh, man! You blew up the oven, and you did it without a bomb. That's great! I see you Hawaiians enjoy a bit of the old ultra-violence."

"I didn't do it on purpose. I'm so in trouble."

"Dude, it wasn't your fault. You didn't, like, take that button off."

"Oh, fuck!"

"Just chill. The kitchen Supervisor will ask you what happened. You'll tell him. He'll tell you to be more careful next time and that's it." Nick put on a Jamaican accent. *"Don't worry, be happy."*

"Sure," I answered. I was positive it wouldn't be that simple.

Nick jumped up and ran to the door. "Dude, I got to tell the others. This is, like, the coolest thing that's ever happened here."

"Fine, go." People would know soon enough anyway. Nick closed the door behind him. I lay back on the bed and buried my head in the pillow. Damn!

I was dreading going into the kitchen the next day, but I had no choice. I walked through the double doors and looked around. The oven was a blackened mess, caked in fire retardant chemicals. Everybody else was doing their jobs, so I began to clean the vats. The Supervisor saw me and began walking towards me. This was it. I was fucked.

"Can I talk to you, Leif?" The Supervisor took me to a deserted corner. "What happened?"

My stomach was spinning like a hula hoop. I considered lying, but decided to tell him about the hose I'd used to clean the oven. It couldn't get any worse.

"Why'd you use the hose?" he asked.

"I've been doing it for, like, two months. I didn't think it was a problem. You've seen me use it."

The Supervisor said nothing.

"What's going to happen now?" I asked.

"We have to buy a new oven."

"Okay." How much Ethics was that worth?

"You will not be cleaning that one."

They'll probably make me scrape the grill clean with my tongue.

"I want you to mop after you clean the vats."

"Okay." Not only the cafeteria but the whole school.

He took a deep breath. "Just be more careful next time." And with that he moved off.

Was that it? I wasn't sure what they were going to do to me, but I knew I was going to be punished somehow. "Be more careful?" That's it? The twisting sensation in my stomach began to go away. I was glad I told the truth about the hose. For once, Istvan was right. Admitting your mistake was necessary for things to begin correcting themselves. Things were going to be fine. And at first, they were.

I cleaned my vats as always and my new second chore was mopping the floor. I got to hang with the Korean kids, so that was cool. They were always nice to me. I was kind of glad I didn't need to clean that blistering hot oven anymore. I guess everyone at Lamia wasn't nuts. People here could be reasonable.

"Oh, no," I moaned the next day when I looked in my mailbox. There was the familiar pink slip again. I reached in and tentatively took it. I read the charge:

Arson violation: Setting the oven on fire.

What?! I didn't do it on purpose. This made it sound like

I was a pyro or something. It said to report immediately to the Ethics Office. I slowly made my way up to the tower. Just when things were going well.

There was one other kid in the waiting room. It was half an hour before he went inside. How did my forced labor involve the Ethics Department? This place pissed me off.

The kid left after about 20 minutes. I waited another half an hour listening to the sound of file drawers closing, before the office door opened. After an hour milling over my situation I was feeling pretty frustrated.

I walked into the cramped little office and sat down. The pudgy faced Ethics Lady looked at the longer version of my ethics violation from the kitchen Supervisor.

"Fire is a serious thing," she began. "Tell me why you set the oven on fire."

I felt a surge of anger in my gut, but controlled it. I explained why I'd used the hose and how a button was missing. I decided to go a step further and say how sorry I was and, if there was anything I could do to make it up, I would. I just wanted to get out of there.

"Why didn't you notice the button was missing?"

"Ah, I just didn't notice. I was careless."

"Why were you careless?"

"I wasn't thinking. That's all."

"Why weren't you thinking?"

"Why was I... you, you don't need to think when cleaning."

"Why is that?"

Christ! What was going on? What was the point of this? I already admitted I'd done it. Suddenly, I realized she wanted me to admit I'd done it on purpose. She wouldn't let it go until I did. I thought of my reminder in my room. "Go along with it until you don't have to." No! Not this time. Fuck 'em. My name was not going on the EIR.

"It was just a mistake."

"How was it a mistake?" Her face was like a Disneyland robot - no expression.

I could feel my anger building again. I am not going to admit it. I almost wished I still had my sharp edged drawing compass. It went on and on. Why? This. Why? Because. Why? That. Why, why, why, why!

This went on for an hour and a half. I was trembling with both anger and frustration. It felt like bees were stinging my stomach - on the inside. Did I see a flicker of a smile on her face? I am not going to confess!

"It's, it's just the way I am," I growled between clenched teeth.

"Why are you the way you are?"

"BECAUSE THAT'S THE WAY THE FUCKING UNIVERSE WAS CREATED!" I screamed. Silence. Gone was that hint of a smile on her face. I was breathing hard. My insides were on fire. I didn't care what they did at this point.

We squared off. She wanted me to confess, but she could see I wasn't going to. The moment seemed to drag on for another hour and a half.

Finally, her eyes broke away from mine and she picked up my file. She began to write.

"I'm writing the fire was an accident."

What? Had I won? I couldn't believe it.

"I'm also writing that, in the future, you are not to be given any dangerous jobs."

"Sure." If cleaning an oven was a dangerous job that was fine by me.

She glanced up from her scribbling. I quickly forced the smile from my lips but not fast enough to go unnoticed. She picked up a thicker file and wrote some more.

"On your permanent record I'm putting that you're accident prone with delinquent tendencies."

"What?"

"That means, when colleges ask for your records, what I'm writing now will be something they will have to consider before accepting you." I could see that hint of a smile again. She returned the file to its drawer and slammed it closed with her foot, sealing my record away. All children fear our permanent records, even me.

Fucking bitch. I glared at her. She couldn't get a confession, so she was going to make my future as difficult as possible. The bees were stinging again.

I'd seen Nazi war reels and always wondered how everyone in Germany just went along with Hitler. Now I knew. Every kid around me was letting themselves be told what to think and what to do because they were afraid. Afraid of what could happen to them if they didn't. They even had our parents eating out of the palms of their hands and they weren't even here! Fear is more powerful than any nuclear weapon or virus and Lamia knew exactly how to wield it.

There was nothing I could do to stop the Ethics Lady. I left the tower clenching my fists so tight my nails were cutting into my palms. Ender Wiggin was right. Teachers are the enemy and the Ethics Lady was the Big Brother of them all. My father had told me on countless occasions that I wouldn't amount to anything, but nothing he had ever said to me welled up as much hatred as I felt for these people. Accident prone? What the fuck does that mean? I felt a new flood of conviction boiling in my veins. I was not going to let them win.

CHAPTER XV
A Letter & a Paper

I was in a pretty dark mood for the rest of the day. I wanted to break something, but then I thought of what I'd already done to the oven and it kind of made me feel better.

Nick, Derk, Jude and most of the other students were gone by that afternoon, flying back to their homes. I didn't mind. I wanted to be alone. I went down to the chapel and played the piano for a few hours. It took my mind off what had happened that morning.

By the next day, I'd almost put the altercation with the Ethics Lady out of my mind, but my stomach still twinged as though it had it's own memory. When I felt the anger pushing its way up into my throat, I just thought about being out on the sea with my board in the waves and I would relax. My sister, Mercedes had taught me this.

After I'd lose a big fight with my sister, I'd lay in bed that night trying to sleep, but all I wanted to do was sneak into her bedroom and smother her with a pillow. Once she was dead my life would be perfect. I would finally be free, but what would happen the next day? This thought always kept me from executing the final solution. The surfing meditation was the only way I could keep from going crazy.

John Peterson picked me up Thanksgiving day and we drove back to Jackskeep.

"How's school?"

I shrugged.

"Your mom told me you've read a lot of books."

"Eh. Whatever." I couldn't remember most of them. They were all books I'd never heard of. Well, not all of them.

"I read *Pinocchio*. Man, that's a screwed up book. I don't know how Disney ever decided to make that into a movie. Pinocchio killed Jiminy Cricket with a hammer, like in the first five minutes. And when Pinocchio turns into a donkey he actually dies. Weird."

"I just read an interesting book," John said, like I hadn't said anything. "It's about a time traveler."

"Like Doc and the Delorean. 1.21 jigawatts!"

"Not really." John didn't get the joke. "There's no time machine. The heroine changed her body chemistry and stood on these cliffs in Scotland as a storm approached. This was how she time traveled."

"Huh? Interesting." I stared out the window at the grey clouds and low rolling hills as John went on about the details of the book. I paid just enough attention so I could acknowledge his points, but nothing else. I didn't really care. The best time travel stories were *Back to the Future* and *Bill and Ted's Excellent Adventure.* No chick in Scotland would ever out do them.

We arrived at the Peterson's house. I was excited to begin cooking, but that was not to be. Everybody jumped right back into the car and we drove to their friend's house, where the food was already prepared. The food was good, but I was a little disappointed I didn't participate in the preparation of the meal. Cooking was a major part of the holiday back home.

Rebecca and I would make the stuffing and shove it into the turkey. Mercedes would mix up some corn bread. I would get the cranberries ready. Istvan would carve the bird when it came out of the oven. Thanksgiving was a family holiday, and this wasn't my family.

That night after dinner, while the guys were watching a football game and the girls were talking chick stuff, John took me out to the porch.

"Hope this was fun for you. It must be hard, being away from home."

"It was great," I lied.

"Take a look." John pointed up into the sky. I looked through the drizzle, but couldn't see anything.

"Uh… what am I looking for?"

"It's right there." I came closer to look up the length of his arm. I still wasn't sure what I was looking at. There was a fuzzy bright blob beyond the clouds.

"What is it?"

"Hale-Bopp." He seemed astonished that I didn't know. "It's a comet. Haven't you seen it on the news?"

"We don't get much news."

"Oh," he nodded. "Well, there it is. The comet only comes around every 4,000 years."

"Cool. Comet action." It was kind of neat, but I couldn't see much through the rain.

"It has this unusual blue flair coming off of it. Can't see it from here, but the news has some great pictures."

"Sweet."

John nodded and we went back into the house.

The next best thing about Thanksgiving, other than that there was no school, was the leftovers. Eating turkey and mashed potatoes for days afterwards seemed to make the holiday last longer. Because the dinner was at somebody else's house, there were none. I knew it wasn't the Peterson's fault, but this was a lousy Thanksgiving. At least I was full for the first time in weeks.

After my first visit to their house they always had a full box of Hot Pockets. It was very considerate of them. I was enjoying a pepperoni one when Mrs. Peterson, walking through the kitchen, stopped to look at me. I immediately thought I'd done something wrong.

"What did I do?"

She came over to look closely at one of my hands.

"My God!" She turned my hand over. "You've lost a lot of weight."

I looked down at my hands. I hadn't noticed, but all the veins were sticking out like an old person.

"How much do you weigh?"

"I don't know." The school didn't have a scale and neither did the Petersons. "I was 165 when I got to Lamia."

"I don't think you are now. Do you want me to make you another one?" indicating my Hot Pocket.

"Sure." I could never say no to free food. I'd get on a scale when I went home for Christmas.

They took me back early on Sunday. Most of the kids came back later that evening. I waited in the lobby for a couple of hours for Katrina. My heart raced when I finally saw her come through the doors and make her way to the stairs. I pretended to read a book so she couldn't tell I was watching. How could she be so perfect?

That night I was playing pool with Jude when Nick came bounding into the Rec Room.

"How was Seattle?" I asked.

"I watched *Clockwork Orange* 10 times, man! It was just like you said. It's the best fucking movie ever!"

Jude gave me a look.

"I thought you said *Leon: The Professional* was the best movie?" Jude said to Nick.

"It's still cool, but *Clockwork Orange* is way better. I, like, brought it back with me. I'm never going anywhere without it."

"I'm glad you liked it," I stated turning my attention back to the pool table. I was on the eight ball but I didn't have a good shot. Fuck it. I aimed and smacked the ball as hard as I could. By some stroke of luck, it went into the corner pocket.

"Game!" I called out.

"That doesn't count," Jude said.

"Why not?"

"You weren't aiming. You have to call the ball."

"We never called the others."

"But you always call the eight."

"I made the shot. Game over, Old Man. I won!"

"No, you just lost!"

"My droogs!" Nick put a hand on each of our shoulders.

"No need for the ultra-violence. How about Leif wins this game, but after this, you always have to call the eight ball?"

"Fine by me," but Jude wasn't so pleased.

"Dude," Nick said, "it's just a game."

"Fine. If he has to cheat to win, then he can have it."

"Thanks," I replied, unperturbed by his jab.

"I'm too old for this crap."

A few days later there was a knock on my door.

"*Help! Help! There's been a terrible accident!*" It was Nick DeLarge, quoting a line from *Clockwork Orange*.

"Oh, God!" I opened the door.

"You have to see this," Nick said before I could get it open all the way. I immediately followed without question. We collected Jude from his room, and then went to Nick's. Derk was already there, with a malicious smile on his face.

"What is it?" I asked. Nick went over to his desk, pulled something out of the drawer and handed it to me. It was a newspaper.

"Where did you get that?" Like TV and radio, you couldn't get a newspaper around here. Lamia printed a bulletin every week telling us about world events: Cyclone Devastates India, Assassination in Bulgaria, Bombing at Olympics, Campers Killed in Spain. They were depressing and I stopped reading them by the third week.

"I stole it from the Ethics Lady," Derk boasted.

"You what?"

"I got sent there today for making this girl cry. Fat bitch narced on me. Anyway, I snatched it when she wasn't looking. Fuck her!"

"Why?"

"Why the fuck not?"

"Jesus, Derk!" Jude said. "Do you know what they'll do to you if they catch you?"

"What do you mean? I was already in Ethics, dickface."

"We should throw it out," Jude said nervously.

"Fuck no!" Derk yelled.

I dropped the paper on the desk.

"It's just a newspaper. Who gives a shit?"

"No, man," Nick said, "Wait until you hear what happened."

"What?"

"You know that comet thing?"

"It's going to hit the earth and kill everybody, like the dinosaurs?"

"No. 40 people in this cult thing thought there was, like, a spaceship in the tail and that it would take them to heaven. They were led by this guy called The Doe. They all killed themselves. There were bodies everywhere. The paper says it's the worst mass suicide in US history."

"Dude. That's pretty fucked up. When did it happen?"

"Almost a week ago."

A week? Strange. That sounded exactly like the gloomy shit Lamia would post.

"I guess they don't want us to know..." my voice trailed off.

"What?" Nick asked.

"Oh, dude," I said, smiling. "I have the best idea." I was tingling with excitement.

"What?" they all asked.

"They obviously don't want us to know about this cult, right? We should, like, go and like tell everybody about it. Make it as gory as possible. It'll piss them off. Especially, the Ethics Lady." I wanted to get back at her for that accident prone bullshit.

Derk grabbed my arm and slapped my palm hard with his other hand.

"Ow!" I pulled my arm out of his grasp before he got the idea to Mercy me, too.

"That's fucking awesome!" Derk cheered. I guess he wanted some payback as well.

"Radical," Nick said.

"What if they find out?" Jude asked.

"How can they, Old Man? By the time they hear about it, every kid at Lamia will know and nobody will remember who started it."

Jude thought for a second then reluctantly nodded.

"Let's do it, my droogs."

Nick read the article aloud so we could get the details.

"Got it?" he asked.

"Derk, throw it in the trash somewhere." I ordered.

"I know, kweef face." He ran off to get rid of the paper.

We spread the word. I went to the Rec Room. Nick went to tell the kids he knew in Form Six. I don't know who Jude told but Derk did his damage up in study hall.

By the next morning, the cult and the suicide were all everybody could talk about. People were even coming up to us, asking if we knew about it. It was glorious and we all felt good. We'd beaten Lamia with the freedom of information. I guess knowing was half the battle. We were all feeling pretty stoked as we walked down to dinner that night.

"We is the man, my droogs," Nick said as we walked down the lower hall.

"No, I stole the paper! I am the fucking bomb!" Derk held up his hands.

We noticed a small crowd near the entrance to the cafeteria, where the official message board was. We pushed through the kids to look. We stopped short in shock. Tacked inside was *the* newspaper. I recognized a small tear in the upper left corner.

"I thought you threw it away," I whispered to Derk.

"I did." He was as shocked as I was. "I dumped it in the bathroom trashcan."

There was an official message next to the paper.

This newspaper was stolen from the Ethics Office. If you have information on the perpetrators, report them immediately.

We walked away quietly.

"Dude," Nick began, "how did they find it?"

"They must go through our trash," I said. "Jesus!"

Derk looked at me. "Fuck."

"So what do we do?" Jude asked.

"Not tell anybody," I said.

"But they know where it came from. What if they trace it back to us? They'll send us to the Trash Room for sure."

"I don't think it will be that bad," Nick reassured.

"Yeah, man. We just blame Derk," I said, half joking.

"I'll kill you! It was your lame ass idea!"

"Dude," Nick said, "the story's been so jumbled up they'll never, like, figure it was us. But we have to promise never to narc on each other. Okay?"

I looked from face to face. It was the only way. We all agreed. I was worried about Jude. He seemed really nervous. He could go and turn us in, even though he was party to it, but, because he narced, he wouldn't be dealt with as severely.

Over the next few days we waited nervously for them to come for us. I was sure every morning there would be a pink slip in my mailbox, but there never was. I started to relax and even felt good about it again. They were so used to people turning others in it must have really pissed them off to have no culprits. The newspaper stayed on the board, though. It was a creepy reminder every time we went to the cafeteria.

I called my parents on the 6th of December.

"Happy Saint Nicholas Day," I said to Rebecca.

"Happy Saint Nicholas Day, my darling."

"It's kind of strange not opening presents today."

"I know. It's lonely without both of my children here."

We did celebrate Christmas, it just wasn't our day to open presents. In Hungary, they always opened their gifts on the 6th. Istvan brought the tradition to America with him. It was always cool to open presents way before the other kids in school. On Christmas, we usually rented a cabin in the rainforest near Honoka'a and camped for a few days. The 6th was a much more important day for me and, being at Lamia, today was like a normal kid being at school on December 25th.

"I guess we'll do a real Christmas at home," I said. "Hope the waves are good. Can we go down to Pine Trees?"

"Actually, we're going to Dallas this year."

"Oh." We did go to my Grandparents sometimes for Christmas. That was cool, but I was looking forward to being in some warm weather and the ocean. I even missed fishing with Istvan.

"I'm sending you your ticket in the mail. It should be there by next week."

"Okey dokey."

"Any special plans for today?"

"Mmm... Not really."

It was a Friday so at least it was the last day of school this week. I talked to Isht for a bit then told my parents I loved them and hung up. That phone call was how I spent Christmas with my family that year. It was the first December 6th that wasn't a happy day for me.

In class, I sat across from Katrina about three times a week. I wanted to make it seem like it was random. I still couldn't get up the nerve to really talk to her. I made progress by asking her questions about what I was working on. It was pathetic, but I was too scared to do anything else.

It was the last week before school let out and I was getting desperate. I had to do something. I was going to hold a conversation with her after class. I was going to make myself do this.

When the bell rang, I spoke up.

"Are you going back home for Christmas?" Stupid question! Of course she was.

"Yeah. We may go to Florida for New Year's."

"Oh. Where exactly?"

"Orlando." She continued putting her books away.

"Do you think I could call you?"

Oh, my God! Had I just said that? I felt my face burn. Oh, shit! She looked a little confused.

"I don't know."

What the fuck! My mind raced for a way out of this.

"What I meant was, I'm going to Dallas, but since Florida's kind of close I thought, ah, we could say hi, or something. You know, close times zones. Hawaii's way out there." That was totally lame. What a loser I am.

"Oh, right." She put her last book away. She could see I was embarrassed and smiled. "Just relax, Leif."

"Yeah." My heart slowed down, but only a fraction. She crossed her arms and looked hard at me.

"You're part of Derk's gang."

"What?" I was confused by the turn in the conversation.

"Aren't you?"

"Yeah, I guess." I'd never thought of it as Derk's gang. Nick was the unofficial leader of our posse.

"He told my best friend she was fat."

Oh, shit. Was that who it was? Goddamn Derk! Why couldn't he bitch out somebody else? Now I was guilty by association. I'm not Derk. I'm a good guy. I was.

"I'm sorry about that." It was the only thing I could say.

"How can you stand being around him?"

"I don't know. He's not that bad."

"He's an asshole."

I involuntarily nodded. I felt bad about talking behind my friend's back, but she was speaking to me. I couldn't tell her she was wrong.

"It's just that he's..." I thought about the best way to describe it.

Every kid in school tries to carve out their own little niche. The Straight A Student, the Jock, the Piano Guy, and so on. We all want to be recognized in some way. Derk wasn't good at anything. The only thing he could do was be the Asshole at Lamia. I could explain this, but she'd never understand.

"He's… you just get used to him."

Katrina slung her backpack over her shoulder.

"Well. I'm glad you can. Merry Christmas."

"Merry Christmas." And with that she left. I watched her gorgeous figure move away. I felt a boner coming on. No! Go down! Go down! Shit! I thought about Fat Rob's ugly, freckled face. The stiffy went away. I breathed a sigh of relief.

I sat there for a moment, thinking. She'd talked to me. She'd asked me questions. I'd fucked up a little, but maybe she'd forget what I'd said about the phone thing. She hadn't given me her number, but I didn't think I could have gotten up the nerve to call. Yet, she knew who my friends were. I felt a spring of hope in my chest. So, was she interested? It really seemed like there could be something there.

I closed my eyes and imagined holding her tight and kissing her. What a great feeling that would be. If I had a fairy godmother I knew exactly what I'd ask for. I opened my eyes, picked up my bag and left the classroom.

Christmas vacation finally came. I packed up my suitcase for the trip to Dallas. Fat Rob was in the room, but he wasn't talking to me. I wasn't trying to sleep. There was a knock on the door.

"There's been a terrible accident!"

Fat Rob gave me a funny look and opened the door.

"Piano Man, what's up?" Nick asked pushing past Fat Rob.

"A little packing action."

"You got a letter, dude." Nick held out an envelope.

"Huh?" I took it from him. "I checked today."

"They must have, like, not sorted it when you came. I was getting my mail when I saw it. Figured I bring it before they closed for the year."

"Thanks, Nick-meister." I'd gotten the ticket already. What was this? The seal was torn so it didn't take long to get the letter out. Nick was poking at Rob's stuff.

"Don't touch that," Rob said.

"Is this a candy-covered bug?"

"Yes. It's gourmet. Put it down." Rob yanked it away from Nick and took it back to his desk.

"Chill out, dude. You are in desperate need of a blow job, man."

I would have laughed at this, but my focus was on the letter.

Hey, Leif. How zit? Your mom told me where I could reach you. Going to school on the mainland? That's got to be strange. I've never left Hawaii.

Hawaii is in mourning right now.
Israel Kamakawiw'ole died yesterday.
Everybody is really sad. all the flags
are at that half whatever thing.
Just thought you'd want to know.

I'm working at McDonalds. It's not
so Bad. Better than school. Anyway,
next time you're over here stop
by and say Hi. Don't take shit from
the Haoles.

od: wallas

Odi had written to me. What a cool thing to do, but then I read the letter again.

"Shit."

"What?" Nick asked.

"IZ' just died." I handed Nick the letter.

"You mean the guy with the unpronounceable name?" Rob asked.

I didn't bother responding. Nick scanned the letter.

"Is this your friend Odi from Hawaii?"

"Yeah. We've been best friends since like, preschool but he was expelled in 7th grade for not doing any of his homework that year."

Odi was probably the only person who hated school more than me.

"I haven't talked to him in a long time."

"No homework!" Nick exclaimed, "Dude, that's hard core." Nick squinted at the letter. "What is a Ha-O-lay?"

"It's How-lee, and ah, it's kind of a Hawaiian thing. It's hard to explain. Yeah. Jeez, man. I can imagine how sad the people are in Hawaii."

"The IZ guy was that big?" Nick asked.

"You have no idea. Israel has been performing for, like, 20 years. In Hawaii, he's like the Beatles and Bob Marley in one person. Literally, too. Every song he wrote was about real things in Hawaii - surfing, sumo wrestlers, Hawaiian sovereignty. I never go to concerts, but when he came to Waimea to play, I took all my savings and bought one ticket. He was a hero. The world is a suckier place with him gone."

Nick gave me back the letter.

"Dude." Nick wandered around my room.

It was sad. There were so few true heroes in the world today. Kids protested the system in the 60's because they had great examples to follow. But who could we follow now? Adam Sandler?

"Nobody cares about Hawaii," Fat Rob said. "Especially some fat guy with a fake guitar."

Anger flared and my stomach burned. Don't diss Israel you motherfucking haole! I calmed myself. He was just trying to piss me off.

"Yeah. It blows," I said.

"Can I borrow this?" Nick held up my pog.

I glanced over at Rob, but he was into one of his books again.

"Why?" I asked.

"I want to show some friends over the break."

"I don't know."

"Come on! I promise I won't lose it."

I didn't really want to lend it out to anybody. It meant a lot to me, but I didn't want to leave it here alone for a month. I couldn't take it to Dallas. One of my younger cousins would probably snatch it. Maybe Nick was a good option for its safekeeping.

"You have to swear, man. It's not like I can replace it. They don't make Menehune Warriors anymore. You have to swear on your mother's name you won't lose it."

"Dude, I swear."

"Pinky swear?" I held out my little finger.

"Pinky swear," he shook my finger.

"Don't lose it."

"I won't." Nick turned and left.

I sat down on the bed. It was really nice of Odi to write, even with the subject of his message.

Israel was dead. The idea was strange. It wasn't a surprise. The guy weighed 700 pounds but, still, he was the greatest musician Hawaii had ever known. I still could remember the first song I'd ever heard of his, "Somewhere over the Rainbow." Just Israel, solo on his uke. I'd even played a few songs of his when I was in the ukulele choir. It was sad that IZ was dead, but I was thankful I'd seen him perform. Nobody born in Hawaii after today could say that. But I could say, I saw him with my own two eyes. I could say, I'd lived in the time of IZ.

CHAPTER XVI
To Return

I was surprised how good it felt to see my mom again. I didn't realize how much I missed her. The feeling was mutual. Rebecca hugged me so hard I couldn't breathe. She said my voice sounded very deep and told me how great I looked. I still had pimples, but I took the compliment. Even my dad acted like he missed me.

I'd always liked my Grandparents' house. It was a square shape with a small courtyard in the center. You could run around the whole house and never have to stop. I wasn't into that anymore, but all my cousins were. They jumped and climbed all over me. My sister and I were the oldest of 15 cousins. My mom was one of six children. Grandpa was one of nine and Grandma was one of seven. It was a huge Italian family.

My grandma was very skinny with a short crop of curly brown hair. Between puffs on her cigarette, she talked nonstop about all the people who lived on her street in New Jersey during the Depression.

"We would go to Philly on the bus every Saturday to go shopping. I went with Marge, who lived five doors down and her brother, Philip, worked at the sandwich shop. The bus ride was only 15 cents and that was both ways. Marge died 10 years ago but Philip is still alive. Marge has three children: Katy, Sue, and Joe..."

She would then go on to tell what jobs they had, how many children *they* had and what they did for a living. For the life of me I couldn't fathom how she kept all that shit in her head!

My grandpa was completely bald, and was either cooking or telling cool World War II stories.

"We were over Formosa in '45," he'd start, chewing on his big cigar, "I was looking down through the bomb bay doors when one of my buddies called to me. Just as I turned there was this loud BANG and a spray of Jap flak came up through the doors and stuck in the ceiling. It came through right were my head was. If my buddy hadn't called over to me, you and I wouldn't be here right now."

Grandpa made the best cookies. There were at least seven kinds to choose from. Cookies like pizzelles, snickerdoodles, and I don't know the name but they looked like huge pretzels. There were dipped in melted sugar. He also made his own ravioli from scratch. You were never hungry there and, after Lamia, it was heaven.

I challenged Grandpa to a game of pool. I lost, but I

expected to. I was always a little scared of my Grandpa. He was the only family member who'd ever hit me. My parents didn't believe in it.

My grandparents had come to visit when I was about nine. I was on the couch fighting with Mercedes about who got to pick the TV channel, when my Grandpa came walking by. Before I knew it he'd backhanded me across the face.

"DON'T HIT YOUR SISTER!"

I was so shocked, not by the pain, but by the action itself that I didn't know what to do. He grabbed the remote, turned on *Wheel of Fortune*, and sat down next to us as if nothing had happened.

I could tell from Mercedes' face that she was as shocked about the smack as I was. We both sat there stock still and silent for the rest of the show.

"Not bad, son," Grandpa said, around his cigar when he sunk the eight ball. "Gettin' some practice in?"

"Yeah. Ah, a little, at school."

"You're better than your father now."

I'd never played Istvan and didn't really want to.

"Thanks. Can we, like, play later?"

"Anytime, son."

I could tell this would be a good Christmas. My dad, on the other hand, never liked it here because there were so many people. Istvan was an only child. My other Grandpa had died 20 years before I was born and Grandma only a few years ago. After Mercedes and me, he was the only one left in his family.

One morning when I was seven, my mom woke me up before sun up and told me there was a family matter we needed to talk about. I trudged downstairs in my pajamas. When we were all nestled in the living room my mom spoke to us.

"I just got a message from Eva in Hungary. Istvan's mom, your grandma, just died." A tear slid down my mom's cheek as she spoke. My sister crawled onto my mom's lap and they hugged. My dad had a strange expression on his face. He was more confused than upset. Should I hug him? I sat on his lap. I tried to feel sad, but it was hard. I couldn't remember her.

My grandma had only visited once, when I was three. That's the first time Istvan had seen her since he was nine. It took her a long time to get papers to leave Hungary. My mom told me stories of how great we got along, even though we didn't understand each other. But, no matter how hard I tried, I couldn't remember her. It's hard to feel sad for a name. I sort of understood how my dad felt. My mom's huge family was always a bit much for Istvan to handle. For me, coming to Dallas had always been a treat.

It used to be the only time we came to the mainland. It was so cool. There was just so much of everything - movie theaters, markets, restaurants; even the cold weather was sort of neat. Yet, after living in the Northwest for so long, it wasn't as special as it used to be.

Once I was shown to my room and dropped my bags off, I went to my grandparents' bathroom and weighed myself. I waited for the ticker to settle. When it finally did, I just stared. That can't be right! I got off and tried again. The same number stared back at me. 145 lbs. I'd lost 20 pounds in four months. Jesus! I guess it was a good thing. I'd wanted to lose weight. I just wished I didn't have to starve to do it.

Later that night my sister arrived from Switzerland. She came bundled up in a huge coat. I was shocked when she took it off. She was a lot bigger than I remembered.

"A lot of good food over there, huh?"

"Dipshit." She turned her back on me and quickly walked off.

My mom followed Mercedes so they could talk about "things." I later found out I was right. Mercedes was eating baguettes and cheese all the time. I thought about my toast with parmesan. It was ironic. We both were in boarding school and eating the same thing, just slightly different quality.

A few days before Christmas, Istvan said he had to get some last minute things and wanted to know if I wanted to come to the mall.

"Sure." I had nothing better to do.

"Let's catch a movie, too."

"Cool."

I put on my coat and we left.

"I'm catching a cold from being around all these kids," Istvan complained as we drove along.

"No you're not, Isht. It's just the heating. It's making my

throat feel funny, too." My dad didn't like being around lots of people because he's also a hypochondriac. He hated handshakes, washed his hands at least 20 times a day, and brushed his teeth so hard he had to change toothbrushes every three weeks.

"It's not the heating. Now I'm going to get sick and I'll have to travel while I'm sick and then I'll get worse..." And so on and so on. I phased him out like usual.

"Goddamn these traffic lights!" Istvan abruptly stopped. "These things are timed by people on the far left of the Bell Curve to be as inconvenient as possible. Now we'll be sitting here for four minutes. *Jesust Christ!*"

"Must have known you were coming," I joked.

"Who?"

"Never mind."

I'd forgotten what Istvan was like driving in cities. I looked down at my watch and timed the light. When it turned green, only 45 seconds had passed. I didn't mention this to him.

"See this guy?" Istvan pointed to a car that had just pulled out in front of us from a parking lot. "He could have waited until I'd gone by, but see how slow he's going? Now watch this."

Istvan moved over to the left lane and passed him.

"See how fast I had to go to get around him? He sped up, you see?"

Istvan flipped the guy off. I tried not to smile. Istvan was so convinced that you almost wondered if he was right. He was sure that everybody and everything was personally against him, determined to slow him down and waste his time.

"Take a good look around you, Leif. In a few years this will all be gone."

"What are you talking about?"

"The Millennium Bug. At 12:00 AM on January 1, 2000, all the computers in the world will fail."

"How's that possible?"

"Let me put it to you this way: computers do all of their calculations based on numbers. Almost all calculations use the computer's internal clock. Back in the 70's, when space was at a premium, instead of programming the year 1976, they just used the last two digits. The 19 never changed. You with me so far? When 2000 comes around, all the clocks will set back to 1900. Calculations like 1999 minus 1900 will confuse the computer and that will be the end of civilization. I should have seen this coming."

"If you know this, then others do. Why don't they fix it?"

"It's too late. Too many computers out there to fix. It's a count down to the end. I'm just sorry Mercedes will have to grow up in the aftermath."

Feel sorry for Mercedes? I guess the biker gangs will still need someone to pump their gas when the world ends. I did my best to ignore the statement. We drove on.

After the mall, we drove around looking for a movie.

"Here's a theater," Istvan said. He always pronounced it "the-A-ter."

I looked up at the marquee.

"Hey, they have a new *Star Trek*."

"I thought you'd want to see *Shine*."

"*Shine*? Isn't that a Jack Nicholson horror movie?"

"No, it isn't. That's *The Shinning*. Look." Isht pointed at a poster near the ticket counter. It was some half naked guy jumping into the air.

"So, what is it?"

"It's about a piano player."

"Okay. Whatever. It's up to you." Actually, I did want to see it, but it was better to let Istvan pick. An unhappy Istvan was an unhappy everybody.

"We'll do both. *Star Trek* starts at 2:30 and *Shine* starts at 5:00. That will work."

My dad only bought tickets for *Star Trek*. We went in and sat down in the massive multiplex. One good thing about the mainland was stadium seating. You never had to worry about some tall dude parking his fat head right in front of you. Musak played quietly through the sound system as we waited for the film to start.

"Mercedes told me that there are, like, commercials before the movies start in Europe," I said to Isht.

"Mmm."

"Yup. Just glad they don't do that here. Commercials suck, even when you have a remote and can change the channel. Definite suckage."

"Be quiet," Istvan said as the lights began to dim. I smiled in anticipation. The projector began to spin up like a snowball rolling down a mountain. Nothing could stop the film from coming now. Watching a movie for the first time was like nothing else, even surfing.

Some people don't understand how I can watch a movie as many as 50 times. They would say, "but you already know what's going to happen." There's more to a film than what happens. After seeing it you can anticipate the good parts and enjoy them more by just knowing that they are coming. The more I watch a movie the more I see. I always discover some new detail.

Good films are like old friends that can transport you wherever you want to go. Until they make interactive hologram stories, films are currently the greatest form of entertainment the world has ever seen. And movie theaters are the vessels that take you there.

Istvan and I watched the *Star Trek* movie. Not bad for a *Next Generation*. The Borg were pretty cool. "Resistance is futile. You will be assimilated." The line made me think of Lamia. After it was over we snuck into *Shine*.

"$4.50 is way too much to spend for a movie," Istvan always said, "I just want to get my money's worth."

Sneaking from theater to theater was one thing my dad and I had been doing for years. Mercedes and Rebecca hated doing it, so it became like a father son thing.

I didn't know what to expect from *Shine*, but I was completely amazed. The acting was incredible and the story was very engaging. What a fucked up father *that* guy had!

As soon as we walked out into the cold night air I wanted to get back and play the piano.

"I'm going to learn that piece," I told Istvan as we got into the car.

"The Rachmaninoff 3rd? It looks very difficult."

"Nah, it'll just take time. Can I get the sheet music? Not for Christmas, but sometime?"

"Talk to your mother." Istvan started the car. As the engine turned over, he looked at me.

"Don't you ever wash your face? You have pimples everywhere. Girls will never like you."

I looked away quickly. Hot anger and frustration bubbled up inside of me. Do you think I don't know I have pimples? I don't need you to point them out. I clenched my stomach trying to squash the bees inside. I could see a ghostly reflection of myself in the car window. Maybe if I grew my hair long I could cover my face with it. That way nobody could see my zits. Isht and I said very little during the rest of the trip.

Christmas Day came and went. I stuffed myself with sausage and ravioli. The pumpkin pie was sweet and creamy. I wanted to keep eating, but after so many months with no food, my stomach had irreversibly shrunk.

Mercedes talked nonstop about how great her school was: Skiing trips to Gstaad (pronounced *Shtad*), amazing parties, how cool her friends were, blah, blah, blah. I wanted to show her the disparity between our experiences. I told her about cleaning the vats. Her response was very sympathetic.

"Oh, well, sucks to be you."

It's comforting to know that some things never change.

My sister was blasting strange music now. She made me listen to it.

"What's she saying? *"Onka un fwa?"*

"Encore Une Fois," she said enunciating. "It's French." She turned the volume up more.

I don't like normal pop and this stuff was even stranger. She used to play *Phantom of the Opera* every time we took a trip in the car. I hated it and wished she'd listen to something else. Now, I wasn't sure if this French crap was any better.

Mercedes also tried to get me to watch this movie called *Sense and Sensibility*. It was a major chick flick. I couldn't understand the old English, but she said it was good so I tried to watch the whole thing. While I sat there in the dark, she brought me a glass of something.

"It's good. You'll like it." I took a mouthful. It felt like somebody was trying to make a pincushion out of my tongue. I ran into the bathroom to spit it out. Mercedes followed me.

"Tastes like shit, man!" I looked at the red liquid trickling toward the drain.

"It's tomato juice. I thought you'd like it." She sounded genuinely shocked.

"Tomato Juice? Blah! You did that on purpose."

"Yeah, don't be so immature," she scoffed and walked off to finish her *Nonsense* movie. She was all "European" now. I'd never be that way.

It was a good Christmas. I got lots of nice presents, including some gloves for the cold. It almost made up for missing St. Nicholas Day. By New Year's all the shit I'd been through at Lamia was fading from my mind. It seemed so long ago and far away, but it wasn't completely gone. Katrina was still in my head.

Every night, before I slept, I would think of Katrina. She was so close, just a state or two over. It would be so nice to run my hands through that silky hair. I almost asked my mom what I should do, but didn't. It was personal and I was going to figure it out myself.

A few days later I was playing on my grandparents upright when a brilliant idea struck me. I'd write her a song! Why hadn't I thought of that before? Their piano was a little out of tune but it would still work. Actually, my dad bought this piano. He didn't buy it for the reasons most people did. He bought it because the brass that the sounding board was constructed out of was worth more than the price he paid. For Istvan, everything was about the return on investment.

I messed around on the piano for a few hours and slowly a song began to emerge. I had some manuscript paper and began to write. It was simple, but very pretty.

I wrote a faster part for the middle before returning to the slow, romantic melody again. She was in the choir so she could appreciate it. I'd call it *Katrina's Theme*. It was perfect. How could she not like it?

"Leif, are you happy?" Rebecca asked a few days into the new year. We sat at the dinner table having some leftover pie.

"Ah, yeah, Bec. What do you mean?"

"I mean at school. I could tell on the phone that you weren't having a good time. You're not used to chores, and after Hector was expelled from school, you didn't have any friends."

"I have friends now. Four of us. Sort of like *Stand By Me*. We're not exactly looking for dead bodies or anything but we're okay."

Rebecca smiled. She knew how important that movie was to me so my comparison was the highest form of reassurance. Why did she always call Odi, Hector. Hector *was* Odi's real name but he never liked it and had always gone by Odi. I'm not sure why he picked that name. He just said he liked the sound of it.

"I'm so happy for you, darling." She squeezed my hand.

I looked at her. "There were some sucky times."

"Now, Leif. I was about to send away your tuition for this coming semester, but I wanted to make sure this is what you want. They don't offer any kind of refund. Your father and I are thrilled that you're reading and making friends and we want you to keep going. But do you want to go back?"

I hadn't expected this. My parents always decided what I was going to do. Now it was up to me? I thought of Ethics and the vats, and Fat Rob and Method Three's. I would be crazy to want to go back. Yet, there were my friends. Nick,

Jude and, I guess, Derk. But, most of all, there was *her*. I had to see Katrina again. She would never become my girlfriend if I left. Katrina was the only one for me.

It wasn't so bad anymore. The oven thing had sucked, but nothing like that was going to happen again. All my troubles had been in the beginning, before I'd decided to pretend to go along with the system. Yeah. I could handle Lamia. My mom was waiting for my answer.

"Yes. I want to go back."

"I'm so proud of you." Rebecca gave me a hug.

"Thanks, Mom."

Movement III

winter

CHAPTER XVII
The New Kids

A shuttle picked me up at the airport and drove me the two hours to Lamia. It hadn't changed. The same brick building, the same grey sky, and the same bland empty landscape.

The posse was already waiting. Derk was the first to see me.

"It's Scuba-Dooby-Doo!"

"My name is not *Scuba*, Derk."

"Where are you, Scuba-Dooby-Doo!" Derk cackled.

I decided not to protest any further. The more attention I drew to the name the more likely he'd always call me that.

"There you are, dude," Nick said, holding out his hand.

I shook it.

"Here I am. How was the break, Nick-meister?"

"No complaints."

I looked at Jude.

"What about you, Old Man? How was... Missouri, right?"

"You mean *Misery*?" Jude complained. "It's boring."

"At least you got to go home."

"It's a house, not my home."

Jude seemed more testy than usual. I guess it would suck to always come home to a house you've never seen before.

"Guess what," Nick said. "You have some competition."

"What?"

I followed him to the chapel. Before we even reached it I could hear music. I opened the door and there was another guy playing the piano. He was very tall with a rounded nose.

"I guess you're not, like, the only Piano Guy," Nick said.

I felt a surge of irritation. This was *my* spot. Even though I didn't want to play just then, I wanted him to leave. But how? I looked over at Derk and smiled. Derk's nature could be useful in this instance.

"Let's go say 'hi' to him." I started across the chapel with the others in tow. The kid stopped playing when he saw us approaching.

"Hi," I said.

"Hey."

"You new here?" Nick asked.

The kid nodded.

"I'm Nick. This is Leif. That's Jude and that's Derk."

"I'm Alex Reinstein."

"A fucking Jew!" Derk belted. "We don't get many of you clip-tips here."

There was a stunned expression on Alex's face. Derk laughed. I smiled. It was so nice when things went the way you wanted. He'd leave now.

"Don't listen to him," Jude said, walking up to Alex. "We heard you playing. Leif here can play the piano, too."

"Oh," Alex said, emerging from his Derk shock. "Let me hear you play something."

"I don't know." I hadn't really practiced lately.

"Concert! Concert!" my posse chanted. I quieted them and sat at the piano. Since Alex was a pianist, I decided on the "Moonlight Sonata." It was the most complicated thing I could play. I played as best I could. I made a few mistakes, but nothing the others would catch.

"Why did you stop?" Alex asked.

"That's it. I'm still learning the rest."

"Stopped before the hard part, huh?"

"No," I said hotly, feeling another flash of irritation. "I'm still working on it." I was definitely going to finish it now.

"Come," Nick said, "We'll show you around." We all left together. As we walked, Nick explained where everything was at Lamia. I said nothing. I didn't want Alex in our group. I was the Piano Guy. Nick's easygoing nature wasn't helping here. I'd have to do something, and soon.

As we were approaching the library Jessica Hopemann emerged, walking in our direction. I saw Alex's eyes go wide.

"Who's that?" he whispered to me.

I smiled before I answered.

"THAT'S JESSICA HOPEMANN, ALEX!" I said, as loud as I could. Jessica Hopemann turned to look at us. Alex's face went totally red and he quickly looked at the floor. Derk let out a big laugh. I saw a small smile on Jessica Hopemann's face before she continued on.

"Look at the Jew's face!" Derk said, cackling. "Like a fucking lobster!" Alex did not look pleased with our posse. So it remained the four of us.

There were other new kids that came that semester, but we didn't pay much attention to them. I got back into my courses. I took chemistry, which was the first class I liked. The Science Room was long and narrow. Glass jars filled with multicolored chemicals studded long shelves that covered three walls. The forth wall was full of cubbyholes devoted to storing student's current and past projects.

I made a motor out of wire and magnets. We'd never done anything like that in Kamuela. When I was done with the engine, I explored the different jars and saw some familiar chemicals from my internet studies. Nitric acid and hydrogen peroxide. That was a great combination for a chemical bomb. I told Nick one day at lunch.

"Dude, could you, like get a hold of that?"

"Maybe, but no. I told you I don't make bombs. That stuff is very powerful. All you have to do is mix it and it explodes. You don't even need a spark. There's enough of it to blow up the whole gym."

"Wow! Would it be more powerful than Oklahoma City?"

I thought for a moment. It would do some damage, but not that much.

"Not by itself. If you added a few containers of gasoline it could. When the bomb goes off, it'll cause the gas to become an aerosol and that could, like, increase the blast by 10 times."

"We could do some major ultra-violence. We could take out half of Lamia." Nick rubbed his hands together maliciously.

"I don't want to hurt people. If you want to blow the school up, wait until I leave."

"But you set the old oven on fire?"

"Not on purpose, you idiot!"

Over the break Lamia acquired a new oven. This one was a little newer than the last one, but it still looked older than me. These people were really cheap.

"You sure it wasn't on purpose?" Nick prodded.

"Shut up!"

Nick laughed. What a weirdo!

"I thought you liked macabre shit?" Nick responded. "You're always asking people what the worst thing they've - whatever."

"That's different." It was. I enjoyed making people squirm, but I don't like hurting people.

Jude sat down with his tray.

"How is it going, my filthy droog?" Nick asked.

"Fine." Jude dove into his potatoes.

"Okay then." Nick turned to me, "What is the worst thing

that's happened to you?"

"You mean other than having to look at your face every day?"

"Ha, ha. Very funny. No seriously, man."

I thought for a moment. Nothing really bad had ever happened to me. I'd never been seriously ill and I never had somebody close to me die. My broken wrist had sucked, but not the worst thing.

"I got it. I'll tell you about the time I almost died."

Jude stopped eating. They both looked at me, waiting for me to begin.

I was 11 years old. Odi and I biked to a nearby sugar cane field. We went there to break the stalks and suck the sugar out. It was kind of tough, like chewing on a bundle of raw spaghetti, but it was fun.

When our jaws were too tired to eat anymore, we came across a canal. These were used to irrigate the cane fields. We followed the canal to a gulch neither of us had ever been to before. It was about 100 feet wide and 50 feet deep. To get the water from one side to the other, the canal fed into a large steel pipe about three feet in diameter with a thin cat-walk on either side.

"Let's float down it," Odi said.

The water was rushing very quickly into the pipe. It would be a cool fast ride.

"Let's do it."

We stripped down to our underwear and jumped into the water. It was cold, but we didn't care. Odi went first and I followed. We whooped and cheered as we floated along. We couldn't see the other end of the pipe, but it would only take a minute to get there. I looked up at the ceiling and saw lots of spider webs. I ducked my head down. As we went further along, the ceiling kept getting lower. Soon the top of my head was bumping the metal.

"The water's getting higher!" I called forward to Odi.

"We'll be through in a few seconds!"

The opening behind us was just a small crescent of light now. The water was really high. I had to turn my face straight up to breathe. I hoped I wasn't breathing in spiders. I felt the water splashing over my mouth.

"Odi!" There was no answer. Then everything went black and there was no more air.

Nick and Jude were mesmerized. Jude's fork was suspended in mid-air. I loved telling stories.

That moment in the pipe was the only time I've ever truly panicked. True panic is not a fun thing. I was screaming. I wasn't choosing to scream. I was screaming involuntarily. It was almost like I was outside myself listening to my own voice.

"WE'RE GOING TO DIE! OH, MY GOD! WE'RE GOING TO DIE! MOM!"

I ran into Odi. He'd stopped somehow. There was a moment of total confusion. The next thing I knew Odi was behind me and I'd found a small pocket of air. My face was jammed up against the metal. I could taste the dirt on the steel. I was gasping for breath. Out of the corner of my eye, I could see Odi was moving away. I saw how he was doing it. The walls of the pipe weren't smooth, but corrugated like a Ruffles potato chip. If you pushed out hard enough, you could get enough leverage to move.

We began to crawl back the way we'd come. Odi led the way. We were concentrating so hard we didn't speak. The water pressure was intense. It was a little easier for me because Odi was taking the full brunt of it. He would slip from time to time, but I always caught him. We moved toward the light.

It had taken us 30 seconds to drift down, but it took us 10 minutes to get out. Finally, we emerged into the light and crawled our way onto the bank. We were panting hard. My entire body was trembling and not just from the cold. I looked over at Odi. Then we began to laugh. I couldn't control it. We laughed and laughed.

"*Oh my God*!" Odi called out, mocking my screams.

"Oh, man! That was so stupid."

We both laughed for a long time. Then we put on our clothes and left. We decided not to tell our parents. They'd probably ground us or something. I was never sure why we got stuck in that pipe. Could we have held our breaths and popped out the other side? Was there a blockage? We never found out.

Odi and I chuckled about it the whole way back, but I knew that what had happened was serious. We'd almost drowned. We came within inches. That was probably the worst thing that has ever happened to me.

"Holy shit!" Jude said.

"Dude," was all Nick could say. "I'd be scared of water forever if that, like, happened to me."

"Eh, it was a long time ago." I finished the last bite of my toast. I saw another new kid searching for a seat. He was in my Form Six Entry, but I'd never spoken to him. I pointed at him.

"Another new one."

"They just keep getting smaller," Jude said, "he's the size of an Ewok."

"Or an Oompa-Loompa," I added.

"You're only, like, an inch taller than him, Jude" Nick said.

"Shut up, *Alex DeLarge*."

The kid saw us and made a beeline for us.

"Oh, great," I said, "Here he comes." I noticed his shoes were undone. He quickly sat down, almost knocking over my water glass.

"I'm James Natlis. I'm new here."

Oh, gee. I never would have guessed.

"Jude."

"Nick."

"Leif."

"*Leaf*?" He said, looking perplexed. "Your name is *Leaf*?"

"Are you making fun of my name, you little dick!?"

"No! Sorry, man!"

I laughed.

"I'm just messing with you."

"Where you from?" Nick asked.

"I'm from Nevada." He spoke quickly and cut the ends of his sentences, like this was an oral test.

"Nevadaage," I said, nodding.

"You wouldn't believe it," James began, "I was in class today and some kid, like, came up to me babbling about a *misunderstood word* or something because I yawned. What's up with that?"

We all laughed. James just looked at us. Was I just like this kid when I arrived? No wonder nobody talked to me.

James was a skateboarder and proud of it. He hadn't been doing well at his last school and his parents sent him here because of the 'unique learning style.' James was almost like a shorter mainland version of me. Even though he couldn't tie his own shoes I liked him better than the Piano Kid. That night, we took him down to the Rec Room to show him the best part of Lamia. I challenged him to pool, but he sucked at it.

"Why are you carrying that?" James asked, looking at my manuscript paper.

I'd been toting "Katrina's Theme" with me, trying to give it to her. Every time I came close, I was always too scared and embarrassed to present it.

"I need to give it to somebody."

"Leif's in love," Nick said in a baby voice.

"Shut up!" I shoved him.

"Why do you walk like that?" James asked me.

"Like what?"

"You walk, like hunched over with your head down."

"I do?"

"Now that you mention it," Nick said, "you kind of do."

I stood up as straight as I could and held my head up.

"Yeah, man. Walk with some pride. You're one of my droogs."

Jude entered the Rec Room and came toward us.

"Where's Derk, Old Man?" I asked. "Haven't seen him in a while."

"I don't know. Ethics again?"

Probably.

"So, what are we going to, like, do?" James asked in his clipped way.

"We could play the Movie Game," I said.

"What's that?"

"Somebody says a movie quote and the rest of us try to guess the movie. Whoever gets it right first gets to say the next quote."

"That's not fair," Jude said. "You have that memory thing."

I shrugged.

"I'll leave the easy ones to you."

"Let's play!" James said, clenching his fists.

"I'll get us started off," I said, thinking of a quote.

"Not something too obscure," Nick said.

I ran through some movies in my head until I got one.

"I ain't through with you by a damn sight. I'm going to

get medieval on yo' ass!"

"Dude, I know it," Nick said, snapping his fingers. Jude and James were completely blank.

"Oh, come on!" I said, "You got to know this." Nick was still snapping.

"Fi...Fi... *Pulp Fiction*!"

"Not Bad. Your turn."

Nick lowered his voice. *"Now you see that evil will always triumph, because good is dumb."*

I laughed. What a great line! The others had no idea.

"You have to know this, Old Man. It's a parody of your favorite movie."

Jude just shook his head.

"What's wrong with you? *Spaceballs*!"

"Right," Nick said.

"This sucks," Jude said, getting up. "Only you can enjoy this game, Leif. I'm too old for this." He walked to the pool table. James looked at us.

"PMS," I said. James' eyebrows furrowed. Then I saw somebody I vaguely recognized walk into the Rec Room. She was medium height with long brown hair and a very mellow expression. Where had I seen her? She was Katrina's best friend. Wait a second! I could give my song to her to give to Katrina. That would be a hell of a lot easier.

"I'll be back," I said, standing up.

"*Terminator II*!" James called out.

"Actually I'm getting up." I walked toward her. I was a little nervous, but nowhere near as bad as when I'd tried this with Katrina.

"Excuse me?"

"Yes," she said, looking at me.

"You know Katrina, right?"

"Yup."

"Could you, like, give this to her?" I handed the song over. The girl looked at it. "Tell her it's from Leif."

She looked a little confused.

"Okay," she said and walked off. I watched her move away. Derk was kind of right. Her ass was sort of wide.

Relief flooded over me. I've done it! Fuck yeah! I felt like celebrating.

"One Clearly Canadian, please," I asked the girl behind the counter. She went to the small refrigerator and handed me the soda and my change. It was so weird that they used 50 cent pieces in the Northwest.

"Thank you." I twisted off the cap.

"You're the only one who does that."

"Does what?"

"Says please and thank you. Nobody else here does."

"Oh." I'd never thought about it. Rebecca always made me do it. Kids at this school were kind of assholeic.

"You're welcome and thanks." I walked back to the table.

"Splurging tonight?" Nick said as I sat down.

"Yup." I took a swig. "Little soda action."

"Why are you saving your money again?"

"I don't know. So I can use it for something cool later."

"I almost forgot," Nick said, digging into his pocket.

"Here," he handed back my Menehune Warrior. "Told you I wouldn't lose it."

"I knew you wouldn't." Actually, I'd prepared a speech about how irresponsible Nick was and a fucking asshole for good measure, just incase. When he handed me the Menehune Warrior, I let the speech evaporate from my mind. I quickly deposited the pog in my pocket. I took a look around, ingesting the sights and sounds of the Rec Room. Things were going great. Writing that song was the best thing I could have done. Soon Katrina would know how I felt about her and maybe she would reciprocate. I felt sure that coming back here was the right choice.

CHAPTER XVIII
Isolation

About a week or so after getting back, on a Wednesday, Nick and I went to check our mail.

"You know what?" Nick said. "I'm going to be a drunkard when I grow up."

I gave him a funny look. He'd said it like it was a career choice.

"What the hell are you talking about?"

"Dude, I'm going to be a drunkard. I can tell."

I wasn't sure what he wanted me to say.

"Whatever."

We arrived at the mailroom. I was surprised to see a manila envelope in my box.

"What did you get?"

"I have no idea." I pulled it out of my box and looked at the return address.

"Oh, it's from Rebecca." I turned it over.

"Dude, I could never call my mom by her first name."

"Not sealed too well." Only the metal tabs were keeping it shut. The sticky flap wasn't sticky.

"Mail kids are clumsy and rip them all the time. Come on. Open it."

"Nah. I'll do it in my room." I never liked opening my mail down here. It always felt like somebody was watching.

We went upstairs to my dorm room. I pulled the metal tab up and looked inside. I smiled.

"Son of a bitch."

"What is it, man?"

I pulled out a thick tan colored music book.

"Rachmaninoff's 3rd Piano Concerto. She got it for me. Didn't think it would be so soon."

"It's music?"

"Yup, the coolest piano concerto. I'm going to learn it."

"Sweet. Oh!" He rifled through his bag. "Here, dude, before I forget again."

"My *Poi Dogs with Crabs*. God, I forgot you had this." I took the CD from him.

"That is some funny shit, man."

"You understood it?"

"Pshaw," he said like it was obvious.

In the past I'd tried to get my cousins to listen to it, but they never got the humor. He was the first mainlander who ever did.

"*Room 1225*," Nick said, in a bad Pidgin accent, "*Do you want cheese on that cheeseburger deluxe?*"

"Wow! Not bad."

"Dude, I want to hear that concerto."

"Sure." We ran down to the chapel. I looked inside to see if it was empty. It was. Sometimes Alex Reinstein was playing when I went to the chapel and it bugged me. I know I didn't own the place, but the piano was my sanctuary.

"I'm not the best sight reader, so bear with me." I opened the music and sat down. I started to play. Actually, it was easy to read. The left and right hands were doing the exact same thing. The melody was beautiful, but sad.

"That's cool," Nick said.

I flipped to the third page and stopped cold.

"Shit."

Nick got up from the first pew to look at the music.

"Dude, that's a lot of ink."

It was crazy. There were endless 16th notes for pages.

"I think I'll work on this later." I closed the book and coughed. It felt like something was caught in my throat. I gave another cough.

"You okay, man?"

"Throat feels kind of dry." I swallowed some spit. "Let's check out the Rec Room, Nick-meister." We left the chapel.

Fat Rob had thought of a new way to bug me over the break. He brought an alarm clock that also played CDs. He put it on his windowsill so it was more in the middle of the room than on his side. In the morning the alarm went off at 6:00, but Rob pretended to be still asleep. The beeping went on and on.

"Goddamn it!" I had to get up and turn it off. While groping in the dark to find the 'off' switch, I accidentally turned on the A.M. radio. Loud static and a faint voice buzzed in the room. I smiled. My turn. I left it like that and jumped back in bed. It was irritating, but I was the one who'd done it. After five minutes he got up and turned it off. Asshole.

I would have reveled in the small victory, but I didn't feel well that morning. My throat was sore and my nose was stuffed up. I had a cold. I'd never liked sore throats, but getting sick was a good thing. No school.

When I got sick back in Kamuela and was sent home, I always wanted to do a *Ferris Bueller*, to sneak out for fun with Odi. Unfortunately, my dad was always home and I never got to try it. He worked as a stock trader these days. He was up at 3:00 every morning to catch the opening of the market in New York. He spent the rest of the day on the computer examining stock trends.

"I'm waiting for the financial collapse," he'd tell me. "When the world is rebuilding itself, I'll buy in and ride the up trend."

He was the only broker who was happy when the market went down. No *day off* for Odi and me, but at least I got out of school. I was sick now and I needed to tell somebody so I didn't have to go to class. I went down the hall to the Resident Director's office. She oversaw this floor.

"Excuse me," I said, lightly knocking on her door. The Resident Director looked up from her desk.

"Leif. I already gave you your allowance."

"No." I made my voice as raspy as possible. "I have a cold."

"Well, let me see, dear." She put the back of her hand on my forehead.

"You are a bit hot." She went back to her desk. "I'll tell your Supervisor that you're not feeling well."

Yes! She wrote down something then came back to me.

"Let's get you down to the infirmary." She locked the door to her office and led me downstairs.

I almost bounded down the steps. No schoolwork. I'd get to relax in my room while everybody was making their dumb Cleared-Lists. And I'd also get out of work detail. You can't let somebody sick into the kitchen.

She took me down to the right wing of the building. This was where many of the faculty lived. Students weren't allowed down here. The linoleum squeaked loudly under my sandals. She unlocked another door and we went down some more stairs into the basement.

The familiar odor of burnt lint assaulted my nostrils as we descended. I heard a roaring from beyond the right wall. The Trash Room. I could almost feel its malignance through the concrete. We hung a left and went through another door. This was a hallway with many closed doors on either side. I saw a boy walking up and down this hall. I'd seen him in Form Eight but I didn't know his name. He was big with very short hair and looked like he was already balding.

"What's up, man?" I asked, walking by him. He looked

at me, but said nothing. We came to the end of the hall. The Resident Director knocked on the door. A skinny woman with 60's style glasses opened it.

"Hi, Marsha," the Resident Director began. "We have a sick boy here."

"Oh," she said, like I was a baby. "Come in here." I went inside. The Resident Director didn't follow. She closed the door behind me.

"Let me see you." She held my face with her hands. She was what you'd imagine Mr. Rodgers' wife being like.

"What's the matter?"

I told her about my throat and my nose. She took my temperature. After a moment, the machine beeped.

"101. You have a fever. Let's find you a nice room where you can get better."

I didn't understand this, but I followed her. What's-his-face was still walking up and down the hall. The nurse unlocked a door on the left and showed me inside. The room was small and Spartan. There was a bunk bed and a small window near the ceiling. I could see grass growing against the glass.

"Now you get better quickly," she said, closing the door.

"Wait, what am I doing?"

"Lamia doesn't believe in drugs, you know that."

"Yeah. So?"

"Well, we don't want others to get sick, do we?"

"I guess not."

"So we keep the sick kids away from the others until

they're better, okay?"

I didn't want to stay here but it did kind of make sense. Like when they quarantined that town in *Outbreak*. I looked around the bare room.

"So, like, what do I do?"

"Get better." She smiled and closed the door.

I turned around and looked at my new room. I guess I wasn't going to be relaxing upstairs. Oh, well. At least I wasn't in class. No Fat Rob down here either. I could conk out and get an uninterrupted nap.

I lay down on the mattress and looked up at the wood beneath the upper bunk. I expected to see some kid carvings, but there was nothing.

As I lay there I felt my upper lip. It was still kind of raw from shaving that morning. Did I really need to shave? I didn't feel like it anymore. I made up my mind. I wasn't going to shave until I had to.

My throat hurt every time I swallowed, but that was the only bad thing about being down here. It was nice to have nothing to do, but soon I was restless.

I looked at my watch, 10:00. I'd only been here two hours. I was probably going to be down here all day, so I'd better think of something to do. I began to play movies in my head. I went through some the ones I had down stone cold, *Tremors*, *Predator*, and *Speed*.

When I was tired of that, I looked at my watch again. 12:00. Man, time was slow down here. I was also getting kind of hungry. I wondered if I go to lunch or they bring it.

I'd ask.

I went to the door and opened it. I was about to step out when What's-his-face stepped in my way.

"Where you going?"

"I was going to ask if lunch comes or-?"

"It comes. Now keep the door closed."

"Dude, chill out." I laughed a little when the door shut. What a freak. I'd be a little pissed too if I was already losing my hair. He must be a kind of Rover or something.

By 2:00 my stomach was growling. When's the fucking food coming? I'd gone through all the movies I knew, but running movies in your head goes a lot faster than watching them for real. I quietly sang a song to myself. It was one Odi and I had come up with. Our school version of "On Top of Old Smokey."

> *"On top of the school house, all covered with sand;*
> *I shot my dumb teacher with a green rubber band.*
> *I went to her funeral, I went to her grave*
> *Some people threw flowers; I threw hand grenades.*
> *It said in the paper that she wasn't dead*
> *So I took a bazooka and blew off her head.*
> *I watched it go up, I watched it come down,*
> *I watched it go SPLAT all over the ground."*

By 3:00 I was bored out of my mind. I'd even settle for a book! I'd ask the Nurse Lady if I could get one. I left my room again, walking toward the nurse's door.

"What are you doing?" What's-his-face rushed up to me.

"I need to talk to the nurse."

He gave me a strange look, like I was planning something devious.

"What?"

"Fine," he finally said and walked me to the door. I knocked and she opened it right away.

"What are you doing?" she asked in that baby voice. "You need to be getting well."

"I know, but could I, like, go to the library to get a book or something?"

"No, sorry. We can't let you get the others sick."

"Okay." I thought for a moment. "Could you get me a book?"

"I have to make sure all the other patients' needs are met. I can't go running off to grab books."

"I'm kind of bored. What should I do?"

She gently pushed me toward my room again.

"Like I told you. You need to get well. Put all your thoughts on that. The mind can make you healthy."

How the hell does it do that? What's-his-face opened my door for me. She guided me into the room.

"Now, don't come out unless it's an emergency. We need to keep your germs isolated."

"Yeah, I get it." What's-his-face began to close the door.

"What about food?" I quickly asked.

"Your meal will come at the end of the day." She smiled and shut the door.

End of the day? Man! I was hungry. I fell on my bed. I

heard the springs rattle then finally settle. That was kind of fun. I arched my back and listened to the springs again. After about 10 minutes of that, I was bored again. I didn't know doing nothing could be so unfulfilling.

The sun was down by 5:00. The little window was dark now. A light suddenly came on overhead. I got up and looked for a switch, but couldn't find anything. I hated the light. I went back to bed. That florescent hum seemed to be getting louder and louder as the minutes dragged on. Where was the food?

I got up and opened the door again. As I expected, What's-his-face was there in a flash.

"I thought she told you to stay in."

"I just wanted to make sure you guys didn't forget I was here."

"We know exactly who and where everybody is. Always."

I blurted a laugh. It quickly degenerated into a cough, but the smile remained.

"This whole prison guard thing is kind of lame."

He did not smile back.

"I take my chore seriously."

"This is your chore?" He'd been here all day. "I thought you were a - what about your class work?"

He put his hand on my shoulder and squeezed very hard.

"Ow!" I cried, but he didn't let up.

"Get back in your room or I'll be forced to lock it." He pushed me back in.

"Jeez, man!"

What's-his-face closed the door hard. What the hell was going on here?

By 10:00 no food had come. I was hungry and bored, but didn't know what else to do. I guess I'd go back to my dorm and sleep. I waited for them to let me out. Nobody came.

At 10:30 the light went out. I got up and listened at the door. Nothing. Was I supposed to sleep down here? I waited for a while, but nothing happened. I walked over to the window. It was cloudy. I waited for a bit of moonlight to see my watch. Finally, some light came. 11:04. I thought about bed check. If they where looking for me, then they would have come. I guess they wanted me to sleep here tonight. No way. I'd wait until late, then sneak back to my own room. This place sucked.

The moonlight was gone now. I lay back on the bed and pulled the thin sheet up to my chin. It smelled like bleach.

With my stomach twisting in hunger, I lay there waiting. There was a low rumble of thunder very far away. Great, more rain. I couldn't wait to get out of here. As the rain began to tap against the small window, I laid on my bunk perfectly still, listening for any signs of movement in the hall outside.

Was that a click at the door? I help my breath and listened. Nothing. Screw this crap. It was definitely time to leave. I gingerly tiptoed to the door. I pressed my ear against it, listening. Not a sound. I hoped What's-his-face was finally gone. I reached down and turned the handle. It would not twist. I strained harder but it didn't budge. It was locked.

CHAPTER XIX
Confessions

Daybreak comes late in winter on the mainland. In Hawaii the time of the sunrise and sunset only varied slightly during the year. We don't even have daylight savings time.

This was day two down in isolation. I tried the doorknob again. It was still locked. I hadn't gotten much sleep after that discovery and my throat was still bothering me. I was so hungry and thirsty. What I wouldn't give for some huli huli chicken. I felt like pounding on the door, but by this point, I knew nobody would open it. *They* were the only ones down here and *they* had locked it.

When there was enough light in the room, I looked for something I could use to pick the lock. I'd seen it done in movies. It couldn't be that hard. I just needed two pieces of metal, one long and another with a bend in it to turn the lock. Even with light I still couldn't find anything. I tried to rip some of the springs off the bed frame, but I could barely bend them. They were too thick anyway. I scoured the corners of the room for some forgotten object, but there was nothing. The carpet was surprisingly clean.

Then I saw something. I picked and pried and pulled up a small carpet staple. This could work. I got up another. They were really short, but they were better than nothing. I put them in the lock and tried. It wasn't as easy as the movies led you to believe. I pushed and twisted, but nothing clicked or moved. After an hour I gave up and lay back in bed.

Even if I could open the door, where was I supposed to go? Maybe I could tell them I needed to finish a course by a certain date. No, they obviously didn't care. I thought and thought, but not one brilliant idea came to my mind. There must be something. Something. Something...

I was jolted awake by the sound of the door opening. I must have fallen asleep. The Nurse Lady came in with that big, phony smile. She was holding a thermometer.

"Let's see how our sick boy is doing."

"Why did you lock the door?"

"Oh, that's just in case one of your friends tried to visit you. We don't want them getting sick." She came toward me. Suddenly I was scared of her. That baby voice and my situation grated like nails on a blackboard.

"Now open up." She pointed the thermometer at me. I didn't feel like cooperating, but if my fever was gone she'd let me go. I opened my mouth. She put the device under my tongue. The little machine beeped. She pulled it out and showed it to me.

"Hundred. Lower, but you still have a fever."

"So I have to stay?" I asked knowing the answer.

"Don't pout. It's raining outside, so there's nothing to do." She turned to leave.

"Wait. Could I get some food and water, please?"

"They forgot to bring it to you? I'm sorry about that. I'll go tell them right now." And she was out the door. I heard the lock click again.

For a brief moment I wanted her back in the room. It was good to talk to somebody, but then I thought about it and was glad she was gone. That voice was giving me the creeps.

At 3:00 the door opened. A girl put a tray down on the floor then shut the door. It was so fast I hadn't even gotten a chance to say anything. I went over and looked down. It was a plastic cup filled with broth, a glass of water and four pieces of bread.

More bread, but I was so hungry I practically inhaled them. The soup was cold and tasted like somebody scooped a bunch of crap off the forest floor and boiled it, but I was too hungry not to eat it. I then downed the water in one breath. That was better. I could hear my stomach making full noises. Now what? I walked back and sat on the bed.

I started to recite chapters from *Poi Dogs with Crabs*. I did all the best ones, Room Service, Mahalo Airlines, Record Offer. When I was done with Rap Replinger I quietly sang some Hapa and Ka'au Crater songs.

I can sing in Hawaiian, but I can't speak it. Only Kamehameha School in Oahu taught Hawaiian and I couldn't go because I was haole. Back at Kamuela, if you couldn't sing the Hawaiian national anthem from memory, you couldn't graduate. The only lines of the American anthem I knew were the ones with the rockets and bombs. There was no reason to learn it. I knew it was weird to sing and talk with nobody around, but it felt good to hear a voice.

By 6:00 the window was dark and nobody else had come to the door. If the Nurse Lady came to check my temperature only once a day that meant I'd have to spend another night down here. Suddenly, one of Fat Rob's riddles was sounding very appealing. At least I could talk to somebody.

I tried the doorknob. It was still open from when the girl had dropped off the tray. I opened it a crack. I looked down the slit near the doorjamb. What's-his-face wasn't there, but another student was patrolling the hall. I'd played pool with him a few times. He was from Puerto Rico or something. I think his name was Luis. I'd try and talk to him and see if he would let me out.

I opened the door all the way. He saw me and came over.

"Hey, Luis, *que pasa?*"

"Get back in there." He towered over me.

"Just relax. I just wanted to say, hi."

"I was told you were already warned."

"What?"

He pushed me inside and slammed the door. The lock clicked a second later. What the fuck!? This was wrong. I rapped on the door.

"Hey!" But there was no answer. "Hey!" I pounded on the door. Nothing. I was about to slam my shoulder into it when I heard something. I turned and looked toward the bed. I thought I'd heard a voice. I walked closer and listened.

"Hello?" I heard a muffled voice through the wall my bunk lay against.

"Hello?" I called back. I pressed my ear to the wall.

"Who's that?" the muffled voice called.

"Leif."

"Who?" It was not easy to hear through the plaster.

"Leif!"

"Oh." Then he said something, but all I caught was, "bed check."

"Who's that?" I asked again.

"Sam!"

Sam? I didn't know any Sam. Wait, it could be Stan, the kid that Derk had insulted.

"Black kid, Stan?" I knew it wasn't P.C but I didn't know how else to ask.

"Yeah!"

Great! Somebody to talk to. It wasn't the best way of communicating, but it was something.

"What are you doing here?" I asked.

I heard something, but couldn't make it out. Was it, stomach pain or headache?

"I have a cold," I said.

There was a loud thump from the other room.

"Stan?" There was no response.

"Stan!" Still nothing. Both rooms were dead silent.

I lay back on the bed and smacked my palm against the bunk above. Shit. I lay there thinking. I got out of bed, crossed to the other side of the room and I knocked on the wall.

"Hello?" I shouted. I pressed my ear to the wall and listened. Nothing. I repeated it on Stan's wall. Nothing. What the hell was going on? Had they heard us yelling and did something to him? Nah, that was stupid.

Then a strange thought occurred to me. What if nobody was there? What if I was hearing things, like in *12 Monkeys*? Was this that cabin fever thing? No, I wasn't fucking nuts. But isn't that what they all said? No. Stan had been in there, but had been released or went to the bathroom.

Just then that glass of water hit me and I had to piss. I went over to the door and knocked.

"Hey! I have to use the bathroom."

There was no answer.

"Yo! Bathroom!" But there was nothing.

Oh, shit. I went back and lay in bed. I was hungry again. I did not want to be here anymore. I wanted to go home. I hate this fucking godforsaken place.

I awoke the next morning. Strangely I felt better, physically speaking. My throat had stopped hurting. I looked around my little cell and noticed a change. My food tray was gone and a metal bowl was there. When did that happen? They must have come in the middle of the night. Creepy.

I looked inside the bowl. Nothing. I tried the door, but it

was locked. Man, I had to piss. I was about to pound and ask about the bathroom when I realized what the bowl was for. No. They didn't expect me to piss in that? But the more I thought about it, the more I realized that was exactly what it was there for.

I had to piss so bad. My bladder was tingling and I was twitching with discomfort. I unzipped my pants and held the bowl underneath. I didn't want it to splash everywhere. Even though I had to go bad, pissing like this wasn't easy. It felt unnatural. I finally finished and put the bowl down.

At least that's done. I just hoped I didn't need to take a major dump. That would suck. There was no toilet paper. I went back and sat on the bed. I didn't feel like movies or Hawaiian comedy. I wasn't in the mood for anything.

I started to pace around the room. I counted the steps. 11. I tried again to make sure. Still 11. I wondered if I could do it in 10? I lengthened my stride and did it in 10. What about 12? That took me two tries, but I got it. I began to walk in a circle. Over and over. I don't know how long I went around. I actually managed to pace the room in seven giant steps one time. Every time I passed the bowl, the piss smell got stronger. Round and round the room I went. There was no reason other than it was something to do.

I was about to look at my watch, but stopped. What's the point? It only made things seem to take longer. I took my watch off, put it in my pocket and sat down on the edge of the bed.

I don't know how it happened, but I started to space out. I

just stared at the opposite wall and didn't think about anything. Its blank white surface was somehow relaxing. I don't know how long I sat there, but then the door opened and I snapped alert.

The Nurse Lady came in holding her thermometer.

"How are you feeling today?"

"Very good, excellent," I said, a little too quickly. "I think I'm all better."

"That's wonderful news." She stuck the thermometer under my tongue. I remembered when I was in grade school Odi had told me to hold my breath if I wanted my temperature to go higher. I didn't know if it worked, but I always held my breath when the school nurse took my temperature. Right now, I was breathing as normally as possible. I'd rather be anywhere than here, even in class.

"No, sorry," she said after the beep. "Still high."

"But I feel fine, really. Can I see the reading?"

"It's still up there. I'll check up on you tomorrow." She turned and walked to the door.

"Please," I begged. "Do I have to stay?" I hated whining but I couldn't help it.

"Don't worry. Just think about getting better and you'll be out of here in no time."

She took my piss pot and left. Shit. Shit. Shit! I sat back on the bed and looked down at the carpet. This was wrong. What was I doing here? I sat there for a long time thinking of my situation, but soon I started examining the carpet near my feet. Interesting. It kind of looked like a planet's surface from orbit. I held my hand like a plane and closed one eye and began to zoom around the room.

"We're coming up on entry interface, *psst*."

"Roger, Challenger. Lift nose to 30 degrees. The window is open, *psst*."

"Houston, we have a problem. We're getting pretty hot up here."

"Lift the nose, you're only at 25 degrees."

"My read says we're at 30."

"You have a malfunction."

"We can't get it any higher. Captain, we're at 3,000 degrees on the outer hull, hull breach in 10 seconds."

"Get your nose up."

"We can't. Ahhhh! BakkkSHHHH!"

"They just broke apart in reentry. I guess we'll need some new astronauts." I laughed and laughed.

"That was funny! Need new astronauts. We're all vaporizing. Holy Shit!"

I stopped flying around the room and stood very still. What the fuck am I doing? I steadied myself and sat back on the bed. I closed my eyes and took a few deep breaths. Whoa, that was weird. Just relax, everything is fine. I began staring at the wall again. I tried to see patterns in the plaster. Was that a mountain range?

Dinner came again later that night. Cold soup, water and bread. I ate it without thinking about how hungry I was. Then I went back and stared at the wall. I could almost see California. If I just squinted a little harder. There it was! I couldn't get San Francisco Bay to show up, but I just pretended it was destroyed in an earthquake.

"Hawaii gets lots of earthquakes," I said, "I was in a five pointer once. That was cool. Hit in the middle of the night. All my drawers shook open. Who are you talking to, Leif? Shut up. You sound like a crazy person."

Day four was the same as day three. Piss pot is suddenly there, stare at the wall, temperature is too high, walk around in a circle, stare at the wall, broth arrives, space out, light comes on, light goes off. This was my life. This was my life. This was my life. This was my life...

On day five I was staring at the wall again. The ridges in the plaster didn't look like California anymore. No, they were New Hampshire. Definitely.

What was there? That lake in *What About Bob*? What was the name again? Lake Winnebago or something?

"I need to go there one day. Why? What do you mean, why? Cause I've never been. Duh."

There was a knock on my door. A knock? I came out of my trance. A knock was new. I slowly walked to the door. I just then noticed how I smelled. If I can smell myself then it must be bad. I'm Stinkor now.

I knocked back.

"Hello?" I called.

"Hello, Leif," a woman's voice said.

The Nurse Lady.

"I'm feeling perfect today, nurse. I'm ready to leave. Come and take my temperature." It was true. My nose and throat were fine. I wanted to get out of here.

"I'm glad to hear you're feeling better."

Wait, that wasn't the nurse. It didn't have any of that bubbly shit. I knew that voice. It was The Ethics Lady. I realized I didn't know her real name.

"Ah, what are you doing down here?"

"I heard you were ill and I thought I'd stop by and see how you're doing."

All the listlessness was gone and I was suddenly tense. Something was not right.

"You don't sound so well. Sounds like you haven't gotten over your fever."

"No," I said firmly, "I'm fine. The door is sort of mucking up my voice."

"I'm afraid I'll have to tell the nurse you need to stay here longer. Perhaps another week."

"No!" Another week? I couldn't take it anymore. "Please," I begged. I'd gladly clean my vats rather than be here.

"You really sound like you want to leave."

"Yes, yes!"

"Very well then. I'll go tell the nurse to let you out today."

"Thank you." She wasn't all that bad. Maybe she just hated her job.

"However, there is a matter we must discuss."

"What?"

"The newspaper. I know it was you who stole it."

"What!?" I'd totally forgotten about the newspaper.

"No true student of Lamia would do such a thing. We can't let stories about cults enter these walls. Children's minds are very fragile and it's our responsibility as educators to protect them from the outside world."

"I didn't steal the paper!" Derk had. I had spread the news, but that wasn't a crime.

"Oh. You really don't sound so well. I'll have to recommend to the nurse that you stay here another week."

Then it hit me. She didn't get a confession for the oven, but she thought she could get one now.

"But – I'll tell my mom about this!" I sounded so 5th grade, but I didn't care.

"We've already told her."

"Huh?"

"I called your mom and told her that you were in our infirmary with a fever. It was a bad one. You were delirious for a whole night and we almost took you to a doctor, but you're fine now, just recovering. Poor thing, you had such strange ideas during the fever."

Oh, my God! I couldn't say anything. My stomach was churning with a swarm of bees. These people were crazy!

"It must be hard living with the guilt," she went on. "It's better to confess about the paper and face your fellow students, rather than hide from it."

Jesus Christ. I couldn't believe this was happening. This was like Freddy Kruger shit. How could they do this? But I'd been here long enough to understand. They needed a culprit and who better than me?

I was about to tell her to go fuck herself with my vat's scrub brush, but held my tongue. I thought about staying down here in isolation for another week. Bread and water, piss bowl, and locked doors. The idea of one more day was too much to bear, but I wasn't going to confess. I'm not a person of any deep convictions, but I did have some principles. But staying down here another week? Pacing and staring at the wall. I couldn't stand this room anymore.

Even though she was on the other side of the door I could feel the Ethics Lady's bulk. Motherfucking bitch! I hated this place!

"Okay." I leaned my head against the door. I really had no choice. "I stole the newspaper and spread the story about the cult suicide to the other students." I had to drag each word out kicking and screaming.

"Why?"

Did she really have to pretend like I'd done it?

"I wanted to be... popular. I thought having the story would make people like me more. I'm sorry."

"Thank you for telling the truth. I'm glad you see that honesty will lead you down the path to becoming a fruitful adult. For punishment, you'll have to clean both courtyards every morning this week before room check. And during that week all TV and Rec Room privileges will be suspended. And for good measure, no playing the piano as well."

I wanted to scream that wasn't fair, but this whole thing wasn't fair. They had to show the others that this action was punishable. Then I remembered that for the past two days the nurse wouldn't show me the thermometer readings. She must have been told to keep me down here so I'd have to confess. I could still feel the bees attacking my stomach.

"I'll tell the nurse that you're ready to go back to class."

I felt really low, like I'd betrayed everything good in the world. Why was this happening to me? I don't know how I could tell, but I knew she was still standing on the other side of the door.

"Now you listen to me you pimply faced delinquent!"

I involuntarily stepped back at the sudden venom in her voice.

"If you incur one more infraction, you'll be working the Trash Room until you graduate. Anything. Your mom is on our side, so don't even bother trying to explain. And, if you tell anybody else about this, not only will you be punished, your friends will be, too. Is that clear or are my words *breaking up in reentry*?"

I felt prickling on the back of my neck. They'd been listening to me in here.

"Crystal clear," I said, trying to keep the fear out of my voice.

"Good." Her tone returned to its normal flatness. "And one more thing, I've talked to your Supervisor and dismissed these as sick days. You are now five more days behind in your courses."

I felt my throat go hot. If there hadn't been a door between us I would have strangled her. The idea of squeezing the life out of her, digging my fingernails into her flesh, of watching those beady eyes roll up into that fat head would have been the best feeling in the world right then. I heard her footsteps fading away down the hall.

"Goddamn it!"

I pounded my fist into my stomach. Fucking bees! I kept pounding. Eventually the stinging subsided and I sat back on the bed. Why? Why? It was all I could think.

An hour later the Nurse Lady came in and took my temperature.

"98.7. You can go now," she said, as if the past five days hadn't happened.

She opened the door and I walked out. The hall looked bigger than I remembered. What's-his-face was back and he unlocked the door to let me out of the right wing. The sound of my sandals on the floor seemed way too loud. I didn't take the stairs, but used the elevator. I didn't care if I wasn't allowed. Fuck them.

The scene at the end of *Shawshank Redemption* where the Warden put Andy in the Hole for two months to force him to launder the Warden's money came back to me. But there was no way to dig myself out of this place like Andy had.

It was 3:00 on Monday. All of the kids were still in class. I'd missed the weekend. Even after all the time down there, right at this moment I felt like being alone. I made my way to the bathroom and jumped in the shower. I just stood there letting the relatively warm water pour down on me. The stench of that room was washing away, but the water couldn't remove Lamia's filth. I'd planned to jerk off the next time I took a shower, but I didn't feel like it now. I don't know how long I stayed there. 20 minutes? 30 minutes? An hour? I hoped I used up all of Lamia's hot water.

Finally, I was tired of it and left. I sat down on my bed and looked around my room. For some reason, it felt as if I'd never left the basement. That cell had followed me up here like a shroud.

The door opened and Fat Rob came in. Just what I needed. He dropped his bag on the bed and turned to leave, but stopped to look at me.

"What's that?" Rob asked.

Rob was pointing at my gut. I looked down and saw several bruises.

"I don't know."

Rob shrugged and left. Fucking asshole. How did I get those? Hunger, I guess. I needed some music. I put on my favorite Beethoven symphony, his 8th. Not many people listen to this one, but he wrote it when he was in the darkest time of his life. His hearing had been going for 15 years and, finally, he couldn't play the piano anymore. This was the piece he wrote to lift his spirits. As the four symphonic movements filled the room I did feel a little better, but even Beethoven couldn't drown out the memory of isolation.

I pulled my watch out of my pocket. 6:00. Dinner time. I was hungry, but I didn't feel like eating. I'd better go anyway. I stood up and got dressed. As I opened the door, I saw my reminder. "Just go along with it."

"Shut the fuck up you stone age piece of junk!"

No, it wasn't my reminder's fault. It was *their* fault. I picked it up and put it in my pocket. Even though I couldn't stand the message, I was going to keep it on me from now on. I had to.

Entering the cafeteria was surreal. Just like any other day, there was the food counter, the drink dispenser and all the students laughing and talking. But something was different. Everything seemed fake. This is what Quaid must have felt like in *Total Recall* when he learned his whole life was just an artificial memory implant.

There were curious glances from the others as I walked to the counter to get food. I paid them no mind. I got my toast and sat down at an empty table. For the past year I'd always felt apart from people, but I never wanted to be part of this group. As I looked around the room I noticed more glances in my direction. What was their problem? I was the one who'd just been imprisoned.

Nick and the posse made their way toward me. I suddenly felt better. I'd almost forgotten I had friends here. They all sat down across from me.

"Good to see you guys," I said. They just looked at me very coldly.

"What?"

"Why the fuck did you tell them, dickhead?" Derk asked.

I was about to ask what he meant when I realized they were talking about the newspaper. I hadn't even bothered to check the EIR on the way in. I wondered if the Ethics Lady had posted it before or after she'd come to see me.

"Everybody's saying that you admitted it," Jude said. Even Nick looked upset.

"They said you were being treated in the infirmary and, like, felt so guilty after all the school had done for you that you, like, told them. Dude, what happened?"

Felt guilty?! It was not funny. I wanted to tell them. I wanted to tell them what was really down there in the bowels of the school, but I remembered her warning. I wondered if there were bugs or cameras in the walls that I couldn't see, but then realized they didn't need them. There were 350 cameras and listening devices all around us at that very moment. Every student would gladly turn his best friend in to Ethics for a pat on the back. These kids were like dead leaves on a forest floor. You couldn't walk anywhere without one crunching loudly under your foot.

By some strange twist, my friends were disconnected from the school's web, but that still didn't mean that others couldn't overhear.

"I can't talk about it."

"What do you mean, fuckface?" Derk asked.

"I can't tell anybody."

"I thought we promised never to narc," Nick said.

"I didn't. I told them I stole the paper and spread the word myself. I didn't mention any of you."

They all looked at each other in surprise. They must have just realized that nobody had said anything about them.

"You took all the blame?" Nick asked "Why?"

"Like they said, I felt guilty and confessed." I spoke with no emotion.

"Come on, man. I know you. That's bullshit. What happened?"

"I can't tell you." I had to stop these questions. "If I do, then it's not just me who needs to worry."

"What the fuck is that supposed to mean, kweef face?"

"It means that I confessed and that's the end of it. You never have to worry about it again." It wasn't their fault, but they were really beginning to aggravate me.

The others just looked at each other again.

"So, then, we're, okay?" Jude asked.

"Yes. You are fine. It's over."

"Well, it's good to have you back, Scuba-Doo," Derk said, reaching across the table and giving me a few light slaps on the face. "I felt bad putting you down behind your back."

"Thanks."

The others, now that they were in no danger, began to tell me about all that had happened while I was away, all of the school nonsense. I responded the best I could, but my mind remained imprisoned in that basement. After dinner Nick talked to me alone.

"What's wrong, dude? You can tell me."

I looked around. I couldn't see anybody, but that didn't mean anything.

"I really want to, but I can't say any more."

"What, did they torture you or something?" Nick smiled.

I didn't laugh. His smile faded away. He waited for my

joke, which would never come. I had to get him off the subject.

"I need some cheering up. What can we do?"

Nick had been here long enough to kind of understand. He wrapped his arm around my shoulder.

"I know just the thing," he said as we walked back upstairs. "I used my little tape recorder while you were gone. Derk and I made some comedy recordings like that *Poi Dog* thing. I think you'll like it."

I could just imagine the crude jokes in store for me. I couldn't help smiling.

"I can't wait."

CHAPTER XX
The Run Away

I called Rebecca a few days after my time in isolation.

"How're you feeling, my darling?"

"Well, I'm not sick anymore, Rebecca." I was not feeling fine.

"I'm so glad to hear it. When they told me you had a fever I was almost ready to jump on a plane to come take care of you, but they said your fever had broken and you were doing better."

I had broken. I had an incredible urge to tell her, but I didn't. I knew what she'd say, "It was just the fever, Leif. You were delirious. Nobody imprisoned you." This was also Lamia's phone.

I had to give it to them. They were crafty Motherfuckers. I reassured Rebecca that I was healthy and told her I loved her. There was nothing else to say.

While my ordeal of isolation was over, it wasn't easy

getting back into the swing of things. If students saw me approaching, they'd cover their bags or belongings with one hand. Sometimes I heard whispers.

"It's Leif, the thief."

I'd heard lots of stupid plays on my name growing up, but this one pissed me off like no other. I wondered if it was the Lamia kids or the Ethics Lady who'd come up with it.

"Hey," Derk said when I sat down at lunch a few days later, "It's Leif, the thief. Please, don't steal my hotdog. Please!" Derk cackled loudly.

"Don't call me that you fucking kweef sniffer."

"What did you call me, dickmouth?!"

"It's bad enough hearing them call me that but you, *you* calling me that, I will not tolerate! Do you get me, Derk, or did your father bash your brains beyond the point of any organized thought?"

Jude's eyes went wide. Nick looked at me horrified. Derk's face turned crimson and the cords in his neck punched through their chubby covering.

"I'll fucking-" Derk began, but Nick put his hand up and stopped him.

"Dude, he's right. You know he's not a thief. Just be cool. Okay?"

Derk glared at me with unbridled hatred. The loathing in his eyes blew out the flame of my own anger. That was a stupid thing to say.

"Sorry, Derk," I said meekly.

Derk continued to glower at me for an interminable

moment. Just when I felt something had to happen, that new kid, James Natlis, sat down with us.

"That was very noble of you," he said to me.

"What?" I glanced at him then back to Derk. This interruption seemed to have defused the situation and Derk was taking long calming breaths.

"Confessing like that. It shows real integrity."

I stared at James for a moment then looked at Jude and Nick. This strange comment seemed to be lost on them.

"Okay," I finally said. What was up with him?

"Do you know of any other infractions in school?" James asked eagerly.

"Other? Other what?"

"You know. Does anybody here know of bad things kids shouldn't be doing?"

The others shook their heads. They seemed to be ignoring him.

"Why do you care?" I asked.

"It's my duty. I'm part of this student community and any infraction hurts all of us."

He had to be joking. This wasn't James. James was a skateboarding kid from Nevada who couldn't tie his own shoes and thought that Misunderstood Words were the dumbest thing. I waited for the telling smile, but none came.

"Sorry, but I don't know anything," I finally said, "And I don't want to. It's none of my business."

"What are you saying? You mean if you knew about an infraction you wouldn't do anything?"

I was about to tell him I wouldn't do shit, when that one word he kept repeating registered. Infraction. I'd only ever heard the Ethics Lady say it like that. Something was funny here.

"Not exactly," I said backpedaling. "Yes, I would tell, but if it was, like, something big, you know? Not every little thing."

"That's not up to us. We must report every infraction. It's for the good of Lamia."

After lunch Nick stopped me in the hall.

"Leif, man, what the fuck?"

"Sorry, I just… lost if for a sec. The whole *thief* thing is really bugging me. I know I shouldn't have… I'm sorry."

Nick shook his head. I'd seen that expression on Istvan's face a thousand times: disappointment. I couldn't take it. I had to change the subject.

"What the hell is wrong with him?"

"Who?"

"James. He's so… *them*."

"I know. He got sent to Ethics right about the time you got sick and now he's convinced that Lamia is, like, the best school in the world."

Nick said this so matter-of-factly.

"Doesn't that, like, freak you out?"

"I've seen it before, dude." Nick spoke like we were talking about an intersection where accidents happened all the time. How could he be so cavalier?

"How do you, like, do it, Nick? I mean, you fit right in. I

can't seem to."

"What choice did I have? Adults have always told me what to do, so why not at Lamia? Dude, it's not like I'm in love with the place like these kids. Things still piss me off. I wish I was more like you. It's a good thing you can't fit in, man. You know?"

I didn't know what else to say, so we went back to class. Nick seemed to have moved past my faux pas but for me, it still clung to my mind like those hitchhiker things when you walk through tall grass. Luckily, the incident with James was a great distraction.

I tried to figure it out. Why would James just go over like that? The only thing that made sense was that he had been brainwashed. I mean, really brainwashed. I thought that was just a movie thing, but this was real. I fingered my reminder in my pocket. Don't forget this is a war, Leif. If you forget, you'll end up like James.

I still didn't understand how they did it. I'd been to Ethics before but never flipped. Maybe that was it. I'd been fighting integration all my life, but James was a normal kid who just wanted to fit in. They probably used that edge to cut out the kid's free will. I'd have to stay away from him from now on. He was an 'other' now.

The Ethics Lady was right about my class work. My sick days didn't count.

"Chop-chop," Connie said, after telling me I was now 37 days behind my scheduled completion at my own pace. I was never going to get my weekends off. I wondered if she knew what had happened to me down there. Either way, I was sure her current attitude would be just the same.

I looked over at Katrina, the only sunny spot in this cloudy hell. She seemed to radiate beauty. I wanted to go sit with her, but after giving her the song, the next move was hers.

I was sure she'd come talk to me at the end of class, but she didn't. She packed up her bag and walked off. I was disappointed and tried to figure out what had happened. I hoped she didn't think I was a thief or something. Perhaps she didn't like the song, maybe? I know it didn't have words, but it was still a nice piece of music. What if that friend of hers forgot to give it to her? That was it. I'd find her and ask.

I began to notice a strange smell in my dorm room. It was kind of rotten, like that juice that comes out of old chicken. I walked over to our trashcan and sniffed. Trash smelled fine. Rob was at his desk reading one of his books. Where was the smell coming from? I walked around the room trying to sniff it out. Finally, I came to Rob's bed. I smelled the sheets. I had to jerk my head away.

"Oh, man! Rob your sheets smell bad." I backed away waving my hand in the air. Rob turned and looked at me, then at his bed.

"It's your bed that smells." He went back to his reading.

"What the hell are you talking about? I do laundry every week."

"It's your bed, not mine, Leif Thief."

It was bad enough having to hear and see him. Now he'd

invaded another one of my senses. Asshole.

What really pissed me off was that he started telling people that it was *my* bed that stunk. He'd let them in the room and say, "Smell that?" They'd nod and then he'd point out my bed. He never let them get close enough to the source to figure it out. I wondered how much thought he put into finding new ways to tick me off.

The vats were waiting for me in the kitchen. I wanted to ask who'd cleaned them while I was sick, but didn't care that much. At least somebody else in this school knew what it was like to wash these things out.

I had to clean the courtyards every morning that week by 6:30. It was cold and dark. I had to pick up trash with my hands and then take it to the dumpsters all the way in back. Every gum wrapper and used tissue I collected made my blood boil. I even found a used tampon. At least I had my new gloves. I couldn't leave until one of the Rovers inspected the courtyards to see if I missed anything. And there was no respite in either the TV Room or at my piano.

Once my cruel and unusual punishment was over, things were back to the way they were, at least from the outside. Inside I felt different. I don't know how, but I felt like something was missing. Like at the end of *Stand by Me* when they come back to Castle Rock. Something was gone.

When I was allowed to return to the Rec Room I found Nick and Jude waiting for me. Derk wasn't hanging around with us much any more. I wondered if it was because of me, but I convinced myself that nothing could truly bother Derk.

Friends just drift in and out of your life, right? Of course, I wasn't sad Derk didn't hang with us anymore. It was always an effort to get along with him.

"Did you see the trailer for that new alien movie?" Nick asked.

"Another *Independence Day*?" I moaned. "Cool effects with a lame story."

"I liked *Independence Day*," Jude said.

"Good for you, Old Man."

"No, man," Nick said, "This one looked really cool. It had this neat spaceship crash. These two dudes were, like, standing there and the ship crashed just a few feet from them."

"Sweet," I said, a little more interested, "What's it called?"

"I can't remember. It had the same guy from *Independence Day*. You know, that black guy from *Fresh Prince.*"

"Will Smith," Jude said.

"That's the one."

"Yeah," I began, "I hope this one's more realistic than *Independence Day*. Hollywood always makes the same mistake with aliens, like making them with tentacles and claws and constantly drooling."

"What's wrong with that?" Nick asked.

"Dude, these aliens are way advanced, right? They have to, like, build all sorts of microcomputer stuff. How the hell can they build it with three fingers and big-ass seven inch claws? And if they drooled all the time, not only would it get on their computer stuff, but they'd get, like dehydrated, Nick."

"I see what you're saying, dude."

"The *Star Wars* aliens aren't like that," Jude said.

"I guess, but they look way too human. I know they have a budget thing, but an alien would look very different from us. Like in the movie rules."

"What are you talking about?" Jude asked.

"You know? The rules all films operate on. Like, ah, with sports movies where the underdog team always loses to the bad team in the beginning, then beats them in the end. The soldier doesn't get killed until he starts showing pictures of his sweetheart back home. You can always tell who the bad guy in a western is because he kicks the dog and the cop can't solve the crime until he's suspended."

"Shit, man!" Nick said, slapping the table, "That's funny!"

"I know. And everybody dies in true stories."

"That's not true," Jude said.

"Think about it. *Braveheart.* Everybody dies. *Schindler's List.* More than everybody dies. Even in that *Fargo* thing, everybody dies. The rules, man. Aliens shouldn't look like humans."

"What about Roswell?" Nick asked. "The Greys and the alien autopsy? They sort of looked like us."

"Dude. Isn't it strange that all these people see UFO's but it's never you?"

"The aliens will take you away!" Jude said in a mad-scientist voice.

Nick and I stared at Jude in shock. I'd never heard him say anything without total seriousness. Even Jude seemed surprised. Nick and I laughed.

"Did you know," Jude began, trying to regain his normal composure, "that Clinton did the 'Macarena' on national TV? Do you still think Dole would have been worse?"

"Are you serious?" I blurted out. Nick and I rolled with laughter.

"See what I mean? Our president was doing a lame ass dance to a stupid song in front of the world."

Jude did have a point.

"I wish I could have seen that," Nick said.

Just then Katrina's friend entered the Rec Room. I had to ask her about the song.

"I'll be back," I said, getting up.

"And I'll be Beethoven!" Nick said triumphantly.

"Oh, God!" But I couldn't help smiling. Back - Bach, funny. I went over to the girl.

"Hey."

"Hi," she answered. All of a sudden I felt very nervous.

"I was wondering if you ever, like, gave the song to Katrina?" I sounded like a little baby. What the fuck was wrong with me?

"Yes."

I waited for more.

"And?"

"I gave it to her." She just looked right back at me.

"Ah, okay." I wanted to know what Katrina said, or whether she liked it, but I felt exposed talking to her friend so I didn't. I walked back to my group and sat back down. Katrina's friend joined some other girls. The group had a small boom box. They put on some chick song. "*Love me love me say that you love me?*" It was annoying.

Nick, Jude and I talked for a while longer, but soon it was time for bed check and we had to get back upstairs. Jude and I waited by our doors as Nick continued on to his hall.

At 10:00 the Rover came to check us off on his clipboard. All the roommates were paired up by their doors except for one. Will was standing alone.

"Where's Stan?" the Rover asked.

"Don't know." Will was a cool guy, but he had more shoes than any dude I'd ever seen. A while back he'd asked me if I wanted to see them.

"Okay. Whatever," I answered. I had nothing better to do at the time. I looked in his closet and was stunned. There had to be 30 pairs, all with their own little space.

"A little shoeage action?" I said, looking down at them, "These all yours?"

"Yup." Then he began telling me all the brands as if that meant something to me. What a strange guy.

The Rover looked troubled by Stan's absence. He told everybody to stay where they were and left the hall. Nobody stayed still. I walked over to Jude.

"What's up?"

"Don't know."

We walked over to Will's room.

"Will, man. What's going on?"

"I'm not sure. Stan is always here."

Then the Rover came back. My skin prickled when I saw who was with him: The Ethics Lady. I was scared as she approached, but she didn't even look at me. She was talking to the Rover.

"Records show he left the Trash Room at 8:02."

Jude and I looked at each other. Shit! Stan had been working in the Trash Room? Jesus. Maybe he really had been down there in isolation with me. I wondered what he did or had confessed to doing.

The Rover opened the door to let the Ethics Lady pass into Stan's dorm. Will was keeping far away from his room, as if to disassociate himself from it. I didn't want to get close to her either, but I wanted to know what was going on.

The Ethics Lady came out. She always looked serious, but her face at that moment was way beyond that.

"A bag and some of his clothes are missing," she told the Rover. "It's only been two hours and 10 minutes. He couldn't have gone far. Get the students into their rooms and then gather all the Rovers. I'll get the Supervisors ready to search for him." She stomped off.

I turned to Jude.

"Search for him? Dude, did he run away?"

"I think so," Jude said in disbelief.

"But it's so far to anywhere and it's dark, too."

"Everybody inside!" the Rover ordered. I wanted to talk more with Jude, but everybody was going into their rooms. I had to do the same.

Either Fat Rob hadn't heard what the Ethics Lady had said or he didn't care. It was probably the latter. I got into bed and thought about the turn of events. They had sent Stan to the Trash Room. I guess Stan couldn't pretend to go along with it any more. I'd never thought about physically running away from Lamia. It had to be 25 miles to the closest town. Man, the Trash Room! No wonder he took off.

Somebody else despised this place more then me. I felt a sense of pride at his boldness. Run, Stan, run! Fucking run! I wish I could've gone with him but I knew I didn't have the guts. I would have to wait out my sentence. I had to endure 106 more days this year at Lamia.

The next day, Jude and I told Nick about Stan, but we didn't whisper it to anybody else. There was no mention of the escape. Lamia went on as if nothing had happened. I'm sure some kids were curious, but it was a subject that nobody explored in fear that they would join Stan. His remaining things were removed and Will now had a room to himself. Stan's name was no longer called out for roll call. Nobody ever saw him again.

Why had he been sent to the Trash Room? Did he make it to wherever he was trying to run? Did they catch him? I never found out the answers to any of these questions. After that night, it was as though Stan had never existed.

CHAPTER XXI
A Recital and a Betrayal

Even though it rained all the time, soccer was still the only school planned event that was fun. It was a slippery and muddy ordeal, but nothing could be done about it. I'd become a forward, even though I wasn't very good at it. Smelly Dylan, Ugly Edward and Scottish Jason were getting annoyed with me. It wasn't my fault, exactly.

I played defense, like always. The ball came to me and, instead of passing, I decided to kick it as far up field as possible. By some miracle I made a goal from our end of the field. Everybody assumed I was an undiscovered talent. Too bad Istvan hadn't been there to convince them otherwise.

Now I was screwing up the game for our team. I didn't have the skill or the stamina to be a good forward. After I missed another pass, Jason came up to me. I had to really concentrate to understand his accent.

"You're not getting the passes."

"Sorry. Maybe I'd be better as goalie or defense again."

"If you can score from there, then by all means."

I moved back and everyone, including myself, was happy. I liked it better back here anyway. Being a forward was hard work. I was always out of breath. Here, I could relax, watch the game and sometimes the ball would come my way. Back here I could become the unofficial announcer.

"And Edward gets the pass," I said like radio announcers from the 40's, "He's coming up on the inside, looks like Jason's going to get it from him. Oh! Jason screws the pooch and eats it. Too bad for Jason. He's been having trouble this year. Edward still has the ball. He's going to the goal. Can Dylan stop him? Nobody knows. It's close. He's there-"

"LEIF, SHUT THE FUCK UP!" Derk called out.

"Why should I?"

"Because you're annoying!"

"That's the funniest thing I've heard in my life coming from *you*!"

Jude and Nick, who were also on defense, laughed.

"I'll fuck you up, kweef face!"

I just laughed.

The teams changed from game to game. Sometimes we had Ugly Edward, sometimes Scottish Jason. Then one day the teams became permanent. Varsity had practice again and we had to play on the smaller field. We were getting ready to pick captains when Big Jae ran up screaming.

"No Captains! Gooks VS. Americans!"

We all looked at each other. I'd only heard the word Gook on Vietnam movies. Wasn't it derogatory? Mopping Alex stood nearby.

"I thought that 'Gook' was something not nice," I said to Alex. He shook his head.

"No. Han Gook is Korea. Gook is me. It is good."

"Really? I always thought it was a bad thing. Okay." Learned something new today. The Supervisor wasn't as excited as Big Jae.

"I don't know. We don't want to encourage racial separation."

"No! Like Olympics. We crush Americans!" The Supervisor turned to the rest of us.

"Is this alright with you?"

"Whatever," was the overall consensus.

"Gooks VS. Americans! Gooks VS. Americans!" Jae whooped, running around.

"That guy has problems," I said to Nick. "I told you about when he pushed me down?"

"Yeah. Several times."

Forming the teams was easy. That kid I'd done that weird staring exam with joined the Korean team. Then I remembered he wasn't Korean, but Japanese. I guess he didn't care, or maybe he didn't understand what was being said.

And so, the game began. The teams were a little uneven in numbers, but in the end it didn't matter. The teams were perfectly matched. I was really surprised. We'd make a goal, they'd make a goal. Back and forth. It was cool. So from that day, it was always Gooks VS. Americans.

In early February, I was playing the piano in the chapel when the music Supervisor approached me. He had one of the afternoon activities. I'd joined his activity before Virus Wars, but he couldn't teach for shit so I dropped it. I told him I needed all my time to practice.

"I see you finished learning 'Moonlight Sonata.'"

"Yup. Now I'm, like, trying the second movement. It's so light and cheerful, compared to the first."

"The third movement is very fast. Not easy to play."

"I'll get to it."

"Listen. On the 11th, we're having a concert of student compositions. I have two compositions already, but I was wondering if you wanted to submit one?"

A concert? I'd never played solo before. The idea of being on a stage by myself with all those people looking at me made my insides squirm. I was about to decline when I had an epiphany. That's why Katrina hasn't talked to me! She has no idea what the song sounds like. It's just a piece of paper to her. If I played it, she could hear it. She'd finally see that I was a person she could be with.

"Sure," I said nodding, "I have a piece I could play."

"Great," the Supervisor took out a piece of paper.

"What's it called?"

Oh, shit. That meant there was going to be a playbill or something with the name in it. If "Katrina's Theme" was on it, everybody would know.

"Ah… 'Lullaby in C.'" Good. She'd know, but nobody else would. Sometimes I'm just too smart.

"Dude, you'll surely win," Nick said, when I told him about it.

"What are you talking about? It's not a contest. It's just a recital."

"But there has to be a best piece."

"This one chick is playing a flute. You can't compare a flute and a piano piece."

"So you're saying their songs are better than yours?"

"No! It's just - you don't understand!"

Nick laughed.

"It's so funny when you get intense, man. Your face is all like, whoa, and you wave your hands. It's because you're Hawaiian."

"Ah, shut up, you drunkard." I couldn't help but laugh.

"I am going to be one," Nick stated emphatically.

"Right."

"Do you know how much booze I snuck from my folks over the break?"

"So what?"

"Have you ever stole liquor?"

"Don't have to. I just ask my parents and they give it to me."

"Really?" Nick looked at me for a long moment.

When I was nine, Rebecca and Istvan sat Mercedes and me down for "the talk."

"Drugs and alcohol are dangerous," Rebecca said.

"That's why, if you want any, we will get it for you. You want to try whisky? Just ask us. You want a cigarette? Just ask. I know you're going to do it one day and I'd feel much better if I knew what it was and where it's coming from. Okay? Whatever you want just ask us."

Had they said you can never have them, I would have tried them anyway because I hate being told what I can't do. Since all I had to do was ask, I never felt the need to sneak it.

"They gave you whatever you wanted?"

I nodded.

"I never felt like smoking pakalolo, but I've tried all sorts of alcohol. I don't care for hard liquor or beer, but I like wine. My dad was a big wine guy before he quit drinking."

"Dude, why would he quit drinking?"

"He read somewhere that if you stop for seven years your liver will, like, be completely repaired or something. He's been drinking since he was seven."

"Seven? Cool."

"He's Hungarian. What the hell can you say? Did you know that in Europe, during the Middle Ages, alcohol was all everybody drank, even kids, because water was, like, dangerous because of parasites and stuff. They didn't know about pasteurization."

"Where do you get this shit from?"

"Discovery Channel."

Nick just smiled and shook his head.

The day of the concert arrived and I was very nervous. My palms were sweating and I kept tapping my feet. The other players were Alex Reinstein and some Form Eight chick I didn't know. I was chosen to play first. Why did I have to open?

There was no backstage or anything so we just had to get up from the pews when our names were called. Nick was sitting with me.

"Dude, just chill."

"This is so fucking stupid." My heart was hammering in my chest. "Why did I agree to do it?"

"I've heard you play, you're a Rembrandt. You'll be great."

I'm not sure what Rembrandt was, but I remembered Red had complemented Andy in *Shawshank Redemption* by saying that, so it must be a good thing.

"Thanks, man."

The music Supervisor stood up and turned to all of us.

"Our first performer is Leif Csuba playing 'Lullaby in C.'"

Everybody clapped. I got up and walked to the piano. Shit. Shit. Shit. I sat down on the bench and looked out at the audience. 20 people. Way too many. It didn't take long to search their faces. Katrina wasn't there. My heart sank a bit. I wanted to delay until she got there, but I had to start. My breath was coming fast. I stopped and took one deep breath, then another. I put my hands over the keys. Just start. Get it over with. So I began.

I thought I was going to screw the pooch right off the bat, but actually I was playing very well. I played the slow beginning just like I wanted it to sound. I almost tripped up in the B section, but recovered and then finished off with the slow part again. I'd never played it that well in practice.

When I was done the small audience applauded. I felt so much better that it was over. I looked out at the audience and saw her. Katrina was a few pews back with her friends. She'd heard some of it. Relief and joy filled me. It was the first time I was truly happy since I'd been locked down in the basement.

I got up from the piano and went back to my seat.

"Viddy well, Viddy well. My little droog is no longer an ugly puppy."

"You weirdo." But I was smiling from ear to ear. Was droog a kind of dog? Nick knew the movie better than I did by this point.

Next was Alex. His piece was okay. Nick asked me about it.

"He's a piano composer," I whispered.

"What's that mean?"

"See how the whole piece is just arpeggios?"

"*Arp*, are what?"

"All he does is play chords, but he doesn't, like, play all the notes at once. Like a wave."

"Oh, yeah."

"What's the melody? Can you sing it?"

"Not really."

"That's what I mean. He's a piano composer. Pianists are afraid of playing a single melody line with their right and chords with their left. They think it's too simple, but nobody like's this shit."

"Yeah. It sucks."

I looked back, but Katrina was gone. She had only come to listen to me. That must mean something. I just had to wait for her to talk to me. Then, I'd see.

Alex finished and people applauded. Next was Flute Girl. She was cute with red hair and she actually played a good composition. I was surprised because I'd never noticed her practicing before.

"How was that?" Nick asked when she was done.

"She was pretty good."

"Yours was the best. You rocked the house, dude."

"I don't know about that, but thanks."

The recital ended and the audience left. The performers had to stay to talk to the music Supervisor before we could leave. He told us how great we were and something about how we made Lamia the great school it was. I didn't really listen. Katrina had come. She had heard the piece I'd written for her. I couldn't wait to get to class the next day and talk to her.

The Supervisor finished his little speech. I was about to leave when Flute Girl came up to me.

"I really liked your song."

"Thanks. You weren't so bad either." She was smiling a lot. I could see Nick waiting for me at the door.

"I'm Cristina," she said, holding out her hand.

"Hello." I shook it.

"How long have you been playing?"

"About a year now."

"Wow! That's really, really good."

"Thanks." Should I sit with Katrina tomorrow or should I let her come to me? No, I should let her come. Be patient. Don't push things. Flute Girl was still standing there.

"Listen," Cristina said, "Umm, I've always wanted to write a duet for piano and flute, but I don't know much about playing piano. You're really good. Do you think we could, like, get together sometime?"

My attention was drawn away from thoughts of Katrina. Duet, huh? I guess I could. It would be a fun challenge. But, that would mean Cristina and I would have to spend a lot of time together. What if Katrina thought we were going out or something? Cristina seemed anxious for my answer.

"I think Alex would be a better guy for something like that."

I saw red creeping into her face. I looked over at Nick. He tapped his watch.

"I have to get going. Good job and take care." I walked over to Nick.

"What'd she want?" Nick asked as we walked out of the chapel.

"Just to help her with some music thing."

The next day I got to class early. I knew that Katrina would sit with me today. I just knew she would. After roll call I watched her approach, but she walked right past me. She sat down at a table behind me. I was confused. She came to hear me, but didn't want to sit with me? Maybe she was nervous like me. That would explain a lot. Maybe she'd only talk to me if I was alone. That was it. I'd spend my free time in the chapel playing. That was a great place to find me by myself.

A few days later I signed out and left the classroom to take a piss. The Upper School bathrooms were kind of dirty, but the middle school ones on the third floor were cleaner so I always used them. I was walking by the middle school when I stopped and looked in. The classroom was right under ours and arranged the same: rows of tables in columns and, in front of each, their blue shirted Supervisor.

All of the Supervisors were at their desks, but nobody was at the tables. I looked at my watch: 2:30. The kids were always here at this time of day. I heard noises from the stairs above that sounded like the cafeteria. I knew the clock was ticking, but I had to check this out. I walked to the end of the hall and went up, following the sound. I came up the stairs to the tower and saw a very strange sight.

The whole middle school was in the corridor. Some kids were sitting, others were leaning up against the wall, and most of them were talking to each other. What the hell was going on? I was about to go up and ask when I heard the slamming of a door and a booming voice.

"There is to be no talking!"

Everybody immediately shut up.

"Now form a line and no sitting!"

The room wasn't big enough for a straight line, so the middle schoolers began to wrap around like a coiled snake. Then I saw her; The Ethics Lady. I realized I was a little exposed on the steps so I ran back down before I was spotted. I'd taken too much time to go to the bathroom so I made my way back to the 4th floor. By the end of class I really had to piss bad.

I told Nick and Jude what I'd seen. We all went up to the tower to look. They were still there. None of us understood what was going on. We quietly made our way back down.

The next day I sat with Jude at dinner. He was trying to explain the history of the Sith.

"I don't remember the Sith ever being mentioned in *Star Wars*."

"They're the opposite of Jedi. Both the Emperor and Darth Vader were Sith."

"What scene did they say this in?"

"It's in the EU."

"The what?"

"It's a book explaining the background of the characters."

"A book? You have to read a book to understand the movie? What the hell? Give me *Star Trek*, man."

Jude shook his head.

"I'm too old for this crap."

Nick came running in and as soon as he spotted us, he came over. He didn't even grab a tray.

"Dude, I know what's going on."

"What?" we both asked.

"You know George Scrubs?"

"Of course. Dumb as Scrubs."

Jude had pointed him out to me right before the Christmas break. He was short with thick brown hair that covered his eyes like the Shaggy Dog. He did look stupid.

"Did you know he had a phone line in his room?"

"How did he manage that?" Jude asked.

"It was just there, I think, but let me tell you what happened. He plugged his modem into it and connected to the Internet. Then he started to download porn."

That would definitely land him in Ethics, but I still didn't get what was going on.

"Here's the thing," Nick continued. "He was doing something wrong and he wanted people to know." Nick scoffed. "So he, like, told his roommate. He told Scrubs he didn't care. Scrubs then told the kids at his table. They told him to leave them alone. Finally, he told everybody in middle school, but nobody cared."

I completely understood their attitudes.

"So, he had, like, nobody else to tell, right? No. So he told his Supervisor."

"What!" I cried. "You got to be kidding!"

"Idiot," Jude said, shaking his head.

"Dude, you know the saying. So he was sent to Ethics, right? The Ethics Lady asked him who else knew about it."

"No fucking way!" I said seeing where this was going.

"Yup." Nick nodded. "Because they all knew and didn't tell, they were all sent to Ethics. The whole middle school!"

"Jesus Christ!" That was impossible, but I'd seen them up there so I knew it was true.

"But," Jude said, "there's 150 kids. It'll take weeks to get through them all."

"Pshaw! And they have to wait there, in the tower until, like, everybody has been dealt with. And those days go against their course work."

"So they'll all fall behind because of this?" I said. "This system sucks."

"Dude, I even heard that Scrubs now has personal Rovers assigned to him." Nick shook his head.

It was incredible. It was more important to keep kids in line than to educate them. Even though I felt sorry for the middle schoolers I was just glad that it wasn't me waiting there. Scrubs's stupidity had fucked over his whole class. What a dumb ass!

About a week later, Ethics had processed about half of the middle school, but it was still crowded up in the tower. At first, kids would take every opportunity to venture a glimpse at this unusual sight but by this time, it had lost its novelty.

Jude and I were playing pool one night. Little James was hanging around the pool table. It kind of bugged me. Other than the fact that Jude and I couldn't freely talk, James would hunch down and make his eyes level with the table so he could see the ball coming right at him. It was distracting.

Nick was in study hall and I didn't even think about where Derk was. I was examining the table for a shot. I saw something that would be hard to pull off, but it was my only option.

"Five in the side."

"You can't make that. That's a two wall bounce."

"You want to bet?"

"I want to see this!" James said, coming around the table and standing to my left. Frickin' kid. I chalked up, drew back the stick, and shot. The cue hit the five, which bounced into the top wall, off the side wall and then just had enough momentum left to fall into the pocket by my left elbow.

"Shit!" Jude said, in disbelief. I was even surprised I'd made it.

"I am the man! Oh, yeah! I guess the Force is with me, Old Man. Just give up. There's no shame in giving up."

"Yeah, Old Man" James said, "Just give up."

Jude said nothing. I aimed for my next ball. It missed the pocket, but I put too much top spin on it and scratched.

"Damn!"

"Too bad," Jude said, taking the cue ball out and placing it on the table. Then he went into the side pocket and took out the five.

"Whoa! What are you doing?"

"You scratched so your ball comes out."

"Only if you make it and scratch at the same time."

"No. Your last ball comes out if you scratch."

"Since when?"

"We've always played that way."

"Bullshit! You want that to be a new rule? Then fine, but we can't change the rules in the middle of the game."

"We were always playing that way!"

"No, we weren't! Put my ball back in the pocket!"

"You scratched!"

"James!"

"What?" James asked startled.

"You've seen us play for a while. Have we ever, like, taken a ball out on a previous shot if somebody scratched?"

"I- I-," he looked from me to Jude. "I don't know the rules that well."

"See?" Jude said, "He doesn't remember your made up rule."

"Don't pull that shit on me. That five is mine!"

"Will you hurry up, ladies," somebody said. I turned to see two kids waiting to get at the pool table.

"You," I said, pointing at one of them, "If you scratch, do you take out a ball from your last turn."

"No."

"See?" I said to Jude, but the other kid in line spoke up.

"Yes, you do."

"What are you talking about, man?" his friend said.

"Your five doesn't count," Jude said to me.

I felt my stomach tingling.

"We'll see about that."

I called out to the kids playing air hockey and asked them. They agreed with me. Jude went to a few of the tables and got kids to agree with him. In five minutes, the whole Rec Room was divided in half, both sides yelling at each whether the five ball counted or not. Jude and I were the ringleaders.

I'm not sure if it was the crowd or what but suddenly I was angrier at Jude than anyone in my life.

"We can use your rule next time!" I called over the yells to Jude.

"We've always used it!"

"NO WE HAVE NOT!" I swung the end of the pool cue into the table. It sounded like a gunshot in the small room. The room went quiet. Most kids backed away from me.

"You're just pissed I made that shot!"

"And you're trying to steal that ball, just like the newspaper!"

My skin prickled.

"What?"

"You heard me, Leif the Thief."

I looked hard at Jude. The bees were swarming in my gut. Motherfucker! I still had the cue stick and was in perfect position to jab out his eye. All I had to do was ram it in. I could almost hear his screams as I broke the end off in his skull like in *Die Hard II*.

I lifted the stick, but stopped. What about Ethics? This would definitely land me in the Trash Room, even if I didn't kill him. And there were parents and all that crap to deal with. But there was another way. I smiled.

"You were the first person I told about the cult suicides, why didn't you report me?"

All eyes were on Jude now. His face went white. That was worse than stealing the paper. Out of the corner of my eye I saw James come stand by me. Jude knew he was trapped.

"This is about you cheating at pool!" Jude said, trying to cover. "That five comes out!"

But he knew it was too late. The damage was done.

"It counts!" somebody yelled.

"No, it doesn't!" somebody else called.

Soon the mob argument was raging again. Jude and I were silent, though. We just glared at each other. During the shouting, Jude had laid his cue stick against the wall. I grabbed it and walked to the kids who'd been waiting to play.

"Your turn." I handed the sticks over. These were the only two playing sticks. I'd rather not play at all, than have Jude win. I walked out of the Rec Room before Jude could do anything. I could hear him yelling at the kids that it wasn't their turn, but I didn't care. The cacophony faded into the distance as I got upstairs. Little James trailed behind me.

"I finally have something to report to Ethics! I can prove I'm a true student of Lamia."

I knew I'd violated the pact we'd taken, but Jude deserved it. He knew I was innocent of that shit, but he publicly humiliated me just to get my five ball out of the pocket. He was the cheater not me.

"Go," I said to James, "Make Lamia proud."

He did a lame salute and ran to the Ethics Office. I could feel the stinging in my stomach fading away, but it wasn't gone. I walked into the chapel, but didn't play. I kicked the piano with the flat of my sandal. The piano rocked, but didn't move. I looked down and saw my Local dangling off the end

of my foot. The end of the plastic toe strap had broken off.
Goddamn that Jude!

CHAPTER XXII
The Law

"Dude," Nick was saying, "That was pretty harsh."

It had been a few days since the fight in the Rec Room. Jude and I hadn't spoken since then.

"I know. But he tried to cheat."

"Leif. Over a *ball*? It was, like, a stupid pool game. You weren't even playing for money."

I was about to continue my defense but Nick's look took the fight out of me. There was no anger, just sadness. My decision to denounce Jude had seemed like a good idea at the time. Thinking about it still made my stomach knot, but as I thought more and more, I wasn't so sure.

"He just pissed me off, man," I said hollowly.

"You're right. That was very uncool, but to, like, condemn him in front of everyone like that. You're always telling me you hate Ethics, but you had him sent there? That's kind of low. Jude's our friend."

I wanted to justify my actions, but every argument I thought of seemed really lame. Nick was right. I shouldn't have done what I did. Jude may have deserved it, but that didn't make it right. At least I hadn't lost my temper and jabbed his eye out.

"Shit," I said.

I'd used the system here to get vengeance on a friend. That was something *they* would do and I was not one of them. I reached into my pocket to squeeze my reminder. You can't forget, Leif. They are the enemy, the system is the enemy. The reminder felt heavy in my pocket.

"How's the Old Man doing?" I asked.

"He spent an hour with the Ethics Lady. Now he has landscaping chores for the rest of the week, mowing and trimming bushes."

The grounds were huge and it was always raining.

"Oh, man."

"Something else, dude. He never liked being called Old Man."

"What? But he never-" I stopped. I guess Jude was trying to be accommodating and nice. I fucked this one up.

"He didn't tell on…?" I pointed to Nick.

"He was cool. He didn't mention Derk or me to Ethics."

That was good, but it didn't make me feel any better.

"Is there anything I could do to fix it? Like, say I'm sorry or something?"

Nick shook his head.

"Damn." I really screwed the pooch.

Jude was still Nick's friend so we all sat at the same table, but it was as though we didn't exist to each other. If Jude looked at me it was a dark, scathing glare. I didn't blame him, but I still felt a twinge of anger for what he'd said in the Rec Room. We both had been upset, but I should have been the bigger guy and just let it go.

I felt more sorry for Nick. To have his best friends be like this must suck. He tried to be cool and jovial, but I could see it eating away at him. It was all my fault. First Derk then Jude. I was like one of those Roman spike things mounted on chariots. Just a few choice words and BAM! I broke apart the wheel of our posse. Fucking stupid.

Istvan had always told me to admit my mistakes right away because things couldn't correct themselves if I didn't. It was hard to do that with him, though. Even if I did something wrong and told him, he would lecture me for hours about how this was the worst thing that could have possibly happened. And if something similar happened later on he would again bring up my previous screw up. This really pissed me off. How could he tell me to own up to my mistakes then never forgive me for them? I guess he was just preparing me for the world. I could tell Jude I was wrong, but he'd never forgive me. Isht was idealistic and ideals will never overcome human nature.

The end of February was approaching. Soon it would be my birthday. It would fall on a Friday this year and I was going to the Peterson's. They said they'd take me to Red Lobster. I was really looking forward to it, but on Monday of that week things started to go wrong.

I left my keys in my room and was locked out. My sneakers were in there and I needed them for soccer. I couldn't find Fat Rob or the Resident Director. The Ethics Lady had told me that if I did anything else wrong I'd go to the Trash Room and I was sure being late for gym would most certainly count. I couldn't run in my sandals because the only thing holding the broken toe strap together was a paper clip, so I played barefoot. Kicking a soccer ball with your bare toes does not feel good. Somebody also stepped on my foot with their cleats.

On Tuesday I failed *Learning How to Study*. I'd just finished the course and went down to the exam room to complete the test. There are no A's, B's, or C's. No grades at all. Either you know it 100% or you don't. Apparently, I didn't know this one and failed my exam.

"Where's your passing form?" Connie asked when I returned from the exam room.

"Didn't pass."

She shook her head.

"You're falling way behind, Leif. You have to do the course all over again before you can retry the exam and that will put you another three weeks behind."

"Great."

"Now, chop-chop."

Every night I was down in the chapel waiting for Katrina to come, but she never did. I couldn't figure out what was going on. I would peek over at her every chance I got in class, but she rarely met my eyes. When she did, she quickly looked away.

On Wednesday, I was down in the TV Room with Nick complaining about my course. It was a weekday so we couldn't watch anything. The room was just a place we could sit and not have to smell Fat Rob's bed.

"This sucks," I said, "Why can't I just go down and take the exam again? Why do I have to start from the beginning?"

"That's just how it works here, dude. I've had to do it."

"It's such a lame course. I had to make a demonstration out of clay. Can you believe that?"

Suddenly, I felt something wet in my nose.

"Oh, shit!" I ran for the bathroom.

"Where're you going?" Nick asked, but I didn't answer.

I managed to grab some toilet paper before the blood began to drip on the floor. I held the TP under my nose.

"What happened?" Nick followed me in.

"Bloody nose."

"But you weren't doing anything."

"I used to get them all the time. My mom said it's a growing thing, but I haven't had one in, like, a year."

"Huh? I never got bloody noses. I got, like, this pain in my side when I breathed sometimes but that's it, man. How long does this last?"

"I don't know." I changed the TP. "Some last for over an hour and a half. This one time, I got one talking to Odi and forgot to change the tissue. When I finally did it had been there so long this six inch blood clot, like, fell out of my nose.

Odi saw it and almost puked."

Nick's face bunched up.

"Ugh! That's sick."

"Yup. Man, this whole week is just going to shit. What's that thing where if anything can go wrong it will?"

"Oh, right," Nick snapped his fingers, "Murphy's Law."

"That's me. Like that book, *Terrible Rotten No Good Very Bad Week.*"

"Never read that one."

"I added the week part. The book was about one day. Maybe God's punishing me for Jude."

"Do you believe that?"

"No. It just seems that way. Only two more days then I get to leave. Then it's only 76 days left until the end of the year."

"You know the number exactly?"

"Yeah."

"Dude." Nick was impressed.

I didn't think things could get worse in class, but they did. The next day, while I was reworking my *Learning How to Study*, a kid came up to me.

"Can I give you a Method Three? It's to pass a course."

Oh, shit. Just what I needed. We went into the back room and he handed me a simple book. Since my first Method Three I'd been forced to do several more but I'd finally figured out a way to get through them. I had to completely disconnect myself from the meaning of the words and just read.

I began the book. I'd only gotten through a page when he stopped me.

"You're not reading right."

"What?" The kid had the blankest expression. "Do I have a Misunderstood Word?"

"No. You're not reading with feeling."

What the hell? How could this kid say that? He sounded like the teacher from *Ferris Bueller*. "*Anyone? Anyone? Anyone...?*"

"Okay," I said to him. I put on my most annoying kids show host voice and began to read.

"And then the happy little bunny began to prance-"

"Stop," he interrupted and held up his hand. "Now you're exaggerating."

No, shit.

"Just read normally."

"Listen. This is how I read. If I have a Misunderstood Word then you stop me, but Method Three's have nothing to do with how much emotion I read with. Get it? Let's finish."

He said nothing and I continued. I wondered if he was upset, but I couldn't tell. I read for a while longer before we finished. I went back to work on my course book; then Connie came up to me.

"A Supervisor just told me that you gave another student a hard time during a Method Three."

Fucking little shit reported me.

"No." I tried to keep my calm. "He stopped me because he said I had no emotion when I read. That doesn't matter."

"If you verbally abuse a student again during a Method Three I'll have to report you to Ethics."

"Sorry," I said not meaning it. What the hell was wrong with this week?

I was in my room that night playing on my computer. I'd found a strange little game with a spaceship that blew up asteroids. I had no idea how it got on there. Isht must have installed it at some point. I was playing Bach's Brandenburg Concertos on my boom box. My favorite was the 3rd. I remember it was used on the first *Die Hard* movie. Fat Rob was reading one of his how-to-whatever books.

"You ready for the Virus Wars trip in April, Leif Thief?"

"Yeah," I said, not paying any attention.

"Are you sure? Your viruses haven't been doing too well."

I'd run out of programs to steal from. I couldn't write my own, but I didn't really care.

"I have a special one you haven't seen," I lied.

I heard Fat Rob sit down on his bed. I would not go near that disgusting piece of furniture anymore. It was too close as it was.

"I don't like classical music," Rob said. "It's almost as bad as country."

I was not getting into a classical music argument again.

"I don't like country either."

To my surprise, Fat Rob didn't say anything more. Good. I couldn't wait until tomorrow afternoon. Tomorrow I'd turn 15 and I'd leave this godforsaken place. I could finally get away from this terrible smell and this shitty week would be over.

The next morning I awoke to a strange feeling. I don't know what it was, but I felt weird. I swallowed a few times, but my throat didn't hurt. My nose wasn't stuffed up either. I just felt off. I didn't know how to describe it so I didn't tell anybody.

Mr. Peterson came at 5:00 to get me. I didn't want to clean the vats on my birthday so I told the kitchen Supervisor the day before that I'd been sent to Ethics and had to clean the bathroom on our floor. He bought it. I just wanted to get away as soon as possible.

We got back to the Peterson's around 7:00 and by 8:00 we were on our way to Red Lobster. I loved this restaurant. We only had a Sizzler on my island, so going to one was always a treat. I usually got the Ultimate Feast. It was Lobster, crab legs, and three types of shrimp. I'd been saving my allowance and had $30 to pay for this meal. It would be worth it.

"So, how's school?" Ruth Peterson asked from the front seat. John was driving and Jack was off with his friends in his Camero.

"Eh, I've had a bad week. And my roommate stopped washing his sheets. His bed really stinks."

She laughed.

"Oh, that reminds me of Stradlater."

"Like what?"

"It's from a book I read when I was a little girl. What you mentioned about your roommate reminded me of it. This boy,

Holden, is at a boarding school and he hates his roommate because he's not very hygienic."

"I completely understand. What did he do about it?"

"Let me think. Mmm, I think he got into a fist fight with him."

"Cool. Did he win?"

"I… no. Stradlater beat him up."

"Figures."

The meal was big and excellent. It was just what I needed. The Petersons were really nice and paid for my food. I got to keep my $30. I was just glad this week was over. I still had that funny feeling, but I had two days to relax and do nothing.

The next morning I felt abysmal. I felt drained and my chest was heavy. I told Ruth and she took me to a doctor. The doctor put a cold stethoscope to my chest and told me to breathe in a couple of times.

"I think you have bronchitis."

"Oh," Ruth said with concern.

"What's that?" I asked.

"It's an infection in your lungs. You need to take antibiotics. I'll write you a prescription."

I'd never had an infection.

"But how did I get it?"

"Many ways. It could have been floating on the wind. Somebody could have coughed and touched a doorknob and you grabbed it right after. Who can say?"

What a completely shitty week. Sick on my birthday to

boot. Rebecca was very supportive when I called her, but Istvan was not.

"I told you time and again, you have to wash your hands all the time. Who knows what shit these kids have. What if it had been something more serious? Do you know how much this will cost, Leif? *Jesust Christ*!"

I couldn't wait for the conversation to be over. The next morning I felt even worse. I had these very painful coughs full of mucous and I could hardly move. I don't think I'd ever been this sick. I'd never even had the chicken pox.

I was lying on the couch unable to move when John came over to me.

"I know your not feeling well, but you have to get back to school."

Fear raced through me. Sick again at school. I couldn't go back down there. I wouldn't.

"No!" I tried to scream, but I was too hoarse. I sat up as far as I could manage. "Please, let me stay!"

John looked surprised.

"I think you'll be okay. You can wrap yourself in a blanket and lie down in the back."

I shook my head violently.

"Honey," Ruth said. "Maybe he should stay. The doctor is here and he only needs to rest."

"What about his school?"

"I'm sure they'll say it's okay," I desperately croaked. "They don't like sick kids near the healthy ones. Please tell them I'm very contagious and shouldn't be moved. Call Bec again and ask. I don't want to go back. Please." Talking this much was a strain, but I had to stay here. I started coughing.

John was confused by my reaction, but agreed to talk to the school. He went upstairs to use the phone. I waited for what seemed like a long time. Every time I closed my eyes I could see that little cell in the basement and smelled burnt lint. Finally, John came down.

"So?"

"Strange people," John said, shaking his head, "They really wanted you to come back, but after I told them you were contagious and your mom thought you should stay here they agreed. But in the beginning they were really adamant, almost angry. Strange."

"So I can stay?" I needed to hear the words.

"Yes, you can stay."

"Thank you so much." I felt an immense tension leave my body. God does love me.

"Just get better," John smiled, flashing his braces at me.

"Thanks."

"Just get better." It sounded so much more reasonable coming from him than the Lamia people.

I don't remember much of the next week. Once I remember my blanket slipping off and I kept telling myself I was cold and needed to get it, but I couldn't. After an hour of telling myself to pick it off the floor I finally gathered the will power to grab it.

The doctor said bronchitis wasn't fatal, but it sure felt like I could die. If I wasn't coughing there was this raspy rattling sound every time I breathed. John and Ruth were very nice about the whole thing. To have some sick kid in their house for a week isn't the easiest thing, but they never said anything that wasn't supportive. Their son, Jack, wandered in from time to time, but we didn't talk. We'd learned by this point we had nothing in common.

One day I was lying in bed thinking about how pretty Katrina was and what to do about getting her to like me when I got a brilliant idea. The song was a nice gesture, but girls like more tangible things. I'd buy her a necklace. What girl wouldn't want a piece of jewelry? I'd ask John if we could stop at a mall before I went back. Leif, you're a genius!

After five days of coughing and incapacitating weakness I was feeling good enough to get up and move around. I went to the doctor on Saturday and he said the pills were working and I'd be myself again in a couple of days. Thank God for modern medicine. I wondered why Scientologists were so against drugs of any kind. Penicillin had saved hundreds of thousands of lives in World War II.

On Sunday I had to return to school. I didn't want to, but I had no more excuses. I was well enough so I wasn't worried about getting sent to isolation.

Before we left Jackskeep we stopped at a mall. John had a few things to get and I went off by myself to find a jewelry store. The lady behind the counter looked at me strangely. I guess not too many 14 year olds came in there. No, I was 15, I reminded myself.

"Can I help you with something?"

"I'm looking for a necklace. Something nice."

"Gold or silver?"

"Well, here's the thing. I only have $30. What can I get for that?"

"We do have one thing." She opened the glass display with a little key. "This is a white gold necklace. A pendant can be hung here."

It was perfect. It was a thin ribbon of metal with a small clasp at one end. It was very pretty. Katrina would definitely love it so it was worth my $30.

"I'll take it," I said without hesitation.

As John drove me back I closed my eyes and smiled. It had been a bad two weeks but things were going to be better. I'd give Katrina this necklace myself. No more using a go-between. It would be hard, but I'd buck up. When she sees the necklace, she'll have to like me. How could she not?

Movement IV

spring

CHAPTER XXIII
Things Lost and Found

During my absence Fat Rob had found another way to piss me off, other than the constant jabber and the smell of his sheets.

"Listen to this, Leif Thief," he said the moment I walked in the door. Rob opened the lid on his radio alarm clock and put in a CD. A moment later some southern guy came on.

"*If you think Madonna's 'Like a Virgin' should be sung at church, you might be a Redneck.*"

"What the hell is this?"

"Jeff Foxworthy. Isn't he funny? I also have a bunch of country music CDs to listen to."

Then I realized what this was. Rob had trapped me the week I'd left. He'd said he didn't like country, but it was just a ruse to see if I did. Now he was going to play this shit all the time. I should have seen it coming. Fuck!

To my surprise, I wasn't interrogated about my weeklong

absence or lying to the kitchen Supervisor on my birthday. I half expected Connie or somebody to lock me up in some small room with no windows, or explain to me why slave labor builds character, or why remaining at Lamia was the best path to a greater education, but nobody did. No pink slip, no mention of my absence. Although I was relieved, it was eerie. This place always kept you off balance.

That first night back I knocked on Nick's door.

"Who is it?" Nick never asked who was at the door. He always opened it right away. I thought I'd have a little fun with him.

"*There's been a terrible accident!*"

The door opened and Nick stood there. His usual carefree expression was gone.

"Where were you, man?"

"I got sick. Bronchitis."

Nick nodded and walked back into the room. I closed the door and followed him. Nick sat down heavily on his bed.

"You okay, man? You seem kind of pissed."

Nick said nothing at first. He just looked at the floor.

"Fucking Ethics Lady. Fucking Bitch!" I'd never heard Nick so angry. He was always so mellow about everything.

"What the hell happened?"

"She took my *Clockwork Orange*."

I looked over his bed. The poster was gone.

"What? Why? It's just a poster."

"That's what I said."

I knew how much Nick loved that thing. Nick's eyes

were still downcast.

"But you've had it for, like months. Why now?"

"Last week, during room check, one of the Rovers found my *Clockwork Orange* tape. They asked why I had an R-rated movie here? I tried to explain, but they said I'd only have it if I intended to watch it."

"That's lame."

"I got sent to Ethics."

Nick's face showed his torture. I didn't know what had happened, but I knew it was bad.

"She made me stomp on my tape until it was broken."

"What the fuck?"

Nick's eyes were closed tight. He looked like he was about to cry.

"And to make sure I didn't forget she came in here and tore my poster in half. Fucking bitch." His voice cracked.

"Jesus Christ! Dude, that sucks." I didn't know what to say. I walked over and put my hand on his shoulder. The Ethics Lady always seemed to know the best way to hurt you. I wondered if this is why nobody had reprimanded me for my absence. The Ethics Lady was indirectly punishing me by hurting my best friend. Either way she was a fucking bitch. Nick was breathing heavily. He needed cheering up.

"And I thought I had a lousy week. You know, coughing up lung matter and blood. I'm still super contagious, but I'm hoping to spread it to all the students here, sort of my way of getting back at the school for all their shit."

Nick was jarred out of his depression.

"What?!"

"Don't worry, it's not like Ebola. Only one in five die of what I have. You have better than a good chance."

Nick's eyes were wide as he began to lean away from me. I tried to keep my face serious, but I couldn't hold back any longer and started laughing. Nick stood up.

"You, you frickin' Hawaiian!" but he was laughing too.

"You should have seen your face! Bronchitis, fatal? Dude."

Nick smiled and shook his head.

"I've never had bronchitis. What is it really like?"

"You won't die, but it still sucks. You have these painful deep coughs and you feel so weak you can't even move. It was like Timmy in *The Secrets of NIMH.*"

"Oh, yeah." Nick nodded. "But I think it's *Secret* not *Secrets of NIHM.*"

"Really? Ah, I like *Secrets* better. Anyway, avoid it if you can."

"I will, dude." Nick seemed normal again, but I could see his smile didn't make it all the way to his eyes. Only time could help him get over the poster and tape, but I felt that cheering him up was repaying him for lifting my spirits after my time in isolation. And it was getting back at the Ethics Lady, too.

A week or so later I heard music as I approached the chapel. Alex was in there again. I felt irritation twitching inside of me, but I went inside anyway. Alex was at the piano playing one of his lame arpeggio compositions, but he wasn't alone. Camila was standing at the piano with her hand on his shoulder. I guess she and Big Jae had broken up or whatever.

"Hi, Leif," she said as I approached.

"Hey."

"I'm almost done," Alex said. "Then it's all yours."

I felt no gratitude towards him. Alex finished his last chord and stood up. Camila smiled and applauded.

"You're so good."

"Thanks, gorgeous." I took his place at the piano.

"So," Camila asked, "which one of you is the better pianist?"

Alex had been taking lessons for years and he could also sight read. I really didn't want to hear him explain his superior playing abilities.

"Oh, Leif here is," Alex said.

We both looked at him. I wondered if he was being modest or sarcastic, but his face was sincere.

"Really?" Camila turned to me.

"Really?" I asked.

"Yeah. Leif just plays with so much more feeling. That's it."

I smiled. To hear that from him meant a lot to me. I felt bad for dissing him.

"Thanks, man," I said.

"Sure. Let's take a walk," he said to Camila. They left the chapel hand in hand.

My respect for Alex quickly dissolved into jealousy. If I was so much better, why couldn't I end up with the girl? I was always told in school that the best person at anything would always get all the opportunities, but it never seemed to work that way. Never. I had to give Katrina that necklace.

The chapel door opened and Nick came in.

"Hey," I said.

"Dude, let's go someplace else."

"I just sat down."

"We always stay in here. Let's, like, walk outside or something."

I thought about it for a second. The piano would always be here.

"Sure."

We left the chapel and walked out to the soccer field. The clouds were still thick and endless, but we were catching a short break in the rain.

"Hey, let's practice karate, Nick."

"Karate. Cool." Neither of us had studied, but we'd both seen it in movies.

"Rules," I said. "No hitting in the face."

"No hitting below the belt."

I took a stance.

"I thought that was a given. It's time for mortal combat."

"Bit of the old ultra-violence."

I put on a Spanish accent.

"*Hello. My name is Aleifo Monchooba. You killed my father. Prepare to die!*"

Nick aimed a punch at my chest. I jumped away.

"*Shoryuken!*" I yelled, as I did a roundhouse kick. I missed.

"*You will not beat me, Ryu,*" Nick said with an Asian accent. "*I am Master Bison!*"

We both kicked at the same time and hit each other. We fell to the ground laughing.

"That was fun," I said, getting up.

"Dude. Let's do that again. You come in from the left. I'll come in from the right."

"Your left or my left?"

"Hey!" Somebody yelled. We both looked up at the road. A Supervisor was approaching.

"What now?" I moaned.

The Supervisor was a squat, toad looking man I didn't recognize, but he knew us.

"Leif, Nick, what are you two doing out here?"

"Practicing karate," I said. "He's Bison. I'm Ryu."

"What?"

"*Street Fighter II,*" Nick said. "One of the best Nintendo games of all time, I don't mind saying."

"Yup. Right up there with *Super Mario* and *Duck Hunt.*"

"I don't care." The Supervisor put his hands on his hips. "Stop it right now and get back in the school or I'll report you to Ethics for fighting."

"No problem, man," Nick said, as calmly as he could. The Supervisor walked away. I made a face behind his back. What a dick! The Supervisor didn't leave, but stopped at the road near a willow to watch us.

"Freak. Why are they always following me?"

"Because you're Hawaiian."

"Shut up."

Nick laughed. We couldn't continue our karate with the S.S watching us so we headed back, but we didn't go inside. We walked around the back of the building. There was nothing interesting to see here, just barren trees. The school loomed large above us.

"You know the movie *Sandlot*?" Nick asked.

"*For-ev-er, For-ev-er*," I said, repeating the best line from the film.

"Funny. You know that big kid?"

"Yeah, well, not personally."

"I met him once."

"No way!"

"Yeah, Pat. I met him one summer. Oh, shit, man! He is the funniest guy in the world."

"Did he play baseball?"

"No. I don't think so. He's a soccer dude."

"Sweet. Was he-?" Something on the ground startled me. I jumped away. "Look out!"

Nick sprang like a cat, landing a good six feet away.

"Wow! I guess white men can jump."

"What is it?" Nick looked around.

"That!" I pointed. We inched closer. I'd never seen one before, but I knew exactly what it was.

"It's a rubber, dude," Nick said. Indeed it was. A blue condom was lying on the asphalt behind Lamia. Nick walked around it.

"Oh, sick!"

"What is it?" I came around to see. Nick's face was all scrunched up.

"It's used and full of jizz!"

It looked like the inside was smeared with hair conditioner.

"*Ejaculation.* I wonder whose it is." There were several couples at Lamia, but I couldn't even begin to guess which one of them this belonged to. Not only was masturbation prohibited, but sex was severely punished. I couldn't imagine these kids wanting to take that risk.

"Wait a second," Nick said. "I know whose this is."

"Who?"

"Jason."

"Scottish Jason? How the hell do you know that?"

"I saw a sealed one just like this on the grass during a soccer game. I think it fell out of Jason's pocket. He's the only one out there with a girlfriend."

"Yeah. I came down to do my laundry one Sunday and caught Jason and Jessica Hopemann playing doctor. I guess they're doing a little more than that now. Nice."

"But look where it is."

I looked around.

"I don't get it?"

"He probably took it off right after he blew his load, right?"

"Yeah?"

"So that means they were having sex here. Probably in the trees over there."

"But it's cold and the grass is always wet."

"Pshaw."

I looked from the trees to the condom. What to do with this information? The funniest thing would be to tell Derk. He would probably bolt out here, grab a stick, skewer the condom, and march it around the school like a bandleader. Maybe that would redeem me in his eyes, but it probably wasn't enough. It would take much more than that. Actually telling anyone would be a mistake.

Word would spread and eventually get back to Ethics. We'd be sent in for questioning. Even if we lied and said that we didn't know whose it was, the Ethics Lady would force us to accuse somebody. If Jason and Jessica Hopemann wanted to break school rules by having sex, I wasn't going to stop them.

"Let's keep this to ourselves," I said.

Small drops of rain were hitting the parking lot giving off that wet asphalt smell.

"Good idea," Nick said, "Time to get back to class."

"Sucks royal dick."

Nick headed back towards the school. I kicked the condom under some Supervisor's car so it wouldn't be found so easily, and ran after Nick to catch up. As we headed back into school I took one last look at the condom.   What a strange thing to find.

CHAPTER XXIV
My Five Cents

Nick and I were eating lunch in the cafeteria. Jude had stopped hanging out with Nick because of me so it was just the two of us, that is until Little James joined us. I tried to avoid him as much as possible, but after letting him narc on Jude, he now assumed we were the best of friends. Whenever he was around Nick and I immediately shut up.

"Did you hear about Austin?" James asked in his clipped way.

Big-head Austin had left Form Six Entry for Form Six a few weeks ago. I didn't really talk to him anymore.

"Nope," I said, shaking my head.

"He tried to get away with masturbation. They'll post it on the EIR tomorrow."

This was a preemptive circulation of the infraction so that when the list appeared tomorrow, Austin's story would get a second breath of life. James: The perfect Lamia student. I didn't hate him, though. Lamia was the enemy.

"Oh, really," I said unconcerned.

"Yeah." James didn't catch my lack of interest. "He tried to do it late at night when he thought his roommate was asleep. He woke up and saw Austin. He then got out his laser pointer. All the sudden, Austin saw a red dot on his thingy. Caught red handed. Get it?"

Nick rolled his eyes.

"Got it."

"Can you believe he was trying to get away with breaking the rules?"

"It's only wrong if you get caught," I declared.

James was appalled.

"How can you say that? The rules are there to protect us. They are what makes this school better than the rest."

Oh my God, this kid was gone.

"You guys follow the rules," James stated.

Nick and I glanced at each other. I was pretty sure Nick jerked off, but I never asked him about it and he never asked me. That's the way it should be.

"So," James went on, "where would kids go so they wouldn't get caught?"

"Well," I began, "the best place to go would be-" Nick gave me a kick under the table. I was about to ask what his problem was when it *hit* me. I was just about to tell James where I went. What the hell was wrong with me?

"Go where?" James prompted.

"I guess if you didn't want to get caught," I said, looking

at Nick, "you could go into the toilet stalls. You could lock the door and stay in there for a long time."

"Have you ever done that?"

"Sick, man! No way."

Good save. I was slipping. James was the last person you wanted to tell anything to. I was glad Nick had reminded me. Come to think of it, it had been a couple of days for me since I last jerked off. As soon as I got the chance I'd get a good whacking in.

Two things pissed me off most about cleaning the vats. One was that I never ate anything that came out of them, but it was my responsibility to get them ready to cook in again. And, two, no matter how clean I got them, the next day they were always revolting. And the next day, and the next day after that. I was like that Greek dude who had to push a huge bolder up a hill every day for eternity.

It was pasta day again. I hadn't eaten any, but I could tell that one of the kids had overcooked it. The inside of the aluminum tub was so caked with it that I had to get a spoon to scrape off all the little bits.

I was a little more pissed than usual by the time I finally got it all washed out. I was on my way out to the cafeteria to mop when the kitchen Supervisor stopped me.

"The boy who normally cleans the grill hasn't come in yet. Take care of it before you mop."

I hated the grill, but what could I say?

"Fine." Fuck this godforsaken place.

The Supervisor nodded and walked off.

I made my way back and began to scrape. There was this two-inch indentation that ran the whole length of the front of the grill. I scraped as much as I could into the groove then pushed the crunchy, liquidy mess into a hole with a collection tray underneath. My hands were smeared with sticky grease and unrecognizable food. At least the grill wasn't still hot like the oven but it still sucked ass.

"What you doing?" I turned to see a short Korean kid standing behind me.

"Cleaning the grill."

"This my job."

Where had he been? We were all fucking working.

"The Supervisor asked me to do it."

"But this my job."

"Get the dude to give you another." I just wanted to finish this and get out of here. The kid was still standing there.

"I clean grill."

What was his problem? Jesus Christ!

"I'm doing it. Do something else."

"But is my job!"

"Leave me alone!"

The kid then tried to grab my scraper.

"What the hell!"

"Is my job!"

I wrenched the scraper away and slashed at him. The dull blade cut his left hand near his thumb.

He yelled something in Korean and cradled his hand.

Little fuck was trying to steal my scraper. My stomach

was stinging in anger. I looked at his hand. In the center of a dark smear of grease was an inch long cut. A trickle of blood was running down his palm.

I was still holding the scraper. I looked at it. I could see a crumpled bit of skin stuck to one corner. What the fuck? I hated the grill, but I'd just cut this kid so I could finish cleaning it? What the hell was wrong with me?

I dropped the scraper on the grill and looked back at the kid. He was staring at me in fear.

"I'm sorry," I said, and made my way to the cafeteria to mop. What the fuck? Why was it getting so hard for me to control my temper? Man, I needed to listen to some Bach and majorly chill out.

Even as I mopped, all I could think about was that slash on that poor little kid's hand and that skin on the greasy scraper. Why had I done that?

I saw Mopping Alex exit the kitchen and make a beeline towards me.

"Why you hurt Kim?" His normally friendly attitude was completely absent.

Oh, shit. The kid was telling people. My concern for Kim immediately evaporated, replaced by fear for myself. I spoke slowly and carefully so Alex would understand.

"I'm having a bad day. I didn't mean to hurt him. I was upset at something else. Please ask him not to report me."

I could see Alex mulling it over. Visions of the Trash Room machined gunned my mind. I had one last ace up my sleeve.

"Don't I always help you and the other ESLs in class?" I pleaded. "I repeat the lessons as many times as you need. The other Americans don't do that? Please, I'm sorry."

Alex nodded with some reluctance. I waited for his response. Please.

"I talk to Kim." Alex turned and made his way back to the kitchen.

I breathed an immense sigh of relief. Fuck. That was too close. Thank God I took all that extra time in class with the ESLs. The next day I tried to tell Kim I didn't mean to hurt him, but he ran away from me. I also tried to thank Mopping Alex for what he'd done but his eyes were full of ice. The rest of the Koreans completely disregarded me while I mopped. I'd bartered away all my good will. At least I didn't get sent to Ethics. I had to keep my shit together.

A few nights later I went to the Rec Room to get something to eat. Nick had study hall tonight and I was alone. I didn't need to save my money anymore. I spent every dollar I had on food to try and quell my constant hunger. I was looking up at the menu above the counter, trying to decide what to get.

> *Pretzel $1*
> *Pretzel with cheese $1.15*
> *Extra slice of Cheese 10 Cents.*

Pretzel with cheese sounded good. I was about to order from the girl when an interesting thought occurred to me. It probably wouldn't work, but I wanted to see what would happen.

"Hello," I said walking forward.

"What can I get you?"

"I'd like a pretzel with cheese, but without the original slice of cheese, just an extra one."

"Huh?"

"I'd like a pretzel, but only with the extra slice of cheese."

"You mean a pretzel with cheese?"

"Not exactly. An extra slice of cheese costs, like 10 cents, right? So I'd like a pretzel with that extra slice so it'll cost $1.10, not $1.15."

"Ah?" She looked very confused. I tried not to smile, but it was hard.

"I don't know if that's…" she didn't know what to do.

"You know what I'm saying?" I asked, as though this was a normal conversation.

"I understand." Clearly she didn't.

I put down my $1.10.

"Pretzel with only the extra slice of cheese, please."

"I need to talk to my Supervisor."

"Go for it." She quickly got out from behind the counter and ran out of the Rec Room.

I couldn't hold it in. I started laughing. Oh, these people were funny. I didn't give a shit about the five cents. I just wanted to fuck with them. I was being polite. I wasn't yelling or acting angry. It's the little things that really count in life.

The girl came back with her Supervisor. He looked down

at me over the counter.

"So what's the problem?" The girl was standing out of the way. She looked relieved to hand this one off.

"No problem," I said, and explained what I wanted. I waited with a pleasant expression on my face while he thought about it.

"I don't think we can do that. An extra slice of cheese implies you have to have a first."

"But a pretzel with cheese is a pretzel with one slice of cheese on it, so why would an extra slice, which is one slice cost five cents less?"

"I don't know. That's just what the rules say it should be. You'll have to pay the $1.15."

"Okay." I put down an extra nickel and the girl heated up my pretzel. The Supervisor, seeing all was well, left.

"Sorry for the trouble," I said to the girl when she handed me my food. She chuckled.

"I've never gotten a request like that before."

I remembered what she'd mentioned about saying please and thank you. I was not like the others.

"Thank you very much," and with that I left.

Even though I didn't get my deal I felt I'd won by pointing out a flaw in the system. Odi would have been proud.

After soccer the next day I went into the bathroom to take a shower. I had an hour before the Virus Wars Club. It was our last meeting before the trip to Jackskeep. I wasn't looking forward to going. I had a program to compete with, but I didn't give a shit.

I had my fantasy of Kellie Martin all ready to go in my mind. I still tried not to think about Katrina when I beat off. I didn't want to demean her in any way.

I pulled back the curtain on the only warm shower stall and stopped in my tracks. Little James was sitting on the floor naked, with his hand wrapped around his hard dick.

"Christ!" I shut my eyes and turned away.

"Oh, no!"

Even with my head turned, the image seemed tattooed to the back of my eyelids.

"Jesus Christ, man!"

"I'm sorry. I'm sorry."

I heard a rustling sound.

"I have a towel on."

I slowly turned around. James had covered himself. He looked utterly miserable. This wasn't embarrassing or funny. This was completely nasty.

"I couldn't help it. I tried your idea, but couldn't do it with my legs bent. This seemed like a better place."

My idea? Then I understood. When James had come to us, it hadn't just been to tell on Big-head Austin, he'd been looking for a way to jerk off *himself!*

"Ah, why didn't you turn on the shower or something?"

"The water bothered me."

I still couldn't get the image of naked James out of my mind, but I did feel sorry for him. He desperately wanted to be the perfect Lamia student, but he couldn't fight his own biology.

"You're going to report me now." It wasn't a question.

"Dude, we don't need to tell anybody."

"But you have to. It's the rules. You must report me."

Shit. The last place I wanted to go was Ethics, even if I wasn't the one in trouble. I'd never reported anybody and I certainly didn't want to talk about masturbation with the Ethics Lady. I couldn't even imagine anybody wanting to fuck that lard ass. I also didn't want to perpetuate this system, but if I didn't, then James would report me for not telling. This place pissed me off. There had to be another way.

"James. You want to be a good student, no?"

James slowly nodded.

"Can I trust you to report yourself to Ethics?"

James looked up at me. This gave him the choice. He could never tell and we could both go on with our lives and, if he did tell, I couldn't be blamed for keeping silent. It was so nice when I found the loopholes.

"Yes," James said. "I am a good student."

He got dressed quickly and left the bathroom. I hoped he wouldn't turn himself in. Some things are nobody's business. I looked at the empty stall. I didn't feel like spanking the monkey anymore and certainly not in that shower. I'd come back another time.

To my disappointment, James did turn himself in. Soon his story was spread throughout Lamia and, to my relief, I was not part of it. I wanted to thank him, but I didn't. Because of him, a new official policy was instigated soon after that.

I found out about it a few days later. I was taking a real shower when the curtain flew open.

"I'm not done!" I yelled, turning to the wall. It was a Rover.

"Sorry, just checking." He closed the curtain and left.

Rovers had been given the authority to randomly check the showers for rule breakers. It pissed me off and I'm sure it did a lot of other guys. I'd have to hold off until the middle of May when I went home. 57 frickin' days! There's nothing wrong with jerking off. I think I'd heard something on the Discovery Channel that it prevented prostate cancer. Maybe if Lamia had TV or radio, they'd know something about the real world.

CHAPTER XXV
The Final Straw

March ended and April began. It was still cloudy as hell, but the rain was coming with less frequency. I carried the necklace in my pocket every day, but I still hadn't given it to Katrina. Every time I tried, I freaked out. My heart tried to break through my ribs and my clothes were instantly damp with sweat. It was almost better not giving it to her so I always had the chance that I could. But I'd spent the money and the year was drawing to a close. Even just a couple weeks with Katrina as my girlfriend would make everything I'd been through worth it. I had to give it to her.

I was playing the piano one night when I lost track of time. I loved to let my mind wander while playing. Sometimes I'd start a piece and not even know I'd finished it. It was like I could control time and space. I'd finished the second movement of 'Moonlight' but for the past few weeks I just kept playing 'Katrina's Theme' over and over.

It was so beautiful and perfect, just like her. I know it was not Beethoven quality but it didn't matter. It was our song. I never got tired of the theme no matter how many times I played it.

When I finally looked at my watch there were only three minutes before bed check. Shit. I closed the lid on the piano and ran up the steps taking them two at a time. As I entered the hall to the dorm, I saw Will crouched behind the entrance.

"What are you doing?"

"Brandon's leading Lauren over here. I'm going to jump out and scare her."

"Cool."

I walked over to my door, but didn't go in. I wanted to see this. I think Brandon was a Form Eight kid who lived down the hall and I wasn't sure who Lauren was, but this was going to be entertaining. I noticed Will was wearing one of his more prize pair of shoes, some brand called *Goochy*. I looked at my Locals. Shoes got you from point A to point C. Who cared how they looked?

A moment later I heard voices from the stairs.

"What does Will want?" I heard a girl ask.

"He just wants to ask you something," a boy replied. That must be Brandon. The voices were getting closer.

"But it's almost bed check."

"It will only take a minute." Will turned to me with a huge grin on his face. I gave him a thumbs-up. Then I saw Brandon come through the hall entrance. A moment later a short girl with dark hair followed. I'd seen her in Form Six.

"I'll get him," Brandon said, and pretended to knock on Will's door. Lauren stood at the entrance because she couldn't come down the boys' hall. Will saw his moment. He jumped up and yelled. Lauren screamed and involuntarily kicked. She made solid contact with Will's balls.

I winced. "Oh, man!"

Lauren covered her mouth when she saw what she'd done. "I'm sorry."

Will stood there for a second then gracefully fell backwards onto the floor. Brandon and I rushed forward.

"Oh my God! Oh my God!" Lauren kept repeating. "I didn't mean to. I just - is he hurt?"

Will's mouth was wide open like he wanted to scream, but no sound emerged. Both hands were between his legs cupping his nuts.

"You wailed him in the nards!" Brandon cried, "Yeah, he's hurt! Will? Will!"

Will couldn't respond.

"Can it hurt that bad?" Lauren asked.

Brandon and I both scoffed. That comment was dumber than Scrubs. There was nothing more painful than getting hit in the balls. It was like the worst side stitch spreading through your body accompanied by sickening nausea. I got hit in the balls during a basketball game and couldn't walk for half an hour. And that wasn't a direct hit. Will must be in a living hell right now. I was just glad it wasn't me. Real glad.

"He shouldn't have scared me like that," Lauren said hotly.

"He didn't deserve this." Brandon pointed to Will's limp form.

The Rover appeared. "Bed check!"

People came out of their rooms.

"I have to go," Lauren said. "Tell him I'm sorry." She ran off.

I looked down at Will.

"Fuck." He was twitching like he was having a seizure.

"What's happening here?" the Rover asked.

I wasn't sure I wanted to be involved with this, in case there was an Ethics Report, so I let Brandon answer.

"He jumped out to scare this girl, but she wailed him in the nuts."

"Ah!" the Rover shuddered. "Can he walk?"

I pushed Will with my foot.

"I don't think so."

The Rover unlocked Will's door.

"Bring him in here." Brandon and I picked Will up under the arms and dragged him into his room. Will was completely limp, his legs dragging on the floor. The only thing Will seemed conscious of was that he was still grasping his crotch.

We dumped him on the bed.

"So, what do we do?" I asked.

"Nothing," Brandon said and walked out. I guess he was right. There was nothing to do. Will would come around when the pain went away. I pulled off Will's shoes and set them in their designated place in the closet. Seemed the least I could do. Before I left I noticed the other empty bed in the room. Stan's empty bed. I'd almost forgotten about him, almost. But I wouldn't forget. Lamia wouldn't win that one. I closed Will's door behind me.

"Do you know what happened to Will?" I asked Fat Rob, closing the door to our room. Cold air enveloped me but I'd come to expect this. "He got totally nailed in the - What the hell is this!?" Rob was walking around the room with a notebook.

"They have names, Leif Thief. This one's Adam and this is Sean."

"What the fuck is this!" The room was swarming with bugs. Moths, crickets and even a few praying mantises.

Fat Rob smiled.

"These are my new pets. I left the window open and kept the light on."

"Get them out!"

"Are you afraid of bugs, Leif Thief?"

"No! But I don't want fucking bugs in my room!"

"If you're not afraid, what's the problem? They are my pets."

Son of a bitch! I started swatting the air. There had to be at least 50 creatures flying around or crawling on the walls.

"Don't you like my pets?"

What the hell was wrong with him? My swatting wasn't helping to get rid of the bugs.

"Isn't she pretty?" Rob asked walking over to a particularly large moth on the wall. "This one is Sara. I named her after my mom."

"Why? Why are you doing this?"

"I wanted some pets," Rob grinned. "Why do you think this has anything to do with you?"

My stomach boiled. I wanted to scream, but I knew it wouldn't do any good. Even if I did complain to the Resident Director or the Ethics Lady, it wouldn't help. All Fat Rob had to say was that he accidentally left the window open with the lights on. The Resident Director would never give me bug spray, or anything remotely flammable, and I was not voluntarily going up to the tower. With my record and Fat Rob's mom being a Supervisor, they'd believe him no matter what I said.

I crawled into bed, but not before checking under the covers for some crawly thing. Then I pulled the sheet over my head. I could hear flapping and buzzing just on the other side of the thin cloth.

It got even worse when Fat Rob's radio alarm went off at 6:00 AM, but instead of beeping it played that Foxworthy CD.

"*If you think Madonna's 'Like a Virgin' should be sung at church, you might be a Redneck.*"

FUCKING ASSHOLE!

My new bug roommates and the fat old one were all I could complain about the next day at breakfast.

"That's fucked up," Nick said after I was done ranting. "You don't look so good."

"I'm really tired. I couldn't sleep. It's the worst feeling waking up to something crawling on your face. Like *Wrath of Kahn* where they put those things in your ears."

Nick winced.

"Dude. Why don't you just ask for another roommate?"

"You can do that?" The thought had never occurred to me. "Pshaw."

That sounded like a great idea. I couldn't stand living with that fat, smelly dickhead anymore. But what if I got somebody worse? Like leaving Kamuela for Lamia. I didn't know how it could get worse, but things always seemed to around here.

"Thanks, but I'll just stick it out." I felt that if I ran away from that room, it would be like conceding defeat. I would never give Lamia a victory. I would stand my ground and fight to the end.

Later, I was admiring Katrina in class when Connie returned an essay of mine with an 'F' written on top.

"This paper is unacceptable," Connie stated.

I scanned the page, but couldn't find any red pen marks indicating spelling or punctuation errors.

"What's wrong with it?"

"It has no mass."

"What?"

"It has no mass."

The paper was about the history and use of TNT. I knew all about it.

"Yes, it does. TNT was first used in artillery shells in World War I. It's made of methylbenzene and sulfuric acid. This one web site was-"

"Web site? So you've never seen it?"

"Ah, TNT? Like, in front of me? No. But I met this guy who-"

"Listening to someone talk about it or reading a web site does not give it mass. You can only understand something if it's real in your mind."

What the hell was she talking about?

"But what about my other papers? You never had any problem with them."

"I was being lenient with you because you were new, but you've been at Lamia for almost eight months now. No more bombs, and no more diseases. You are only to write about things that actually have substance in your mind. And no more papers on surfing. Is that clear?"

"But it's what I like."

"I'm going to allow you to rewrite this paper with a more appropriate subject."

"But-"

"Do you want to rewrite every paper you've ever turned in?"

"Come on!"

"Is this a problem that Ethics has to deal with?"

I felt a tingling in my gut. This was so unfair. I swallowed the fire building up.

"No."

"Good. Why don't you write about the dangers of drugs. You have mass on that. Now, chop-chop." She turned and walked back to her desk.

Oh, so their books and doctrines had mass, but nothing

else did. Son of a bitch! I hate this fucking place. I turned back to look at Katrina. Well, I didn't hate it completely. God, she was beautiful.

The burning in my stomach began to fade. I crumpled up my TNT essay. I patted the pocket which held my reminder. "Go along with it until you don't have to." I pulled out a fresh sheet of paper and began to write.

I really didn't want to go on the Virus Wars trip, but I was part of the club and I was committed. The problem was I couldn't get my virus off the computer. None of my floppies would copy and the Supervisor didn't have any spares.

"Goddamn it!" I said, slamming the door to my room. I didn't notice that Fat Rob was there.

"What is it, Leif Thief?"

I didn't want to talk to him, but couldn't help complaining.

"My disks won't work in the IBMs."

"Told you Macs suck."

I sat down at my desk trying to think of something. I'd already asked William and Curtis but neither had an extra. What the hell was I going to do?

"I have a disk," Rob said.

I turned and looked at him.

"Really?"

Rob reached into his desk and pulled out a floppy. "I'll copy it for you and get you the disk before we go."

Why was Rob being nice to me? There had to be some ulterior motive for wanting me to compete with my virus. He probably knew my program was shit and wanted to see me embarrassed in Jackskeep when I ran my virus against the super nerds. That was it. Sorry, Fat Rob, not going to work this time because I don't care if I lose.

We left early Saturday morning for Jackskeep. It was a crappy convention. There were only five other kids there besides us. The Supervisor had told us there would be at least 50, but it seemed there weren't that many uber geeks in the Northwest.

The others battled their programs and soon it was my turn. This other kid loaded his disk into the computer then I loaded mine. The screen flashed *Disk Error*. What? I called the guy over who was heading up the competition. He had thick glasses and a pinched nasal voice. He sounded like a white version of Steve Urkel. He came over and typed a few commands.

"I'm sorry," he said, "Your disk won't work here."

"Why?"

He pushed up his glasses.

"Bad disk. Do you have another?"

"No."

He marked something down on a clipboard. "I'm afraid you're disqualified. Next up!"

Disqualified? How could-? I looked at Fat Rob. He was smiling at me. Rob had never copied my program. He'd just given me a broken disk. The Motherfucker! My stomach burst into flames. I took a deep breath and tried to calm it. "Just relax, Leif. You don't really give a shit anyway."

The Supervisor came up to me.

"What happened?"

"My disk was screwed up." I was still glaring at Fat Rob.

"Coming here is like a final exam for our club. I'm afraid I'll have to give you a fail on this."

What was he talking about?

"I thought this was just a fun thing. Extra-curricular whatever."

"It takes the place of a study hall so counts as an outside course like art or gym. I'm afraid you'll have to retake this again next year."

What? You never said - I began to shake with rage. The bees were back in my stomach, stinging with an increased ferocity. I saw a freshly sharpened pencil on the desk. I picked it up. I wanted to jam it up the Supervisors nose like in *Total Recall*. Let's see him retake that, fucker!

No. It wasn't the Supervisors fault. It was Fat Rob's. He wasn't looking at me, but he still had a smirk on his face. My insides were on fire. He'd known it was a bad disk and now I had to do this stupid club thing all over again. The stinging spread up into my throat. This was the last straw. My decision was clear and with no ambiguity. Fat Rob had to die.

During the whole return trip I was silently seething. We got back to Lamia in the early evening. I immediately went to the third floor and crept over to the Science Room. I checked the handle. It was unlocked. I opened it up.

"Hello?" Nobody was there. Stupid to keep this place

open. I closed the door and locked it.

I found two small glass beakers and moved them into holders. I put on some heavy gloves and took the nitric acid and the hydrogen peroxide off the shelf. I would pour them into the vials, tape them together, and wedge them in between the springs of his bed. When he sat his fat ass down, BOOM! No more riddles, no more smell, and no more Fat Rob. Hopefully the blast would kill all the remaining bugs. I just had to make sure I wasn't in there when it went off. I was a minor so couldn't go to jail and I'd most assuredly be expelled. Good. Fuck Lamia and fuck Rob!

I opened the container of nitric acid and gingerly poured it into a vial. I did the same with the peroxide. I screwed the two lids on and used electrical tape to hold the bomb together. I was done. My own personal grenade.

I giggled with excitement. My first bomb. I'd actually built one! It was beautiful. I couldn't wait to see Rob's charred guts splattered on Lamia's walls. Too bad it wouldn't hurt. Maybe it would only rip his limbs off and he would be crippled for life. Oh, I was just too fucking good!

I picked up the bomb to look at it. The days last light glinted and refracted off the exposed glass almost like metal. I suddenly thought of the metal of my drawing compass and all the terrified faces of my 6th grade classmates. Odi wasn't by my side but standing with them. The same look of fear etched onto his face.

I looked back down at the device I'd just created. What

was I doing? This was a bomb. A bomb! I laughed aloud. I was about to kill somebody. Jesus Christ!

I found a cubbyhole with a model of a suspension bridge inside. A thick layer of dust indicated it hadn't been used in a long time. I carefully placed the bomb at the far back. What if the bomb had gone off in my hands or while I was trying to place it? I hated Fat Rob more than anybody besides the Ethics Lady, but I didn't want to kill him. I didn't want to kill anybody. I'm not a bad person. I'm not.

I put the chemicals back in their places and left the Science Room. My stomach was still hot. I needed to calm myself. "Just think about surfing, Leif. Think about a cool Hawaiian breeze and a kick ass set."

The stinging slowly lessened. I was out in the water, a board beneath me and a wave behind me. The bees were gone. I'd almost lost my temper again. Jesus Christ.

I wouldn't kill him but I was going to get back at Fat Rob. Something that would piss him off as much as he pissed me off and keep him from doing anything to me for the rest of the time I was here. I wanted to get him sent to isolation or the Trash Room. I wanted him to know I'd done it. I wasn't sure how, but I'd put all my brainpower into figuring it out. It was Fat Rob's turn now.

CHAPTER XXVI
The Door and the Window

Finding something on Fat Rob turned out to be much harder than I imagined. I'd always done my best to ignore him but as my investigation into his personal life progressed, I was becoming more and more discouraged.

He'd been here since he was six. This was the only school he'd ever attended. He'd never been late or missed a class. Not only that, he'd always finished his courses on time if not early. He'd never skipped or welched on work detail. He was a member of the student council, a fact that surprised me because I didn't know there was one, and worst of all, he'd never been sent to Ethics.

To any authority figure he was the model Lamia student, or any student for that matter. He was one of those kids adults are always telling you to be more like. Only I seemed to know who Rob truly was. Finding a way to bring him down didn't seemed possible. Maybe that's why he fucked with me. He knew he could do anything he wanted and never get in trouble. The only thing I could do in the mean time was keep the gears of my mind in idle and wait for an opportunity to hit the gas.

An announcement was made that the school would need to undergo a thorough cleaning. Not only the inside, but every acre needed to be mowed, trimmed or raked. Connie cancelled my weekend trips to Jackskeep for the rest of April so I could help.

One Sunday morning, I was assigned to the left wing. Even though this was the girls' side, the top floor of their dorm had been under construction since the beginning of the year, so nobody lived there. I knew it would be dirty and dusty. Even with it being cloudy and cold, I'd rather be outside than in there.

"These boards need to go to the third floor," the Supervisor told me.

I looked at the pile of wood. There had to be dozens of four foot by two foot particle boards in the truck. I picked one up and faltered under its weight. It was really heavy. I grabbed it as best I could and shuffled inside.

There was no elevator. I had to drag the particle boards up three flights of stairs. By the seventh board my left arm was starting to ache. This had happened before. After I broke my wrist, my left arm could only take so much before it completely gave out and was useless for the rest of the day. Soon I wouldn't even be able to pick up a pencil.

I was sweating and my palms were burning from the

rough edges of the wood. The other guys with me were all Form Seven and Eight. They probably picked me for this because I looked older than I was.

By the tenth board, my left arm was on fire. I couldn't fucking carry these things. When I made it to the top, I moved out of the way to catch my breath. I leaned against a support and looked around. There were cables dangling from the ceiling. All that was left of the walls were wooden frames.

There were kids up here wiring outlets and stapling carpets. This was not work for students. We should be studying normal things and having fun on our weekends. This was exploitation. If only our parents really knew.

"We need some music up here," I heard a boy say. A second later some rap song was filling the third floor. I think it was called 'No Diggity, No Doubt,' but who knows with these rap songs.

Cradling my arm, I walked into the room where the music was playing. A girl was washing windows and a skinny haole kid was rapping along to a boom box plugged into the wall. The kid could not dance at all. He turned to me.

"I like this low piano part here." He made a motion like he was playing the piano. I couldn't help but smile. He looked like a complete goof. What the hell was a *diggity*?

"What are you doing, Leif?" I heard somebody call out. I turned to see the Supervisor approaching. Great.

"You were supposed to be helping with the construction, not standing around listening to music."

"I can't do it anymore," I said holding up my arm, "I broke my wrist a few years ago and I can't lift heavy things."

The Supervisor looked skeptical.

I knew it would hurt, but I had to show them. I grabbed my left hand with my right and gave a sharp yank. The arm made a loud crack as I dislocated my wrist. Fuck, that sucked. The Supervisor stared at the sunken space where my wrist should be.

I held my arm up to his face.

"You see."

The Supervisor pulled away.

"Fine. We'll find something else for you."

I popped it back in as he led me downstairs. We made our way to the chapel. There was a large ladder resting on the floor. It was very long and went from the door almost to the piano. Sitting on a pew was Big Jae. A young Supervisor I'd never seen before, with short brown hair and intense blue eyes, was trying to throw a rope over one of the rafters.

"We found another guy for you." The construction Supervisor called out.

"Thanks," the young one said turning his attention back to the rope.

I went over and sat with Big Jae. The shoving incident was a long time ago and, after all I'd been through, I wasn't scared of him anymore.

"What are we doing?" I asked Big Jae.

"He changing light bulb. We hold ladder."

Holding the ladder? I didn't want to, but I had to work

somewhere.

"I've almost got it… there!" the Supervisor called as the rope flew over the rafter and fell back to the ground.

"Dude, not bad," I said.

"Thanks. What's your name?"

"Leif."

"I'm Andrew. Let's do this."

Andrew tied the rope to the ladder and we pulled it up until the top was resting against the beam. The ladder wobbled up its length. It had to be at least 60 feet tall.

Big Jae and I held the base of the ladder while Andrew climbed. It was hard to keep it steady, but not as hard as hauling those particle boards up the stairs. After Andrew changed the bulb he'd slowly climb down and we'd shift the ladder over for the next light.

Most of my attention was focused on the base of the ladder, fighting to keep both its feet on the ground but sometimes I stole a glance upwards. Man, he was high up! I wasn't afraid of heights, but I would never risk my life for this place.

Andrew was just about to get the fourth bulb when I heard a shout from the chapel entrance. I turned. The Ethics Lady was charging toward me.

"Leif! What are you doing?"

Sweat was beading my forehead from the physical effort. This was not the time for questions.

"Holding the ladder," I said between my teeth.

"Let go!"

"What?"

"You are not allowed to do jobs like this! You're accident prone! Let go!" She grabbed my shirt and yanked me away.

Big Jae cried out as the base of the ladder wobbled away from him.

"Hold it!" Andrew called.

"No can hold!"

"Get off me!" I cried trying to get out of her grasp, but she held fast.

Andrew rushed down the ladder as quickly as he could. He was about 10 feet up when the top of the ladder came off the beam. The rope couldn't hold the weight and the ladder slipped sideways. Andrew jumped and landed hard on the concrete, knocking his head into a pew. I could only stand there and watch as the massive ladder fell away.

It was almost graceful until it landed on the piano. There was a loud bang as the top broke in half under the impact and the front leg collapsed. The piano slammed to the ground, all the notes ringing at once. The ladder clanged to a rest on the floor. The ringing notes faded away into the walls. The chapel was completely silent. I just stared. No. My piano was gone. No!

Andrew got to his feet rubbing his head. He looked at the devastation then back at us.

"What are you doing?" he asked the Ethics Lady.

"He's accident prone," the Ethics Lady said still holding my shirt. "He can't be doing dangerous jobs like this. Look what happened."

Andrew looked incredulous.

"I was up there! Why didn't you just wait for me to get down?"

My eyes hadn't left the remains of my piano.

"You destroyed my piano!"

Fire burned inside me like my blood was gasoline. I was going to kill her! I didn't have a weapon. Maybe if I slammed my palm up at her nose I could shove a jagged piece of skull into her brain.

"You broke piano," Big Jae said to the Ethics Lady.

"Shut your mouth, Gook, or you'll be in the Trash Room for a week."

Big Jae cringed away.

"You shut up!" I yelled. I didn't care anymore. She was fucking crazy! "You did this, not me. You're the one whose accident prone you crazy bitch!"

"That's it, Csuba," she said, grabbing my arm like a vice. "You broke the piano, almost killed a Supervisor and disobeyed my explicit orders. You will be removed from your room to Isolation and you'll have double shifts in the Trash Room for the rest of your school life!"

My insides swarmed. I was in a perfect position for the kill. I made a fist and drew back my arm for the upward strike. I was finally going to make her and that stinging feeling go away.

"You will not do that," Andrew said to the Ethics Lady. The remark caught me off balance and stayed my arm. I turned and looked at him. So did she.

"Excuse me?"

He walked up to her.

"He did nothing wrong. I will inform the faculty what really happened here."

"This boy is a violent delinquent. This is the only way to turn him into a fruitful adult."

"There will be three of us with a different story."

I locked eyes with Andrew. He wanted to help me. Why? No Supervisor had ever helped me. Maybe he could tell what I wanted to do to her. I still wanted to kill her, but Andrew was going out on a limb for me, a limb with an Everest drop beneath it. Andrew's deep blue eyes seemed to plead for my help. I couldn't let him down. I let my arm fall to my side and looked at Big Jae. He looked from me to Andrew.

"It you fault!" Jae finally said, pointing at the Ethics Lady.

She looked at both of them, then at me. I could see my own hatred mirrored in her eyes, but I was not scared and she could see it. Without fear she had no power. She was just a fat, ugly, bitch.

She broke my gaze and looked at Andrew.

"This was an accident. The ladder slipped. It was lucky you got down in time."

"Yes," he said flatly, "The ladder slipped."

Big Jae nodded. Andrew looked at me. For now, it had to be this way.

"Yes. It was an accident," I said.

"I'll find you somebody else to hold the ladder."

The Ethics Lady dragged me out of there and toward the cafeteria.

"So, will I still become a fruitful adult?"

She said nothing. Her face was like stone. It felt good knowing she'd lost control, even if it was momentary. A Supervisor had stood by me and had challenged the Ethics Lady. Who the hell was that guy?

She marched me into the kitchen and over to a Supervisor.

"Do you have any strong boys?"

"I think so."

"I need that boy for another job."

"Clint!" the Supervisor called out. Clint put down the spray hose and came forward. "New job for you."

"Do you have anyone on the boilers?" she asked.

The Supervisor shook his head.

"Use him."

The Ethics Lady let go of my arm. She gave me one last glare then walked off with Clint. A plastic crate of vegetables was in her way. She kicked it under the closest counter and stomped out through the swinging doors. The crate slammed into the wall and an onion rolled out onto the floor. I remembered she'd always kicked the drawers shut in her office. She must have some weird tick about kicking things.

I looked at the vats. They were filled with baked beans and foul smelling jambalaya. Her parting shot. My stomach began to burn again. Even though I was not in the Trash Room, like she wanted, I hadn't won.

My piano was destroyed. Despair mixed with the anger.

Like sand, it seemed to find the cracks and rub the already bruised areas raw. My piano was gone. I'd never play it again. I wish I could have heard 'Katrina's Theme,' one last time.

By the time I was done with the vats my anger had subsided, but the sadness remained. I tried to find Andrew, to thank him, but I couldn't. Nobody seemed to know who he was. People just shrugged when I asked. Like Stan, it was as though he'd never existed. Even Big Jae had no idea. Fucking Ethics lady! Fucking Lamia! I hated this Godforsaken place! I needed to be around friends.

Nick was not alone in his room. Derk was there. I would have preferred to show just Nick, but Derk was still technically part of the posse.

Nick, Derk and I stood in the chapel looking at the devastation.

"You were right, Leif," Nick said looking at the remnants of the piano.

"Ah, I wish I could have seen it!" Derk said smiling.

I walked over to the broken piano. Wood fragments scattered the floor nearby. I reached down and picked one up. It was wood grain on one side and glossy black on the other. I could see a distorted reflection of myself.

"Son of a bitch."

"So the ladder just fell?" Nick asked. I wanted to tell him the truth, but knew I couldn't. It would only make the situation worse than it was.

"Yeah. Right on the piano."

"Too bad the Ethics lady wasn't here and it didn't, like, fall on her."

I almost smiled.

"Too bad."

"NEEEER KABOW!" Derk's sound effects traced the path of the ladder with his hands as accompaniment. "I guess you're not the Piano Man anymore, Scuba-Doo."

"Shut up."

Derk laughed and slapped me hard on the back. I guess seeing something I loved destroyed was payment enough for Derk to forgive me.

"So what are you going to, like, do with your spare time?" Nick asked.

I shrugged. I didn't know. I'd never imagined my piano being gone. The more I thought about it the more the despair began to replace the anger. My piano was gone.

"I know," Derk said, "You can get some other hand motion in. Get it?" He cackled and moved his right hand back and forth.

I hadn't masturbated in almost a month. This thought only made me feel worse.

"Sounds good, Derk. Anybody going to be in your room around 9:00?"

Nick laughed.

"Hey! I'll fuck you up!"

I looked back at my ruined piano. I took a sharp breath. I was not going to cry. Not here. I thought of the movie *NeverEnding Story*. If you lost hope walking across the

Swamps of Sadness, you'd sink and disappear. I knew I'd sink before my second step, but there was a silver lining. I'd seen something no kid at Lamia had ever seen. I'd seen the Ethics Lady lose all her power, but my piano was the price.

"Dude," Nick began, "I just got a new CD. *The Verve.* There's this kick ass song called 'Bittersweet Symphony.' It has strings. I think you'll like it, Leif."

"I don't feel like it."

"*The Verve* are fucking pussies!" Derk interjected. "You'll never get a chick to suck your cock listening to that shit."

"You're one to talk, Derk," Nick responded. "You like Madonna."

"Shut up! I'll fuck you up!"

I couldn't help smiling. I never would have guessed that Derk liked Madonna. I thought of Fat Rob's stupid radio CD player and that Foxworthy shit. I'd rather listen to 'Like a Virgin' for the rest of my life than one more of his Redneck jokes!

Then it hit me like a crashing wave. The Radio! I knew how to get back at Fat Rob. It was so easy! I went over it quickly in my mind. It would work! I'd have to go someplace I didn't want to go, but it was the only way.

"I'll find you guys later!" I said and rushed out of the chapel. My insides were tingling with excitement. This was it. The payback for all the shit he'd done to me. You fucked with the wrong guy, Fat Rob. I made my way up to the Ethics Office.

When I was done in the tower, I came back down to the room and sat at my computer. Fat Rob was reading his dumb books again. I could hear him whispering lessons to the wall.

The plan was set. I quivered with anticipation. I just had to wait for them to come. They never took long.

As if on cue, there was a knock on the door.

"Could you get that, please?" I asked.

I heard Fat Rob get out of his seat. I pretended to be typing on my computer, but all my attention was on the sounds from the door. I heard it open.

"Mom?" Rob asked surprised. "What are you-" then his voice trailed off.

I couldn't hold back, I had to look. There was Rob's mom. She was skinny with dirty blonde hair and dark rimmed glasses. Standing next to her was the Ethics Lady. She stomped past them both and picked up Fat Rob's CD playing alarm clock.

"Is this yours?"

She held it up.

"Yeah?" Rob said, completely confused.

"Why did you bring that up here?" his mom said in a whisper.

The Ethics Lady flipped a switch. A male voice came out of the alarm.

"*...the first burial in space occurred when a Pegasus rocket carried the remains of 24-*"

The Ethics lady yanked the plug out of the wall, abruptly cutting off the broadcast.

Rob's face went pale. He'd brought that thing to torture me with crappy CDs. He probably never even noticed the A.M. radio receiver. Since he'd always gone to Lamia he'd probably never filled out the admission papers, which clearly stated that students weren't allowed to have radios under any circumstance.

"I would have told you sooner," I said innocently to the Ethics Lady, "But I didn't know it had a radio until I heard him listening to it today."

"But," Rob began, "Mom, please-"

"No talking," the Ethics Lady said, cutting him off, "You know the rules. Radios are strictly forbidden. I assume you bought this for him, Sara?"

"Yes. But I didn't know he had it here-"

"Silence. I want you in my office right now." She pointed her fleshy finger at Fat Rob.

"And for you, a Supervisor letting her son bring a radio into the dorms is unforgivable. You will be seriously dealt with. You are to come to my office tomorrow morning at 8:00. Is that clear?"

Sara was looking at the Ethics Lady's feet.

"Yes, ma'am."

Rob was glaring at me. I mouthed the words "Bye Bye."

The Ethics Lady wrapped the cord around the radio and bundled it under her arm. As she walked by Fat Rob's bed she wrinkled her nose.

"And wash your son's sheets. They smell filthy."

Rob's mom quickly collected the bed sheets and left,

pulling Fat Rob with her. The Ethics Lady and I were alone in my room. She looked at me for a long time.

"That was a good thing you did, Leif. I knew you could be a true student of Lamia if you wanted to be." And with that she left the room.

True student? Did they actually believe their own crap? These people were really fucked up. I leaned back and closed my eyes. I'd done it. It had been tough voluntarily walking into her office, especially after what happened in the chapel, but this victory completely made up for any discomfort.

I got up and went to my stereo. What music best fit this moment? The 4th moment of Beethoven's 5th would do nicely. I put the CD on and listened to the orchestral explosion. Perfect. What do the Klingons say? *"Revenge is a dish that is best served cold."*

I'd used the system here again. I regretted the first time when I'd gotten Jude sent to Ethics. I knew I'd never regret this. There was one last thing I had to do. According to the rules, it was my duty to spread this story around to make an example. Under normal circumstances I would never do anything of the kind, but Fat Rob deserved everything the system he loved so much had to offer.

I didn't feel like running around the school telling everybody I met. I wanted to be with Nick and, well, I guess Derk, to enjoy the victory. I'd tell Little James. He'd be glad to wander the halls passing the news. It would give him a chance to redeem himself a little. It was their system, let them wallow in their own fucking misery.

CHAPTER XXVII
Stalker

It was almost May and I was running out of time to get the necklace to Katrina. I finally came up with a solution. To get to the cafeteria or the Rec Room, you had to walk through the lobby. I'd wait down there for an hour after soccer on the off chance she'd come by alone. Then I'd give it to her. I'd been trying this strategy for about a week now with no success.

On the upside, Fat Rob's punishment was the irreparable tarnishing of his perfect record and an extra scullery chore for two weeks. I would have preferred the Trash Room, but scullery had been his chore last year and I remember he said he hated it. The Ethics Lady must have known, too. I'm not sure what happened to his mom, but I didn't care. Fat Rob stopped talking to me and I gladly reciprocated.

No more redneck jokes, no more smell, and no more talking. I never would have thought two people who hated each other could be the perfect roommates. It was as though we were invisible to each other. There were still bugs in the room, but they were slowly dying off. I piled all the carcasses on his dumb books.

"Can I ask you something?" Nick said one night in his room. "What's your best day?"

"Huh? What do you mean?"

"You're really into the dark side of life. You're always asking what's the worst thing you've, like, ever seen or talking about bad experiences, but you never talked about the things you like. What's the best day you've ever had?"

Was I really that negative? Never thought about it.

"Sorry."

"Nah, man. That's what makes you, you."

Great. I'm turning into Istvan. No way in hell. I can talk about good things.

"Okay. I know what my best day was. It was two years ago in Hawaii."

In the end of January, our school took an overnight field trip to Kiholo, a small bay on the west coast. We were supposed to do all these scientific measurements on rocks and trees and count how many turtles we could spot, but the teacher forgot his equipment, so we did nothing.

Odi and I went exploring. We found Hawaiian petroglyphs under some kiawe trees. It was the fun of school without the stupid work. That evening I was hanging out with this one girl, when she asked me straight up if I wanted to be her boyfriend. I'd never had a girlfriend before so I said yes.

The next morning Odi woke me up at 6:30. I grabbed my

board and we went looking for waves. I was used to shore break, but this area had a small reef so the waves were much easier to ride.

The waves were three foot backs, but the wind was off shore, which kicked up the faces. There were already a couple of kids from school out there. Odi stayed closer in, but I went out really far and waited for a macking set. When a big one did come I was in perfect position. I took off and turned left. Just then a gust of wind hit and the wave barreled. I crouched down and was in the tube. The water was falling over my right arm like a cool waterfall. That moment seemed to last forever. Just the sound of the water and the wind rushing past my ears. Then I was out. When the crashing noise of the wave faded, I heard yelling. I looked over and Odi was cheering for me.

"Tube, Brah! Tube!"

"I caught a tube!" It was my first and it was everything I'd ever hoped it would be. I heard more yells and noticed the other kids were cheering for me, too. No kid other than Odi liked me, but they were cheering for me.

Just then the sun came up over the flank of Mauna Kea catching the mist from the crashing waves. The air around me glowed like gold. The breeze was so cool on my face. I'd caught a tube, had a girlfriend, and my classmates were cheering for me. I knew, even then, that this was the best moment of my life.

"Wow, man," Nick said when I was done, "That's pretty sweet."

Yes, it was. I'd forgotten about it until now. While telling the story I almost felt like I wasn't at Lamia. I wished I could relive that time in my life. Not to change, just to do it again.

"What about you, Nick? What's your best day?"

"The day you told me about *Clockwork Orange*."

I laughed.

"Come on. What's it really?"

"No, that's it. Nothing has ever changed my life like that movie."

"Really? But it's so fucked up."

Nick's face got serious.

"Dude. Your favorite movie is *Stand By Me*, right?"

"Yeah?"

"Why?"

"I don't know. It's just, those kids were my heroes, even when I was four years old. I wanted them to be my friends. I even styled my hair like Gordy."

"It's the same for me and Alex DeLarge."

"Why? He so, gone and you're-?" Nothing like that psycho.

"But *Stand By Me*? Those kids smoked, swore all the time, stole, and lied to their parents. They were, like, not the best kids, man."

"I'd never thought about that." Pretty strange idols.

"You may not get it, but I see parts of Alex I like. I want to be like him. Just like you and those kids."

I don't exactly know how, but Nick made sense. I felt bad for dissing his movie. Especially after what the Ethics Lady had done to it.

"Sorry, man."

"Dude, don't be. I wouldn't have known about it if it wasn't for you."

After Odi, Nick was the only true friend I'd ever had. There were so many things I wanted to say to him at that moment but didn't know how. I put my hand on his shoulder.

"Thanks, man."

It was now my second week of waiting for Katrina. I stood off to the side near the entrance to the chapel so people wouldn't keep asking me what I was doing. Nick wanted to know where I was, but I told him I was busy. Talking about girls made me feel uncomfortable.

I had the necklace in my pocket and was ready if I saw her. It was tense waiting for her, but this was going to work. I was sure.

I'd hand it to her and she'd be surprised, maybe even a bit startled, but then she'd smile and say how sweet it was. Then we'd start going out. We could keep in touch over the summer. Then next fall we'd be together and everything would be perfect because she was perfect.

I was waiting in the doorway of the chapel working out what I was going to say when I saw her. Oh, shit! Katrina was walking across the lobby. She was wearing jeans and a tight white T-shirt. She was so gorgeous! My heart began to jackhammer in my chest. I have to do this. I have to do this, now! I took a few quick breaths. This was it. One last try. I was just about to walk out when one of her friends approached from the other direction. I stopped. They were talking. Then Scottish Jason appeared and joined the group.

Damn! I slipped back into the chapel, looking out from around the door. My heart was still pounding. Maybe they would leave and I'd get my chance. I waited, but they kept talking. Go away! I just want to give her the necklace!

I saw Jason glance in my direction. I ducked my head back and held my breath. When I peeked around again they were all looking at me. Oh, Shit! Shit! I quickly moved out of sight. Without a piano I couldn't fake a reason to be in the chapel. Shit! I hid behind a pew. I felt embarrassed and guilty. Stupid! Dumber than Scrubs!

After an intolerable wait I got up and checked outside. The lobby was empty. Good. I'd try again tomorrow. I reached into my pocket for the necklace. Its pale silvery surface gleamed in the defused light breaching the high windows. Once she had it in her hand she had to like me, even after this. I just knew it.

I had the necklace in my pocket the next day on my way to soccer so I could go straight to the lobby when the game was over. It was just like any other day, cloudy with a bit of rain. I told Nick about mayonnaise bombs on our way to the game.

"All you need to do is seal it in a jar and heat it to over 500 degrees, like in a fire. BOOM!"

"Awesome!"

"Just don't stand too close."

"Leif!" Scottish Jason called to me from behind, "I have some goalie tricks for you." He motioned for me to come.

"I'll see you out there, Nick-meister." I ran back. Jason was a master player. Any tip from him was gold. I went through the door. Smelly Dylan and Ugly Edward were waiting with Jason.

"What's up, man?"

Dylan and Edward grabbed my arms and shoved me back against the wall.

"What the hell?!" Jason put his hand over my mouth and slammed the back of my skull into the wall. I felt pain radiate out through my whole head. It wasn't as bad as my concussion, but it was close.

"Shut up," Jason said calmly. I struggled, but my arms were held fast. The proximity to Dylan's stench was overpowering. Jason took his hand off my mouth. What the hell had I done?

"I saw you stalking Katrina," he said menacingly.

"What?" I went cold inside. This was the last thing I'd expected him to say.

"Don't lie." The others squeezed my arms tighter. "I saw you spying on her. Katrina is scared of you."

Scared? I wasn't stalking her. I wanted to give her a necklace, but it was none of their business.

"I wasn't spying! I was - waiting for somebody. I had to give-"

"Bullshite!" Jason shoved my head back into the wall

again. He squeezed my cheeks hard.

"If you don't stop following her and staring at her in class, she'll sue you for sexual harassment. But first, you'll be sent to the Trash Room."

Jason leaned in closer.

"She doesn't like you. Nobody will ever like you. Do you understand?"

Jason brought his knee up into my balls. Crushing pain gripped my stomach and I felt puke surge up my throat. Dylan and Edward pushed me to the floor. Jason then gave me a kick in the ribs. My diaphragm locked up. I couldn't breathe. I couldn't breathe! I heard the door swing shut.

I was going to suffocate! After what seemed like a lifetime, I finally pulled some air in. I lay there doubled up. I was too stunned and in too much pain to do anything. I was shaking all over.

Just then a kid came downstairs. He gave me a funny look, then jumped over me and walked out the door. I had to get out of the way. I crawled out of the door and onto the grass.

When I moved, the pain only seemed to magnify. My stomach was heaving. I couldn't hold it. I threw up on the grass. The rancid taste of vomit clung to my tongue like old milk. I gasped several times. Finally, my breath slowed down and my trembling stopped. As long as I didn't move, the pain wasn't unbearable. Slowly, I began to comprehend what had just happened.

Sexual harassment? I'd barely spoken to her. I'd never

even touched her. I wasn't stalking her. I just wanted to give her a gift, a white gold necklace. Then Jason's last words bloomed in my mind like a grotesque flower. *"She doesn't like you. Nobody will ever like you."*

The fear and pain I felt began to fade away. A deep sadness draped over me, like a cold wet blanket. My heart began to ache like never before. Katrina didn't like me. She never did. It was over. There was no hope.

Like an ice sculpture shot by a rifle, the perfect image I had of Katrina shattered and fell to the ground, its thousands of shards cutting me to ribbons. Nothing seemed real. Nothing made sense. *She doesn't like me.*

"Dude, you okay?" I looked up to see Nick standing over me. "Soccer is starting."

Soccer? Nick held out his hand. I took it and he pulled me up. I wobbled and he caught me.

"What happened?"

I tried to speak, but couldn't. What could I say?

Nick led me to the field. I watched my feet as I walked. One foot in front, then the next. Nothing mattered anymore. Nick was asking me what was wrong. I still couldn't talk.

I don't remember how the game went. Who cared? I just stood there in the defense area. The pain in my groin and ribs had migrated to my chest and head. It felt like I was splitting in two. *"Nobody will ever like you."*

Thoughts swirled around in my head like a backed up toilet after a crap. In the end, one question stuck and wouldn't go down. How could she do this? How could my

Katrina do this to me? My stomach began to burn. How could she?

The moment the end whistle blew I walked off the field. I had to get away from this place. Nick ran up to me and grabbed my arm.

"What happened, man?"

I had to get away.

"Let go."

"What's wrong, man?"

"LEAVE ME ALONE, YOU CRAZY FUCK!" I screamed, punching him as hard as I could. Nick stumbled away, clutching his chest where I'd struck. If he touched me again, I'd rip him to shreds. I glared at Nick, then turned and walked away. I reached into my pocket for the necklace. It pulled it out, but it was tangled with my reminder.

"God-fucking-damn it!"

I shoved the stupid reminder back into my pocket. The necklace didn't seem to shine like it had before. I entered the door that would take me down to the basement.

I stood at the entrance to the Trash Room. The furnace was raging. The smell and the buzzing of the flies were almost pleasant. I walked into the room. Roaches crunched under my sneakers like *The Temple of Doom*. I marched straight up to the furnace. The heat was intense. I could see the hairs on my arms curling and withering, but I didn't care. I shoved the necklace through the slats. The thin ribbon of silvery, pale metal disappeared into the crackling flames. I hoped it melted completely. Fuck you!

The bees began to swarm in my stomach, stinging every inch of my intestines. How could Katrina do this? It didn't make sense. Katrina would never do anything like getting that fuck to beat me up. It must have been Jason's idea. That had to be it. He must have convinced her to go along with it. He tricked her into thinking that I was the bad guy. Now there was nothing I could do or say to change her mind. Jason! The Motherfucker! My side still hurt every time I took a breath.

"Nobody will ever like you, Stalker."

Fuck you, Jason! I am not a stalker! The idea of revenge began to clot in my mind, blocking all other thoughts. As I left the Trash Room a plan for vengeance slowly began to take shape. I knew how to get back at him. It was high time I found out just how dumb George Scrubs really was.

There were only 10 days left until the end of the year. This was going to be my last week at Lamia. I'd make sure of it.

CHAPTER XXVIII
The Last Warrior

I ate breakfast alone. I brutally tore off pieces of toast with my teeth. I quickly glanced over at Katrina. She sat at a table with some of her friends and *Jason*.

"You'll get yours soon, fucker! I've already set your fate in motion."

Jason must have said something funny because Katrina started laughing. How did he convince her to go along with him? My jaw was clenched so hard my teeth ached. I hated this godforsaken place! My stomach burned so much I couldn't eat anymore.

I got up, leaving the rest of my toast on the plate. I was still hungry, but I didn't care. I couldn't be in the same room as they were. I hope she saw me leave. I wanted her to know what she'd done. I am not a stalker.

I went into the Phone Room to call home. It was early in Hawaii, but I had to do this now.

"Hello?" It was Istvan. Figured.

"Hey, Isht."

"I have a new joke for you."

I didn't feel like it, but he was already going.

"This guy's out fishing and a space capsule lands in the water nearby. It opens up and a marlin jumps out. The guy realizes this is an alien marlin. It swims up to him and says, 'take me to your leader.' Get it?"

I tried, but I didn't.

"Get it?" Istvan went on, "Let me put it to you this way: fishing leader on the end of the line?"

"Jesus Christ."

"Yuck! Yuck! Yuck! Yuck!" Isht laughed.

I couldn't help but smile. His jokes were always so lame. Other than sneaking into movies, fishing was the only real thing we did together. Aside from my nausea, it consisted of interminable hours of boredom punctuated by intense periods of screaming.

"Reel, goddamn it, reel! Keep the drag up, Leif! Guide the line, don't let it bunch! Pump with you legs! Don't lose it! Reel, goddamn it, reel!"

"Is Bec there?"

"She's still in bed, I think."

"I need to talk to her."

"The world doesn't revolve around you. People have other things to do than wait on you every moment of the day. Why can't you be more like Mercedes?"

I felt the stinging grow in my stomach.

"Can you see if she's up, please?"

I heard him put the phone down. While I waited I tried to calm myself. I needed to be clear for this.

"Hello, this is Rebecca."

"Hi."

"Hello, darling."

"Bec, there's something I have to tell you." I took a deep breath. "I don't want to come back to Lamia." By this point I didn't care if they were listening.

"Why? What happened?"

"I can't go into it. Not right now. Please. I want to leave. I can't stand it anymore."

"Tell me what happened."

"I can't. Please."

"It can't be that bad. You're doing so well. They tell me…"

"Bec-" I interrupted.

"You've read over 25 books," she kept talking. "I never would have imagined…"

"Rebecca-" She still wouldn't stop.

"You're doing it all by yourself without help. I can't-"

"*Mother, please!*" I cried. She stopped. I never called her "Mother" unless I meant it.

"Please help me. Please, Mom." The line was silent for a while. I waited for her to say something.

"You really want to leave?"

"Yes." I said it with as much conviction as I could muster. I waited for her response.

"Let me talk it over with Isht. Call me back later."

"I'll call you when classes are done."

"I love you."

I hung up and made my way to the fourth floor.

All during class I kept looking at the clock waiting for 4:00 to roll around. Every time I turned away from the clock it was as though time held still, waiting until I looked again.

I plodded ahead with my stupid courses. I was almost done with my last one for the year: *Learning Techniques for Adulthood.*

> *As alumni, it's your duty to send money*
> *to Lamia so future students may enjoy*
> *the same advantages you've received.*

Who wrote this shit? Obviously it was somebody who never went here. I almost laughed out loud when I read my next assignment. I had to give somebody a Method Three. After this I would be certified to give them at anytime. Just what I always wanted.

I asked somebody sitting in Form Six. I wasn't going to be an asshole like my first Method Three. I gave them an easy book, but not a fucking kiddy story and let them read. I asked them to define words I was sure they knew and in 15 minutes we were done. The kid knew I'd gone easy on him, but he still signed me off as being thorough. He didn't want to be taken away from work for three days either. Just like that, I'd given my first Method Three. I did not feel proud.

I returned to the Phone Room after classes.

"Hello?" It was Istvan again.

"It's Leif."

"I'm so disappointed in you. All that money wasted for nothing. Do you want to be a gas station attendant?"

My whole body shook with rage.

"I'm not -" I gritted my teeth. "Is Bec there?"

I heard him sigh. "I give up on you." He yelled for Rebecca. "Don't talk too long. I'm waiting for a call from a man who wants to charter my boat."

"Okay."

"Leif?" Rebecca asked as she got on the line.

"Yeah."

"Well, we talked it over for a while. I really wish I knew what was going on."

"I don't want to talk about it now."

"I take it you don't want to come back to school here either."

It was funny to think that I'd once thought Kamuela would be worse than this place. That didn't mean it still didn't suck.

"If there's no other option."

"All schools will be about the same. So here it is. Do you want to become a concert pianist?"

This question caught me off guard.

"I - I'm not sure."

"Well. You have two choices. You can continue with high school, graduate, and go to college like everyone else. Or, you can drop out of school and train to become a pianist.

That means spending at least the same amount of time each day practicing the piano that you would have spent in school studying and doing homework. It wouldn't be a vacation."

A concert pianist? I liked playing the piano. It seemed like a good alternative.

"But. There's a down side," Rebecca continued. "If you can't make it as a pianist you'll have no high school education. It will be very hard to get work and impossible to get into college."

I hadn't thought about that.

"I want you to consider it carefully. This is your choice. When you've made your decision, give me a call. It's good you called today."

"Why?"

"The school's been asking me to send next year's tuition. I was just about to send it off."

Jesus, that was good timing. Lamia had a "no tuition refund" policy. Why did they want the money so early? Then I finally understood. *The money.* Since my arrival, I'd been asking myself why Lamia was so screwed up. Why they made such a big deal about Tylenol, Cleared-Lists, Rovers and all that crazy shit. Now I knew. It had nothing to do with any of that, because that was *crazy.* They just wanted our money. They had to brainwash kids and their parents into believing their crap so we wouldn't realize the truth. That's why they had forced child labor, cheap kitchen equipment, made us eat rotting food, and all that other shit we had to pay for at this school. They wanted to keep as much money as possible for themselves. It was all about the money. How could a little thing like money be the cause and the solution to all of life's problems?

The familiar burning was building in my stomach. I felt the lump in my pocket where my reminder was. It wasn't over yet. I could still beat them. One way or another I'd get out of this godforsaken place.

A sob on the other end of the line startled me. Rebecca was probably disappointed in me, too.

"What?"

"Well. I wasn't sure I should tell you this, but I have to. I learned about it a few hours ago."

This was about something else. The hairs on my neck stood up.

"What?"

"I have some very bad news. I know it will be hard for you, but it's hard for me, too, being a mother." She took a deep breath. "Hector. Hector Wallas was killed yesterday."

Hector? Who the hell was - then I remembered. He never went by his first name. Something cold gripped my chest.

"Odi? Odi is dead?"

All other sounds in the room died away.

"I'm so sorry."

"What happened?"

"You know the waterfall about a mile from our house?"

"Yeah, by Buster Brown, where I broke my wrist."

"Yes. Well, Hector and a couple of kids climbed to the top to jump. He slipped on the rocks, knocked himself unconscious, and he fell off. The waterfall held him under. The other kids ran for help. They found his body downstream early this morning. His poor mother. I don't know what I'd do if I lost you or Mercedes."

Odi was dead? How could he be dead? He was back home like he always was. I'd received a letter from him. He worked at McDonalds. Dead?

"Are you okay, honey? He's been your best friend since preschool."

I heard Istvan talking in the background.

"Istvan needs me to get off. I'm so sorry, Leif."

"When did this happen again?"

"Yesterday afternoon around 1:00 or 2:00."

I was breathing hard. How could this happen?

"Call me anytime if you need to talk, Leif. I'm here. I love you, so much."

I hung up without another word and sat there for a long while. Odi was dead? It couldn't be. He was going to turn 15 in a couple of weeks. He'd never even left Hawaii. Dead? Why?

I made my way to the chapel. I needed to think and play the piano- oh, shit. The wreckage awaited me. I'd forgotten. I just wanted to play my music. Fucking Lamia. Fuck! I didn't know where to go. I left the chapel and stood in the lobby. I remembered the first day I'd walked through those doors. This place had filled me with so much hope. Now it was all gone.

I heard footsteps to my left. Even though I was surprised,

it wasn't unexpected. There was Scottish Jason being led by a Rover. His clothes were rumpled and his face was downcast. The Rover had a tissue in his hand and in the tissue was a blue condom.

On Jason's heels was another Rover. He was leading George Scrubs. He looked more confused than guilty. I almost smiled. My plan had worked perfectly.

After leaving the Trash Room, I'd gone to the cafeteria and found Scrubs. He sat alone at a table. His shaggy dog hair twitched every time he blinked. If he was half as dumb as the stories I'd heard, then my plan would most certainly work. I grabbed a tray, quickly dumped some food on it, and made my way towards him.

"Is anyone sitting here?" I asked him.

Scrubs looked at me then around at the empty seats.

"Not yet. My friends are coming."

I'd never seen anyone sit with him. To a "true" Lamia student, Scrubs was like Kryptonite.

"I'll only be a sec, I have some work to do." I sat down. I gave it about five seconds before I launched into my spiel.

"Man, you wouldn't believe what Edward told me."

"Who?"

"Edward, plays soccer a lot, upper schooler?"

"Oh, yeah," Scrubs nodded. He didn't know any upper schoolers. Perfect. I shook my head in mock disbelief.

"Live porn, man. How cool is that?"

Scrubs was immediately attentive. He tried to clear the hair out of his eyes without success.

"Live porn?"

"Maybe I shouldn't have mentioned it," I continued. "I don't want to get anyone in trouble." I made as if to get up.

"Wait, wait, wait!" Scrubs said, "I won't get anyone in trouble. I swear!"

I settled back into my seat.

"Ok, but this is just between us, right?"

"Oh, yeah."

"Well, Edward found were Jason and Jessica Hopemann go to have sex."

"Jessica Hopemann!" Scrubs cried.

"Keep it down, man."

"But she's the hottest girl in school!" He knew one upper schooler.

"I know. They've been having sex behind the school near the parking lot in the trees. Probably right after class and before sports. All you would need to do is find a nice hiding spot and wait for the show."

"Wow!" I couldn't see his eyes very well but I was sure they were as wide as saucers. He was hooked. After the porn incident where he got the whole middle school sent to Ethics, he had his computer confiscated. I knew he wouldn't be able resist a chance to see more porn.

I could only take a guess as to when Jason's sexcapades took place, but after class seemed like the most logical time. I bet Scrubs would wait out there everyday until it happened.

"But this is just between us, right?"

Scrubs nodded. "I know."

"Well, I have some work to do." I got up to leave.

"Wait," Scrubs said, "What's your name?"

I smiled. I'd hoped that would come up.

"I'm Smel - Dylan," and with that I left. Close one. I highly doubted Dylan referred to himself as *Smelly Dylan*. I glanced over my shoulder. Scrubs was smiling to himself. It worked! Man, Scrubs was dumb!

I could have just gone to a Rover with the information about Jason but rejected the idea. I didn't want to involve myself anymore with Ethics. Scrubs was dumb enough to forget he had permanent Rovers assigned to him and would lead them right to Jason. Scrubs wouldn't get into too much trouble with Ethics so I didn't feel bad about manipulating him. When Scrubs was asked how he learned of it, Smelly Dylan, A.K.A me, would get the blame. And if I was lucky, Ugly Edward, too. Fuckers deserved it after helping Jason beat me up. The more they denied it the more trouble they would be in. Leniency was granted only to those who confessed.

Now, as Scrubs and Jason were herded towards Ethics, I wished I could have felt good about it, but after that phone call, I didn't feel good about anything. I wasn't sure what the punishment for sexual activity was, but it was right up there with drugs. Probably expulsion. Good.

I heard more steps approaching from downstairs. It was probably another Rover with Jessica Hopemann. I felt a little guilty about her, but she chose the wrong horse and now would have to ride him all the way to the glue factory.

I turned and froze. There was the other Rover, but he wasn't leading Jessica Hopemann as I'd expected. He was leading Katrina.

As they passed, she looked up and our eyes met. Too many emotions swirled around inside those dark circles to distinguish any one, but none of them were good. I watched her disappear up the stairs.

She must have known about Jason and his girlfriend and didn't tell. I looked toward the cafeteria, but there was no Rover and no Jessica Hopemann. The subterranean hallway was silent. Where the hell was she? I wondered if they'd posted this infraction on the EIR already. I went to the bulletin board and scanned the EIR. A new entry was freshly tacked behind the glass.

> *Jason Gadai: Ethics Violation– On the*
> *afternoon of May 5th Jason Gadai was*
> *caught engaging in sexual activities with–*

A cold shock passed through me and I caught my breath.

> *–in sexual activities with Katrina Skinner.*

She was the one having sex with Jason? The confusion raged in me like a tornado, blowing away everything I thought I'd known. Only one thing made sense. It must have been Katrina's idea to beat me up not Jason's. It was always her.

I was disgusted and sick. Why had she come to my recital? Why had she given me that smile at the graduation? Why? Bitch! All girls were fucking bitches. I turned away.

I couldn't look at her name. She was the ugliest girl in the world right then.

An unfathomable emptiness engulfed me. It was all gone. My friends were gone. My piano was gone. Katrina was gone. Odi was gone. The school system had taken everything from me. Odi would still be alive if it wasn't for them. He would have been in class if they hadn't expelled him. They had killed him. They killed everything. There was nothing left, only the school.

The stinging in my gut intensified. School was the antithesis of everything that made kids happy in life and Lamia was the epitome of schools, their representative. I thought of all the misery I'd had to wallow through for the past 10 years and especially this last year. The stinging in my stomach spread outward to my hands and feet. I couldn't take it anymore! School had to be destroyed. Lamia had to be destroyed. I was the only one who could see it and the only one who could do anything about it.

I bounded up the steps to the third floor and went straight to the Science Room. It was late afternoon, but why did it matter? With the dark clouds, every hour of every day looked the same in my life.

The bomb was right were I'd left it. I grabbed it and descended all the way to the basement. My flopping Locals were the only sound as I walked along the maze of dimly lit halls. Everything was so clear. Like when I held that drawing compass over that boy's face, I knew what needed to be done.

Even before I saw it, I could smell and hear the Trash Room. The heart of Lamia. The source of the fear that kept this school standing.

As I turned the last corner that would take me there, I looked to my left. Just beyond the wall was the isolation ward where I'd been imprisoned. My hatred for Lamia brimmed over as memories of that place raged through me like a flashflood. All traces of doubt were gone. I'd never been so sure of anything in my entire life.

I pushed open the large metal door and stood there. The fire and the flies matched what I felt inside. The stinging was in my head now, puncturing the back of my eyes.

I pulled back to chuck the bomb. They were not going to win. Without this place, this greedy institution would cease to be. No more brainwashed kids, no more slave labor, and no more Method Three's.

Wait. The blast would be too big. I wouldn't be able to get away in time. As I thought about it, I felt no fear. So what? I didn't need to run. There was no reason. What was my future? Years of school and a 99% chance of becoming nothing? No. A passage from *Ender's Game* solidified my resolve. *Death is the only true escape.*

I walked down the short, nine steps to the Trash Room floor. The flies clung to me, but, as the heat increased, they lifted off and circled. I felt tickling on the tops of my feet from the crawling roaches, but I didn't care. Nothing mattered anymore.

I stopped a few feet from the heart of Lamia. The full

heat of the fire was trying to force me back, but my own fire would not retreat. All I had to do was drop it. The blast would radiate out at 25,000 feet per second and destroy everything here. For the first time, there would be no consequences for me. My dyslexia would never hold me back, I'd never have to see another pimple on my face, and I'd never feel alone again. And I would never be a gas station attendant! The stinging inside would finally go away and never return. There's no shame in giving up.

I held out my hand. I just had to loosen my fingers. It was so easy. I would die one day anyway. What's the difference between today and 60 years from today? The world will probably destroy itself by then anyway. It didn't matter. I wasn't afraid. I knew what death was like. Nothingness. The blast would tear the flesh from my bones before I could blink. There would be no pain.

Nobody would really miss me. The world had been here before me and it would keep going after. My sister had only ever hurt me. Rebecca didn't love me, not really. It was biological. Like Little James masturbating, she had no choice. And Istvan, I was sure he wished I'd never been born. As much as I hated Jason, he was right. Nobody would or could ever love me. My stomach was a cauldron of lava.

All that time I'd wasted watching movies. Why? Those characters were not my friends. They weren't even real. Nothing good was real. Lamia was real because only evil things existed. There was no justice in the world. How could there be?

Fuck this godforsaken place! I am not a stalker! I am not a thief! I am not accident prone! I am not a delinquent! I am not! I am not!

I began to loosen my grip on the bomb. I screamed at the furnace.

"I am not! Fuck you! FUCK YOOOOU!"

A sob choked my throat. Only two fingers held on. I breathed sharply. Tears welled in my eyes.

I am not. I am not. Why can't anybody see? I am not. My arm trembled. The grenade was just barely dangling. I am not. I am not. Why?

Tears now streamed down my cheeks. I hadn't cried since the compass. I remembered Odi coming over to put his arm around my shoulder.

"It's not your fault. I know you."

I could see his face so clearly. That scraggly black hair, the goofy grin, his Asian eyes. I could hear his laugh, like that day on the bank of that canal after we'd escaped from the water pipe. We'd both made it but now I was the only one left. Odi was gone now and I was not. Why?

I reached into my pocket with my other hand and pulled out my reminder. It's silvery face shone back at me. I rubbed the engraving with my finger. Menehune Pog Warrior. My slammer for flipping Passion Orange Guava caps. This had been Odi's.

When the pog craze hit my school Odi and I were late to jump on the bandwagon. We rushed to Hioshi's Store to buy some. We looked at the normal ones, but they didn't do anything for us.

"Look at these," I said, my face pressed to the counter. Odi came over to look. We were fogging up the glass. A silver and a gold Warrior. They were the coolest pogs I'd ever seen.

"They're sweet, Leif, but they're four dollars each."

I pulled my money out.

"I have six."

"I have three."

"We can get them. Nobody will beat us with these."

"But what if they do? Four bucks is choke money."

"I got an idea. We make an agreement. If you, like, lose yours I'll challenge that person and use mine to get it back and you do the same."

"Okay. Pinky swear?"

We shook pinkies and bought them. Odi got the silver and I got the gold. We began to challenge people at school and were winning a lot of pogs. Soon very few people wanted to face us. We were the champions of the pog wars. Then I lost mine to a girl. I was really pissed. Not just to lose the Warrior, but it was like lemon juice in a paper cut that a girl had beaten me. I was bummed all that day, but after class, Odi came up to me.

"Here's your *da kine*," he said, holding the Gold Warrior out. I was totally shocked. Odi had kept his word and challenged her, risking his own silver to win back my gold. He was always dependable.

"You keep it, man. Give me the silver. You're the gold winner right now."

"Really? Thanks, Leif."

"Don't mention it, Odi. Next time I'll get the gold. Next time." But there never was.

Right after that the school banned pogs because they said it was like gambling, but Odi and I still kept ours. We played each other every day after school to be defiant. We played until the day he was expelled. Maybe that's why 8th grade had sucked so much. Odi had always been there with me, fighting the good fight. Then he was gone. Odi was gone.

My reminder. The pog was something from Hawaii, something the school hated, but mostly it was Odi's and mine. We'd started this fight together. Odi was the best person I'd ever known. Why did he have to die and these people got to live? Why? Their whole purpose was to turn kids into what they thought they should be, not what we *could* be. There was no perfect school and there never would be. School was an institution and by its nature could never tolerate the things that made kids worthwhile.

I looked down at the pog in my hand. The firelight danced across its surface. Odi was a good guy and he'd wanted to be around me. I must be worthwhile. I didn't really want to die. Not for this place. School would be over in a few days. I didn't know what would happen after, but I wanted to find out.

"Don't take any shit from those haoles, Leif." I could almost hear Odi.

I tightened my grip on the grenade before it fell. Not like this. After 10 years of fighting, I was not going to give up. I looked down at the bomb. I should take it apart, but it was my first. I didn't know what I'd do with it, but I'd think of a perfect place to deposit it.

I looked around the Trash Room. I didn't know where or how I was going to die, but I didn't want it to be in this hell. I shook off a layer of ash that had collected on my feet and brushed away the roaches that had begun climbing up my legs. Unlike *The Temple of Doom* I couldn't tear the heart out of Lamia, but I was here and could stop it temporarily.

I pulled the flue handle so the smoke would suffocate the fire. They'd probably restart it tomorrow, but, like the oven, this fire probably hadn't been out in 20 years. I was proud.

The stinging in my stomach was abating. I straightened up and put the reminder back in my pocket. I wiped the last of the tears away.

The alternative to school would be harder, almost impossible, but it was my choice not theirs and that made all the difference. I would become a pianist no matter how difficult it was. I was not going to give up.

CHAPTER XXIX
The Grownup and the Old World

I stood in the early morning light waiting for the shuttle that would take me to the airport. All of my belongings were in two large suitcases and a carry-on. I'd been hoping for this moment for a long time, but it was still strange to think I was leaving Lamia.

I'd gone to the Peterson's one last time to drop off some things like my computer and boom box. I never really understood how kind they were to me until I was older; even Jack, for letting me crash in his room all those weekends.

I called my mom from the Peterson's to tell her that I'd made my choice.

"I'm glad you took the time to think about it."

"Yeah. I'm sure, but I'm a little freaked out."

"It's a big decision. I'd be more worried if you weren't."

"Okay." While this was what I wanted, a problem had been nagging at me.

"How do we solve the under 16 thing? I thought it was, like, the law that I had to stay in school until then."

"School's only mandatory if you're in this country."

"Right."

"Isht and I have made arrangements with Eva. Do you remember her?"

"Vaguely." She had been my Grandmother's best friend in Hungary. I'd seen a few pictures and had heard my mom talk about her, but I'd never met her.

"She found a flat in Debrecen and talked to the Franz Liszt Music Academy about you taking private lessons," my mom went on.

"So I'll live in Hungary?" I didn't see that coming but it made sense. Istvan was born in Debrecen.

"You'll stay there for nine months until you turn 16 then you'll come back to Hawaii."

Nine more months. I'll have been away from home for more than a year and a half by then.

"Now that you've made your decision, I'll tell Isht to call Eva to make the final arrangements. I'll purchase your ticket and send it to you."

"Okay." I could live in Europe for a while. If Mercedes could do it, I could.

"Are you guys going to meet me there?"

"Well, here's the thing. Mercedes is coming back to finish high school in Kamuela."

"Really? I thought she liked it over there?"

"She did, but her boyfriend's a senior and he's graduating.

She doesn't want to be there without him so she's coming home."

Didn't even know she had a boyfriend in Switzerland. I understood her decision. Without Katrina I had no incentive to stay here either. I guess we weren't so different. My mom went on.

"Because she's enrolling back in Kamuela we can't go to Hungary."

"So if you're not going - I don't get it?"

"Do you want to live there by yourself and study piano? If you don't, that's perfectly all right. But it's up to you."

By *myself*? Whoa! This is intense.

"Really?"

"Only if you want. Hungary is so far and I don't know what I'd do if something happened to you there. You'll always be my little boy."

Little boy? I'm not so sure I was. It had nothing to do with physical changes like those my mom had told me about when I was eight. Children never have to make difficult decisions. That's what's so great about being a kid.

If I went to Hungary I would be totally responsible for myself. I'd be on my own. It hit me then. I wasn't a kid anymore. Not an adult yet, but not a kid. It was sad to know it was over, but good and bad things never last forever.

"Yes. I'll go to Hungary. You don't have to worry. I can take care of myself."

"Are you sure?" It almost sounded like she wanted me to change my mind. It would be nice to go home but I had to move on.

"*I'm positive*. Like Marisa Tomei in *My Cousin Vinny*."

My mom laughed. It was settled. I would be going to Hungary. I'd live by myself until I was 16 and become a pianist. I wondered if I could have honestly made this choice if I hadn't gone through all that I did.

Connie went over my schedule for next year during one of my last few class days. She informed me that I could be in Form Six by October if I pushed myself. I went along with it. I'd been worried after the call in the Phone Room that they would know I wasn't coming back, but I saw no indication they knew. Probably by this late in the year, all the kids had been brainwashed so no electronic surveillance was required.

As I left that single large classroom for the last time a funny thought dawned on me. Form Six Entry was a limbo grade, so this whole year I never actually was in high school. I was a middle school dropout. I guess it would never matter that I'd didn't pass my typing test.

When I looked at my reflection in the bathroom mirror my cheeks were so sallow. I must weigh only 130 or close to it. I still had pimples, though. At least my hair was long enough to cover my forehead and part of my cheeks. Why won't they go away? I washed my face every day. Why did it look so dirty? I couldn't see well from where I stood so I climbed on the counter to get closer.

"Damn," I said aloud.

My whole face was covered with fine blonde hair. I hadn't shaved since isolation because I didn't think I had to.

I'd never noticed until now. This looked weird. I guess I did have to shave. I'd have to get used to it just like I'd gotten used to my new voice.

I went to the library to return my last reading book, *The Bronze Bow*. I'd liked that the kid took on the Roman Empire but that crap about love conquering all in the end was crap. Jessica Hopemann sat by herself in the back of the room. Even though Jason deserved what he got, I felt bad for her. Jessica Hopemann had done nothing wrong, but when the music stopped, she was the one without a chair.

"Hey," I said walking up to her. She looked up from her book. Her cheeks were dry but her eyes looked like she'd been crying.

"I'm really sorry about what happened."

She nodded slowly.

"I..." I felt an overwhelming urge to tell her it was my fault this whole thing had happened. I was leaving tomorrow anyway and maybe her anger towards me wouldn't make it hurt so much. But anger is just an excuse not to deal with the pain. You had to admit the pain to yourself first before things could begin correcting themselves.

"...I know what it feels like. I really do. It sucks that the hottest girl in school can get so bummed out. What hope is there for the rest of us?"

The corners of her mouth turned up for a brief moment. I saw a little light in those beautiful blue eyes of hers.

"Take care," I said and walked away.

"Bye, Leif," I heard her say. I turned to wave.

She knew my name. Jessica Hopemann knew *my* name. My resentment toward women dropped down a notch. All girls were still fucking bitches, but she was kind of cool. Maybe one day a girl like that would like me. I'd never do anything to lose her if she did. Jason was dumber than Scrubs.

I found Nick on my last night at Lamia and told him I was sorry for hitting him after the soccer game. He didn't really forgive me until I told him I'd built a bomb. I never told him why though.

"I can't believe you actually, like, built one, dude." Nick said. "Bit of the old ultra-violence, I see."

"I had to do it sometime."

"You got balls, man. It's because you're Hawaiian."

"Could be."

"I have to, like, go up there and check it out, man."

I'd found the perfect place to hide it but that still didn't mean it couldn't go off.

"Just be careful. Remember what I told you about people who mess with-"

Derk jumped over the back of the booth and landed hard, startling me.

"What the fuck are you fuckers talking about?"

I gave Nick a look. I could see he understood that the bomb thing was just between us.

"I invented a new game," I said to Derk.

"Double Mercy?" Derk darted toward my hands but they were under the table long before he got close. I smiled and shook my head.

"Too slow."

"Fuck, man," Derk said dejected. "Okay, so what's this dumb game of yours?"

"It's the 'Rather Or' game."

"The *'Rather Or' game?*"

"Yeah. Like, Derk, would you rather get a hand job from Scrubs or screw the Ethics Lady?"

"Fuck you, Leif! Fuck you!" Derk cringed. Nick and I laughed.

"Okay, Dick mouth," Derk said, regaining his composure. "Would you rather smell a jar of farts or a jar of kweefs? Ha!"

I guess that was the best Derk could do.

"I got one for you, man," Nick said to me, "Would you rather have Derk jerk off all over your room or make-out with Fat Rob?"

"Ah! Sick, man!"

We all laughed. It was just like old times. Well, almost. I looked over at the pool table. Jude was playing a game with Little James. Some things could never go back to the way they were.

At about 9:45 we made our way back to Nick's room. Soon Derk and I had to get to our own hall for bed check.

"I'll see you, Nick-meister," I said, giving him a hug.

"Give some of those young devotchkas a bit of the old in

out, this summer in Hungary."

I'd told Nick and Derk I was only going for the summer.

"Viddy well."

"That's how pussies say good bye!" Derk yelled, grabbing me in a headlock and giving me a noogy.

"Let me go, you dick!" I cried. Derk just cackled and put on his dumb voice.

"Ooh, does it hurt? Does it hurt?" I finally pushed him off me. He was an asshole, but in some strange way, a good friend, too.

"I'll see you next year, dude," Nick said, as I walked out the door with Derk.

It had been easy lying to Lamia that I wasn't coming back, but not to Nick. Yet I had to.

"Yeah, man. Next year."

Nick was the only good friend I had left and I'd never see him again. For a brief moment, I wished I wasn't going.

Nick called out as we rounded the corner to our hall. "Me and my droogs will rule Lamia! Nobody can stop us! I am Nick DeLarge!"

I laughed. I'd miss that weirdo. He probably would become a drunkard.

"Well, Scuba-Doo," Derk said when we got to his room, "Good luck and show all those commies what America is all about."

"I don't think Hungary is communist anymore."

"What am I? Fucking Carmen San Diego? Get the fuck away from me, you fucking kweef face."

Ah, Derk. What more could you say? I guess that was his way of saying goodbye. I smiled and walked away. Bed check was any second now. I stood alone by my door and waited for the Rover. I looked up and down the hall. My last bed check and my last night here. Felt like I'd been here forever. Fat Rob and his mom had packed up all his crap and left earlier that day. I didn't know if his move was permanent or not, but I didn't care. Five minutes after my head hit the pillow I was out. It was the best sleep I ever had at school.

Standing outside at dawn the next morning, I could see the shuttle turn off the main road and begin winding its way up the hill. I was thankful the mornings here weren't cold anymore. I guess spring was sloughing off its winter coat.

I was going to Hungary to live by myself. Who would have thought? I looked at my itinerary again. Most of it had been written by Istvan in his block printing.

ARRIVE IN BUDAPEST, CHANGE MONEY TO FORINT. GET TAXI TO TRAIN STATION: BUY VONAT TICKET TO DEBRECEN . 3 HR TRIP . EVA WILL PICK YOU UP.

Hope she could recognize me because I had no idea what she looked like. He also gave me some basic Hungarian words. Mom filled in the pronunciations.

THANK YOU : KÖSZÖNÖM *Kuss oh nom*

PLEASE : KÉREM *Kay rem*

HELLO : SZIA *See ya*

That's how you said hello? *See ya*? Funny. I'd probably have to learn Hungarian. That's cool. I'd always wanted to know another language. I looked at the last word on my itinerary. At this one I actually laughed out loud.

GOOD BYE: HELO *Hello*

The shuttle pulled up. The driver, a tall black man with shiny white teeth got out. His thick British accent surprised me.

"Get your bags for you?"

"Thanks."

He loaded them into the back. I opened the sliding door and got in. The inside was nice and toasty warm. No more open windows and cold rooms.

I noticed a newspaper on the seat next to me and looked at the front page.

> 126 day hostage crisis at the
> Japanese Embassy in Peru ends.
> One hostage died.

Interesting. I had no idea that was going on. The driver closed the sliding door and got behind the wheel.

"Heading off to the airport, right?"

"That's it."

The driver put the shuttle in gear and we drove away. I looked up one last time at the Ethics tower. Good and Bye. Soon we were gliding down the long weeping willow tree tunnel.

"Are you from England?" I asked

"Kenya, but not bad," he said smiling. "I did live in the UK for several years. Name's Godfred. You want to hear the radio?"

I smiled. "Sure."

A second later loud rock filled the shuttle. It was a little early for that kind of music, but I kind of enjoyed it. It was some song about never being kept down. We reached the bottom of the hill as the song ended.

"That was 'Tubthumping' by *Chumbawamba*," the DJ said.

We turned onto the main road and Godfred accelerated. I looked back. Lamia was slowly shrinking into a point on the horizon. It was like I was escaping from a black hole. Just a few more minutes and that godforsaken hell would be gone from view.

"Not a cloud in the sky," Godfred said. "Looks like it's going to be a nice day to fly."

I was about to go to the Old World, like the defectors in *Hunt for Red October*, but the other way around. Too bad Hungary didn't have any oceans. I missed surfing.

We drove past a small hill and the orange light of the

rising sun made me squint. It was so nice to see the sunlight again. The school was gone now and we were speeding away toward my unknown future. That wasn't a bad thing. There needs to be more mystery in the world.

No more school, *for-ev-er*. I was finished. I wasn't standing before everybody, a proud graduate like I'd imagined, but things rarely go the way you think they will. Could you really grow up if they did? Whatever. I'd been wishing for this moment for as long as I could remember and now it was here. I wasn't sure if it was finishing school or finishing Lamia which made this moment feel so sweet.

I reached into my pocket and took out my pog. I wish you could have felt this, Odi. I rubbed my thumb over the engravings. The pog would always be my reminder. Not just of my war against the system and Lamia, but of true friends who were always with you. Enemies, religions, and even countries come and go. It's those who struggle along side you that gives life meaning and makes it worthwhile.

The sun was higher now and the landscape was glowing in its golden rays. Small green buds freckled the seemingly dead branches of the passing trees. If life had a soundtrack, the last movement of Beethoven's 6th symphony would be playing right now.

I put the pog back in my pocket. I thought about those final moments in the Trash Room. That had been the worst day, but I was glad I didn't give up because Godfred was right. This was a good day. Today was the best day of my life.

Coda

What was that buzzing? I jolted awake. It was the intercom. Somebody at the gate. I looked at the clock. 5:49 AM. Why did the postman always have to come so goddamn early in this country? But it was Hungary. What the hell could you say?

I flung the covers aside and ran to the intercom.

"One moment, please!" I yelled in Hungarian.

I'm too old for this crap. I grabbed a shirt and ran out of my room, trying not to step on the pages of my new woodwind composition that were scattered around the floor. If I didn't get to the gate and sign, they'd stuff my package into some forgotten back room at the Egyetem like that huge warehouse at the end of *Raiders of the Lost Ark*. I'd have to sign 20 million documents just so they'd begin to look for it.

I flung the front door open and jumped outside. It was snowing again.

"*Busz!*" I muttered as the cold enveloped my body like a frigid glove. I didn't want to fall on the icy steps like I'd done last time so I placed each foot purposefully on the slick concrete.

When I reached the ground I took off at a run. The postman looked bored and impatient as I approached. It was almost like my parcel was forcing him to go out of his way. If he didn't like this job why didn't he just quit? I fumbled for my keys and opened the first gate.

"*Egy pillanat, kerem,*" I said to him.

I shuffled to the next key on the ring and opened the second gate. This city had more fences than a nuclear waste dump.

The postman looked at a clipboard.

"Csuba, Leif?" he asked, butchering my first name into a multi-syllable mess.

"*Leaf*," I corrected, snatching the clipboard from him. It's been me every time you've delivered a package. Dumber than Scrubs! At least in Hungary they always pronounced my last name right.

After I signed, the postman handed me a manila envelope.

"*Koszonom*," I said, thanking him. He didn't even grunt a response. He got back in his truck and took off down Komlossy Street.

I locked the fences, rushing back for the warmth of my flat. Once inside, I made a mad dash back to my warm bed and wrapped myself in the covers. I pulled open the metal tabs of the envelope and tore the sticky flap up. Inside was a letter, a folded clipping from the *Jackskeep Herald,* and something that looked like an extra large CD case. I took the case thing out first.

It was *Shine*. I recognized the half naked piano man jumping on the front. Must be the soundtrack, but then something caught my eye on the cover. Widescreen DVD? What the hell was a *DVD*? I opened the case and looked inside. It was just a CD. What's this widescreen crap?

I flipped it over and there was a yellow sticky note written by my dad.

A NEW GADGET FOR YOU. I'LL SHOW YOU
WHEN YOU GET HOME. KEEP PRACTICING,
PIANIST.

SZERETLEK FIÚ

"*Love you, my son.*" That was considerate of him. New gadget, huh? Cool. I put the DVD thing on the nightstand. I read the letter next.

Dear Leif,

How are you, Darling? I missed having you at home for St. Nicholas Day again. We'll be together this year for sure. I received the videotape of your concert. It looked like there were over a hundred people there. I was blown away. The Rachmaninoff Prelude was my favorite. We are so proud of you. The waves are great for surfing right now. I hope they still are by the time you return. Just a few more weeks and you'll be in my arms again. I can't wait to see you. Mercedes wants to take you to see *Titanic* She thinks you'll like it. We'll go to the clambake at the Mauna Kea Resort the week you get back. I miss you terribly.

Love,
Mom

P.S.
Someone sent this news clipping. I
think they meant it for you.

Clambake? Awesome! There was nothing better than all-you-can-eat lobster. Except fish and poi, freshly pounded poi. It would be nice to get some normal food again. Not that Hungary is a bad country. *Palacsinta* and *rétes* are some of the greatest foods on the planet, but not chocolate covered cottage cheese or pizza with ketchup and a fried egg on top. Some things were never intended to work together.

I turned my attention to the clipping. I hadn't noticed before, but written on the back, in pencil, was the phrase:

There's been a terrible accident

I unfolded the clipping to reveal a grainy photograph. The picture was unmistakably of the Lamia School. Just the sight of that place gave me the creeps. There were police cars and emergency vehicles parked in front. It took me a moment to realize that the entire top tower that housed the Ethics Office was gone.

Local officials report that an
explosion ripped through the
Lamia School early Friday
morning, destroying the

institution's 5th floor. Investigators believe the blast was triggered by two volatile chemicals that mixed and ignited when the filing cabinet they were stored in was closed with excessive force. No students were injured, but one woman was killed in the resulting explosion. The woman's identity has not been released. The school will remain closed until further notice.

I read the article one more time to make sure I hadn't misunderstood it. It happened. The entire tower? Impressive.

I leaned over the bed and took my pog out of the nightstand drawer. I laid the article down and set the pog on top of it. Perfect. I think I need a few more hours of sleep before I start practicing.

I settled back into bed and pulled the covers tighter around me. It had been very cold, but now I could feel gentle warmth spreading from my stomach throughout my body.

I looked from the letter I'd just received to the snow falling outside my window. *My* window in *my* flat. I was living in Hungary by myself. I was studying music, giving concerts and composing. Most importantly, I was finished with school. Wow! I was so glad I survived to see this day. And in that moment I knew beyond a shadow of a doubt. I smiled and closed my eyes. I was not going to be a gas station attendant.

THE END

PAUL Y. CSIGE is a traveler, fisherman, surfer, writer, and filmmaker who holds degrees from Berklee College of Music and The New York Film Academy. He has worked in both television and film industries for several years as an editor, and director. He was commissioned by the Kamuela Philharmonic to compose a full orchestral overture and successfully adapted the book *Voyage: The Discovery of Hawaii* by renowned historian and artist Herb Kawainui Kane into an award winning feature film. He has combined his creative experience in story telling through music and films to produce this fictional memoir. He currently lives in Kailua Kona, Hawaii.